STORIES WANTING

ONLY TO BE HEARD

THE UNIVERSITY OF GEORGIA PRESS ATHENS

SELECTED FICTION FROM SIX DECADES OF

The Georgia Review

Stories Wanting Only to Be Heard

EDITED BY STEPHEN COREY

with Douglas Carlson, David Ingle, and Mindy Wilson

∽ Foreword by Barry Lopez

© 2012 by the University of Georgia Press

Athens, Georgia 30602

www.ugapress.org

All rights reserved

Designed by Mindy Basinger Hill

Set in 10/15 Minion Pro

Printed and bound by Thomson-Shore

The paper in this book meets the guidelines for permanence and durability of the Committee on Production Guidelines for Book Longevity of the Council on Library Resources.

Printed in the United States of America

16   15   14   13   12   P   5   4   3   2   1

Library of Congress Cataloging-in-Publication Data

Stories wanting only to be heard : selected fiction from six decades of the Georgia review / edited by Stephen Corey with Douglas Carlson, David Ingle, and Mindy Wilson ; foreword by Barry Lopez.

     p.   cm.

ISBN-13: 978-0-8203-4254-2 (pbk : alk. paper)

ISBN-10: 0-8203-4254-8 (pbk : alk. paper)

1. Short stories, American. 2. American fiction—20th century. I. Corey, Stephen, 1948– II. Georgia review.

PS648.S5S76 2012

813'.0108—dc23   2011037561

Publication of this book was made possible, in part,
by the President's Venture Fund through generous gifts
of the University of Georgia Partners.

Contents

Barry Lopez

ONE RAINY FALL EVENING SOME YEARS AGO IN NEW YORK, ABOUT twenty of us got together in an Italian restaurant in SoHo to celebrate Lewis Lapham's twentieth year as an editor at *Harper's* magazine. The gathering was to have been a surprise, but when Lewis came through the door with a colleague and saw us milling around several large dining tables—members of the magazine's staff, one of its benefactors, and several freelance writers—he looked more delighted than surprised. He'd suspected something was up.

During his early years at the magazine Lewis had encouraged my work, and I'd since written a number of major pieces for him. When I arrived at the restaurant, I learned I was one of three of the magazine's regular contributors who intended to stand up that evening and formally thank him. Lewis's early editorial support, in my case, had consistently countered the insecurity young writers very often feel around their developing self-image, and I'd heard others say the same about the salutary effect of his editorial guidance on their writing. I assumed that my fellow contributors in the room that night felt exactly as I did, that we all hailed Lewis as a mentor. Perhaps, too, I harbored a conceit: when I offered my own toast that evening, I would be representing more *Harper's* writers than just myself.

As it happened, I was the last of the writers to speak, but I rose to my feet with a measure of doubt and self-consciousness. I'd listened carefully as the other two talked about their relationships with Lewis, and I'd had difficulty identifying with their remarks. One struck me as too ironic, and the other seemed indifferent to the moment. Was I a naïf, flying in from so far out of town (rural western Oregon) that the notion of editorial camaraderie so strongly on my mind that night would now strike everyone as jejune? Would my carefully prepared sentences now seem sentimental? I couldn't risk trying to recast everything, so I went ahead as planned, despite my misgivings, probably trimming my adjectives a bit and not emphasizing quite so much—or presuming too much upon—the ideals I felt should underlay the editorial process at this esteemed magazine. I attempted, I suppose, to strike a tone somewhere between earnestness and sophistication, a sense of my being above it all—and I sat down despising myself for having curbed my remarks. Many years later, Lewis assured me I had not betrayed any straight-from-the-heart feelings I might have had that evening but rather had only been self-conscious about my idealism, a kind of hopefulness about humanity that Lewis had always appreciated in my work but that back then had seemed slightly out of tune with other, more urbane sentiments in the room. He could have added, of course, that, yes, I had been a bit naïve about the world that night.

What has proved most memorable for me about that evening is the difference between myself and the other writers who spoke. We shared a few polite words with each other but had no real rapport. The situation would have been different, I thought, had contributors who were friends of mine been in the room. Had that been the case, though, I would never have gotten a lesson about what good editorial direction means at a publication like *Harper's*. Lewis was a great editor partly because he had faith in writers with markedly different notions about the world, with different ideas about what it means to write, and with clearly divergent voices. Conversely, these dissimilar writers all trusted Lewis to do right by them. The divergence of style and opinion was one reason the magazine flourished the way it did under him. He loved controversy and provocation, any challenge to received wisdom or to the status quo—as long as it was well written. (He had edited my first piece for *Harper's*, about time I'd spent in an Eskimo community in Alaska, to make it more controversial than I cared for— the only time he ever did this—and I learned quickly the sort of edge he preferred to see in an essay.) His intent was to serve a readership, not a clique of writers.

I begin with this anecdote, about how different from one another writers whose work appears in the same journal can be, to stress two points I believe worth noting about the collection you hold in your hands. The unifying theme of *Stories Wanting Only to Be Heard* is *The Georgia Review* itself, specifically the cultural leanings and aesthetic tastes of its editorial staffs over the years. Its theme, therefore, is neither a topic nor a cause nor a particular type of fiction; the fiction in this collection, in fact, is driven by disparate imaginations working across a range of styles. Among these writers are even some, I am guessing, who would like to point out why someone else's fiction here doesn't really suit them; but this point is moot. What the editors have assembled in *Stories Wanting Only to Be Heard* is a book meant to serve an audience, not a particular cadre of writers. Furthermore, I have to assume the editors' hope is that this specific collection of fiction will serve an audience considerably larger than those who are regular readers of *The Georgia Review*. Reading each of these pieces, I came to the conclusion that the anthology accomplishes exactly this. Its appeal is to discerning minds, whatever journals, magazines, or books they might (or might not) be perusing regularly; to minds that, above all, have been paying close attention to the American experience; to the minds of readers who enjoy the sensations that come from finding their culture artfully delineated and enunciated.

The history of *The Georgia Review*, as Stephen Corey writes in his introduction, is a southern history. More and more in recent decades, however, the magazine has extended a welcome to voices from the country's other regions (as you will discover), to writers who grapple in their stories with the mysteries of trying to live out basic human needs and emotions—self-respect, love, the desire to make a wise choice, the longing behind various human appetites and desires—and to do so in cultural landscapes with which many of us might be unfamiliar. Each one of these stories captures something formidable, for me, about the effort each one of us makes to survive. You look up from the last word on the last page of a story, drift away, think of some element from the daily call sheet of threats we all know now—financial loss, cultural disintegration, biological compromise, spiritual demise—and realize that the story you have just finished speaks directly to one of these dilemmas. To surviving them.

We read, in part, to survive, to carry on in the belief that our lives have meaning. Whatever might motivate any of us as writers, we each hear, I think, a particular entreaty from readers: to show them what survival does (or does not) look like. Show us, the reader asks, some believable aspect of human determination, the great Carrying On, in a world as fraught, as beset, as ours.

In *Stories Wanting Only to Be Heard*, it is the book as a whole that speaks. For reasons of taste or aesthetic preference, you might not carry through to the end with every story, but you will see, if you see nothing else, the actual rather than the putative value of a distinguished literary journal, a magazine that takes the looming fate of the reader into editorial consideration. The readers matter as much as the writers at America's best magazines, and for the stories in this anthology, dramatic substance regularly trumps literary fashion.

All those years ago, in a neighborhood restaurant in SoHo, I learned what I have found, all over again, in these pages. Some editors, some magazines, care what happens to us. All of us.

Acknowledgments

FIRST AND FOREMOST, TO MY COEDITORS—DOUG CARLSON, DAVID INGLE, and Mindy Wilson—for their long hours and smart observations as we made our way through all the reading and meetings that led to the final contents of this collection; to all the past editors of *The Georgia Review*, whose endless reading and countless decisions over the years gave us the material from which to choose: John Donald Wade (1947–1950), John Olin Eidson (1950–1957), William Wallace Davidson (1957–1968), James B. Colvert (1968–1972), Edward J. Krickel (1972–1974), John T. Irwin (1974–1977), Stanley W. Lindberg (1977–2000), and T. R. Hummer (2001–2006); to the authors and their heirs/executors/assignees for their cooperation in seeing this book into print; and to the staff of the University of Georgia Press, in particular director Nicole Mitchell, acquisitions editor Regan Huff, and managing editor Jon Davies, for supporting our project and shepherding it into print.

S.C.

STEPHEN COREY

Introduction: Single Sittings

THE INAUGURAL ISSUE OF *THE GEORGIA REVIEW* (SPRING 1947) INCLUDED short fiction—"Astute Mr. Rufus Treowth" and "Night Watch," both by one LeGarde S. Doughty of Augusta—as has every quarterly issue since, with the exception of a handful of special numbers such as a forty-year poetry retrospective (Fall 1986). This nearly perfect record, I like to think, indicates a commitment to the form . . . but what exactly *is* the form?

The short story is part of a family whose members are sometimes easily distinguished from one another and sometimes not: myth, epic, saga, tale, fable, novel, novella, novelette, short-short, flash fiction, and no doubt others. As we consider these designations—that word itself forces us to recall *design*, which leads us to think both of making and of breaking down into essential parts—we are most quickly led to thoughts of length, historical age, relation to so-called truth or reality, and what I would call tone or attitude. Almost every assertion we might make about one relative in the family—"a myth captures a particular culture's view of . . ."; "an epic attempts to raise itself to . . ."; "in a fable we often sense an air of . . ."—can at times be applied to another member of the clan. Only the matter of length can ever be discussed with generally accepted certainty—notions of the "one-page novel" and the "world's longest short story" being imaginatively intriguing but ultimately perverse—although even here gray areas abound. Where lies the tipping point from short story to novella or from novella to novel? (*Novella* has been widely adopted to resolve the question "longish short story or novel?" but its use tends to create two questions while only partially answering one.)

When I was a kid in elementary school—in an era so long ago and seemingly far away that we hadn't even heard of electric typewriters, to say nothing of computers—we had access to a mail-order book club, which was a wonder to those of us who were avid early readers. Every month or so the teacher would pass out copies of a small newsprint catalogue, and I would always order as many titles—most cost twenty-five to fifty cents—as I could persuade my parents to fund. One of the books I remember most vividly was *Ten Classic Tales by Edgar Allan Poe*—yes, his name had been made a part of the title—with its adult-creepy stories and its terrifying pen-and-ink illustrations. At the age of eleven and twelve in particular, I read the tales in that collection again and again: "The Black Cat," "The Pit and the Pendulum," "The Tell-Tale Heart," "A Descent into the Maelstrom," and the rest.

One story not included in that literally little volume—it would have measured no more than 4 × 6 inches, though the gruesome cover drawing of a gaunt, haunted-eyes Poe probably magnified my sense of the size—was "The Purloined Letter," a work from the headier side of Poe's oeuvre, where strange events that engender a heightened pulse and some looks over the shoulder are replaced by intellectual ruminations on puzzling, detective-worthy mysteries. In this tale, which I did not read until years later, the Parisian living quarters of a blackmail suspect are surreptitiously turned upside-down by local authorities in a futile search for the incriminating titular document. C. Auguste Dupin, Poe's pre–Sherlock Holmes Sherlock Holmes, is told about the case by a police prefect and immediately solves it: determining that the culprit is "both a mathematician and a poet," and thereby a long imaginative stride ahead of the authorities, Dupin rightly surmises that the letter has been "hidden" in the one place the police would not think to look: in plain sight. (Specifically, on a decorative card rack hanging from a fireplace mantel.)

So, we are here sleuthing for an answer to the question posed above—what exactly *is* the short-story form?—and to complete the search I'll turn briefly to Poe's critical writings. In "The Philosophy of Composition," he puts forth some of the best-known theoretical statements about the nature of strong writing and its potential effects on readers:

> If any literary work is too long to be read at one sitting, we must be content to dispense with the immensely important effect derivable from unity of impression—for, if two sittings be required, the affairs of the world interfere, and every thing like totality is at once destroyed.

Poe speaks primarily of poetry in this particular essay, holding up and analyzing "The Raven" as an instance of a compact work whose author is aware that "all intense excitements are, through a psychal necessity, brief," but he is also careful to reemphasize his broader claim: "there is a distinct limit, as regards length, to all works of literary art—the limit of a single sitting." And in an essay on Nathaniel Hawthorne's *Twice-Told Tales*, Poe reminds us of this vital factor that makes "the brief prose tale" such a favorite of his:

> As the novel cannot be read at one sitting, it cannot avail itself of the immense benefit of *totality*. Worldly interests intervening during the pauses of perusal, modify, counteract and annul the impressions intended. But simple cessation in reading would, in itself, be sufficient to destroy the true unity. In the brief tale, however, the author is enabled to carry out his full design without interruption. During the hour of perusal, the soul of the reader is at the writer's control.

I would never claim that anyone has the final say on the definition or the value of the short-story form. However, for present purposes (and from my aesthetic perspective) I suggest that Poe's remarks constitute the "purloined letter" we are seeking—that is, we should bypass any convoluted and hairsplitting flummery about genre, engaging directly with the "immense benefit" of what lies before us: *short* storytelling.

So our offer to you, with *Stories Wanting Only to Be Heard*, is twenty-eight single sittings . . . twenty-eight intense excitements . . . twenty-eight totalities.

However, these sittings will be not just single but *singular* as well, taking you to diverse places—and into diverse emotional states and moods in the company of diverse characters: to World War II Germany, to the Strand bookstore in New York City, to an isolated restaurant off an interstate exit in the deep South, to Tokyo, and to the less populated regions of North Dakota; to a dozen varieties of hope and love, to as many of sadness and pain and grief and not a few of humor—sympathetic, vicious, ironic, intellectual, and more; to charmingly innocent (yet still wise) young boys in the Midwest, to an undertaker's movingly dysfunctional family, to a frightening yet eloquent would-be pedophile, to a creek-rock-selling southern graduate student with a stuttering wife who wants to be a radio announcer, to Jane Austen on a motorcycle, and to Marilyn Monroe in a checkout line.

Samuel Johnson famously said that "nothing odd can last"—a sentiment to which I feel a sort of bedrock connection, although with the proviso that one must figure out how to define *odd* and *last*. I and my *Georgia Review* colleagues Doug Carlson, David Ingle, and Mindy Wilson believe that all the stories we've selected for this volume stand the test of the time span with which we were dealing, offering themselves to readers as forcefully now as they did in various decades past. The source of this durability lies in the stories' unique elements of plot or character, of setting or narrative structure, of diction or tone, of imaginative subtlety or brashness—which means that what might have been mere oddness has been transformed by the writer, smartly yet almost alchemically, into work with a memorable *style*,

> the heart of a hand and eye,
> knowable yet unpredictable,
> the shapes and shades we acquire
> both with and against our wills.

The twenty-eight authors and their stories gathered here harbor, innately, a simple but immense desire to be heard. We editors have faith that you readers will be overcome, repeatedly, by your own undeniable want: to listen, and then listen again, one sitting at a time.

JESSE STUART

From the Mountains of Pike

"THIS WILL DO THE TRICK, SAL," PA SAID TO MOM. "LOOK! SEE WHAT
I've got! This is the deed for the Sid Beverley property. All made ready to
sign! I'll show Permintis Mullins something. He'll never outshine Mick
Powderjay when it comes to tradin'!"

Pa held the clean unsigned deed for Mom to see. Mom was hooking a
rug while she waited for us to return. She didn't look up when Pa held the
deed for her to see. She kept on working on her rug.

"What's the matter, Sal?" Pa asked. "This is the deed for that property!
Don't you want us to have it? Don't you want to see me buy it? Why don't
you back me up like a good wife backs up her trading husband?"

Mom still didn't speak. She kept on hooking her rug while the night
wind sang around our house. Wind flapped the loose shingles on the roof.
Wind rattled our loose window sashes. We heard it moan through the
barren branches of the apple trees in our front yard. Pa wouldn't have any
kind of shade but apple trees. He said they were good shade trees and they
bore fruit too. Mom couldn't understand this, since we had seven hundred
eighteen acres of land in The Valley. We owned all of The Valley but two
farms. Permintis Mullins owned seventy-three acres. Sid Beverley owned
one hundred and sixty acres. But Sid Beverley had moved from The Valley
back to Pike County in the high mountains. And Pa and Permintis had
tried to buy him out and he wouldn't sell. Not then.

And what had caused all the excitement was a letter we got at The Valley
post office in the four o'clock mail. I had gone to the store for groceries,
and John Baylor, who runs our post office and store, gave me the letter.
When I saw it was from Sid Beverley I knew the letter must be important.
Important to Pa. I rode the horse home in a hurry. Pa was delighted when
he read that Sid Beverley said he was ready to sell. Said he was happier
back in the mountains where he was born and grew to manhood. Said
something about going home to drink the water from the well of his youth
and it tasted so good and things like that. How much fresher and better
the air was. How much friendlier the people were. The smile left Pa's face

when he read where Sid said he was writing Permintis Mullins and telling him too the farm was for sale. Said in the letter he was writing both at the same time. "I'm telling you that I'm writing Permintis," the letter said. "I'm telling Permintis I'm writing you. I know you don't get along too well. But both of you are my friends and I'm ready to sell my farm in The Valley."

When Pa read this he stood a minute and looked into the open fire. That's the place Pa looked when he was in a deep study. And when he looked into the fire he didn't speak to anybody. Then Pa shouted: "Adger, put the saddles on the horses in a hurry." I ran to the barn to saddle the horses. We had a car but in March our roads were impassable. We had to ride horseback when we traveled any distance. I didn't ask Pa any questions. I knew he'd hatched something. After I'd saddled the horses and run back to the house, I heard Mom say: "Don't do it, Mick."

But Pa and I ran hack to the barn, led our saddled horses from the stalls. Pa climbed upon Moll's back like a young man. His foot in the stirrup and his other leg high up over Moll's back, he dropped into the saddle and we were off. I followed him. I knew something was in the wind. A big trade was on. He was off to beat Permintis Mullins.

"As fast as we can go to Blakesburg," he said. "Nine miles and an hour and a half to get there. We got to get there before the clerk's office closes. It closes at six. And we've got muddy traveling."

We made it all right. We had ten minutes to spare. But when we asked for the deed, it took more than ten minutes to make it. We were on the safe side now. Jack Willis, Greenwood County's clerk, belonged to Pa's party. Pa had ridden horseback every day and part of the night for one week before the election to help elect Jack Willis.

"Sure, Mick," he said. "I'll favor you. You favored me. I'll never forget you. Got this office by forty-four votes and I think this work you did put me over. Yes, I'll make that deed."

Permintis Mullins rode his horse day and night for you too, I thought. But I didn't speak my thoughts. He belongs to the same party too. And I wondered if Jack Willis wouldn't tell Permintis the same thing if he'd come to have a deed made in the night. I wondered if Pa would think to ask if Permintis had been there before we arrived. Pa never left a stone unturned when he traded. This was one reason Permintis Mullins didn't like Pa. I'd heard Mom and Pa talk on winter evenings when they sat before the fire, how Sid Beverley, Permintis Mullins, and their wives and Pa and Mom had come from Pike County when they were young married couples. How they all worked with each other in the beginning. They were all traders. How they left Pike County where about everybody was a good trader and had all come to Greenwood County where there weren't many land, cattle, and horse traders. They'd heard great stories of the poor traders in this county and they came to get rich. And when Pa got ahead of Sid Beverley, Sid got sick at heart and went back to Pike County. I knew it wasn't the fresh air, the water from the family well he drank when he was a boy, and the friendliness of the people that called him back. It was Pa's doing so much better than he did. It was Pa's getting most of The Valley that hurt him. It was Pa's getting up at midnight and getting there first that beat Sid Beverley.

It was when Pa tried to buy Permintis Mullins' farm that Permintis turned on him. From that hour, Pa and Permintis never stood by one another again. And they never traded with each other. Viola Mullins, Permintis' wife, never came to see Mom again. Permintis' boys, Cief, Ottis, and Bill, never spoke to my brother Finn and me again. The big rift came between us when Pa got enough ahead by his trading to "buy Permintis out." Pa had insulted Permintis. And if anybody on earth knew the Mullinses we did. If anybody knew the Powderjays, the Mullinses did. They knew we had often carried "hardware" pieces. We knew they did too. They knew we had used them in Pike County before we left. We knew they carried them there and had used them too. We didn't want to get into it with each other. How many dead there would have been, would have been anybody's guess.

"Say, Jack," Pa whispered when Jack had finished making the deed, "I want to ask you something. Don't ever mention I've asked you this. But I want a truthful answer right from the shoulder."

"You'll get it, Mick," Jack Willis told Pa. "I won't lie to you."

"Has Permintis Mullins been in here this afternoon?" Pa asked. "Have you made a deed for him for this Sid Beverley property?"

"He's not been here, Mick," Jack said.

"Thank you, Jack." Pa's face beamed with happiness. "I know you'd tell me the truth."

Then Pa pulled a big fat billfold from his hip pocket. He took enough bills from it to paper a small room. He started peeling off the ones with his big thumb to pay for the deed.

"I wouldn't take a penny for that deed, Mick," Jack said. "I know you've made the green lettuce in your day by trading. I know you got more lettuce than I'll ever have working in this office and getting myself elected every four years. But I wouldn't take a penny from you. It's a pleasure to serve you, Mick. It's a pleasure to have you for a friend. You're the greatest trader in Greenwood County. There's never been one as good and I don't think there ever will be."

Pa loved these words. His face turned redder than the cold March winds had ever made it. He looked at Jack Willis and smiled. Jack stood there looking at Pa, a large square-shouldered man, with a clean, folded, unsigned deed in his big stubby hand. Pa didn't insist that Jack take the money for the deed. With the other hand he slipped the big billfold into his hip pocket and buttoned the pocket and kept it there. That's where Pa kept his big money. He kept his "chicken feed" in a little pocketbook in his front pocket.

"Jack, you're a good man and a reliable friend," Pa said. "I appreciate this from the bottom of my heart. Appreciate it more than I have the words to tell you. My wife doesn't like the way I work all night when a trade is on. She can't understand it. But I have often told her if I go first, the one thing I want her and my sons to remember about me is I was a great trader. I want them to remember the grass didn't grow under my feet. That the early bird always got the worm and I was the early bird."

"You're that, Mick," Jack agreed as we left his office.

With the deed in his inside coat pocket, Pa went down the courthouse corridor laughing. His laughter echoed against the stone walls and returned to us, deafening our ears. When we got back to our horses, unhitched them from the posts, and were in the saddles again, Pa said: "See how men respect you, Son, when you do something in life. Boy, I'll make that Permintis Mullins live hard. He'll die when I get that Sid Beverley farm. His mouth has been watering for it ever since Sid went back to Pike. And I don't blame him," Pa shouted as we galloped our horses from Blakesburg. "Sweet meadows, timbered hills, good tobacco ground . . . who wouldn't want it?"

I didn't say anything. I rode along beside Pa.

"I want you boys to learn something from me while I'm alive and trading," Pa said. "You boys don't realize what a great trader I am. And you won't know it until after I'm gone."

"I've loved you for thirty years with all my heart," Pa said as he stood before Mom with the deed in his hand.

"Second to trading, Mick," she said. "I play second fiddle. It's your trading you think about. It's been your life since I've been married to you. All you do is trade and brag about it. Some of these times, somebody is goin' to be just a little smarter than you."

Then Pa laughed as I had never heard him laugh before. He put the deed in his inside coat pocket, pulled a cigar from his vest pocket, bit the end from it with his tobacco-stained teeth, wet the cigar with his tongue. Then he put it between his clean-shaven lips, pulled a match from his hatband, struck it on his thumbnail, and held the flame to the end of the long black cigar. He pulled enough smoke from the cigar into his mouth at one time to send a cloud of smoke to the ceiling. With the cigar in his mouth, he looked up at the smoke, put his thumbs behind his suspenders, pulled them out, and let them fly back and hit him while he laughed, smoked, and listened to Mom.

"You're too proud of yourself, Mick," Mom warned. She had stopped hooking her rug now as she sat there watching Pa walk up and down the room. "You know Permintis Mullins is a dangerous man. You know he's a proud man. When you hurt his pride, you do something to him. He's liable to explode. You know the Mullinses back in Pike County, don't you?"

"And you know the Powderjays too, don't you?" Pa snapped. "You're married to one. We had pride back in Pike County too. And we got it now. That's why I own The Valley. I'll have Permintis Mullins hemmed. I'll own land all around old Permintis. And if he's got any pride left in his bones he'll come to me like a man. We'll set a price 'give or take.' And when he sets the price, I know he can't 'take it.' I'll get it all. What kind of pride do you call that, Sal?"

Pa laughed louder than he did before.

"We've been together thirty years, Mick," Mom said. "Even if you do stay on the road and trade, I want you to be with me a while longer. I just have a feeling something is goin' to happen to you. I don't know what. I do know Permintis Mullins!"

"Not anything is goin' to happen," Pa assured her.

Pa had stopped laughing now. He had taken his big thumbs from behind his suspenders. He didn't blow smoke at the ceiling. He held the cigar in his hand and looked at Mom. Mom didn't often talk to him like this. "We're goin' to have this farm before Permintis Mullins knows what's goin' on. I'm leaving here tonight. Adger is goin' with me. Finn is goin' with us to Auckland and bring the horses back. We're goin' to get that five o'clock train up Big Sandy. We're heading for Pike County tonight. Sid and Clara will be signing this deed for me at about noon tomorrow if the train's on time."

Mom looked at Pa and then she looked at me. Mom didn't know what to say.

"It's the early bird that gets the worm," Pa bragged. Then he started laughing again.

"I've heard you say that so much, Mick," Mom said. "But I'm afraid, Mick."

"Not anything to be afraid of," Pa boasted, as he walked toward the dresser and opened the drawer.

"No, Mick," Mom said, getting up from her chair. And then she smiled. "You don't need that. Not you. Anybody who can trade and make money like you, can protect himself with his big strong fist."

Pa closed the dresser drawer. He looked at Mom and smiled. Then he pulled her close to him with his big arms around her.

"Now you're talking like the little girl who used to love me," he told her. "That's the way I love to hear you talk. That puts the spirit in me. I'll have that farm now or I'll know the reason. Adger, get Finn out of bed. Have him dress and let's be on our way."

When I returned with Finn, Pa was still holding Mom in his big arms. He wasn't acting like the trader now. He was acting like a man in love when he held my beautiful mother in his arms. And I knew why Mom had bragged on him. She didn't want Pa to take his piece of hardware with him. She knew Pike County and she knew Pa. She knew Pa had as much spirit and pride as any man in Pike County. She knew if any man asked Pa to count to ten and then draw, Pa would do it. She knew there wasn't a Mullins of the name who could bluff my father.

Pa squeezed Mom tight and kissed her goodbye and we were off into the night. Finn and I rode old Ned double. Pa took the lead on Moll. It was past midnight. The moon was down. We rode through the mud and the night wind. We rode by starlight. It was four in the morning when we reached Auckland.

"Now, be careful goin' back," Pa advised Finn. "Don't go to sleep in the saddle. Don't get Moll's bridle rein tangled around you and let her drag you from Ned's saddle. Go home and get some sleep."

"Don't worry about me, Pa," Finn replied. "I'll get the horses home all right. I won't go to sleep in the saddle. I worry about you. Up all night and not any sleep. I've had some sleep."

"We'll get a little sleep on the train," Pa told him. "Business is business, you know, and when a deal is hot it's better to forget sleep. There'll be time enough for sleep when I have this deed signed. I'll sleep peacefully coming back on the train tonight. Be sure and meet us here with the horses."

"I won't forget," Finn said as he mounted old Ned.

We stood there in the starlight, not far from the depot, and watched Finn ride away. Then Pa turned toward the railroad station and I followed him. When Pa stood at the window getting our tickets, I just happened to look back and there sat Permintis Mullins. His eyes were about half-closed. He sat there dreaming like a lizard half asleep in the morning sun. I didn't say anything. Not to Pa. I'd let him see Permintis for himself. It made my heart skip a few beats to see him there.

"Here's your ticket," Pa said, looking up at about the same time.

When he saw Permintis Mullins, he froze like my Irish setter, Rusty, when he sees a bird. Pa didn't move a muscle. His big gray eyes narrowed down. When Permintis Mullins awoke from his half sleep with Pa's eyes on him, he jumped up from his seat. He muttered something we couldn't understand. I think he called Pa a bad name under his breath. He sat back down and looked at Pa. Neither one spoke. He knew what Pa was after. Pa knew what he was after. When Pa did move he walked outside the station and I followed.

"What do you know about that." It was hard for Pa to believe. "Do you reckon Jack Willis lied to me?"

"I'll bet he came later and went to Jack Willis' home and got Jack out of bed," I said. "That's how he got his deed. You know he's got one too."

"You reckon he has?" Pa looked strangely at me.

"Think I saw it in his inside coat pocket," I told him.

"Let's get our heads together and do some thinkin' before we get on the train." Pa wasn't laughing now. "Let's get on the same coach so we can watch 'im."

"But Pa, you don't want any trouble with 'im," I pleaded.

"We're not goin' to have any trouble," Pa assured me. "I just want to get close enough to watch him. Want to be close enough to feel any move he makes. Want one of us to keep an eye on him at all times."

"Suppose he's not got a piece of hardware along?" I said.

"I'd a had my piece along if it hadn't been for your mother's soft-soapin' me right before I left," Pa explained. "Even a woman when she loves a man with all her heart is liable to get him hurt. Hurt by a dangerous character like that Permintis Mullins."

Permintis Mullins was a big Pike County mountaineer. He had a clean-shaven bony face. His handlebar moustache looked like a long black bow tie, tied under his nose with both ends of the tie sagging. He wore a big black umbrella hat. He was a big man but he wasn't built like Pa. He wasn't broad shouldered. He was tall. He had long arms and big hands. He was long legged and wore tight-fitting pants that bulged at the knees. Permintis had the eyes of an eagle. They were beady black eyes that pierced when they looked at you.

"When we get off this train at Bainville, let's make a run and get the first taxi," Pa suggested. "Take it all the way to Sid Beverley's. It's just three miles from the railroad station. I've been over that road many a time."

"You make the plans, Pa, and I'll follow 'em," I said.

"All we want to do is beat old Permintis there," Pa whispered.

When the train pulled up, we stood there waiting for Permintis. I happened to turn around and he was standing behind watching us. "Come on, Pa," I said.

And Pa followed me onto the coach. When we walked in and got a seat in the smoker, Permintis followed us. He sat on the other side of the aisle just a little behind us. When he sat down, I saw the deed in the inside pocket of his unbuttoned coat. Maybe it was my imagination, but I thought I saw the prints of a holster on his hip. I was sure he'd brought his hardware piece along.

When breakfast was called and Pa and I went to the diner, Permintis followed us. He sat about the middle of the diner. Pa and I got up in the front corner so we could talk.

"He's goin' to Sid Beverley's sure as the world," Pa said. "I wonder when he got that deed. We were the last ones in Jack Willis' office before he closed. After the way Jack talked to me, I don't believe he would get out of bed to make a deed for that scoundrel."

"But he voted for Jack too, Pa," I said. "He belongs to our party and he rode day and night the last week of the election to help Jack Willis. I understand he says he elected Jack. Said his work gave Jack the extra forty-four votes."

Pa couldn't believe it. He couldn't believe we were on the train eating breakfast in one end of the diner and down midway sat Permintis Mullins. All of us heading for Sid Beverley's place on Wolfe Creek.

After breakfast we went back to our seats in the smoker. Strange, but Permintis finished his breakfast same time we did. When we sat down, Permintis had to walk past us. Pa scanned him carefully.

Just before noon, about the time we reached the border of Pike County, Pa got up to light a cigar and stretch his legs. Permintis got up too. He stood up and watched Pa, though he didn't speak. And everybody riding on this coach watched the strange actions of Pa and Permintis.

When the conductor called "Litchfield" Pa stood up again.

"Bainville's the next stop," Pa whispered. Then Pa walked out into the aisle while the train stopped. Permintis got up too. Pa walked in the opposite direction since he was a little shy of Permintis. Then we heard "all aboard" from outside. Pa walked back to our seat and sat down. He was so restless he couldn't wait. He didn't like Permintis Mullins' black eagle eyes trained on him all the time either. When Pa got seated the train was moving again.

"Where's Permintis, Pa?" I said, looking back.

"Men's room, maybe," Pa said, puffing on his cigar. Then, Pa looked back. "Do you reckon he got off this moving train?"

"There he goes, Pa," I shouted as I looked from the window. "He's running down the street."

"Let me off'n here," Pa screamed, jumping up.

"But the train is moving now, Pa," I said, holding him by the arm. "You can't get off. Not now."

"We're tricked," Pa shouted.

Everybody started looking at us and the conductor came running and grabbed Pa by the arm. "What's the matter with you?" he asked Pa. "Are you trying to commit suicide? You can't leave this train when it's moving like this."

"But that scoundrel," Pa screamed, shaking his head. "That Permintis Mullins! He's tricked me!"

"What fellow?" the conductor asked. "What did he do? Relieve you of your wallet or something?"

"Not that, Conductor," I said. "I'll explain it to you. He and my father are here to buy the same piece of land down in Greenwood County and it's owned by Sid Beverley on Wolfe Creek. The other fellow got off at Litchfield and is trying to beat us to Wolfe Creek. We're on this train and can't get off before Bainville. Which is closer to Wolfe Creek, Litchfield or Bainville?"

"Bainville, of course," the conductor said, smiling at Pa. "It's only three miles from Bainville to Sid Beverley's on Wolfe Creek. It's thirteen miles from Litchfield to Sid Beverley's. I know this country well. I live in Litchfield."

"Can we get a taxi in Bainville?" Pa asked.

"They'd laugh at you if you asked for a taxi there," said the conductor as he looked over his bright-rimmed glasses at Pa. "Bainville's not big enough to support a taxi."

"Can Permintis Mullins get one in Litchfield?" I asked.

"He can't get one there either," the conductor said.

Everybody on the coach had become interested in our problem. They listened when the conductor talked with us. There were whispers from one end of the coach to the other. And there was much laughter which Pa didn't like. His face got as red as a ripe sourwood leaf. The fire died in his cigar. Pa put it in his mouth and chewed the end. When the conductor left us to call the next station, Pa and I hurried to the end of the coach.

When the train stopped, we were the first to get off. "Taxi! Taxi!" Pa screamed. Somebody laughed at Pa. "Can I get somebody to drive me to

Sid Beverley's on Wolfe Creek? I'm in a hurry." There wasn't any bidding. Not a single bid.

"Come, Adger," Pa shouted. "Not any time to lose. We've got to hoof it! We can beat him if we hurry! I know the way! Come on!"

We started off. I never saw Pa move like he was moving now. He threw the cigar down. I hoped, as we trotted along down the muddy road, somebody might come along with a wagon and pick us up. I wondered how Permintis was going to cover his thirteen miles if his road was as muddy as this one. And I hoped it was.

"Now is the time to beat Permintis," Pa grunted with a half breath. "Pray for a ride and keep going. Let's strike while the iron's hot. Early bird . . ."

"He's got thirteen miles of this muddy road," I grunted. "We've got three. . . . We can beat 'im . . ."

"But we lost time on that awful slow train," Pa stammered, for he was short of breath. "Permintis pulled a fast one."

After one mile on this muddy road, we stopped. We didn't talk, to save our breath. We doubled time on the second mile. We reached the mouth of Wolfe Creek. Then we crossed the bridge.

"Back to my homeland," Pa grunted. "Changed so I don't know it. Not my homeland any longer. The Valley . . ." And Pa stopped talking, saved his breath, and increased his speed.

When we turned the first big bend in the Wolfe Creek road, Pa stopped. "Yonder's where Sid lives," he moaned as he wiped streams of sweat from his face.

As we hurried the last quarter mile, our breath coming short and fast, we saw three men come from Sid's big log house. We stopped short when we saw them get in a car. They started driving toward us. To our surprise the car pulled up close beside Pa, who was spattered with mud, and stopped.

Permintis rolled the window down and stuck his head out. "Would you like to have this, you old land-hawg?" Permintis shouted, holding up a paper for Pa to see. Then, he laughed slyly as he pulled his head inside and rolled the window up. The driver gunned the car.

Pa was stunned. We stood there in silence looking at each other and at the car as it moved slowly along, flinging two streaks of yellow clay into the bright March wind from the rear wheels.

"Wonder if he got that farm?" Pa said, breaking our silence as Permintis' car crossed the Wolfe Creek bridge and was out of sight. "Let's go see what happened!"

Sid Beverley, six feet five inches tall, and a big man for his height, opened the door when we walked onto his porch. His frosted crabgrass-colored hair was ruffled by the March wind. His blue eyes sparkled.

"Welcome home, Mick," Sid greeted Pa. "Welcome, Adger! Back to the land of your people. Come in! I've been waitin' for you all mornin'! Permintis told me you were on your way!"

We walked into the house, where Clara took Pa's hand. "How is Sallie, Mick?" Clara asked, but Pa didn't answer her.

"I come to buy that farm from you, Sid," Pa said, turning to Sid.

"Well, the early bird always gets the worm, Mick," Sid told Pa. "You've traded enough to know that!"

"It beats all I ever heard tell of," Pa grunted as he wiped streams of perspiration from his red face with a big blue bandanna. "Do you mean that Permintis outsmarted me?"

"Call it anything you like," Sid said calmly. "Permintis telegraphed the Sheriff of Pike County to meet the train at Litchfield with a car, a notary public, and a witness for a land deal."

"That scoundrel," Pa shouted as he shook his fist in the direction Permintis had gone.

I looked at my father as he stood there before Sid Beverley. The light that had always been in his eyes when he was about to make a good trade was gone. And then, I remembered how many times Mom had warned him that someday an earlier bird would get the worm.

HARRY CREWS

A Long Wail

THE OLD MAN LOOKED OUT THE WINDOW AT THE DARKENED FIELDS
slipping past in the rain and said, "Tonight, you ring the bell before supper.
I want to eat with him one more time."

Sarah Nell sat stiff on the seat, both hands holding firmly to the steering
wheel, and did not answer. Out of the corner of her eye she could see her
father's twisted profile. No matter how hard she concentrated on the road,
his face was always there like a piece of gravel under the lid.

The old man turned on the seat toward her, half of his face melting away
into shadow.

"You ain't fer it, are you?" he asked.

"You're Pa, so I ain't against it," she said. "It's you that's got to care it around,
that's going to bed with it and gittin up with it, so I cain't be against it."

"You always was a sensible girl," he said.

"I just don't know about tollin Gaff in and shutting the door on him like
you'd pen a hog. He ain't gone understand that."

"He don't have to understand," said the old man. "I'm the only one who
has to understand. I'm sick to death of doctors."

"Don't put it on him," she said. "Dr. Threadly's a good man."

"He's a fool and I'm worse. When it gits that time, you go. That's all there
is to it. All there ever was to it." His voice was soft, the words slightly blurred,
as though coming from a great distance. "Remember your Ma, an how he
wagged his wonderful tongue over her an how we follered her right on
down to the grave with him still talking."

Sarah Nell caught at the word "Ma" and held it to her as though it were
a talisman. She moved her lips over the sound of it, breathing it into the
darkness and sucking it back again until finally the sound and the word
became an odor and an image; and the image burned cleanly before her:
hot blue eyes, dry and faded with pain, set above high cheekbones over
which the thin flesh stretched like parchment.

"But Ma never rung a bell for Gaff," she said, the words bursting from her lips before she knew she would say them. "Never a bell for Gaff to take me to Big Creek Church."

"That was your Ma, and she had me," he said. "Besides, women can walk up face to face with things that men can only back up to."

"I'll pray," she said softly, almost inaudibly.

"For me?" he asked.

"No," she said. "For Gaff and me."

She turned the car into the lane leading down from the big road, through old, winter-naked pecan trees, past the lot where the hesitant bray of a mule joined the sound of the wind. A great, brindle-colored mastiff waited at the yard fence. He had not barked when they drove up, and sat now with his huge head hanging forward. The old man spoke to him softly as he passed through the gate and the dog raised himself, long and lean, his belly curving sharply upward from his chest. The old man lifted his arm in the direction of the mule barn and the mastiff turned and walked away in the rain.

In the kitchen her father sat silently with his elbows on the faded oilcloth of the table, his chin propped in his hands, while Sarah Nell set out cold meat and bread.

"Is they clabber?" he asked through the web of his fingers.

"Yessir," answered Sarah Nell.

"Set it," he said.

She set the clabber out and put an earthen bowl beside his plate. In the yellow light of the kerosene lamp, the surface of the clabber took on a bluish tinge. He turned his eyes on the bowl and gently his fingers drummed the bandages partially covering his mouth where cancer had broken through in an open sore. Slivers of cheek and segments of gum had been removed leaving the right side of his face concave as though his jawbone had been half split away. As it always did when he was about to eat, his odor grew stronger, the heavy, half-sweet odor of decay that swarmed about him like flies.

"Git that syrup, too," he said, the words far away, muffled by the bandage.

She took the syrup bucket down from the screen-wire safe, pried up the lid with a case knife, and set it beside him. Before she could sit down at her place, he said without looking up from the bucket, "Ring the bell for Gaff."

She stepped out onto the porch, and the night air met her cold and clean. She stood a moment breathing deeply against the scent in her nostrils, but it was no good. On her tongue was the taste of decay and it drew her mouth like alum. The rain had stopped, but a mist still hung in the air as fine as fog. There were no stars now, no moon. The lamp from the kitchen window gave enough light to see the triangular rod of iron hanging from a piece of hay wire at the end of the porch. She struck it three times with an iron cylinder. The sound came back again and again, bouncing out of the black forest of pine that bordered the field at the back of the house.

"I ain't there, I'm here."

Sarah Nell shrank into herself, the breath catching at the base of her throat, her hand still poised to strike. The voice had come out of the darkness at the edge of the porch.

"Gaff?"

"Yeah. I've already come. I was just waiting out there for the bell." The voice was at the steps now; then the sound of his booted feet was on the porch and she saw him, tall, his felt hat pushed back, his brow very smooth and damp.

"How . . . ?" she began.

"Seen the lights of the automobile when it come up," he said.

"He's waiting," she said.

Gaff went into the kitchen ahead of her, stooping slightly in the door, the black hat still on his head.

"That was quick," her father said without looking up from the clabber he had dipped and was now stirring.

"I was out there waiting," said Gaff.

Sarah Nell sat at the table opposite her father. Gaff remained standing just inside the door.

"You had your supper?" asked her father.

Gaff shifted his weight and reached up and pulled his hat farther down on his forehead.

"No sir, I ain't," he said, "But I don't . . ."

"Git him a plate Sarah Nell."

Gaff was rock-still now, his back pressed into the wall by the door.

"I ain't hongry," he said evenly.

"You said you didn't eat," said her father, still without looking at him. "Set and be welcome."

Sarah Nell set a plate, a bowl, and a spoon at the end of the table, and then the three of them sat very still, their plates empty, while the old man loosened the bandage at the right side of his face so he could eat. Both Gaff and Sarah Nell looked directly at him, at his fingers working slowly and delicately as though unwrapping a fine and treasured secret.

He was the first to eat and the clabber had to be kept in the left side of his mouth because the right cheek had been partially cut away to expose the grinding teeth.

"You want some of this clabber?" asked the old man, gesturing toward the bowl at his elbow.

"No sir, I don't," said Gaff. He had put a biscuit in the middle of his plate and was making an effort to keep his eyes on it, but the naked, working spot in the old man's face was too fascinating, and his eyes would invariably come off his plate and slowly move up the denim work shirt to the dry, seamed neck to the teeth.

"It's mighty good with a little syrup."

"Yessir," Gaff said, his eyes trying to make it back to the biscuit, "But I really ain't too hongry."

"You ain't, huh?"

"No sir, I ain't and if it's the same to you, I'll just step to the door and smoke till you ready to talk."

"No, no," said the old man quickly. "Smoke there if you like. And's for talking, now's as good as any."

Gaff took out a book of cigarette leaves and a can of tobacco.

"Did you start breaking the back field yet?"

"Yessir, I did."

"And did you get the cloth on the beds all right?"

"Yessir."

"Any sign of blue mold?"

"No sir."

The old man had cleared his mouth of food and his words were more distinct now.

"Good, good. You're a worker Gaff. Always have been. What you need is a wife."

The cigarette broke in Gaff's fingers, and the tobacco dribbled off onto his lap. He looked at Sarah Nell. She sat stiff in her chair, her cheeks ashen, looking directly across the table at her father.

"Sir?" said Gaff.

"You a young man and you able," he said. "You cain't expect to go on working another man's land in a cabin without a woman for the rest of your life." He had begun spooning clabber into his mouth again. There was a brittle silence over the table for a long minute. Then he looked up over his poised spoon and asked, "Can you?"

Sarah Nell and the old man watched Gaff across the table, and he, still holding the torn cigarette paper between his fingers, stared at the biscuit in his plate. Finally he pushed his chair back slowly and took off his hat. The band across his forehead where the hat had been was red and damp with sweat.

"They is some that has," said Gaff.

"Do you want to be one that has?" asked the old man, pushing the clabber bowl across to Gaff.

Gaff reached for the spoon and without lowering his eyes began to dip clabber.

"No," said Gaff.

"When you take Sarah Nell to Big Creek Church tonight, you oughto start looking," he said. "They's lots of girls just waiting."

Gaff stopped dipping.

"When I take her where?"

"I want you to drive her over there to the revival. The roads is bad with the rain."

"Tonight?" asked Gaff.

"She wants to go," said the old man.

Sarah Nell, her face set like a gray mask, leaned forward and with a steady hand ladled two spoons of syrup into Gaff's bowl.

"Clabber and syrup makes right good eatin'," she said. "It's a wonder anything could look so bad and be so good."

A loud silence hung in the room. Gaff picked up his spoon, stirred the clabber, looked at Sarah Nell, then stirred again, his face as gray as hers. A drop of sweat broke from his forehead and trembled at the end of his nose. Only the old man had the color of life in his face.

"It *is* a wonder," said Gaff.

The old man moved his chair closer to the table, leaned on his elbows, and said, "Sarah Nell and me was talking on the way from town."

"You was, huh," said Gaff.

"Would you like another one of these biscuits, boy?" asked the old man.

"No sir, I ain't finished this un yet."

"We was talking about you and the doctor. Tell Gaff what the doctor said, Sarah Nell."

"About the doctor and *me*?" asked Gaff.

"Tell him, Sarah Nell."

"Doctor Threadly says Pa has to have his tongue taken off."

Gaff's mouth opened, worked over a word, then closed. His pink underlip caught the light and trembled.

"His tongue?" he finally managed to say.

"That's the next thing," said Sarah Nell woodenly.

"The doctor says," said the old man, his mouth doing the best it could with a smile, "that if I don't have it taken off I'll die."

Gaff opened his mouth as though he would speak, but instead put a spoon of clabber into it.

"That's mighty good eatin once you get started," Sarah Nell said. Gaff raised his eyes to hers and she saw his throat work over the clabber.

"It's mighty good, thank you," said Gaff. "You going to have it taken off?"

"No, I ain't," said the old man.

"I'll have another one of them biscuits," said Gaff.

The old man looked past Gaff to the door, and his vision was distant, stretching past the porch, past the field and even the night, down to the forest of pines. "Since the first frost of November in this country, living on land I growed out of as a boy, I been a stranger. Not eating with anybody, not talking with anybody, and follered by a scent that'ed sicken a hog." His eyes suddenly snapped back, and Gaff met them steadily, sucking at a front tooth, and wiping his mouth with the back of his hand. "Now I'm supposed to fix it so I cain't even holler when I hurt."

"And Pa and me was just talking on the way this evening," said Sarah Nell, her face still ashen, but her eyes bright and moist.

"And I just wanted to set again . . ." said the old man, his voice trailing off, his eyes wandering to the door again, ". . . to set to the table again. . . ."

"It was mighty good," said Gaff. "That syrup's got a good taste."

"That syrup's a tad too sharp, son," said the old man. "You biled it too long."

"You think so, huh," said Gaff, dabbing his finger on the rim of the syrup can and touching it to his tongue.

"Next year you cook it slower and not so long. It'll lose that tart."

"I'll do that," Gaff said. "I will."

"I smell myself," said the old man. "You'd think I couldn't smell it wouldn't you? To be able to smell it after all this time." He shook his head slowly, and pulled the clabber to his bowl again.

"We'd best be going, Miss Sarah Nell," said Gaff.

She went around the table to her father and kissed him on the scarred side of his face.

"Goodbye, Pa."

"Bye, Sarah Nell." He did not look at her.

When Gaff opened the door, the huge dog was sitting on the other side of the screen, his yellow eyes dull and unblinking. Gaff pushed back the screen and the dog walked through to the old man and lay at his feet. As they were going through the door the old man spoke again.

"Take the dog too," he said.

"Sir?" asked Gaff, already standing on the porch, but still holding the door open behind him.

"Take him out of here," said the old man.

Joe Gaff looked from the dog to Sarah Nell, who refused to meet his eyes, and then back to the dog.

"It ain't me that can make him leave you, sir," Gaff said.

The old man looked at the dog for a long, still moment and then raised his arm and pointed toward the door and the night.

"Go out of here. Git," said the old man.

The dog raised himself slowly and passed through the door between Gaff and Sarah. Outside, the wind was up again and it was raining. They left the dog standing by the car shed, tail and ears drooping, his body slicked black with rain. The car was already past the mule lot, halfway down the lane between the rows of pecan trees, before they heard the dog howl the first time, a long, moon-reaching wail breaking over the night.

Gaff turned to Sarah Nell as though he would speak, but did not. Instead, he pulled his hat lower over his eyes and guided the old car carefully through the mud out of the lane onto the big road.

"Pa always was a fool about clabber," Sarah Nell said, her wooden voice breaking over the last word.

JAMES LEWIS MACLEOD

The Jesus Flag

IF GOD, IN CURSING LOT'S WIFE, HAD TURNED HER INTO A PILLAR OF sugar, instead of salt, Mrs. Wilhelper would have fit the bill. With her tight bun hairdo and squat body resembling a bush, she was five feet three inches of sweetness as determined as a dump truck. She had two sayings—"Too Sweet for Words" and "Perfectly Marvelous"—which she unloaded on every aspect of the universe as relentlessly as a manure spreader covering a green field.

"Clara's just Too Sweet for Words," said Mrs. Wilhelper to her daughter, Mugsie. They were seated at an imitation early-American breakfast table under a large still-life of fruits. Stirring her breakfast coffee with a plain-patterned silver spoon engraved *W*, Mrs. Wilhelper regarded Mugsie.

"Don't you think so, dear?" she asked, adding as if there might be room for misconstruction, "Clara's just too sweet for words?"

"Ummm," said Mugsie. Long ago she had outgrown the desire to scream, to strip off her clothes, to run around the table at the banality of her mother's conversation. This was probably the millionth and first time she had heard the same views expressed in the same words, yet she had adopted an almost predestinarian fatalism about the whole thing. She had learned to let her mother clank on, assuming agreement, until her view of the universe was exhausted.

Mugsie was not an unattractive girl with her straight red hair and bright brown eyes; however, she dressed severely, purposely out of fashion. She had been christened Estella Carolina, but her father, who had hoped for a boy, called her Mugsie. It fit, even though she was a girl, for her mind was as hard as any man's.

The girl was educated and teaching school at a branch of the state university ten miles away. Mrs. Wilhelper realized that her daughter was an intellectual but always treated her as if she were normal. The daughter repaid the compliment by treating Mrs. Wilhelper as if she were human.

"Clara's a nut, but, at least, she's interesting," answered Mugsie. With that she rose briskly from the table, pecked her mother on the cheek, and grabbed a briefcase from under the table; her flat heels ground efficiently and speedily out of the room.

Mrs. Wilhelper's friends said Mugsie was on flame for knowledge. This was merely Southern rhetoric but it affected Mrs. Wilhelper strangely. She had a vision of a dry haystack going up in flames, a loss to nobody but cows. What Mrs. Wilhelper wanted was grandchildren, yet she was not one to stand in the way of talent. She dismissed the misfortune of Mugsie from her brain, concentrating on the silver spoon with the *W* on it that Clara had polished so beautifully.

Clara loved to work. She dressed herself in a long white apron to go about cleaning with the love of an artist.

"Work for the night is coming," Clara would say brightly to Mrs. Wilhelper as she sat on the porch. Mrs. Wilhelper thought of herself in the old tradition of being a lady. A lady was decorative, ornamental, useless, closely identified with the beatific vision whose chief duty was to sit and be admired.

Clara had no such views. She was the late Mr. Wilhelper's sister, recently come to live with them, and she had no intention of letting work lie on her hands. She had polished the Victorian sideboard in the dining room with a mixture of beeswax and yellow oil until the sideboard fairly shone. She had aired the mattresses, beat the rugs, ironed the linen, and the day before had just finished polishing the silver, including the spoon with the *W* that Mrs. Wilhelper was holding admiringly in her hand at the breakfast table.

Mrs. Wilhelper admired the virtues of Clara. She preferred to overlook the social vices, of which there were a number. Clara was a religious fanatic. Mrs. Wilhelper had seen her in operation once.

Clara had stood tall (six feet), erect (she had been trained by a Victorian mother), dressed in black linen topped by a cameo (the cameo had belonged to Mr. Wilhelper's mother) by the orange and green neon sign of Metcalf's Clothing Company on the corner of Main Street and Greene. Against her leg there was propped a briefcase in which she dipped to pull out tiny pocket Bibles, offering them to passers-by.

Holding out the tiny Bibles she asked, "Have you found Jesus?" as if religion were a game of hide-and-seek.

If the passers-by had found Jesus, she thrust the Bibles into their hands telling them, "Then this will help you on your way."

If the passers-by had not found Jesus, she said, "It's all here. The path of salvation. Take it. Read about it. Take it."

She would thrust the Bibles into their pockets if the passers-by would not take them in their hands.

Mrs. Wilhelper had considered thrusting Bibles, or anything for that matter, into strange men's pockets as obscene, but of course she was too much of a lady to say so.

If this had been all, Mrs. Wilhelper would have thought nothing of it. Plenty of families were under the domination of hard-lipped, religious-minded old women. But this was not all. The clincher was the Jesus Flag, an original idea conceived by Clara and, as far as Mrs. Wilhelper knew, practiced only by her in the civilized world.

Clara had originated the flag as a signal to let Jesus know a soul was falling from grace so that He might rescue the perishing. She waved it in dire circumstances when she felt the aid of Jesus was vitally needed. Having called Christ's attention to the sinner in peril, Clara, more or less, considered her work done.

"I don't do a thing," said Clara piously, stroking her white apron, "grace saves and grace alone."

The flag was known all over the state. When the governor had made a commencement speech to the graduating class of the State University, Clara had risen up and waved the flag right there—right there, Mrs. Wilhelper thought, right there, pointing specifically in her mind to an imaginary scene so that she could work up a hotter indignation.

Mrs. Wilhelper was glad Clara had been married (even though she had had no children) so that the Wilhelper name had not been in the papers whose headlines generally ran: "Auntie Appeals to God to Save the Governor."

The picture in her own paper, her own paper, the *Union-Times*, had shown Clara standing on a chair beside a puzzled young man in a mortar board hat whose tassel obscured his nose. She was holding the flag in both her hands like a classical statue of Victory or something Greek.

The flag was a green cross on a red background with John 3:16 embroidered in black beneath the cross. Clara had designed it herself.

Mrs. Wilhelper sometimes wondered if Clara knew the modern value of publicity, but generally decided she was too unworldly to know the modern implications. People said it cost the governor plenty. The opposition had circulated underground pictures of Clara and the flag with the caption underneath: "Pray for the State Under J. P. Gilmore." It seemed to have no effect on Clara.

Mrs. Wilhelper put the silver spoon with the *W* back on the table, groaned inwardly, and got up to go sit on the front porch. Lately she had become fond of an old wicker chaise longue at the end of the porch in the shade of an oak tree. She could count on Clara's coming down to do the work.

"Making myself useful as well as ornamental," Clara would say briskly.

"Darling, you're too sweet for words to do all this," Mrs. Wilhelper would say as she watched Clara grab a brush to scrub the porch.

"Work's good for the spirit," Clara would respond happily digging into an offending black path on the shiny surface of the paint.

That evening the mother, the aunt, and the girl sat on the front porch to enjoy the sunset. The aunt sat in a captain's chair, painted white, commanding a view of the pasture in front of the house. Her straight back, hands carefully folded in her lap, gave her an almost royal silhouette. The girl sat in a wooden rocking chair, painted green, next to her aunt. Mrs. Wilhelper lay in the chaise longue by the oak tree.

"Isn't it a perfectly marvelous view," said Mrs. Wilhelper referring to the sky in the process of sunset as the pattern of the oak tree fell across her legs, its intricate shadow promising a grotesquely Celtic day after night's unyielding cancer had eaten light away.

"Striking," said the aunt, as the hard yellow sun folded the sky into a brilliant coarse texture, and the white clouds spun themselves into ragged cones of orange cotton, resembling cotton candy sold at county fairs.

"Pleasant," said the girl. The statement was generous for her. She was not given to growing weak over sunsets.

Mrs. Wilhelper noticed the generosity of the statement. Though she was as dedicated to sweetness as a Vestal virgin, she was nobody's fool. She was sharp in a shrewd, earthy way. Noticed things.

The girl had spent an unusual amount of time with her elders since the aunt had arrived. If the mother had been the sole occupant of the house, the girl would have been inside, reading a book, flaming for knowledge. The mother wondered what had happened to the flame as she shifted uncomfortably on the chaise longue, trying to get her legs back in the shade of the tree and away from an unusually vital last shot of the sun before its departure.

The girl, swaying gently in the green rocker, was burning—even consumed—with curiosity about the Jesus Flag. She dared not ask directly. Manners forbade it and she had horrifying visions of what a direct attack might set off. A revivalistic retaliation. A Puritan Sermon. A Shouting Methodist. So she said politely, "The world situation seems to be getting worse."

"Yes, I think they'll have to drop the bomb eventually," said the aunt.

"Don't think about it," said the mother.

The flag did not appall Mugsie as it did her mother; if anything, she felt it added color to the world. She had the intellectual's delight in eccentricities coupled with the intellectual's desire to analyze them. She wanted to see how, when, and under what circumstances Aunt Clara flew the Jesus Flag. She did not often have the opportunity to examine so unusual a curiosity, abnormal psychology not being her field.

Moving the green rocker gently back and forth on the porch in the soft solemnity of the night, she felt disappointed there had not been even one sign of evangelism so far. Vaguely she had relied on the horrors of the world situation, the atrocities so faithfully recited each night over television, to spur so religiously sensitive a soul as her aunt to fly the flag.

Perhaps, the girl reasoned as she stood up from the rocker to bid them good night, her aunt felt Jesus was already informed of the state of the world by modern communications methods, whereas the aunt worked on an individual basis among the unpublicized.

The girl's bedroom consisted chiefly of books and a bare four-poster bed. Her mother had done her best to make it feminine and she had done her best to make it sexless. Lying down on the bed, which she had carefully de-chintzed, she arranged the white pillows beneath her head to settle down to consider the problem.

She would have to force her aunt's hand.

The more she thought about it, the more determined she became. It was not an irrational desire. If push came to shove, she could rationalize it in the name of science by submitting a report to the psychology department.

Poking the white pillows to make a more comfortable gap for her head, she began to recite in her mind all the horrors she could think of to spur the old lady to fly the flag. It was not difficult, for she had a naturally tough mind, yet she was not unkind enough to wish to shock her aunt too deeply.

She decided to start gently, playing the campaign by ear. Having decided, she got up to turn the lights out so she could undress. She preferred to turn the lights off to undress rather than deprive herself of the night breezes by shutting the blinds.

The next night the round mahogany dining table was set formally with a silver epergne in the middle of the table directly beneath the crystal chandelier. The first layer of the epergne was filled with ferns, the second layer with white roses.

The three of them sat around the shiny centerpiece. The mother was in the hostess' position, the girl in the man's position, the aunt in the middle.

"Isn't this salad just perfectly marvelous," said Mrs. Wilhelper drawing out the words into breathy loops of airy contentment. She was especially proud of the salad. She had made it herself out of grated cabbage and topped it with a yellow syrup swimming with cinnamon. The rest of the food—a pie, a soufflé, a grilled steak—had been prepared by the aunt.

"Delicious," said the aunt, who had acquiesced in the matter of the salad.

"Appetizing," said the girl, eyeing the yellow mess suspiciously, its turgid liquidity demanding moral effort. She fastened her eyes resolvedly (she knew her mother would object) on a white rose (she knew there was a worm in it) and determined (in the name of science) to begin.

"There was a rape yesterday," she said.

She interpreted the ensuing silence as nonbeing awaiting being and described the rape vividly, including a pair of bloodstained rayon panties that, under laboratory analysis, would clinch the case for the prosecution lawyers, until the mother squealed from the hostess' position, "Not at the table, dear, not at the TABLE."

The aunt munched on as contentedly as a cow. When a low-flying plane shook the house, drowning all conversation in the rattling of the chandelier, jolting a rose from the epergne onto the mahogany table, the aunt asked to be caught up on the backwash: "I missed the part about the panties," she said, poking for further information.

The girl gave it again in detail. Nothing happened, but the question showed the aunt was amenable, involved, paying attention.

Like a good fisherman, Mugsie, having baited the hook, determined to catch the fish. She placed her eyes carefully on the white rose and began casting with tales of beatings. The aunt's serenity on beatings warmed her to consequent murders. The aunt's tranquil acceptance of murder stymied the girl momentarily. She regarded the worm in the white rose and was caught up in perversion.

"Homosexuality is very prevalent today," said the girl.

"Anyone we know?" said the mother.

"I wonder why the Apostle Paul was against it," said the aunt, as if she were ignorant. The girl told her descriptively. They had homosexuality with the soufflé, incest with the steak, and sodomy with the pie, disturbed only by the mother's periodic yappings of, "Not at the table, dear, not at the TABLE," as if it were all right to wait until they got into the parlor.

"I knew a case in '05," said the aunt, carefully manipulating the last cherry from her plate onto her fork and finishing up her pie.

It was useless. There seemed to be nothing under the sun that could shock the aunt and no perversion she was unacquainted with. The girl summed this up as the result of the aunt's having lived in boarding houses where the atmosphere was morbid, the caliber of the gossip notorious.

Awaiting the hostess' signal to rise from the table, the girl moved her center of attention from the white rose to her mother. Mrs. Wilhelper, in a kind of trance, had taken a handful of ferns from the epergne and was making a wreath arrangement of the spidery green skeletons on her plate.

When they finally rose from the table, the light of the chandelier caught the silver centerpiece, and the girl noticed her aunt's cleaning had left no black paths of dirt unexplored even in the most creviced parts of the highly chased ornamentation.

"That was a perfectly marvelous meal, Clara," said the mother as the group passed a red velvet love seat in the hall on their way to the porch.

"Yes, and think, just think, of all the people starving in China," said the aunt piously, as if she were giving an invitation to the girl for a further recital of horrors.

"Just think," said the aunt again.

"Not now, love," said the mother who thought she had had as much as she could take.

"But just think," protested the aunt as the mother hurried on her way past the group to the chaise longue, as if there were a disease sitting on the love seat in the hall.

The girl decided to overlook the bid to discuss the Chinese. She had a mental picture of starving Chinese children groaning on the ground, each weighing thirty pounds, their tremendous heads with eyes slightly askew stuck on very small bodies like concentration-camp pictures which, the girl felt, would greatly satisfy her aunt.

She began to wonder just who had been hooked at the dinner table and if her aunt were not profounder than she had heretofore considered.

That night in her bedroom the girl lay on the four-poster bed with the two pillows propped sturdily under her head, considering the aunt from various angles like a prism held up to the sun of her mind. For stability in the middle of her mental readjustments she fixed her gaze steadily on one of the bedposts which had a carved pineapple at the top.

She considered her aunt's having a highly original mind which she, the girl, would discover. The thesis of the original mind would certainly explain a lot. It would explain not only the absurdity of the flag, but her inability to be shocked, her resolute desire to face the plight of the Chinese, her familiarity with murder, her acquaintance with sex perversions.

The girl remembered that the aunt had not brought up the sex perversions, as she had the Chinese, but the girl did not blame the aunt for not dwelling on them, since she was born in the nineteenth century.

The pineapple assumed gigantic proportions in the girl's mind as she groped towards a picture of a completely untrained, undisciplined native mind realizing its existential situation. She could see her aunt in an absolutely shaking essay which she, the niece, would write.

She could see the essay now: "Educated by herself, her untrained mind nevertheless groped with the great problems of our age. Natively realizing her existential situation of futility, her flag became her chief contribution to the absurdity of the universe. Her expression of it in Judeo-Christian terminology is merely the recognition of the limited symbolism in which her experience had to move."

This theory clarified much. On one hand her aunt might be a self-educated folk genius paralleling in the intellectual realm what Grandma Moses did for art, her name ringing eternally in the halls of fame of primitive Americana. On the other hand she might belong in an institution.

The girl's eyes followed the straight line of the bedpost from the pineapple down to where the wood met the sheet. She had to plumb her aunt's depth.

On consecutive nights after dinner the three of them took up their positions on the porch. The aunt, hands carefully folded in her lap, sat in the captain's chair. The girl sat in the green rocker. The mother lay in the chaise longue by the oak tree trying to keep her legs out of the sun.

"I was reading an article by Turgenev," said the girl.

"By who?" queried the aunt.

"Did I remember to turn the hose off?" asked the mother.

The girl, moving in the solemn rhythm of a summer rocker, threw out names like sparks hoping one would catch fire. She ran out Malraux, Gide, Dostoevsky, Dante, Fiske, and Darwin like a Greyhound bus caller hinting beyond the mereness of names to some existent reality waiting expectantly for the traveler. She gave a brief survey of current intellectual thought. She gave up when she found out the aunt had never heard of Freud, though, in probing the aunt's existential situation, she did strike a spark in telling her Kafka's tale of the boy who metamorphosed into a roach.

The aunt hung on every word of the roach story. Every night beneath the orange cotton sky the aunt, hands carefully folded in her lap, royally erect in the captain's chair, would wait for a lull in the conversation.

"Now tell us the roach story, Mugsie," she would beg.

The girl had the feeling she was telling a child a favorite bedtime story that could be repeated endlessly. Since the girl had decided the aunt was as shorn of intellectuality as a sheep, she couldn't decide whether her interest in the roach was traceable to a dirty mind or the right instincts in an untutored one.

The aunt particularly liked the part where the boy turned into a roach. The girl, ceasing rocking, would tell it in words she felt the aunt could understand. She dramatized it for further effect upon the peasant mind. She would open her large brown eyes wide, screw down the corners of her mouth, and say histrionically, "And he woke up and found he was a ROACH."

The aunt's bright little eyes would blink appreciatively like a child's when the wolf was mentioned in "Red Riding Hood." The girl, unmoving in her rocker, would smile bravely. The mother in the chaise longue looked nauseated.

The girl concluded the aunt must be like a child and simply enjoyed a delicious state of terror as greatly as children enjoy scrawling "I am starving to death slowly" on the cellar wall in red paint to symbolize blood.

Dismissing the aunt's original mind, the girl resumed her old position of trying to get the aunt to fly the flag. The rocker continued to be her battle station every night for assaults upon the captain's chair which remained immovable, unshaken, occupied. The chaise longue was a bystander in agony, yet the mother remained fixed in it, constantly redistributing herself to keep her legs out of the sun and in the shade of the oak tree.

"Nietzsche says God is dead," the girl said.

"I've seen quite a few corpses in my time," the aunt volunteered as if she had strength to face it.

"I thought He rose," said the mother.

The girl pointed out to the aunt in a carefully chosen vocabulary of two to three syllables that God was dead, morals foggy, the world an open wound, capitalism a failure, nationalism a disease, patriotism a vice. She broached the idea of a Black Mass, but found her aunt was a Baptist.

As the summer passed, the girl, each night swaying rhythmically in the green rocker, made a discovery. She had started out to shock the aunt, but the result was she had expressed herself so fully that now she felt comfortable with the aunt as with no one else. She dismissed as nebulous the idea of the aunt's ever flying the flag again. She now used the aunt for therapy and began to enjoy her home as never before.

Every evening the group would take their stations to watch the sunset, and the girl, her eyes like obscene yellow lights whose motored passion rapes the night, would address the captain's chair: "I am reading a man who is a silly, ignorant, stupid ass," she would declare, spitting out the words in carefully enunciated contempt.

"Really?" the aunt would say, her ears perking up like those of a fox hearing the distant yapping of a dog pack.

"A jackass," the girl would say flatly.

"You don't mean it," the aunt would say in a tone implying she would be delighted to have it proved.

"The hell I don't," the girl would say in the tone of an officer gathering his men for assault.

"Now, dear," the mother would say, hoping to shut her up though she knew it was useless. The two were as made for each other as fire and straw. For her sins she had to watch the combustion nightly, though it was true nobody forced her to stay in the chaise longue.

When the summer ended, they all went into the parlor.

The girl became harder and more well-defined as if she were aware error emerged from preciseness and truth through definition. Her eyes solidified to rock, piercing the coverings of ideas as easily as a man's lusting eyes piercing skirts to evaluate the living mysteries therein. She toughened into a tartar and gained a reputation.

Soon the girl was giving a series of lectures that terrified the state, the old lady accompanying the girl on her drives to the various small towns where she lectured. The mother did not accompany them, explaining, "I'll just stay here and enjoy peace and quiet for a change."

The girl had a black 1963 Chevrolet with red upholstery. The aunt sat on the right front seat always clutching her black leather handbag with the tulip clasp which, the girl knew, but no longer cared, contained the Jesus Flag. They were two hours from Doomsboro, where the girl was to lecture, the aunt looking calmly out of the window.

They passed a general store with a red Coca-Cola sign, two brick houses, and a Sinclair gas station. After the gas station there was a herd of cows in a green pasture. The aunt watched the cows, seemingly unaware that a brown and white cow was defecating, or, perhaps, unaware that the brown and white cow should do anything else.

Next to the cow pasture the realization came to the girl like a bolt of lightning out of her subconscious, where knowledge had lain passively for months generating energy. She could not conceive of her own stupidity. Insight flashed into her brain and she felt it was illuminating her entire body, yet she drove on, moving the gears from fourth into third and back again as straight-faced and solidly as any Indian.

She saw her aunt's innocence crawling out of a pit so depraved her own world view was merely titillating. She saw her serenity was not betrayal but the last word in acceptance of a view as stark and straight as from the pineapple to the sheet. That her aunt had been a master psychologist squeezing her like a pimple till the pus and core shot out.

The girl passed a white Cadillac convertible and looked slyly at her aunt, who was studiously regarding the remains of a dead dog by the roadside. Pressing the accelerator efficiently, firmly on the floor, she ironed out the tremors in her voice as sleekly as a good maid turning a wedding gown.

The aunt, noticing a sudden spurt in speed, transferred her eyes from the dead dog to the niece.

"What are you gonna lecture on tonight?" she asked, gently sharp in a tone like a harpsichord speaking of rabbits eating grave grass in the moonlight.

"Think I'll reaffirm man's basic position; stress hope, that sort of thing," said the girl's voice smoothly normal.

"Sounds like your mother," said the aunt metallically.

"Mother's pretty sharp in her own way," said the girl sanctimoniously.

By the time they neared the outskirts of Doomsboro, the Jesus Flag had been flying for thirty-eight minutes. The girl had timed it on her watch. Iron-armed, the aunt held the flag out of the right side window to catch the breeze the car was creating as it moved along its path. The tulip-clasped handbag had fallen on the floor and was a black splotch on the red floor upholstery.

The aunt's black-linened arm out the window was as stiff, long, and straight as a poker. If the girl skimmed anything, the arm would be broken. She couldn't risk passing the little green Volkswagen trailing a battered hearse in front of them. The black Chevrolet, chromium gleaming, fell into line at thirty miles an hour behind the Volkswagen and the hearse, while a red '55 Buick came up behind to tail them into the city.

The girl was not unconscious of the scene they were creating, yet there was no sense of amusement in her. She was driving, grim-faced and glorious, through the South Carolina countryside in a procession resembling, on the left, a part of a funeral; on the right, a parade in which people waved flags ridiculously behind hearses. In this way she would enter the city to the acclamations of jeering adolescents. She was determined neither to stop nor to veer.

SIV CEDERING

Family Album

THIS IS THEIR WEDDING PICTURE. PAPPA WEARS A TUXEDO, AND MAMMA is wearing a white satin dress. She is smiling at the white lilies. This is the house Pappa built for Mamma, when they were engaged. Then this house, then that; they were always making blueprints together.

Mamma came from Lapland. She was quite poor and dreamed of pretty dresses. Her mother died when Mamma was small. Pappa met her when he came to Lapland as a conscientious objector. He preached in her church. There he is with his banjo.

Pappa was quite poor too; everyone was in those days. He told me he didn't have any shoes that fit him, one spring, and he had to wear his father's big shoes. Pappa said he was so ashamed that he walked in the ditch, all the way to school.

Pappa was one of eleven children, but only five of them grew up. The others died of tuberculosis or diphtheria. Three died in a six-week period, and Pappa says death was accepted then, just like changes in the weather and a bad crop of potatoes. His parents were religious. I remember Grandfather Anton rocking in the rocker and riding on the reaper, and I remember Grandmother Maria, though I was just two when she died. The funeral was like a party: birch saplings decorated the yard, relatives came from all around, and my sister and I wore new white dresses. Listen to the names of her eleven children:

Anna Viktoria, Karl Sigurd, Johan Martin, Hulda Maria, Signe Sofia, Bror Hilding, Judit Friedeborg, Brynhild Elisabet, John Rudolf, Tore Adils, and Clary Torborg.

We called the eldest Tora. She was fat and never got married. Tore was the youngest son. I remember sitting next to him, outside by the flagpole, eating blood pancakes after a slaughter, and also calf-dance—a dish made from the first milk a cow gives after it has calved. Tore recently left his wife and took a new one. He once told me that when he was a boy, he used to ski out in the dark afternoons of the North and stand still, watching the sky and feeling himself get smaller and smaller. This is Uncle Rudolf in his uniform, and this is Torborg, Pappa's youngest sister. Her fiancé had tried to make love to her once before they were married, and—Mamma told me—Torborg tore the engagement ring off her finger, threw it on the floor of the large farmhouse kitchen, and hollered, loud enough for everyone to hear: "What does that whoremonger think I am?" He was the son of a big-city mayor and well educated, but you can bet he married a virgin. Don't they look good in this picture? Three of their five children are doctors. They say that Torborg got her temper from Great-grandfather. When he got drunk he cussed and brought the horse into the kitchen. This is the Kell people from the Kell farm. I am told I have the Kell eyes. Everyone on this side of the family hears ghosts and dreams prophecies. To us it isn't supernatural; it is natural.

Mamma's oldest brother Karl went to America when he was eighteen. There he is chopping down a redwood tree, and there he is working in a gold mine. He married a woman named Viviann, and they visited us in Sweden. Let me tell you, the village had never seen anyone like her. Not only had she been married and divorced, but she had bobbed hair, wore makeup, and had dresses with padded shoulders, matching shoes, and purses. Vanity of all vanities was quoted from the Bible. So of course everyone knew the marriage wouldn't last—besides, they didn't have any children. Uncle Karl is now old and fat, the darling and benefactor of a Swedish Old Folks Home in Canada. Silver mines help him. This is Mamma's second brother. He had to have a leg amputated. I used to think about that leg, all alone in heaven. This is Aunt Edith. She once gave me a silver spoon that had my name written on it. And this is Aunt Elsa who has a large birthmark on her face. I used to wonder what mark I had to prove that I was born. Mamma's father was a Communist and he came to Lapland to build the large power plant that supplies most of Sweden's electricity. He told me, once, that he ate snake when he was young and worked on the railroad. His wife Emma was a beauty and a lady, and when the household money permitted, she washed her face with heavy cream and her hair with beer or egg whites. My hair? Both grandmothers had hair long enough to sit on.

I am talking about my inheritance—the family jewelry that I wear in my hair, so to speak, the birthmark that stays on my face forever. I am motherless in Lapland, brought down to size by the vastness of the sky. I rock in the rocker of old age and ride the reaper, while some part of me has already preceded me to heaven. I change one husband for another, and toss my ring, furiously moral at any indignation. I am a pacifist, I am a Communist, I am a preacher coddling my father's language and abandoning my mother tongue forever. I eat blood pancakes, calf-dance, snake, and I bring the horse into the kitchen. I build new houses, dream of new dresses, bury my parents and my children. I hear ghosts, see the future and know what will happen. If I step on a crack and break my mother's back, I can say the shoes were too large for my feet, for I know, I know: these are the fairy tales that grieve us. And save us.

T. C. BOYLE

I Dated Jane Austen

HER HANDS WERE COLD. SHE HELD THEM OUT FOR ME AS I STEPPED into the parlor. "Mr. Boyle," announced the maid, and Jane was rising to greet me, her cold white hands like an offering. I took them, said my good evenings, and nodded at each of the pairs of eyes ranged round the room. There were brothers, smallish and large of head, whose names I didn't quite catch; there was her father, the Reverend, and her sister, the spinster. They stared at me like sharks on the verge of a feeding frenzy. I was wearing my pink boots, "Great Disasters" T-shirt, and my Tiki medallion. My shoulders slumped under the scrutiny. My wit evaporated.

"Have a seat, son," said the Reverend, and I backed onto a settee between two brothers. Jane retreated to an armchair on the far side of the room. Cassandra, the spinster, plucked up her knitting. One of the brothers sighed. I could see it coming, with the certainty and illogic of an aboriginal courtship rite: a round of polite chitchat.

The Reverend cleared his throat. "So what do you think of Mrs. Radcliffe's new book?"

I balanced a glass of sherry on my knee. The Reverend, Cassandra, and the brothers revolved tiny spoons around the rims of teacups. Jane nibbled at a croissant and focused her huge unblinking eyes on the side of my face. One of the brothers had just made a devastating witticism at the expense of the *Lyrical Ballads* and was still tittering over it. Somewhere cats were purring and clocks ticking. I glanced at my watch: only seventeen minutes since I'd stepped in the door.

I stood. "Well, Reverend," I said, "I think it's time Jane and I hit the road."

He looked up at the doomed Hindenburg blazing across my chest and smacked his lips. "But you've only just arrived."

There really wasn't much room for Cassandra in the Alfa Romeo, but the Reverend and his troop of sons insisted that she come along. She hefted her skirts, wedged herself into the rear compartment, and flared her parasol, while Jane pulled a white cap down over her curls and attempted a joke about Phaetons and the winds of Aeolus. The Reverend stood at the curb and watched my fingers as I helped Jane fasten her seat belt, and then we were off with a crunch of gravel and a billow of exhaust.

The film was Italian, in black and white, full of social acuity and steamy sex. I sat between the two sisters with a bucket of buttered popcorn. Jane's lips were parted and her eyes glowed. I offered her some popcorn. "I do not think that I care for any just now, thank you," she said. Cassandra sat stiff and erect, tireless and silent, like a mileage marker beside a country lane. She was not interested in popcorn either.

The story concerned the seduction of a long-legged village girl by a mustachioed adventurer who afterward refuses to marry her on the grounds that she is impure. The girl, swollen with child, bursts in upon the nuptials of her seducer and the daughter of a wealthy merchant, and demands her due. She is turned out into the street. But late that night, as the newlyweds thrash about in the bridal bed—

It was at this point that Jane took hold of my arm and whispered that she wanted to leave. What could I do? I fumbled for her wrap, people hissed at us, great nude thighs slashed across the screen, and we headed for the glowing EXIT sign.

I proposed a club. "Oh, do let's walk!" Jane said. "The air is so frightfully delicious after that close, odious theatre—don't you think?" Pigeons flapped and cooed. A panhandler leaned against the fender of a car and drooled into the gutter. I took Jane's arm. Cassandra took mine.

At *The Mooncalf* we had our wrists stamped with luminescent ink and then found a table near the dance floor. The waitress' fingernails were green daggers. She wore a butch haircut and three-inch heels. Jane wanted punch, Cassandra tea. I ordered three margaritas.

The band was re-creating the fall of the Third Reich amid clouds of green smoke and flashing lights. We gazed out at the dancers in their jumpsuits and platform shoes as they bumped bums, heads, and genitals in time to the music. I thought of Catherine Morland at Bath and decided to ask Jane for a dance. I leaned across the table. "Want to dance?" I shouted.

"Beg your pardon?" Jane said, leaning over her margarita.

"Dance," I shouted, miming the action of holding her in my arms.

"No, I'm very sorry," she said. "I'm afraid not."

Cassandra tapped my arm. "I'd love to," she giggled.

Jane removed her cap and fingered out her curls as Cassandra and I got up from the table. She grinned and waved as we receded into the crowd. Over the heads of the dancers I watched her sniff suspiciously at her drink and then sit back to ogle the crowd with her black satiric eyes.

Then I turned to Cassandra. She curtsied, grabbed me in a fox-trot sort of way, and began to promenade round the floor. For so small a woman (her nose kept poking at the moribund Titanic listing across my lower rib cage), I was amazed at her energy. We pranced through the hustlers and bumpers like kiddies round a Maypole. I was even beginning to enjoy myself when I glanced over at our table and saw that a man in fierce black sideburns and mustache had joined Jane. He was dressed in a ruffled shirt, antique tie, and coattails that hung to the floor as he sat. At that moment a fellow terpsichorean flung his partner into the air, caught her by wrist and ankle, and twirled her like a toreador's cape. When I looked up again Jane was sitting alone, her eyes fixed on mine through the welter of heads.

The band concluded with a crunching metallic shriek, and Cassandra and I made our way back to the table. "Who was that?" I asked Jane.

"Who was who?"

"That mustachioed murderer's apprentice you were sitting with."

"Oh," she said. "Him."

I realized that Cassandra was still clutching my hand.

"Just an acquaintance."

As we pulled into the drive at Steventon, I observed a horse tethered to one of the palings. The horse lifted its tail, then dropped it. Jane seemed suddenly animated. She made a clucking sound and called to the horse by name. The horse flicked its ears. I asked her if she liked horses. "Hm?" she said, already looking off toward the silhouettes that played across the parlor curtains. "Oh yes, yes. Very much so," she said, and then she released the seat belt, flung back the door, and tripped up the stairs into the house. I killed the engine and stepped out into the dark drive. Crickets sawed their legs together in the bushes. Cassandra held out her hand.

Cassandra led me into the parlor where I was startled to see the mustachioed ne'er-do-well from *The Mooncalf*. He held a teacup in his hand. His boots shone as if they'd been razor-stropped. He was talking with Jane.

"Well, well," said the Reverend, stepping out of the shadows. "Enjoy yourselves?"

"Oh, immensely, father," said Cassandra.

Jane was grinning at me again. "Mr. Boyle," she said. "Have you met Mr. Crawford?" The brothers, with their fine bones and disproportionate heads, gathered round. Crawford's sideburns reached nearly to the line of his jaw. His mustache was smooth and black. I held out my hand. He shifted the teacup and gave me a firm handshake. "Delighted," he said.

We found seats (Crawford shoved in next to Jane on the love seat; I wound up on the settee between Cassandra and a brother in naval uniform), and the maid served tea and cakes. Something was wrong—of that I was sure. The brothers were not their usual witty selves, the Reverend floundered in the midst of a critique of Coleridge's cult of artifice, Cassandra dropped a stitch. In the corner, Crawford was holding a whispered colloquy with Jane. Her cheeks, which tended toward the flaccid, were now positively bloated, and flushed with color. It was then that it came to me. "Crawford," I said, getting to my feet. "*Henry* Crawford?"

He sprang up like a gunfighter summoned to the OK Corral. "That's right," he leered. His eyes were deep and cold as crevasses. He looked pretty formidable—until I realized that he couldn't have been more than five three or four, give or take an inch for his heels.

Suddenly I had hold of his elbow. The Tiki medallion trembled at my throat. "I'd like a word with you outside," I said. "In the garden."

The brothers were on their feet. The Reverend spilled his tea. Crawford jerked his arm out of my grasp and stalked through the door that gave onto the garden. Nightsounds grated in my ears, the brothers murmured at my back, and Jane, as I pulled the door closed, grinned at me as if I'd just told the joke of the century.

Crawford was waiting for me in the ragged shadows of the trees, turned to face me like a bayed animal. I felt a surge of power. I wanted to call him a son of a bitch, but, in keeping with the times, I settled for cad. "You cad," I said, shoving him back a step, "how dare you come sniffing around her after what you did to Maria Bertram in *Mansfield Park*? It's people like you—corrupt, arbitrary, egocentric—that foment all the lust and heartbreak of the world and challenge the very possibility of happy endings."

"Hah!" he said. Then he stepped forward and the moon fell across his face. His eyes were like the birth of evil. In his hand, a riding glove. He slapped my face with it. "Tomorrow morning, at dawn," he hissed. "Beneath the bridge."

"Okay, wise guy," I said, "okay," but I could feel the Titanic sinking into my belt.

A moment later the night was filled with the clatter of hoofs.

I was greeted by silence in the parlor. They stared at me, sated, as I stepped through the door. Except for Cassandra, who mooned at me from behind her knitting, and Jane, who was bent over a notebook, scribbling away like a court recorder. The Reverend cleared his throat and Jane looked up. She scratched off another line or two and then rose to show me out. She led me through the parlor and down the hall to the front entrance. We paused at the door.

"I've had a memorable evening," she said, and then glanced back to where Cassandra had appeared at the parlor door. "Do come again." And then she held out her hands.

Her hands were cold.

GARY GILDNER

Sleepy Time Gal

IN THE SMALL TOWN IN NORTHERN MICHIGAN WHERE MY FATHER LIVED
as a young man, he had an Italian friend who worked in a restaurant. I will
call his friend Phil. Phil's job in the restaurant was as ordinary as you can
imagine—from making coffee in the morning to sweeping up at night.
But what was not ordinary about Phil was his piano playing. On Saturday
nights my father and Phil and their girlfriends would drive ten or fifteen
miles to a roadhouse by a lake where they would drink beer from schoopers and dance and Phil would play an old beat-up piano. He could play
any song you named, my father said, but the song everyone waited for was
the one he wrote, which he would always play at the end before they left
to go back to the town. And everyone knew of course that he had written
the song for his girl, who was as pretty as she was rich. Her father was the
banker in their town and he was a tough old German and he didn't like
Phil going around with his daughter.

My father, when he told this story, which was not often, would tell it
in an offhand way and emphasize the Depression and not having much,
instead of the important parts. I will try to tell it the way he did, if I can.

So they would go to the roadhouse by the lake and finally Phil would
play his song and everyone would say, Phil, that's a great song, you could
make a lot of money from it. But Phil would only shake his head and
smile and look at his girl. I have to break in here and say that my father,
a gentle but practical man, was not inclined to emphasize the part about
Phil looking at his girl. It was my mother who said the girl would rest
her head on Phil's shoulder while he played, and that he got the idea for
the song from the pretty way she looked when she got sleepy. My mother
was not part of the story, but she had heard it when she and my father
were younger and therefore had that information. I would like to intrude
further and add something about Phil writing the song, maybe show him
whistling the tune and going over the words slowly and carefully to get
the best ones, while peeling onions or potatoes in the restaurant; but my
father is already driving them home from the roadhouse and saying how

patched up his tires were and how his car's engine was a gingerbread of parts from different makes, and some parts were his own invention as well. And my mother is saying that the old German had made his daughter promise not to get involved with any man until after college, and they couldn't be late. Also my mother likes the sad parts and is eager to get to their last night before the girl goes away to college.

So they all went out to the roadhouse and it was sad. The women got tears in their eyes when Phil played her song, my mother said. My father said that Phil spent his week's pay on a new shirt and tie, the first tie he ever owned, and people kidded him. Somebody piped up and said, Phil, you ought to take that song down to Bay City—which was like saying New York City to them, only more realistic—and sell it and take the money and go to college too. Which was not meant to be cruel, but that was the result because Phil had never even got to high school. But you can see people were trying to cheer him up, my mother said.

Well, she'd come home for Thanksgiving and Christmas and Easter and they'd all sneak out to the roadhouse and drink beer from schoopers and dance and everything would be like always. And of course there were the summers. And everyone knew Phil and the girl would get married after she made good her promise to her father, because you could see it in their eyes when he sat at the old beat-up piano and played her song.

That last part about their eyes was not of course in my father's telling, but I couldn't help putting it in there even though I know it is making some of you impatient. Remember that this happened many years ago in the woods by a lake in northern Michigan, before television. I wish I could put more in, especially about the song and how it felt to Phil to sing it and how the girl felt when hearing it and knowing it was hers, but I've already intruded too much in a simple story that isn't even mine.

Well, here's the kicker part. Probably by now many of you have guessed that one vacation near the end she doesn't come home to see Phil, because she meets some guy at college who is good-looking and as rich as she is and, because her father knew about Phil all along and was pressuring her into forgetting about him, she gives in to this new guy and goes to his hometown during the vacation and falls in love with him. That's how the people in town figured it, because after she graduates they turn up, already married, and right away he takes over the old German's bank—and buys a new Pontiac at the place where my father is the mechanic and pays cash for it. The paying cash always made my father pause and shake his head and mention again that times were tough, but here comes this guy in a spiffy white shirt (with French cuffs, my mother said) and pays the full price in cash.

And this made my father shake his head too: Phil took the song down to Bay City and sold it for twenty-five dollars, the only money he ever got for it. It was the same song we'd just heard on the radio and which reminded my father of the story I just told you. What happened to Phil? Well, he stayed in Bay City and got a job managing a movie theater. My father saw him there after the Depression when he was on his way to Detroit to work for Ford. He stopped and Phil gave him a box of popcorn. The song he wrote for the girl has sold many millions of records and if I told you the name of it you could probably sing it, or at least whistle the tune. I wonder what the girl thinks when she hears it. Oh yes, my father met Phil's wife too. She worked in the movie theater with him, selling tickets and cleaning the carpet after the show with one of those sweepers you push. She was also big and loud and nothing like the other one, my mother said.

WILLIAM FAULKNER

A Portrait of Elmer

I

Elmer drinks beer upon the terrace of the Dome, with Angelo beside him. Beside him too, close against his leg, is a portfolio. It is quite new and quite flat. Sitting so among the artists he gazes across the boulevard Montparnasse and seems to gaze through the opposite gray building violetroofed and potted smugly with tile against the darkling sky, and across Paris itself and France and across the cold restless monotony of the Atlantic itself, so that for the twilit and nostalgic moment he looks about in lonely retrospect upon that Texas scene into which his mother's unselfish trying ambition had haled at implacable long last his resigned and static father and himself, young then still and blond awkward, alone remaining of all the children, thinking of Circumstance as a tireless detachment like the Post Office Department, getting people here and there, using them or not at all obscurely, returning them with delayed impersonal efficiency or not at all.

He remarks on this. Angelo awaits his pleasure with unfailing attentive courtesy as always, with that spirit of laissez-faire which rules their relationship, claims the same privilege himself and replies in Italian. To Elmer it sounds as though Angelo is making love to him, and while autumn and twilight mount Montparnasse gravely Elmer sits in a warm bath of words that mean nothing whatever to him, caressing his warming beer and watching girls in a standardised exciting uniformity of dress and accompanied by men with and without beards, and he reaches down his hand quietly and lightly and touches the portfolio briefly, wondering which among the men are the painters and which again the good painters, thinking *Hodge, the artist. Hodge, the artist.* Autumn and twilight mount Montparnasse gravely.

Angelo, with his extreme vest V-ing the soiled kaleidoscopic bulge of his cravat, with a thin purplish drink before him, continues to form his periods with a fine high obliviousness of the fact that Elmer has learned no Italian whatever. Meaningless, his words seem to possess an aesthetic significance, passionate and impersonal, so that at last Elmer stops thinking *Hodge, the artist* and looks at Angelo again with the old helpless dismay, thinking How to interrupt with his American crudeness the other's inexhaustible flow of courteous protective friendship? For Angelo, with an affable tact which Elmer believed no American could ever attain, had established a relationship between them which had got far beyond and above any gross question of money; he had established himself in Elmer's life with the silken affability of a prince in a city of barbarians. And now what is he to do, Elmer wonders. He cannot have Angelo hanging around him much longer. Here, in Paris, he will soon be meeting people; soon he will join an atelier (again his hand touches lightly and briefly the briefcase against his leg) when he has had a little more time to get acclimated, and has learned a little more French, thinking quickly *Yes. Yes. That's it. When I have learned a little more French, so that I can choose the best one to show it to, since it must be the best. Yes yes. That is it.* Besides, he might run into Myrtle on the street any day. And to have her learn that he and Angelo were inseparable and that he must depend on Angelo for the very food he eats. Now that they are well away from Venice and the dungeon of the Palazzo Ducale, he no longer regrets his incarceration, for it is of such things—life in the raw—that artists are made. But he does regret having been in the same jail with Angelo, and at times he finds himself regretting with an ingratitude which he knows Angelo would never be capable of, that Angelo had got out at all. Then he thinks suddenly, hopefully, again with secret shame, Maybe that would be the best thing, after all. Myrtle will know how to get rid of Angelo; certainly Mrs Monson will.

Angelo's voice completes a smooth period. But now Elmer is not even wondering what Angelo is talking about; again he gazes across the clotting of flimsy tables and the serried ranks of heads and shoulders drinking in two sexes and five languages, at the seemingly endless passing throng, watching the young girls white and soft and canny and stupid, with troubling bodies which he must believe were virginal, wondering why certain girls chose you and others do not. At one time he believed that you can seduce them; now he is not so sure. He believes now that they just elect you when they happen to be in the right mood and you happen to be handy. But surely you are expected to learn from experience (meaning a proved unhappiness you did get as compared with a possible one that missed you) if not how to get what you want, at least the reason why you did not get it. But who wants experience, when he can get any kind of substitute? To hell with experience, Elmer thinks, since all reality is unbearable. I want what I think I want when I think I want it, as all men do. Not a formula for stoicism, an antidote for thwarted desire. Autumn and twilight mount Montparnasse gravely.

Angelo, oblivious, verbose, and without self-consciousness, continues to speak, nursing his thin dark drink in one hand. His hair is oiled sleekly backward; his face is shaven and blue as a pirate's. On either side of his brief snubbed nose his brown eyes are spaced and melting and sad as a highly bred dog's. His suit, after six weeks, is reasonably fresh and new, as are his cloth topped shoes, and he still has his stick. It is one of those slender jointed bamboo sticks which remain palpably and assertively new up to the moment of loss or death, but the suit, save for the fact that he has not yet slept in it, is exactly like the one which Elmer prevailed on him to throw away in Venice. It is a mosaic of tan-and-gray checks which seems to be in a state of constant mild explosion all over Angelo, robbing him of any shape whatever, and there are enough amber buttons on it to render him bulletproof save at point-blank range.

He continues to form his periods with a fine high obliviousness, nursing his purplish drink in his hand. He has not cleaned his fingernails since they quitted Venice.

II

He met Myrtle in Houston, Texas, where he already had a bastard son. That other had been a sweet brief cloudy fire, but to him Myrtle, arrogant with youth and wealth, was like a star: unattainable for all her curved pink richness. He did not wish to know that after a while those soft distracting hips would become thicker, heavy, almost awkward; that straight nose was a little too short; the blue ineffable eyes a trifle too candid; the brow low, pure, and broad—a trifle too low and broad beneath the burnished molassescolored hair.

He met her at a dance, a semipublic occasion in honor of departing soldiers in 1917; from his position against the wall, which he had not altered all evening, he watched her pass in a glitter of new boots and spurs and untarnished proud shoulder bars not yet worn thin with salutes; with his lame back and his rented tailcoat he dreamed. He was a war veteran already, yet he was lame and penniless, while Myrtle's father was known even in Texas for the oil wells which he owned. He met her before the evening was over; she looked full at him with those wide heavencolored eyes innocent of any thought at all; she said, "Are you from Houston?" and "Really," with her soft mouth open a little to indicate interest, then a banded cuff swept her away. He met Mrs Monson also and got along quite well with her—a brusque woman with cold eyes who seemed to look at him and at the dancers and at the world too even beyond Texas with a brief sardonic perspicuity.

He met her once; then in 1921, five years after Elmer had returned from his futile and abortive attempt at the war, Mr Monson blundered into three or four more oil wells and Mrs Monson and Myrtle went to Europe to put Myrtle in school, to finish her, since two years in Virginia and a year in the Texas State University had not been enough to do this.

So she sailed away, leaving Elmer to remember her lemoncolored dress, her wet red mouth open a little to indicate interest, her wide ineffable eyes beneath the pure molasses of her hair when he was at last presented; for suddenly, with a kind of horror, he had heard someone saying with his mouth, "Will you marry me?" watching still with that shocked horror her eyes widen into his, since he did not wish to believe that no woman is ever offended by a request for her body. "I mean it," he said; then the barred sleeve took her. I do mean it, he cried silently to himself, watching her lemoncolored shortlegged body disseminating its aura of imminent fat retreating among the glittering boots and belts, to the music become already martial which he could not follow because of his back. *I still mean it, he cries soundlessly, clutching his beer among the piled saucers of Montparnasse, having already seen in the* Herald *that Mrs Monson and Myrtle are now living in Paris, not wondering where Mr Monson is since these years, not thinking to know that Mr Monson is still in America, engaged with yet more oil wells and with a certain Gloria who sings and dances in a New Orleans nightclub in a single darkish silk garment that, drawn tightly between her kind thighs and across her unsubtle behind, lends to her heavy white legs an unbelievably harmless look, like drawn beef; Perhaps, he thinks with a surge of almost unbearable triumph and exultation, They have seen me too in the papers, maybe even in the French one: Le millionnaire americain Odge, qui arrive d'être peinteur, parce-qu'il croit que seulement en France faut-il l'âme d'artiste rêver et travailler tranquille; en Amérique tout gagne seulement*

III

When he was five years old, in Johnson City, Tennessee, the house they were temporarily living in had burned. "Before you had time to move us again," his father said to his mother with sardonic humor. And Elmer, who had always hated being seen naked, whose modesty was somehow affronted even in the presence of his brothers, had been snatched bodily out of sleep and rushed naked through acrid roaring and into a mad crimson world where the paradoxical temperature was near zero, where he stood alternately jerking his bare feet from the iron icy ground while one side of him curled bitterly, his ears filled with roaring and meaningless shouting, his nostrils with the smell of heat and strange people, clutching one of his mother's thin legs. Even now he remembers his mother's face above him, against a rushing plume of sparks like a wild veil; remembers how he thought then, Is this my mother, this stark bitter face? Where [is] that loving querulous creature whom he knew? and his father, leanshanked, hopping on one leg while he tried to put on his trousers; he remembers how even his father's hairy leg beneath the nightshirt seemed to have taken fire. His two brothers stood side by side nearby, bawling, while tears from tight eyesockets streaked their dirty faces and blistered away and that yelping scarlet filled their gaping mouths; only Jo was not crying, Jo, with whom he slept, with whom he didn't mind being naked. She alone stood fiercely erect, watching the fire in dark scrawny defiance, ridiculing her wailing brothers by that very sharp and arrogant ugliness of hers.

But as he remembers she was not ugly that night: the wild crimson had given her a bitter beauty like that of a Salamander. And he would have gone to her, but his mother held him tight against her leg, binding him to her with a fold of her night gown, covering his nakedness. So he burrowed against the thin leg and watched quietly the shouting volunteers within the house hurling out the meagre objects which they had dragged for so

WILLIAM FAULKNER

many years over the face of the North American continent: the low chair in which his mother rocked fiercely while he knelt with his head in her lap; the metal box inscribed Bread in chipped curling gold leaf and in which he had kept for as long as he could remember a dried and now wellnigh anonymous bird's wing, a basket carved from a peachstone, a dogeared picture of Joan of Arc to which he had added with tedious and tongue-sucking care an indigo moustache and imperial (the English made her a martyr, the French a saint, but it remained for Hodge, the artist, to make her a man), and a collection of cigar stubs in various stages of intactness, out of an upstairs window onto the brick walk.

She was not ugly that night. And always after that, after she had disap-peared between two of their long since uncounted movings and there was none of the children left save himself, the baby—after he saw her one more time and then never again, when he remembered her it was to see her again starkly poised as a young thin ugly tree, sniffing the very sound of that chaos and mad dream into her flared nostrils as mobile as those of a haughty mare.

It was in Jonesboro, Arkansas, that Jo left them. The two boys had before this refused the gambit of their father's bland inactivity and their mother's fretful energy. The second one, a dull lout with a pimpled face, deserted them in Paris, Tennessee, for a job in a liverystable owned by a man with a cruel heavy face and an alcoholcured nose and a twenty-two-ounce watch chain; and in Memphis the eldest, a slight quiet youth with his mother's face but without her unconquerable frustration, departed for Saint Louis. Jo left them in Jonesboro, and presently Elmer and his mother and father moved again.

But before they moved, there came anonymously through the mail ("It's from Jo," his mother said. "I know it," Elmer said) a box of paints: cheap watercolors and an impossible brush bristling smartly from a celluloid tube in which the wood stem would never remain fixed. The colors them-selves were not only impossible too, they were of a durability apparently impervious to any element, except the blue. It compensated for the others, seeming to possess a dynamic energy which the mere presence of water liberated as the presence of spring in the earth liberates the hidden seed. Sultry, prodigious, it was as virulent as smallpox, staining everything it touched with the passionate ubiquity of an unbottled plague.

He learned to curb it in time, however, and with his already ungainly body sprawled on the floor, on wrapping paper when he could get it or on newspapers when not he painted blue people and houses and locomotives. After they had moved twice more however the blue was exhausted; its empty wooden dish stared up at him from among the other glazed discs, all of which had by now assumed a similar dun color, like a dead mackerel's eye in fixed bluish reproach.

But soon school was out, and Elmer, fourteen and in the fourth grade, had failed again to make the rise. Unlike his brothers and sister, he liked going to school. Not for wisdom, not even for information: just going to school. He was always dull in his books and he inevitably developed a fine sexless passion for the teacher. But this year he was ravished away from that constancy by a boy, a young beast as beautiful to him as a god, and as cruel. Throughout the whole session he worshipped the boy from a distance: a blind and timeless adoration which the boy himself wrote finis to by coming suddenly upon Elmer on the playground one day and tripping him violently to earth, for no reason that either of them could have named. Whereupon Elmer rose without rancor, bathed his abraded elbow, and emotionally free again, fled that freedom as though it were a curse, transferring his sheeplike devotion once more to the teacher.

The teacher had a thick gray face like heavy dough; she moved in that unmistakable odor of middle-aged virgin female flesh. She lived in a small frame house which smelled as she smelled, with behind it a small garden in which no flowers ever did well, not even hardy Octoberdusty zinnias. Elmer would wait for her after school on the afternoons when she remained with pupils who had failed in the day's tasks, to walk home with her. For she saved all her wrapping paper for him to paint on. And soon the two of them, the dowdy irongray spinster and the hulking blond boy with almost the body of a man, were a matter for comment and speculation in the town. Elmer did not know this. Perhaps she did not either, yet one day she suddenly ceased walking home through the main streets, but instead took the nearest way home, with Elmer lumbering along beside her. She did this for two afternoons. Then she told him not to wait for her anymore. He was astonished: that was all. He went home and painted, sprawled on his stomach on the floor. Within the week he ran out of wrapping paper. The next morning he went by the teacher's house, as he had used to do. The door was closed. He went and knocked, but got no answer. He waited before it until he heard the school bell ringing four or five blocks away; he had to run. He did not see the teacher emerge from the house when he was out of sight and hurry also toward the still ringing bell along a parallel street, with her thick doughlike face and her blurred eyes behind her nose glasses. Then it became spring. That day, as the pupils filed from the room at noon, she stopped him and told him to come to her house after supper and she would give him some more paper. He had long since forgot how at one time his blond slow openwork inner life had been marked and fixed in simple pleasure between walking home with her by afternoon and coming by her house in the mornings to walk with her to school until she stopped him; forgetting, he had forgiven her, doglike: always with that ability to forgive and then forget as easily; looking, he did not see her eyes, he could not see her heart. "Yessum," he said. "I will."

It was dark when he reached her door and knocked; high above the reddening bitten maples stars flickered; somewhere in that high darkness was a lonely sound of geese going north. She opened the door almost before his knock had died away. "Come in," she said, leading the way toward a lighted room, where he stood clutching his cap, his overgrown body shifting from leg to leg; on the wall behind him his shadow, hulking, loomed. She took the cap from him and put it on a table on which was a fringed paper doily and a tray bearing a teapot and some broken food. "I eat my supper here," she said. "Sit down, Elmer."

"Yessum," he said. She still wore the white shirtwaist and the dark skirt in which he always saw her, in which he perhaps thought of her in slumber even. He sat gingerly on the edge of a chair.

"Spring outside tonight," she said. "Did you smell it?" He watched her push the tray aside and pick up a crust which had lain hidden in the shallow shadow of the tray.

"Yessum," he said. "I heard some geese going over." He began to perspire a little; the room was warm, close, odorous.

"Yes, spring will soon be here," she said. Still he did not see her eyes, since she now seemed to watch the hand which held the crust. Within the savage arena of light from the shaded lamp it contracted and expanded like a disembodied lung; presently Elmer began to watch crumbs appear between the fingers of it. "And another year will be gone. Will you be glad?"

"Ma'am?" he said. He was quite warm, uncomfortable; he thought of the clear high shrill darkness outside the house. She rose suddenly; she almost flung the now shapeless wad of dough onto the tray.

"But you want your paper, dont you?" she said.

"Yessum," Elmer said. *Now I will be outside soon* he said. He rose too and they looked at one another; he saw her eyes then; the walls seemed to be rushing slowly down upon him, crowding the hot odorous air upon him. He was sweating now. He drew his hand across his forehead. But he could not move yet. She took a step toward him; he saw her eyes now.

"Elmer," she said. She took another step toward him. She was grinning now, as if her thick face had been wrung and fixed in that painful and tragic grimace, and Elmer, still unable to move, seemed to drag his eyes heavily up the black shapeless skirt, up the white shirtwaist pinned at the throat with a bar pin of imitation lapis lazuli, meeting her eyes at last. He grinned too and they stood facing one another, cropping the room with teeth. Then she put her hand on him. Then he fled. Outside the house he still ran, with the noise in his ears still of the crashing table. He ran, filling his body with air in deep gulps, feeling his sweat evaporating.

O and thy little girlwhite all: musical with motion Montparnasse and Raspail: subtle ceaseless fugues of thighs under the waxing moon of death:

Elmer, fifteen, with a handleless teacup, descends steps, traverses sparse lawn, a gate; crosses a street, traverses lawn not sparse, ascends steps between flowering shrubs, knocks at screen door, politely but without diffidence.

Velma her name, at home alone, pinksoftcurved, plump sixteen. Elmer enters with his teacup and traverses dim quietness among gleams on nearmahogany, conscious of tingling remoteness and pinksoftcurves and soft intimation of sheathed hips in progression, and so on to the pantry. Helps to reach down sugar jar from where it sits in a pan of water against ants, but sees only in white cascade of sugar little white teeth over which full soft mouth and red never quite completely closed and her plump body bulging her soiled expensive clothing richly the aromatic cubbyhole in the halfdark. Touched sugar hands in the halfdark hishing cling by eluding, elude but not gone; bulging rabbitlike things under soiled silk taut softly, hishing ceaseless cascade of tilted sugar now on the floor hishing: a game.

It whispers its blanched cascade down the glazed precipice of the over-flowed cup, and she flees squealing, Elmer in lumbering pursuit, tasting something warm and thick and salt in his throat. Reaches kitchen door: she has disappeared; but staring in vacuous astonishment toward the barnyard he sees a vanishing flash of skirts and runs after across the lot and into the high odorous cavern of the barn.

She is not in sight. Elmer stands baffled, bloodcooling, in the center of the trodden dungimpregnated earth; stands in baffled incertitude, blood-cooling in helpless and slowmounting despair for irretrievable loss of that which he had never gained, thinking *So she never meant it. I reckon she is laughing at me. I reckon I better try to scrape up that spilled sugar before Mrs Merridew gets home.* He turns toward the door, moving. As he does so a faint sound from overhead stops him. He feels a surge of triumph and fright that stops his heart for the moment. Then he can move toward the vertical ladder which leads to the loft.

Acrid scent of sweated leather, of ammonia and beasts and dry dust richly pungent; of quiet and solitude, of triumph fear change. Mounts the crude ladder, tasting again thick warm salt, hearing his heart heavy and fast, feels his bodyweight swing from shoulder to shoulder upward, then sees yellow slants of cavernous sunlight latticed and spinning with golden motes. Mounts final rung and finds her, breathless and a little frightened, in the hay.

In the throes of puberty, that dark soft trouble like a heard forgotten music or a scent or thing remembered though never smelt nor seen, that blending of dread and longing, he began consciously to draw people: not any longer lines at full liberty to assume any significance they chose, but men and women; trying to draw them and make them conform to a vague shape now somewhere back in his mind, trying to imbue them with what he believed he meant by splendor and speed. Later still, the shape in his mind became unvague concrete and alive: a girl with impregnable virginity to time or circumstance; darkhaired small and proud, casting him bones fiercely as though he were a dog, coppers as though he, were a beggar leprous beside a dusty gate.

IV

He left his mother and father in Houston when he went to the war. But when he returned, someone else had the house, as usual. He went to the agent. A bright busy bald youngish man, the agent stared at Elmer's yellow hospital stick in a fretful hiatus, visibly revolving the word Hodge in his mind. Presently he rang a bell and a brisk pretty Jewess smelling of toilet water not soap, came and found the letter [they] had left for him. The agent offered Elmer a cigarette, explaining how the war kept him too busy to smoke cigars. Our War, he called it. He talked briefly about Europe, asking Elmer a few questions such as a clothes dealer might ask of a returned African missionary, answering them himself and telling Elmer a few facts in return: that war was bad and that he was part owner of some land near Fort Worth where the British government had established a training field for aviators. But at last Elmer read the letter and went to see his people.

His father had liked Houston. But his mother would want to move though, and sitting in the daycoach among the smells of peanuts and wet babies, nursing his yellow stick from whose crook the varnish was long since handworn, he remembered and thought of that Joblike man with pity tempered by secret and disloyal relief that he himself would no more be haled over the face of the earth at what undirected compulsion drove his mother. From the vantage point of absence, of what might almost be called weaning, he wondered when she would give up: this too (compensating for the recent secret disloyalty) tempered by an abrupt fierce wave of tenderness for her bitter indomitable optimism. For he would return to Houston to live, now that his parents did not need him and hence there was none to expect him any longer to do anything. He would live in Houston and paint pictures.

He saw his father first, sitting on the small front porch; already he had known exactly what the house would look like. His father was unchanged, static, affable, resigned; age did not show on him at all, as it never had, on his cunning cherubic face, his vigorous untidy thatch. Yet Elmer discerned something else, something his father had acquired during his absence: a kind of smug unemphatic cheeriness. And then (sitting also on the porch where his father had not risen, also in a yellow varnished chair such as may be bought almost anywhere for a dollar or two) without any feeling at all, he listened to his father's cheery voice telling him that his mother, that passionate indomitable woman, was dead. While his father recited details with almost gustatory eulogism he looked about at the frame house, painted brown, set in a small dusty grassless treeless yard, recalling that long series of houses exactly like it, stretching behind him like an endless street into that time when he would wake in the dark beside Jo, with her hand sharp and fierce in his hair and her voice in the dark fierce too: "Elly, when you want to do anything, you do it, do you hear? Dont let nobody stop you," and on into the cloudy time when he had existed but could not remember it. He sat in his yellow varnished chair, nursing his yellow varnished stick, while his father talked on and on and dusk came for two hundred unhindered miles and filled the house where his mother's fretful presence seemed to linger yet like an odor, as though it had not even time for sleep, let alone for death.

He would not stay for supper, and his father told him how to find the cemetery with what Elmer believed was actual relief. "I'll get along all right," Elmer said.

"Yes," his father agreed heartily, "you'll get along all right. Folks are always glad to help soldiers. This aint no place for a young man, nohow. If I was young now, like you are—" The intimation of a world fecund, waiting to be conquered with a full rich patience, died away, and Elmer rose, thinking if his mother had been present now, who refused always to believe that any flesh and blood of hers could get along at all beyond the radius of her fretful kindness. Oh, I'll get along, he repeated, now to that thin spirit of her which yet lingered about the house which had at last conquered her, and he could almost hear her rejoin quickly, with a kind of triumph, That's what your sister thought—forgetting that they had never heard from Jo and that for all they knew she might be Gloria Swanson or J. P. Morgan's wife.

He didn't tell his father about Myrtle. His father would have said nothing at all, and that brisk spirit of his mother's energy would have said that Myrtle wasn't a bit too good for him. Perhaps she knows, he thought quietly, leaning on his stick beside the grave which even too seemed to partake of her wiry restless impermanence, as clothes assume the characteristics of the wearer. At the head was a small compact palpably marble headstone surmounted by a plump stone dove, natural size. And above it, above the untreed hill, stretched an immeasurable twilight in which huge stars hung with the impersonality of the mad and through which Adam and Eve, dead untimed out of Genesis, might still be seeking that heaven of which they had heard.

Elmer closed his eyes, savoring sorrow, bereavement, the sentimental loneliness of conscious time. But not for long: already he was seeing against his eyelids Myrtle's longwaisted body in the lemoncolored dress, her wet red halfopen mouth, her eyes widening ineffably beneath the burnished molasses of her hair, thinking Money money money. *Anyway, I can paint now* he thought, striking his stick into the soft quiet earth *A name. Fame perhaps. Hodge, the painter*

V

Angelo is one of those young men, one of that great submerged mass, that vigorous yet heretofore suppressed and dominated class which we are told has been sickened by war. But Angelo has not been sickened by war. He had been able to perform in wartime actions which in peacetime the police, government, all those who by the accident of birth or station were able to override him, would have made impossible. Naturally war is bad, but so is traffic, and the fact that wine must be paid for and the fact that if all the women a man can imagine himself in bed with were to consent, there would not be time in the allotted three score and ten. As for getting hurt, no Austrian nor Turk nor even a carabinier is going to shoot him with a gun, and over a matter of territory he has never seen and does not wish to see. Over a woman, now—He watches the seemingly endless stream of women and young girls in hushed childish delight, expressing pleasure and approbation by sucking his breath sharply between his pursed lips. Across the narrow table his companion and patron sits: the incomprehensible American with his predilection for a liquid which to Angelo is something like that which is pumped from the bowels of ships, whom he has watched for two months now living moving breathing in some static childlike furious brooding world beyond all fact and flesh; for a moment, unseen, Angelo looks at him with a speculation which is almost contempt. But soon he is immersed again in his own constant sound of approbation and pleasure while autumn, mounting Montparnasse, permeates the traffic of

Montparnasse and Raspail, teasing the breasts and thighs of young girls moving musical in the lavender glittering dusk between old walls beneath a sky like a patient etherised and dying after an operation.

Elmer has a bastard son in Houston. It happened quickly. He was eighteen, big blond awkward, with curling hair. They would go to the movies, say twice a week, since (her name is Ethel) she was popular, with several men friends of whom she would talk to him. So he accepted his secondary part before it was offered him, as if that was the position he desired, holding her hands in the warm purring twilight while she told him how the present actor on the screen was like or unlike men she knew. "You are not like other men," she told him. "With you, it's different: I dont need to be always. . . ." In the sleazy black satin which she liked, staring at him with something fixed and speculative and completely dissimulate about her eyes. "Because you are so much younger than I am, you see; almost two years. Like a brother, Do you see what I mean?"

"Yes," Elmer said, statically awash in the secret intimacy of their clasped faintly sweating hands. He liked it. He liked sitting in the discreet darkness, watching the inevitable exigencies of human conduct as established and decreed by expatriate Brooklyn button- and pants-manufacturers, transposing her into each celluloid kiss and embrace, yet not aware that she was doing the same thing even though he could feel her hand lax and bloom barometrically in his own. He liked kissing her too, in what he believed to be snatched intervals between mounting the veranda and opening the door and again when noises upstairs had ceased and the tablelamp would begin to make her nervous.

Then they went to four movies in succession, and then on the fifth evening they did not go out at all. Her family was going out and she did not like to leave the house completely untenanted. He was for starting the kissing then, but she made him take a chair across the table while she took one opposite and told him what type of man she would someday marry; of how she would marry only because her parents expected it of her and that she would never give herself to a man save as a matter of duty to the husband which they would choose for her, who would doubtless be old and wealthy: that therefore she would never lose love because she would never have had it. That Elmer was the sort of man she, having no brothers, had always wanted to know because she could tell him things she couldn't even bring herself to discuss with her mother.

And so for the following weeks Elmer existed in a cloying jungle of young female flesh damply eager and apparently unappeasable (ballooning earnestly at him, Elmer with that visual detachment of man suffering temporary or permanent annihilation thought of an inferiorly inflated toy balloon with a finger thrust into it) though at first nothing happened. But later too much happened. "Too much," she told him from the extent of her arms, her hands locked behind his head, watching his face with dark dissimulate intentness.

"Let's get married then," Elmer said, out of his mesmerism of enveloping surreptitious breasts and thighs.

"Yes," she said. Her voice was detached, untroubled, a little resigned; Elmer thought *She's not even looking at me* "I'm going to marry Grover." This was the first he had heard of Grover.

I'm not running away, Elmer told himself, sitting in the inkblack boxcar while the springless trucks clucked and banged beneath him; it's because I just didn't think I could feel this bad. The car was going north, because there was more north to go in than south. And there was also in his mind something beyond even the surprise and the hurt and which he refused to even think was relief; what he told himself was, Maybe in the north where things are different, I can get started painting. Maybe in painting I can forget I didn't think that I could feel this bad. And again maybe he had but belatedly reached that point at which his sister and brothers had one by one broken the spell of progression which their mother had wound about them like the string around a top.

Oklahoma knew him; he worked in Missouri wheatfields; he begged bread for two days in Kansas City. At Christmas he was in Chicago, spending day after day erect and sound asleep before pictures in galleries where there was no entrance fee; night after night sitting in railroad stations until the officials waked them all and the ones who had no tickets would walk the bitter galeridden streets to another station and so repeat. Now and then he ate.

In January he was in a Michigan lumbercamp. For all his big body, he worked in the roaring steamopaque cookshack which smelled always soporific of food and damp wool, scrubbing the bellies of aluminum pots which in the monotonous drowse of the long mornings reminded him of the empty wood dish of blue in the paint box of his childhood.

At night there was plenty of rough paper. He used charcoal until he found a box of blue washing powder. With that and with coffeedregs and with a bottle of red ink belonging to the cook, he began to work in color. Soon the teamsters, axmen, and sawyers discovered that he could put faces on paper. One by one he drew them, by commission, each describing the kind of clothing, dress suit, racecourse check, or mackinaw in which he wished to be portrayed, sitting patiently until the work was finished, then holding with his mates gravely profane aesthetic debate.

When February broke, he had grown two inches and filled out; his body was now the racehorse body of nineteen; sitting about the steaming bunkhouse the men discussed him with the impersonality of surgeons or horseracers. Soon now the rigid muscles of snow would laxen, though reluctant yet. Gluts of snow would slip heavily soundless from the boughs of spruce and hemlock and the boughs would spring darkly free against the slipping snow; from the high blue soon now the cries of geese would drift like falling leaves, wild, fantastical, and sad. In the talk of sex nightly growing more and more frequent about the bunkhouse stove, Elmer's body in relation to women was discussed; one night, through some vague desire to establish himself and formally end his apprenticeship to manhood, he told them about Ethel in Houston. They listened, spitting gravely on the hissing orange stove. When he had finished they looked at one another with weary tolerance. Then one said kindly: "Dont you worry, bub. It's harder to get one than you think."

Then it was March. The log drive was in the river, and over the last meal in the bunkhouse they looked quietly about at one another, who perhaps would never see the other faces again, while between stove and table Elmer and the cook moved. The cook was Elmer's immediate superior and czar of the camp. He reminded Elmer of someone; he coddled him and harried him and cursed him with savage kindness: Elmer came at last to dread him with a kind of static hypnosis, letting the cook direct his actions, not joyously but with resignation. He was wiry and hightempered; when men came in late to meals he flew into an almost homicidal rage. They treated him with bluff caution, shouting him down by sheer volume while he cursed them, but not offering to touch him. But he kept the kitchen clean and fed them well and mended their clothes for them; when a man was injured he tended the invalid in a frenzy of skillful gentleness, cursing him and his forebears and posterity for generations.

When the meal was over, he asked Elmer what he intended to do now. Elmer had not thought of that; suddenly he seemed to see his destiny thrust back into his arms like a strange baby in a railroad waitingroom. The cook kicked the stove door to savagely. "Let's go to that goddam war. What do you say?"

He certainly reminded Elmer of someone, especially when he came to see Elmer the night before Elmer's battalion entrained for Halifax. He sat on Elmer's bunk and cursed the war, the Canadian government, the C.E.F. corps brigade battalion and platoon, himself and Elmer past present and to come, for they had made him a corporal and a cook. "So I aint going," he said. "I guess I wont never get over. So you'll just have to do the best you can by yourself. You can do it. By God, dont you take nothing off of them, these Canucks or them Limey bastards neither. You're good as any of them, even if you dont have no stripes on your sleeve or no goddam brass acorns on your shoulders. You're good as any of them and a dam sight better than most, and dont you forget it. Here. Take this. And dont lose it." It was a tobacco tin. It contained needles of all sizes, thread, a pair of short scissors, a pack of adhesive tape, and a dozen of those objects which the English wittily call French letters and the French call wittily English letters. He departed, still cursing. Elmer never saw him again.

Soldiering on land had been a mere matter of marching here and there in company and keeping his capbadge and tunic buttons and rifle clean and remembering whom to salute. But aboard ship, where space was restricted, they were learning about combat. It was with hand grenades and Elmer was afraid of them. He had become reconciled to the rifle, with which a man aimed and pulled the trigger with immediate results, but not this object, to which a man did something infinitesimal and then held it in his hand, counting three in the waiting silence before throwing it. He told himself that when he had to, he would pull the pin and throw it at once, until the stocky sergeant-major with eyes like glass marbles and a ribbon on his breast told them how the Hun had a habit of catching the bomb and tossing it back like a baseball.

"Nah," the sergeant-major said, roving his dead eyes about their grave faces, "count three, like this." He did something infinitesimal to the bomb while they watched him in quiet horrified fascination. Then he pushed the pin back and tossed the bomb lightly in his hand. "Like that, see?"

Then someone nudged Elmer. He quit swallowing his hot salt and took the bomb and examined it in a quiet horror of curiosity. It was oval, its smug surface broken like a pineapple, dull and solid: a comfortable feel, a compact solidity almost sensuous to the palm. The sergeant-major's voice said sharply from a distance: "Come on. Like I showed you."

"Yes, sir," Elmer's voice said while he watched his hands, those familiar hands which he could no longer control, toying with the bomb, nursing it. Then his apish hands did something infinitesimal and became immobile in bland satisfaction and Elmer stared in an utterly blank and utterly timeless interval at the object in his palm.

"Throw it, you bloody bastard!" the man beside him shouted before he died. Elmer stared at his hand, waiting; then the hand decided to obey him and swung backward. But the hand struck a stanchion before it reached the top of the arc and he saw the face of the man next to him like a suspended mask at his shoulder, utterly expressionless, and the dull oval object in the air between them growing to monstrous size like an obscene coconut. Then his body told him to turn his back and lie down.

How green it looks, he thought sickly. Later, while he lay for months on his face while his back healed and young women and old looked upon his naked body with a surprising lack of interest, he remembered the amazing greenness of the Mersey shores. That was about all he had to think of. These people didn't even know where Texas was, taking it to be a town in British Columbia apparently as they talked to him kindly in their clipped jerky way. On a neighboring cot and usually delirious was a youth of his own age, an aviator with a broken back and both feet burned off. It's as hard to kill folks as it is to get them, Elmer thought, thinking *So this is war*: white rows of beds in a white tunnel of a room, grayclad nurses kind but uninterested, then a wheelchair among other wheelchairs and now and then lady lieutenants in blue cloaks with brass insignia; thinking *But how green it looked* since it was quiet now, since the aviator was gone. Whether he died or not Elmer neither knew nor cared.

It seemed greener than ever when he saw it again from shipdeck as they dropped down with the tide. And with England at last behind, in retrospect it seemed greener still, with an immaculate peace which no war could ever disturb. While they felt through the Zone and into the gray Atlantic again he slept and waked, touching at times his head where endless pillows had worn his hair away, wondering if it would grow out again.

It was March again. For eleven months he had not thought of painting. Before they reached midocean it was April; one day off Newfoundland they learned by wireless that America had entered the war. His back did not hurt so much as it itched.

He spent some of his backpay in New York. He not only visited public and semipublic galleries, but through the kindness of a preserved fat woman he spent afternoons in private galleries and homes. His sponsor, a canteen worker, had once been soft pink and curved, but now she was long since the wife of a dollarayear man in Washington, with an income of fifty thousand. She had met Elmer in the station canteen and was quite kind to him, commiserating the mothy remnant of his once curling hair. Then he went south. With his limp and his yellow stick he remained in New Orleans in an aimless hiatus. Nowhere he had to go, nowhere he wanted to go, he existed not lived in a voluptuous inertia mocking all briskness and haste: grave vitiating twilights soft and oppressive as smoke upon the city, hanging above the hushed eternal river and the docks where he walked smelling rich earth in overquick fecundity—sugar and fruit, resin and dusk and heat, like the sigh of a dark and passionate woman no longer young.

He was halted one day on Canal Street by a clotting of people. A hoarse man stood on a chair in the center of the throng, a fattish sweating prosperous man making a Liberty Loan speech, pleading on the streets for money like a beggar. And suddenly, across the clotting heads, he saw a slight taut figure as fiercely erect as ever, watching the orator and the audience with a fierce disgust. "Jo!" Elmer cried. "*Jo!*"

money we earn, work and sweat for, so that our children   not have to face what we are now   able to earn this money? By the protection which this country, this American nation showing the old dying civilizations   freedom   she calls on you what will you say

The crowd stirred in a slow hysteria and Elmer lunged his maimed body, trying to thrust through toward where he still saw the fierce poise of her small hat. "For Christ's sake," someone said: a youth in the new campaign hat and the still creased khaki of recent enlistment; "whatcher in such a rush about?"

boys over there   finish it before others must die   duty of civilization to stamp forever

"Maybe he wants he should enlist," another, a plump Jewish man clutching a new thousand dollar bill in his hand, shrieked. "This var— In Lithuania I have seen yet O God," he shrieked in Elmer's face.

"Pardon me. Pardon me." Elmer chanted, trying to thrust through, trying to keep in sight the unmistakable poise of that head.

"Well, he's going in the wrong direction," the soldier said, barring the way. "Recruiting office is over yonder, buddy." Across his shoulder Elmer caught another glimpse of the hat, lost it again.

price we must pay for having become the greatest nation   Word of God in the Book itself

The crowd surged again, elbowing the filaments of fire which lived along his spine. "This var!" the Jew shrieked at him again. "Them boys getting killed already O God. It vill make business: In Lithuania I have seen—"

"Look out," a third voice said quickly; "he's lame; dont you see his stick?"

"Yes, sure," the soldier said. "They all get on crutches when assembly blows."

"Pardon me. Pardon me." Elmer chanted amid the laughter. The black hat was not in sight now. He was sweating too, striving to get through, his spine alive now with fiery ants. The orator remarked the commotion. He saw the soldier and Elmer's sick straining face; he paused, mopping his neck.

"What's that?" he said. "Wants to enlist? Come here, brother. Make room, people; let him come up here." Elmer tried to hold back as the hands touched began to push and draw him forward as the crowd opened.

"I just want to pass," he said. But the hands thrust him on. He looked over his shoulder, thinking, I am afraid I am going to puke, thinking, I'll go. I'll go. Only for God's sake dont touch my back again. The black hat was gone. He began to struggle; at last his back had passed the stage where he could feel at all. "Let me go, goddam you!" he said whitely. "I have already been—"

But already the orator, leaning down, caught his hand; other hands lifted and pushed him up onto the platform while once more the sweating man turned to the crowd and spoke. "Folks, look at this young man here. Some of us, most of us, are young and well and strong: we can go. But look at this young man here, a cripple, yet he wants to defy the beast of intolerance and blood. See him: his stick, limping. Shall it be said of us who are sound in body and limb, that we have less of courage and less of love of country than this boy? And those of us who are unfit or old; those of us who cannot go—"

"No, no," Elmer said, jerking at the hand which the other held. "I just want to pass: I have already been—"

"—men, women, let everyone of us do what this boy, lame in the very splendor of young manhood, would do. If we cannot go ourselves, let everyone of us say, I have sent one man to the front; that though we ourselves are old and unfit, let everyone of us say, I have sent one soldier to preserve this American heritage which our fathers created for us out of their own suffering and preserved to us with their own blood; that I have done what I could that this heritage may be handed down unblemished to my children, to my children's children yet unborn—" The hoarse inspired voice went on, sweeping speaker and hearers upward into an immolation of words, a holocaust without heat, a conflagration with neither light nor sound and which would leave no ashes.

Elmer sought for another glimpse of that small hat, that fierce disdainful face, but in vain. It was gone, and the crowd, swept up once more in the speaker's eloquence, as suddenly forgot him. But she was gone, as utterly as a flame blown out. He wondered in sick despair if she had seen, not recognising him and not understanding. The crowd let him through now.

Dont let the German Beast think that we, you and I, refused, failed, dared not, while our boys our sons are fighting the good fight bleeding and suffering and dying to wipe forever from the world

He shifted his stick to the palm which had become callous to it. He saw the Jew again, still trying to give away his thousand dollar bill; heard diminishing behind him the voice hoarse and endless, passionate, fatuous, and sincere. His back began to hurt again.

VI

Musical with motion Montparnasse and Raspail: evening dissolves swooning: a thin odor of heliotrope become visible: with lights spangling yellow green and red. Angelo gains Elmer's attention at last and with his thumb indicates at a table nearby heavy eyes in sober passive allure, and a golden smile above a new shoddy fur neckpiece. He continues to nudge Elmer, making his rich pursed mouthsound: the grave one stares at Elmer in stoic invitation, the other one crops her gold-rimmed teeth at him before he looks quickly away. Yet still Angelo grimaces at him and nods rapidly, but Elmer is obdurate, and Angelo sits back in his chair with an indescribable genuflexion of weary disgust.

"Six weeks ago," he says in Italian, "they fetched you into the political dungeon of Venice, where I already was, and took from you your belt and shoelaces. You did not know why. Two days later I removed myself, went to your consul, who in turn removed you. Again you did not know how or why. And now since twenty-three days we are in Paris. In Paris, mind you. And now what do we do? We sit in caffees, we eat, we sit in caffees; we go and sleep. This we have done save for the seven days of one week which we spent in the forest of Meudon while you made a picture of three trees and an inferior piece of an inferior river—this too apparently for what reason you do not know, since you have done nothing with it, since for thirteen days now you have shown it to no one but have carried it in that affair beside your leg, from one caffee to another, sitting over it as though it were an egg and you a hen. Do you perhaps hope to hatch others from it, eh? or perhaps you are waiting until age will make of it an old master? And this in Paris. In Paris, mind. We might as well be in heaven. In America even, where there is nothing save money and work."

Musical with motion and lights and sound, with taxis flatulent pale-vaporous in the glittering dusk. Elmer looks again: the two women have risen and they now move away between the close tables with never a backward glance; again Angelo makes his sound of exasperation explosive but resigned. But musical with girlmotion Montparnasse and Raspail and soon Angelo, his friend and patron forgotten in the proffered flesh, expresses his pleasure and approbation between his pursed lips, leaving his patron to gaze lonely and musing through the gray opposite building and upon that Texas hill where he stood beside his mother's grave and thought of Myrtle Monson and money and of Hodge, the painter.

Someone died and left the elder Hodge two thousand dollars. He bought a house with it, almost in revenge, it might be said. It was in a small town innocent of trees where, Hodge said in humorous paraphrase, there were more cows and less milk and more rivers and less water and you could see further and see less than anywhere under the sun. Mrs Hodge, pausing in her endless bitter activity, gazed at her husband sedentary, effacing, as inevitable and inescapable as disease, in amazement, frankly shocked at last. "I thought you was looking for a house that suited you," Hodge said.

She looked about at those identical rooms, at the woodwork (doorframes and windows painted a thin new white which only brought into higher relief the prints of hands long moved away to print other identical houses about the earth), at walls papered with a serviceable tan which showed the minimum of stains and drank light like a sponge. "You did it just for meanness," she said bitterly, going immediately about the business of unpacking, for the last time.

"Why, aint you always wanted a home of your own to raise your children in?" Hodge said. Mrs Hodge suspended a folded quilt and looked about at the room which the two older boys would probably never see, which Jo would have fled on sight; and now Elmer, the baby, gone to a foreign war.

It could not have been nature nor time nor space, who was impervious to flood and fire and time and distance, indomitable in the face of lease contracts which required them to rent for a whole year to get the house at all. It must have been the fact of possession, rooting, that broke her spirit as a caged bird's breaks, Whatever it was, she tried to make morningglories grow upon the sawfretted porch, then she gave up. Hodge buried her on the treeless intimation of a hill, where unhampered winds could remind her of distance when she inevitably sickened to move again, though dead, and where time and space could mock at her inability to quicken and rise and stir; and he wrote Elmer, who was lying then on his face in a plaster cast in a British hospital while his spine hurt and the flesh inside the cast became warmly fluid like a film of spittle and he could smell it too, that his mother was dead and that he (Hodge) was as usual. He added that he had bought a house, forgetting to say where. Later, and with a kind of macabre thoughtfulness, he forwarded the returned letter to Elmer three months after Elmer had visited home for that brief afternoon and returned to Houston.

After his wife's death Hodge, cooking (he was a good cook, better than his wife had ever been) and doing his own sloven housework, would sit after supper on the porch, whittling a plug of tobacco against tomorrow's pipe, and sigh. Immediately that sigh would smack of something akin to relief, and he would reprimand himself in quick respect for the dead. And then he would not be so sure what that sigh signified. He contemplated the diminishing future, those years in which he would never again have to go anywhere unless he pleased, and he knew a mild discomfort. Had he too got from that tireless optimist an instinct for motion, a gadfly of physical progression? Had she, dying, robbed him of any gift for ease? As he never went to church he was intensely religious, and he contemplated with troubled static alarm that day when he too should pass beyond the veil and there find his wife waiting for him, all packed up and ready to move.

And then, when that had worn off and he had decided since he could not help that, to let Heaven's will be done since not only was that best but he couldn't do anything about it anyway, three men in boots came and, to his alarmed and pained astonishment, dug an oilwell in his chickenyard so near that he could stand in the kitchen door and spit into it. So he had to move again, or be washed bodily out of the county. But this time he merely moved the house itself, turning it around so he could sit on the veranda and watch the moiling activity in his erstwhile henyard with static astonishment and, if truth be told, consternation. He had given Elmer's Houston address to one of the booted men, asking him if he would mind looking Elmer up next time he was in Houston and telling him about it. So all he had to do then was to sit on his front porch and wait and muse upon the unpredictableness of circumstance. For instance, it had permitted him to run out of matches tonight, so instead of shredding his whole plug for smoking, he reserved enough to chew until someone came tomorrow who had matches; and sitting on the veranda of the first thing larger than a foldingbed which he had ever owned, with his most recent tribulation skeletoned and ladderlatticed high again the defunctive sky, he chewed his tobacco and spat outward into the immaculate dusk. He had not chewed in years and so he was a trifle awkward at first. But soon he was able to arc tobacco juice in a thin brown hissing, across the veranda and onto a parallelogram of troubled earth where someone had once tried to make something grow.

The New Orleans doctor sent Elmer to New York. There he spent two years while they fixed his spine, and another year recovering from it, lying again on his face with behind his mind's eye the image of a retreating shortlegged body in a lemoncolored dress, but not retreating fast now, since already, though lying on his face beneath weights, he was moving faster. Before departing however he made a brief visit to Texas. His father had not changed, not aged: Elmer found him resigned and smugly philosophical as ever beneath this new blow which Fate had dealt him. The only change in the establishment was the presence of a cook, a lean yellow woman no longer young, who regarded Elmer's presence with a mixture of assurance and alarm; inadvertently he entered his father's bedroom and saw that the bed, still unmade at noon, had obviously been occupied by two people. But he had no intention of interfering, nor any wish to; already he had turned his face eastward; already thinking and hope and desire had traversed the cold restless gray Atlantic, thinking *Now I have the money. And now fame. And then Myrtle*

And so he has been in Paris three weeks. He has not yet joined a class; neither has he visited the Louvre since he does not know where the Louvre is, though he and Angelo have crossed the Place de la Concorde several times in cabs. Angelo, with his instinct for glitter and noise, promptly discovered the Exposition; he took his patron there. But Elmer does not consider these to be painting. Yet he lingered, went through it all, though telling himself with quick loyalty, It wont be Myrtle who would come here; it will be Mrs Monson who will bring her, make her come. He has no doubt but that they are in Paris. He has been in Europe long enough to know that the place to look for an American in Europe is Paris; that when they are anywhere else, it is merely for the weekend.

When he reached Paris, he knew two words of French: he had learned them from the book which he bought at the shop where he bought his paints. (It was in New York. "I want the best paints you have," he told the young woman, who wore an artist's smock. "This set has twenty tubes and four brushes, and this one has thirty tubes and six brushes. We have one with sixty tubes, if you would like that," she said. "I want the best," Elmer said. "You mean you want the one with the most tubes and brushes?" she said. "I want the best," Elmer said. So they stood looking at one another at this impasse and then the proprietor himself came, also in an artist's smock. He reached down the set with the sixty tubes—which, incidentally, the French at Ventimiglia made Elmer pay a merchant's import duty on. "Of course he vants the best," the proprietor said. "Cant you look at him and tell that? Listen, I vill tell you. This is the vun you vant; I vill tell you. How many pictures can you paint vith ten tubes? Eh?" "I dont know," Elmer said. "I just want the best." "Sure you do," the proprietor said; "the vun that vill paint the most pictures. Come; you tell me how many pictures you can paint vith ten tubes; I tell you how many you can paint vith sixty." "I'll take it," Elmer said.)

The two words were *rive gauche*. He told them to the taxi driver at the Gare de Lyon, who said, "That is true, monsieur," watching Elmer with brisk attentiveness, until Angelo spoke to him in a bastard language of which Elmer heard *millionnaire americain* without then recognising it. "Ah," the driver said. He hurled Elmer's baggage and then Angelo into the cab, where Elmer already was, and drove them to the Hotel Leutetia. So this is Paris, Elmer thought, to the mad and indistinguishable careening of houses and streets, to canopied cafes and placarded comfort stalls and other vehicles pedaled or driven by other madmen, while Elmer sat a little forward, gripping the seat, with on his face an expression of static concern. The concern was still there when the cab halted before the hotel. It had increased appreciably when he entered the hotel and looked about; now he was downright qualmed. This is not right, he thought. But already it was too late; Angelo had made once his pursed sound of pleasure and approbation, speaking to a man in the dress uniform of a field marshall in his bastard tongue, who in turn bellowed sternly, "*Encore un mililonnaire americain.*" It was too late; already five men in uniform and not were forcing him firmly but gently to sign his name to an affidavit as to his existence, and he thinking *What I wanted was a garret* thinking with a kind of humorous despair *It seems that what I really want is poverty*

He escaped soon though, to Angelo's surprise, astonishment, and then shrugged fatalistic resignation. He took to prowling about the neighborhood, within his hand the book from which he had learned *rive gauche,* looking up at garret windows beneath leads and then at the book again with helpless dismay which he knew would soon become despair and then resignation to the gold braid, the funereal frock coats, the piled carpets, and the discreet lights among which fate and Angelo had cast him, as though his irrevocable horoscope had been set and closed behind him with the clash of that barred door in the Palazzo Ducale in Venice. He had not even opened the box of paints. Already he had paid a merchant's duty on them; he could well have continued to be the merchant which the French had made him and sold them. Then one day he strayed into the Rue Servandoni. He was merely passing through it, hopeful still with fading hope, when he looked through open doors, into a court. Even in the fatal moment he was telling himself *It's just another hotel. The only difference will be that living here will be a little more tediously exigent and pettily annoying* But again it was too late; already he had seen her. She stood, hands on hips in a clean harsh dress, scolding at an obese man engaged statically with a mop—a thin woman of forty or better, wiry, with a harried indefatigable face; for an instant he was his own father eight thousand miles away in Texas, not even knowing that he was thinking *I might have known she would not stay dead* not even thinking with omniscient perspicuity *I wont even need the book*

He didn't need the book. She wrote on a piece of paper the rate for the rooms; she could have made it anything she wished. He told himself that, housed again, static, dismayed, and relieved, while she nagged at him about his soiled clothes, examining and mending them, prowling furiously among his things and cleaning his room furiously (Angelo lived on the floor above him) while she jabbed French words and phrases into his mouth and made him repeat them. *Maybe I can get away some night,* he told himself. *Maybe I can escape after she is asleep and find an attic on the other side of town;* knowing that he would not, knowing that already he had given up, surrendered to her; that, like being tried for a crime, no man ever escapes the same fate twice.

And so soon (the next day he went to the American Express Co. and left his new address) his mind was saying only Paris. Paris. The Louvre, Cluny, the Salon, besides the city itself: the same skyline and cobbles, the same kindlooking marbles thighed as though for breeding—all that merry sophisticated coldblooded dying city to which Cézanne was dragged now and then like a reluctant cow, where Manet and Monet fought points of color and line; where Matisse and Picasso still painted: tomorrow he would join a class. That night he opened the box of paints for the first time. Yet, looking at them, he paused again. The tubes lay in serried immaculate rows, blunt, solid, torpedolike, latent. There is so much in them, he thought. There is everything in them. They can do anything; thinking of Hals and Rembrandt; all the tall deathless giants of old time, so that he turned his head suddenly, as though they were in the room, filling it, making it seem smaller than a hencoop, watching him, so that he closed the box again with quiet and aghast dismay. Not yet, he told himself. I am not worthy yet. But I can serve. I will serve. I want to serve, suffer too, if necessary.

The next day he bought watercolors and paper (for the first time since reaching Europe he showed no timorousness nor helplessness in dealing with foreign shopkeepers) and he and Angelo went to Meudon. He did not know where he was going; he merely saw a blue hill and pointed it out to the taxi driver. They spent seven days there while he painted his landscape. He destroyed three of them before he was satisfied, telling himself while his muscles cramped and his eyes blurred with weariness, I want it to be hard. I want it to be cruel, taking something out of me each time. I want never to be completely satisfied with any of them, so that I shall always paint again. So when he returned to the Rue Servandoni, with the finished picture in the new portfolio, on that first night when he looked at the tall waiting spectres, he was humble still but no longer aghast.

So now I have something to show him, he thinks, nursing his now lukewarm beer, while beside him Angelo's pursed sound has become continuous. Now, when I have found who is the best master in Paris, when I go to him and say Teach me to paint, I shall not go emptyhanded; thinking *And then fame. And then Myrtle* while twilight mounts Montparnasse gravely beneath the year turning reluctant as a young bride to the old lean body of death. It is then that he feels the first lazy, implacable waking of his entrails.

VII

Angelo's pursed sound has become continuous: an open and bland urbanity, until he sees that his patron has risen, the portfolio under his arm. "We eat-a, eh?" he says, who in three weeks has learned both of French and English, while Elmer has not yet learned how to ask where the Louvre and the Salon are. Then he indicates Elmer's beer. "No feeneesh?"

"I've got to go," Elmer says; there is upon his face that rapt, in-turned expression of a dyspeptic, as though he is listening to his insides, which is exactly what Elmer is doing; already he moves away. At once a waiter appears; Elmer still with that rapt, not exactly concerned expression but without any lost motion, gives the waiter a banknote and goes on; it is Angelo who stays the waiter and gets change and leaves a European tip which the waiter snatches up with contempt and says something to Angelo in French; for reply and since his patron is going on, walking a little faster than ordinary, Angelo merely takes time to reverse his sound of approbation by breathing outward through his pursed lips instead of inward.

And now musical with motion Michel also, though it is in the Place de l'Observatoire that Angelo overtakes his patron, where even then he still has to trot to keep up. Angelo looks about, his single eyebrow lifted. "No eat-a now?" he says.

"No," Elmer says. "The hotel."

"Otel?" Angelo says. "Eat-a first, eh?'

"No!" Elmer says. His tone is fretted, though not yet harried and not yet desperate. "Hotel. I've got to retire."

"Rittire?" Angelo says.

"Cabinet," Elmer says.

"Ah," Angelo says; "cabinet." He glances up at his patron's concerned, at once very alert and yet inwardlooking face; he grasps Elmer by the elbow and begins to run. They run for several steps before Elmer can jerk free; his face is now downright alarmed.

"Goddamn it, let go!" He cries.

"True," Angelo says in Italian. "In your situation, running is not what a man wants. I forgot. Slow and easy does it, though not too slow. Coraggio," he says, "we come to her soon." And presently the pay station is in sight. "Voila!" Angelo says. Again he takes his patron's arm, though not running; again Elmer frees his arm, drawing away; again Angelo indicates the station, his single eyebrow high on his skull, his eyes melting, concerned, inquiring; again he reverses his sound of approbation, indicating the station with his thumb.

"No!" Elmer says. His voice is desperate now, his expression desperate yet determined. "Hotel!" In the Garden, where Elmer walks with long harried strides and Angelo trots beside him, twilight is gray and unsibilant among the trees; in the long dissolving arras people are already moving toward the gates. They pass swiftly the carven figures in the autumntinged dusk, pass the bronze ones in solemn nowformless gleams secretive and brooding; both trotting now, they pass Verlaine in stone, and Chopin, that sick feminine man like snow rotting under a dead moon; already the moon of death stands overhead, pleasant and affable and bloodless as a procuress. Elmer enters the Rue Vaugirard, trotting with that harried care, as though he carries dynamite; it is Angelo who restrains him until there is a gap in the traffic.

Then he is in the Rue Servandoni. He is running now, down the cobbled slope. He is no longer thinking *What will people think of me* It is as though he now carries life, volition, all, cradled dark and sightless in his pelvic girdle, with just enough of his intelligence remaining to tell him when he reaches the door. And there, just emerging, hatless, is his landlady.

"Ah, Monsieur Odge," she says. "I just this moment search for you. You have visitors; the female millionaires American Monson wait you in your chamber."

"Yes," Elmer says, swerving to run past her, not even aware that he is speaking to her in English. "In a minute I will—" Then he pauses; he glares at her with his harried desperate face. "Mohsong?" he says. "Mohsong?" then: "Monson! *Monson!*" Clutching the portfolio he jerks his wild glare upward toward his window, then back to the landlady, who looks at him in astonishment. "Keep them there!" he shouts at her with savage ferocity. "Do you hear? Keep them there! Don't let them get away. In a minute I will—" But already he has turned, running toward the opposite side of the court. Still galloping, the portfolio under his arm, he rushes up the dark stairs while somewhere in his desperate mind thinking goes quietly *There will be somebody already in it. I know there will* thinking with desperate despair that he is to lose Myrtle twice because of his body: once because of his back which would not let him dance, and now because of his bowels which will give her to think that he is running away. But the cabinet is empty; his very sigh of relief is the echo of his downwardsighing trousers about his legs, thinking Thank God. Thank God. Myrtle. *Myrtle.* Then this too flees; he seems to see his life supine before the secret implacable eyeless life of his own entrails like an immolation, saying like Samuel of old: Here I am. Here I am. Then they release him. He wakes again and reaches his hand toward the niche where scraps of newspaper are kept and he becomes utterly immobile while time seems to rush past him with a sound almost like that of a shell.

He whirls; he looks at the empty niche, surrounded by the derisive whistling of that dark wind as though it were the wind which had blown the niche empty. He does not laugh; his bowels too have emptied themselves for haste. He claps his hand to his breast pocket; he becomes immobile again with his arm crossing his breast as though in salute; then with a dreadful urgency he searches through all his pockets, producing two broken bits of crayon, a dollar watch, a few coins, his room key, the tobacco tin (worn silver smooth now) containing the needles and thread and such which the cook had given him ten years ago in Canada. That is all. And so his hands cease. Imbued for the moment with a furious life and need of their own, they die; and he sits for a moment looking quietly at the portfolio on the floor beside him; again, as when he watched them fondle the handgrenade on board the transport in 1916, he watches them take up the portfolio and open it and take out the picture. But only for the moment, because again haste descends upon him and he no longer watches his hands at all, thinking Myrtle. Myrtle. *Myrtle.*

And now the hour, the moment, has come. Within the Garden, beyond the dusk and the slow gateward throng, the hidden bugle begins. Out of the secret dusk the grave brazen notes come, overtaking the people, passing the caped policemen at the gates, and about the city dying where beneath the waxing and bloodless moon evening has found itself. Yet still within the formal twilight of the trees the bugle sounds, measured, arrogant, and sad.

FRED PFEIL

The Idiocy of Rural Life

The bourgeoisie . . . has thus rescued a considerable part
of the population from the idiocy of rural life.

—Marx and Engels, *Communist Manifesto*

A PATIENT STOICAL MAN, THE FARMER WAITED THROUGH HIS WORK
into the evening, until after washing up out back, rubbing the cold spring
water over his face and hands, before he walked into the kitchen of the
white frame house and asked his wife: You seen them cars outside there
today?

Sure did, said the Farmer's Wife, a worrier, from the stove. Often—as
now—her pale eyes were shadowed with a vague anxiety, and her thin
lips quivered white as she turned to look at him.

Whole afternoon, she said. I was out there peeling apples for this
pie—she nudged a thumb to where it sat on the counter, round and
brown —and just looked up and there they was.

He nodded. Then walked in unhurried strides, his face impassive, past
her and out of the kitchen and through the small living room, where he
brushed the gauzy curtains of a front window aside with one large hand.
Fifty feet away, across the yard, the cars still moved up the road, chrome
glinting, glass glaring like moving shields in the stark heat of this strange
dry spring.

Still there? his Wife called behind, wiping her hands in her apron.

The Farmer let the curtain drop, turned his head in profile to her, nodded. He raised up and went over to the maple rocker they had bought the
year before from Sears, sat down in it, and began to unlace his boots.

Probably some folks gettin together up on Old Saddleback for some
kind of do, he said, glancing at her haunted eyes. I wouldn't pay no attention to it. Chances are it don't amount to nothin at all.

While they sat at the kitchen table eating pork, okra, pie, the traffic
noise reached them as a slight constant roar, like the sound of a distant
plane. Afterwards, while she picked up the dishes, he went in to watch TV.

At this hour, in his time zone, the Farmer had a choice between *Welcome Back Kotter* and *Little House on the Prairie*. Being a farmer, he chose the latter, though tonight it was a rerun he had seen during the regular season. In this show a deadly blizzard attacks Walnut Grove, the small town in Kansas near the Ingalls family farm, trapping beautiful children, clothed in attractive homespun, in the little wooden schoolhouse. Michael Landon, with his dark curly hair, his boyish yet resolute face, rescues them and leads them home, in the middle of the nineteenth century and the days of the frontier.

By the time she came in the show was over. Outside, the cars must have turned their lights on; a pulse of muffled light swept through the windows regularly.

He watched her look around the room, eyes drifting from grandfather clock to pole lamp to the old armchair where he sat—everything, thanks to the headlights, strange. When her eyes met his she started to talk.

Gettin low on a few things, she said. Oughtta get to town pretty soon.

Fine, he said. Anytime.

You still thinkin you're gonna have to go see Boles this year? she said.

He scraped his hand across the stubble on his chin and watched the TV. *Baretta* was starting now. Don't know, he said. Depends on what they want for seed and fertilizer. Pretty soon, we'll see.

He watched the beginning of the episode. Tony Baretta is chasing a flashy black pimp down an alley of the city. Then he heard her strained voice.

I don't like the idea of this kind of thing goin on when you're not here, she said. What if one of them cars was to stop and somebody come right in here?

When he turned and smiled at her, crow's-feet formed in the corners of his gray eyes. Well, he said, I guess the way they're goin now, car behind that one'd smash right into the back of it, now wouldn't it. Then there'd be hell to pay.

Her tight mouth opened, released a high squealing chitter which ceased abruptly, even as he joined it with his own guffaws. She stared at the window, at the sweeping lights, rubbing her fingers around and around on the arms of the rocking chair until, rising, he stepped over and rested a work-worn hand on her thin arm.

Just don't you worry, honey, he said. It ain't goin to keep on; and it ain't no business of ours.

The air is thick, rich gold with the dust of hay as the old robust farmer and his strapping sons climb down from the hay wagon and tractor and walk—tired, dusty, happy—homeward through the mown field to the white frame house on whose front porch they sit and are regaled by the old farmer's comely wife, age oddly indeterminate, bearing gold bottles of Miller's beer as someone sings "When it's time to relax, one thing comes clear, if you've got the time, we've got the beer," while the farm family raise their bottles to their lips in the gold air.

The Farmer woke at the first music of the GE digital clock radio, rose and dressed to the Farm Report—*Alfalfa, 43; Oats, 40; Soybeans, 72; Wheat, 59; and in Poultry*—as his wife still tossed and rolled in restless sleep. Then he heard the noise from outside, and remembered.

So he stepped out without his customary coffee, and walked over the soft dew-fresh grass until he stood at the edge of the drainage ditch not more than two yards from them, watching them snap past. The string of cars stretched into mist on either side. On the right, towards Saddleback, a few red taillights winked a glow through the last of night, caught in the trees.

The Farmer looked across the road, at the shed with his own car and the wheat field beyond, powder-green in the wet air. It needed fertilizer, extra water soon. How the hell was he gonna get across to it?

He lowered as if to an invisible chair, hands braced on his knees, so he could glimpse, blur after blur, the occupants of the cars. Hey, he said—first in a soft call, finally in a hoarse shout—how the hell you expect me to get across here to my field? How the hell you expect me to get across here to my field?

When he realized nobody heard him the Farmer stood, wheeled around, and walked past the house to the barn, where he fed the chickens and milked the cows, holding his face as still as theirs, calming down. In all the hen boxes there were only three eggs.

By the time he came back out the sun was a good inch free of the horizon, and his wife was outside, her back turned to him, standing by the front corner of the house watching the cars pass, a pale shape tipped with the brown of her hair. Slowly, heavily, he walked up to her, dreading the fear he would find on her face.

But when she turned, he was surprised to find her looking far less frightened than he'd counted on. You picked up anything on them? she said.

For a second he thought of telling her about the bottom field, how they were blocking it; but if she did know there was no use repeating it, if not there was no use getting her upset. No, he said.

A light, elusive smile crossed her smooth face. What kinda cars they drivin, she said.

He looked. The fog had burned away so he could see maybe forty from the rise on the left to the hill on the right, where they went up into the woods: station wagons, compact cars, medium-sized models, sporty compacts and sports cars, family and luxury sedans, coupes, convertibles and luxury automobiles . . .

Well, he said, all kinds, I guess. He scratched his head, sneaked another quick look to the side: No trucks . . .

She grabbed his arm, turned him straight ahead again. No, she said, staring fiercely. The *makes*.

He looked; and, as the day's first real heat touched his head, saw that they were Fords.

Against black we see first one ordinary watchband, then a dazzling host of them, of shapes, sizes, elasticities, and light tones; and the urbane yet concerned voice of a skilled announcer asks how we would like it if we lived in a country where we could only buy just that first kind of watchband and no other, some unnamed other place under the oppression of the lone watchband, only one thing to buy, instead of here where you can pluck out of the glittering heap of watchbands the very one that is right for only you before you line up at the register to pay. This ad is a public service of the Ad Council, a "nonprofit" organization headed by representatives of United Airlines, General Mills and General Foods, ITT and IBM, General Electric, etc., etc.

Soon the day was starched with heat; in the west meadow where the Farmer went, choosing to mend fence, the heat stood breathing close and sour in his face as he strung, stretched, clipped wire, pounded a few posts deeper down. Yet he made it all day without so much as going in for lunch, scrutinized only by his own idling cows jostled together under the meadow's few trees, stopping only to slap at sweat bees.

Late in the afternoon, he propped the spool of wire on one shoulder, swung the sledge from his free arm, and started back across and down the ridge that sloped to his barn, house, and the dirt road beyond. The second the cars came into view he could see how much they had slowed down; to twenty mph anyways, and still no end to them in sight. And he could see, framed by the two oaks in the front yard, the tiny figure of his Wife.

She was, he found once he was all the way down, sitting close to the spot where he'd hunkered that morning to yell at the cars. All day plumes of dust must have drifted from the road to the lawn; dust lay in a dull brown all over the grass, over her aproned lap.

Her face was rapt; her brown, normally troubled eyes remained fixed and calm; rather than follow each car out of sight, she let them fill and refill her field of vision, like someone thirsty drinking glass after glass. When at last she turned to him her eyes looked yellow; for a second he was afraid she did not recognize him.

Ever notice how Ford makes their cars animals? she said, and pointed a finger like a gun at the road: Pinto; Mustang; Bronco; Thunderbird.

Above his head he heard a high breeze shiver the oak leaves. Shoot, he said, and snorted. How bout Torino? You heard of a animal called Torino? You know of a animal named LTD?

The Farmer and his Wife stared at each other with dull angry eyes.

You been sittin out here all day, he said. I suppose you know how I'm gonna get over there, tend that goddamn wheat?

Her mouth grew a slow, sly smile though her eyes did not change. They'll let you through, she said.

How you know? the Farmer said as once more sweat broke out on him, as though hot water had been flung on his face. You been talkin with them? You the one's so scared some one of them'd stop to see you; they stoppin to see you now?

The Farmer's Wife rose, slapping the dust off her apron and housedress before looking at him again almost in her old way, without the smile. I just think they will, she said. Just a feelin, that's all. Now come on, she said, reaching for his hand. Let's go on in, news is on. They might have somethin to say about all this, you never know.

So he allowed himself to be led in, seated in his armchair; the TV was on, had been on the whole time. While she got supper he watched the news, featuring a farmers' strike. The farmers have their tractors drawn around the Governor's mansion and stand sullenly in flannel shirts, arms crossed on chests. The Governor comes out to speak in a gray suit, white shirt, and tie, and says I will go to Washington; I will tell them that the farmer feeds us all; and a thin ragged cheer floats from the crowd, followed by a commercial for Union Carbide.

She wafted in with two shiny silver trays from which he could discern no smells, flopped a dish towel in his lap, and set one tray on top of it.

There, she said, indicating the content of each bin: there's your crispy chicken leg and thigh, your green peas with pearl onions, your apple brown betty for dessert—

The Farmer looked down at the food, like pictures on TV, and closed his eyes and let a wave of feeling pass over him. You get the same for yourself? he heard his voice say.

Oh no, she said. I got loin of pork.

He opened his eyes and watched her awhile, eating in her rocking chair. She attacked her portions with apparent relish, without benefit of a fork, dipping her fingers in her tray and mouth with her eyes fixed on the TV, an episode of *The Waltons*. John-Boy is upstairs in the Walton farmhouse recording in his journal the events of this episode from the days of the Depression which now begin to unfold, brought to you by General Foods. By Gulf-Western, By Zenith color TV.

Since when you bought this stuff? the Farmer said.

Her thin hand stopped halfway to her mouth, then redeposited a Tater Tot in her tray. Her eyes looked somewhere between the TV set and his chair.

Oh, she was saying, I don't know when. She was laughing now, with that smile on again: All this weird stuff we got goin around now, I just thought we might's well eat somethin new too. How you like it?

Don't know, he said feeling sick with her lie. Ain't yet tasted it. But she had turned her face back to the set.

Sadly the Farmer dipped his head, pinched a chicken leg's gold crunchy crust, and lifted it toward his mouth. Grease like some hot secret spurted through the chicken skin over his hand, John-Boy and Pa on the TV jog the mules across the hill toward home, Pa nodding sagely, and the Farmer heard at that selfsame moment once again the deep-throated murmur of the cars outside, and felt this strange conjunction so—hot skinny chicken, her deception, the cars outside, the pictures on the screen—that his lap trembled beneath the towel, his broad thighs buckled and spread apart, sending kelly-green peas up in the air, brown betty to the floor, soft side down.

Aw, he cried, Hell's bells.

Hey, she said, rising swiftly: don't worry about it, okay? She set her emptied tray down on the floor and came and stood over him; she passed a hand through his short-cropped hair, down the back of his bull neck. I'll get it later, she said. How bout if you and me do somethin different for a change?

He looked down in time to see one of her small feet squash a pea. Like what? he said, voice trembling.

Like go to bed a little early for a change? she said.

Ain't even dark yet, the Farmer mumbled, feeling his face go hot; but already, once again, she had him by the hand and was leading him out of the room, into the bedroom, again leaving the TV on.

What they did then, there in the bedroom with the red sun going down, was indeed different enough from usual that when it was done, while she was all giggly happy, he set his shamed body and mind running toward sleep but did not manage to arrive before her voice, silky, thrilling, reached him one last time.

And we're out of food and practically a dozen other things too, why I can hardly think what all, you just remember now, we go to town first thing tomorrow—you hear?

I hear, he groaned—and fled below the voice, beneath even the slow rolling of wheels outside, so far down he never noticed when she got up from the bed and went back outside, humming in the dark.

The background, brown, textured, woody, suggests a farm or cabin, soft dream of rural interiority. Likewise, the man wears suede tones and conveys in voice and manner a certain sturdiness, though he is not husky enough to be an Outdoorsman, too polished for a Farmer, as he slides across the background (through whose window you glimpse wildflowers? gnarled

oak tree in bloom?), moving his calm jaws. He says some people want the
lightness of white bread. Others want the firmness of wheat and whole
grain. Roman Meal gives you both, he says, showing you gray-brown rug-
ged grains in the iron scoop; flour in a barrel; honey in a jar. Where did
the grains grow, in whose field, by what methods; where and how do these
ingredients come together to compose the loaf he hefts in his hand? And
his shirt of raw cotton, open almost to the pectorals—where and by whom
was it made? Who decided he should have black hair? The Roman Meal
people, he says, thought you'd like to know.

There was just room enough for his car, a Plymouth V-8, ten years old,
to squeeze by the Fords inching the other way on the dirt road. He drove
the mile to the main road slow and cautious, sweat crawling down his
face and dampening the Sears plaid short-sleeve shirt he was wearing to
town. Beside him on the seat, his Wife, cool and dry in some lime slacks
and blouse he had not seen before, began reading aloud from her book.

During barbarous ages, she read, if the strength of an individual declined, if he felt himself tired or sick, melancholy or satiated and, as a consequence, without desire or appetite for a short time, he became relatively
a better man, that is, less dangerous. . . . She stopped reading, peered over
the top of the paperback at him: What do you think of that?

Think of it? The Farmer squinted fiercely at the road, the space the
Fords left him; the morning sun shone hard, straight at the windshield of
the car. Ain't nothin to think of it. Bunch of trash is what it is.

I just knew you'd say that, said his Wife. That's just the kind of thing
you'd say. And it's Nietzsche, in case you're interested.

I don't give a hair of my behind what it is, the Farmer was about to say;
but they had reached the hard road, where he saw a sight that silenced him.
In the westward, left-hand lane of the hard road, the Fords lined up to turn
left stretched off to vanishing point; then, in his full shock, he turned to
his Wife and saw her eyes staring off at them shining, her tongue tracing
the line of her lips.

I don't know where you gettin that trash anyways, he said, looking back
at the road and turning the car right, onto the macadam: Neechuh. People
in them cars puttin that trash in your head or what.

Oh *God*, she said. Why can't you just leave me alone? And with that, poked her nose back in the book again the rest of the way in, inking in passages now and then with a purple felt-tip pen.

He dropped her off at the Safeway and went to the Agway, where the fellow told him No he hadn't heard a thing about it. To which the Farmer replied as how he hadn't really figured it was anything to amount to anything anyway; just curious was all.

The fellow slapped the sacks he had hauled up to the counter: All right then. That be all today?

That's all I guess, the Farmer said.

Cash or charge, the fellow said.

Charge, said the Farmer.

The fellow reached down under the counter and went through the slips until he found his. Then he took a stub of pencil from behind his ear and figured on the slip for a while, his round face wadded in a frown, while the Farmer's eyes traveled over the dusty outlines of bags and barrels in the cool dark of the warehouse, thinking nothing, waiting for the calculation to end.

I hate to tell you, the fellow said when he looked up, in a voice without sorrow: You're already over.

Figured as much, the Farmer said quite levelly, looking straight on back at him. Goddamn prices the way they are. He moved a step closer to the counter, so close now his belt buckle touched the wood. Gotta have that stuff, he said.

The fellow's eyes seemed to lose focus, turn watery. You been to see Boles yet this year? he said.

No, said the Farmer. Not yet this year. I'll be goin directly now.

The fellow's mouth knit and firmed, though his eyes stayed the same. All right then, he said. I'll put you down and let you ride. He wrote a few more numbers on the slip and turned it around for the Farmer to sign. I'll be hearin from you then just as soon as you see him, he said.

That's right, the Farmer said, hefting to his shoulder a sack of potash, popping fresh sweat on his brow. Already the fellow was scuttling around the counter wheeling a dolly.

Here now, he was saying brightly, smiling again: Lemme give you a hand there gettin that in the car.

In the parking lot at Safeway he watched a checkout boy watching her cross the asphalt with her bags, bend to stuff them in the back, get in herself, still looking dry and cool; only high on her cheekbones he saw blazes of red.

You gonna go see Boles soon? she said staring out as though to someone on the hood, and lighting a cigarette.

Yeah, he said in a much higher voice than usual. He had never seen her smoke before.

I couldn't buy *half* what we need with what you gave me, she said and puffed, tapping the ash off on the floor. I had to take back half the things *after* they were rung up. *Very* embarrassing, as you can imagine.

I'll be goin directly, the Farmer said.

As soon as they reached the main highway again, he realized his mistake: the Fords, fender to fender, still jammed the right side of the road. Oh Christ, he heard his wife sigh, what a—

He wrenched the Plymouth into the left lane and gunned it as she shouted his name; the car popped, shuddered, raced up the road. Three times before they reached the turnoff cars moving legally in the lane came straight at them and he had to sound the horn as loud and long as he could to send them off the road to the berm in time. But even as his car fishtailed and scudded up the wrong side of the dirt road, not one of the Fords pulled out after him.

He wheeled the car into the shed and shut it off and looked at her taut face. You could have killed us both, she said.

Naw, he said, smiling, feeling good for the first time in days. Not much chance a that.

They crossed between two Fords easily; the line was now still, though the cars all had their engines on. A thin blue haze of hydrocarbons, faint as gunsmoke, reached as high as the first boughs of the oak, and the ditch was strewn with Big Mac wrappers, DQ cups, Coke bottles and cans, though all the car windows were up. The grass beneath its dust blanket had turned a dying yellow.

You mind puttin this stuff away? she said when the bags were on the kitchen table, with a vestige of her old tone. I think I'd like to go and lie down for a bit. She draped a forearm over her brow: It's just so hot.

Yeah, the Farmer said. Sure. He thought of touching her but instead stood looking at his hands until she was out of the room. Then he took all the strange frozen boxes out of the bags—Spinach Soufflé, Turkey Tetrazzini, Cannelloni in sauce, Potatoes au gratin, Lobster Newburg—put as many as would fit away in the freezer, the rest in the fridge, piled the books she had stowed in the bags' bottoms on the table for her—*Critique de la raison dialectique?*—and, after some hesitation, went out to doze himself for a few hours in the known, deep shadows of the barn with the animals.

In less than twenty years, from 1950 to 1969, the number of farms in the United States has declined by half—from 5.4 to 2.7 million. This decline is not due to a drop in agricultural activity, but from the rapid process of concentration of U.S. agriculture into large-scale capitalist enterprise. Thus in 1969 a little over 2 percent of U.S. farms consisted of at least 2000 acres. And these large farms accounted for 40 percent of U.S. farmland. At the other end of the scale 23 percent of the farms in 1969 were less than 50 acres, and another 17 percent were between 50 and 99 acres. Taken together, these two groups—or 40 percent of the farms—operated less than 100 acres each and accounted for less than 5 percent of total farmland.

So shortly thereafter the Farmer found himself waking in dark morning beside his sprawled Wife, fallen asleep with the reading light on again, her fingers marking the 246th formulation of the *Philosophical Investigations*; found himself hauling on his overalls and tiptoeing out, turning back only once to let his hand come back and almost rest on her hair, as his eyes lighted on the passage without meaning to; something about knowing someone's pain.

Outside the Fords had their headlights on, each shining directly into the taillights of the next a matter of inches away. The line no longer moved; so the strangely refracted glow, the radiance suffusing the stream, seemed the product of the massed, purring engines of the cars, gas-burning generators of light. Crossing the line this time he had to step up and over a Torino's bumper; the dark backlit outlines in the car did not honk.

Shortly after he had reached the hard road and turned east, darkness began to leak out of the sky. Soon it was the same time he usually got up; he turned on the Farm Report in the car—*Alfalfa, 43; Oats, 40; Soybeans, 72*—and found the litany of prices conjured up his Wife the way she used to be, eyes closing and opening in slow fatigued anxiety as he moved around the bed and dressed. The image held him all the way to the airport, a goodly distance away.

The jet took off into a swollen sun, then banked to the northeast so that he, in a window seat on the right, could see it rising orange and monstrous in the haze of the day before. He thought of that sun shining on his fields all day, of spreading gray fertilizer and hoping for rain, of the way weather worked before the Fords came. But soon the high vibration of the machine he sat in soothed him; gradually he assumed the indifference of an object, as one does in planes, rousing only to eat a yellow square of hot soft stuff he did not bother to think of as eggs.

Hours later, as the plane touched down again and taxied the runway, the Farmer felt a new and general sadness creeping over him as his sense of self returned—a sadness he realized he had been holding back in his mind for a few days now anyway. The feeling something was over, things were changed and would not come back, stuck inside him like a pit in a peach. Still, he told himself, scanning the profile of the gray city as it passed, just have to keep goin on.

So, willful as an animal, consciously blind to the concourse crowds and noise, he forced his way as usual through the terminal, grabbed the first cab he could, shot Boles's address in the cabby's ear like a poem he had memorized and would soon forget.

The cab moved over beltways, expressways, freeways, on- and off-ramps; occasionally the Farmer, staring fixedly out the window, would see a Ford in the clog of traffic, but he tried not to count.

The cab dropped him off downtown at the foot of a giant alabaster building where, Boles had once told him, everyone worked for the same company he did. You see ads for them on TV sometimes, showing couples on stretches of beach or sunsets on wheat fields or sunrise on forests and saying Working to make America stronger, or better, or things like that.

The Farmer took an elevator to the eighty-fifth floor, Boles's floor. It let him off into a magenta room with lime stripes and a slim secretary who said in a voice of cool disapproval, May I help you please?

Like to see Mr. Boles, he muttered, dropping into what seemed to his nervous haunches to be a bottomless chair.

Do you have an appointment, said the secretary, examining a fingernail.

Believe I do, he said, almost inaudibly.

She frowned at him and pressed the intercom. Mr. Boles, she said, there is a gentleman in overalls out here to see you, sir. Says he has an appointment. Then she listened to the button in her ear, said Yes sir, and swiveled in her chair back toward the Farmer with a smile: Yes, Mr. Boles will see you now. Walk right in, please.

Obliged, he mumbled and lurched to his feet, swiping the Harvester cap from his head.

Well, Boles said in the inner office, without rising from his massive desk: Hello again.

Hello Mr. Boles, the Farmer said.

What can I do for you, said Boles.

The Farmer stared at Boles's name and title on the edge of his desk, wrung the cap in his hand, tried to smile; failed. Need some seed and fertilizer money, he said. Plus a little for provisions the next month or so.

He stopped; Boles said nothing; he went on. All I'm askin for, he said—

Boles raised one slim hand, palm out. I must tell you, he said. The answer this time must be no. We can offer you no advance funding this year.

He pressed a button on the console on the right-hand edge of the desk; a map of the earth slid down the wood-lined wall. On the map in various areas emblems of food were stuck. A teapot covered Kenya; soybeans dotted Brazil; a steer head loomed over Central America; a chicken stalked Pakistan; pineapples rested on the Philippines; etc., etc., etc. In his own region the Farmer saw a representation of a milk can and stalks of corn and wheat, but now Boles rose and lifted them off the map.

We're relocating many of the sources of our agricultural supply, he said, and seemed about to replace the stalks and can on their new home.

But the Farmer, to his own surprise, lifted his eyes straight at Boles; and Boles stood still with the little images in his hand. You know anything about these Fords keep comin up my road? the Farmer said, astonished at himself.

Boles frowned, staring off, and slid the emblems into his suitcoat pocket. Fords? he said. Fords . . . No, he said, sliding back into his chair; I can't tell you why Fords. He spoke softly and slowly, as though talking to himself: Although certainly there would be increased traffic in the vicinity I can't tell . . . Fords . . . Fords, you say?

That's right, said the Farmer.

Hmm, Boles said, tossing his head casually back and to the side: Frankly, that worries me. We've got some nice little plans for your part of the country, your neck of the woods, whatever you want to call it—you know, that Saddleback you've got up there is a *very* important hill—and I don't like to hear about a lot of Fords in there, no sir. I don't like hearing about it one bit.

What kinda plans, the Farmer said, amazing himself again.

Across the desk Boles pursed his mouth and looked at him with sharp blue eyes. Then he leaned forward suddenly. Listen, he said. You've been a good tenant, client, whatever you want to call it; I'm gonna give you a break.

He settled back in his chair and swiveled it slightly from left to right and back. The plan is to wait about another month, he said, until you're really low and the stuff's burning up in the fields; it won't rain either, see? Then we come and make you an offer on the whole shebang. And that offer's gonna seem real nice.

His eyes were gleaming; his left-hand index finger shot up in the air: Don't take it. Ask us to make a second offer, maybe a third. I'm telling you this for your own good; you mention it to anyone, I can kiss this job goodbye. But you keep your mouth shut and play your cards right and you won't ever have to farm again, all right?

He jumped up from the seat and bent over the desk with his hand out like a chopping blade. Don't forget now, he said as they shook hands: I'm telling you because you're a good man and for telling me about the Fords. But don't forget to leave my name out of it, okay?

My great-grandfather, recently over from Sweden, is working out of the Wetmore lumber camp, stripping the bark off shag hickory trees. He goes out in the morning with a gunny sack and a short saw and an eight-inch double-handled blade, and comes in at night with the bag full of bark. This is in western Pennsylvania, the northern tip of the Appalachians, 1904. The company pays him so much per pound and sells it to the chemical plant over in Coudersport where they do something with it, he doesn't know what; but the money is good enough that, with the help of my great-grandmother, who cooks for the men at the camp, he will be able to buy a small ramshackle farm in four years' time, up what will be called Farmer's Valley where he will live until his death in 1958.

So on this midsummer afternoon he is working in the forest down a hill towards the Smethport road, metal voices of locusts off behind him, last shade-cool of the woods fading away. Then, he hears another noise, or set of noises, popping and crackling from down on the road. He rests his blade and saw on the sack and walks to the edge of the woods and looks down. On the road, about a half-mile away, is a black box tapered a bit at the front end, moving forward on four wheels mounted on the outside edge of the carriage, trailing great clouds of dust behind it and a thinner, higher plume of smoke, all traveling at least as fast as a good horse at a gallop. My great-grandfather takes out the red print bandanna he bought last time he went down to town and wipes his brow and watches closely, without expression, until the first car he has seen is gone; then he goes back up in the woods to work.

On the way back there were not only the immobile Fords but other equipment, earthmovers, caterpillars scraping, already at work, flagmen everywhere in the dust; it was twilight before the Farmer reached his home again. From the kitchen, where she had left her note, he could hear the livestock calling out back from the barn: hens clucking with hunger and irritation at the cars, cows lowing to be milked and fed. They made at least as much sense as her note, in block capitals, held before his eyes.

THE CONTRADICTIONS IN OUR SITUATION ARE IRRECONCILABLE. I'M SORRY.

    KATE

The floor, table, and counter space were covered with empty boxes with pictures of serving suggestions on their fronts, with spine-broken books whose pages fluttered in the breeze swept through the screen. Could it be about to rain? Boles had told him no. For a minute he thought of going after her, finding the car she was in, even started toward the front door. Then he stopped; it would be easier, after all, this way.

He went out back, pumped some water into his cupped hands, washed his face. Seemed silly to feed or tend the animals, too, if all they were going to do was die. So he let them yell, and walked on past the barn to the south field he'd put alfalfa down in a few weeks ago.

Now, though the first stars had come out, there was still enough light left to show him the bright clean green of the sprouts coming up: the coolest, most beautiful green in the world. He felt refreshed just looking at it; though it too would die. And be paved over? he wondered, idly.

In the middle distance, some two hundred yards away, the Fords on the road were turning on their lights. The Farmer sat down in his field, and felt the warmth of the earth soaking into his body. He reached over, plucked a green sprout from the ground, ate it. Cool green taste filled his mouth, eyes, mind. He ate another. Another. Another. When he had finished the row he obeyed another sudden urge, and lay down on his stomach against the earth.

After a while, a cry rang out of the night—carried over the sounds of insects and cars with the aid of an electrified bullhorn, which helped alter the sound of her voice considerably.

JIM, she called. CAN YOU HEAR ME? I DIDN'T GO WITH THE CARS LIKE YOU THOUGHT.

The Farmer rolled over on his back; the cars' lights were so bright you could find stars only in a small portion of the sky. *Sure*, he thought, somewhere far back in his mind. *Hear you just fine.* His large hands stroked, sifted, patted the warm ground.

SOME OF THEM—US—SOME PEOPLE LEFT THEIR CARS, the voice said. THERE'S QUITE A FEW OF US HERE, ACTUALLY. AND IF YOU WANT TO, JIM—

The electric voice went on; but the Farmer no longer listened. In that place back in his skull, a voice still went on saying things like *sure enough, uh huh, yeah, yeah, yeah*; but he had lost the habit of speech. He lay on his back while the voices talked on until finally, after they both stopped, he felt the moment he had been waiting for, with or without knowing it, all along: when, his belly full of warm green stuff, his eyes could see the sparks of light up there and—thanks to the cars—the glow around the edges of the sky like the whole thing was a big TV screen, the world's biggest, which he kept right on watching for a very long time.

FRED CHAPPELL

The Snow That Is Nothing in the Triangle

"IF A MAN CONSTRUCT AN EQUILATERAL TRIANGLE ON A SHEET OF paper, what is in the triangle?"

Silence, consternated head-wagging. . . . Nothing is in the triangle. What did Herr Professor Feuerbach want his students to answer? They were not yet so disturbed as they would later become at his bizarre behavior, as when he would enter the classroom with an unsheathed sword and seriously threaten to behead any student who could not solve the problem that he would propose. But they were beginning to know that things were not straight, not clear.

"You will say, Nothing," Feuerbach went on, "but that is wrong. The correct answer is *Snow*. It is snow inside the triangle."

Snow.

They looked at his unclean sparse hair, dressed, or rather not dressed, in the old long fashion, falling in raddled strings on his shoulders. He was not much older than his students, the youngest man ever appointed to such a position at the Gymnasium in Erlangen, yet his thin and greasy hair was white and his long fingernails tough and horny like the talons of a man in his seventies.

"Ha, but wait—you will not be quite wrong either. For snow is nothing, yet it is a Substantive Nothing. If a man plunge into a snowbank up to his neck, or even over his head, has he fallen into Nothing?" He nodded, heavily grave. "He has, yes he has fallen into Nothing, and who can tell what consequences will ensue?"

They no longer called him *the Pope of the Theorems*, referring to his magisterial brilliance as a geometrician and to his physique. His body, like that of the famous English poet of seventy-five years before, was crushed into the shape of a question mark, and he got himself about with obvious pain. But his manners had become so odd that the students no longer called him anything but *Feuerbach*, as if his true name were descriptive beyond the power of other words. For a brief time he had been called *old Feuerbach*, but then they had discovered that he really was only thirty-two years old. In any case, he seemed no age at all, but rather outside time, like a topological proposition that could not be proved.

"That it is snow in our constructed triangle is true, indubitable, but you gentlemen are not to noise this fact abroad. It is to be our secret." As soon as he had said this, he began to look about the classroom apprehensively. Then, with a sudden expression of alarm, he crossed to the door and flung it open. The hallway was empty, but he looked up and down it with the greatest intensity, as if suspecting that something escaped his gaze.

The students stirred uneasily. It had been hard to believe that their Herr Professor F. was the same man who had produced the most beautiful theorem in plane geometry since the time—perhaps—of Euclid. It bore his name, the Feuerbach theorem: "For any triangle, the nine-point circle is tangent to the incircle and to each of the three excircles of the triangle." And there was a further lovely corollary, because the nine-point circle also passes through the three feet of the altitudes of the triangle and the three points bisecting the joins of the orthocenter to the three vertices. This was a theorem so elegant that some of the students had decorated the flyleaves of their textbooks with drawings of it.

Now Feuerbach trotted back and perched his crooked little shape on the edge of his desk. "Secret secret secret," he cooed, and leaned forward in earnest confidentiality. "*Secret* is another word that, gentlemen, you must never utter. Do you know why?"

He waited; they waited.

"Because it is destructive to your health. Do you not observe the shape of my body, gentlemen, which is twisted like a curve in space? That is because there is a logically unbreakable linkage between the word *secret* and the prison cell and the triangle full of snow which is Nothing. Oh you may try"—and now he leaned forward even more, and they feared that he might tumble—"you may try, gentlemen, gentlemen, to cut the veins in your feet, but they will not let you die. No, you cannot bleed to death that way—there is a guard who coughs and shuffles and then they take you to the infirmary and bind up the veins again and you are alive after all. Of twenty of you, only one may die, that much is clear. Look, I will demonstrate."

He tipped to the floor and scurried back to the blackboard. He seized a piece of chalk, but he had already covered the board with partial constructions, numbers, mottoes, Greek and Latin abbreviations, scraps of poetry. He stood looking at this wilderness of scrawl in bafflement.

Peremptorily, he turned back to the class and indicated the whole of the board with a languid hand. "Klaus Hörnli will now solve this problem," he said.

The eleven students turned involuntarily to survey the back of the classroom. There was no Klaus Hörnli among them, and no unknown person in the room. Finally one of them dared to say, "There is no Klaus Hörnli here, Herr Professor."

He put the chalk down and rubbed his hands together briskly. "So. You see. By now it is evident, it is evident as daylight, is it not? There is no Klaus Hörnli among us." His voice quavered and his cheek trembled with irrepressible sorrow. "And he was the best of us, gentlemen, the very best." He brightened triumphantly. "But that is our proof. Klaus is absent from us, while I am here. The snow that is Nothing in the triangle has rejected me, but it has accepted Klaus. *Quod erat*, gentlemen. This is clear, this is clear as daylight."

Again the feckless student ventured to demur. "Herr Professor, I am afraid that we do not completely understand."

"Why can you not understand? It is clear, it is evident, a fool, even an idiot, can understand." Anger stopped his voice in his throat for a moment. His face reddened; he coughed, gagged. Then his whole body shuddered convulsively as if it might tear apart. But then settled. Suddenly now he seemed to be possessed by a peaceful gravity. His expression softened, his eyes were wise and glistening.

"Let us begin again from the beginning. Here is the basic proposition. Two young men are walking along the street. A quite ordinary day, and these two young men are merely walking along, chatting as any of you gentlemen might be chatting with one of your friends." He stopped and looked at them anxiously. "Do you understand where we are? Do you comprehend our premise?" Klaus Hörnli was the other young man with Feuerbach. Blond Klaus, high-spirited, sardonically witty, that is the way of young and brilliant students, when suddenly two policemen—two agents, that is—in dark unseasonable overcoats, you would not have

known them for policemen, you could not decipher, decipher—"Gentlemen, how could a geometrician be an anarchist? Is not anarchy disorder?
But do not the propositions of Euclid—including even the famously
troublesome fifth proposition—follow one another with the inevitability
of the leaves falling in autumn? Let us begin again from the beginning.
Two young men walking, and let us say that the town is Hof, a wealthy
and respected town with a reputable Gymnasium," *anarkhos*, without a
ruler, no constructions without a ruler, he Klaus Hörnli was no anarchist,
he Karl Feuerbach was no anarchist, "Gentlemen, you have mistaken the
loose and spirited talk of students in the beer gardens for plots and con-
spiracies; that is a false conclusion as I will now demonstrate," he went
back to the blackboard but could not find the chalk anywhere, meanwhile
they were questioned endlessly, taken from their cells and asked to eluci-
date faulty conclusions to problems without being given the necessary
premises, there was a guard or there were many guards who paced the
corridor outside the blind doors of the cells, all these guards in delicate
health, coughing and snuffling and sputtering, racking their poor lungs
for bits of phlegm to swallow down again, shuffling always, not lifting their
feet, with a dull sound that kept erasing the thoughts of him *Hörnli* Feuerbach in the cell, the feet wiping out the clear mathematical propositions,
a hexagon would appear shining white on black paper and then the feet
would come shuffling and the hexagon would disappear, that was in early
fall, the first fall in the prison cell, and when the snows began the sound
of falling snow was quite loud, much louder than you would expect, it
sounded like the shuffling of the feet of many guards in the corridor there,
the snow that fell into the interiors of any closed construction and filled
it up with the sound of shuffling, the lines no longer discernible on the
black paper covered over with snow, Feuerbach flapped his arms helplessly
at the blackboard then turned around and came back to his desk, in the
cells bitter cold and dank, many of us fell ill, twenty of us all told, "Do you
understand, from a group of twenty, one by one, or as it might be in some
cases, by twos and threes, abstracted subtracted distracted distracted from
the numerical order of their lives?" and put into cells by featureless heavy
men and loutish foul guards and asked to fabricate in a pitiless given time
and without any proper tool a geometry of anarchism, "The mind, gentlemen, the mind is not anarchical, geometry for instance as it occurs in

nature, the snowflake let us say with its infinitely varying but unvarying hexagon, is a clear proof the mind is not anarchical, for the mind has in it all the shapes of geometry and does not require that nature supply it with example, but here let us say in the snowflake nature reaches out to touch us reassuringly, gentlemen, to suggest that the mind is not mistaken in apprehending intimations of a high and eternal order, an order though we can but guess at it as certain and clear as the Pythagorean theorem," but then all the little hexagons of the snow filled up the greater hexagon in the mind with the sounds of coughing and shuffling until gradually gradually by minute gradations, you understand, the Greater Proposition began to show clear, in burning letters it appeared in his mind on the blank paper, melting away the detritus of snow on top, letters of yellow fire, IF ONE MAN DIE THE OTHERS SHALL BE FREED, there was no doubting this intuition written in pure fire, the way such intuitions must have come in antique time to Plato, to Euclid, to Aristotle, and no doubting the further certain corollary, that he Karl Wilhelm Feuerbach must be the man to die, the cough and shuffle of snowy hexagons fell upon these burning letters but could not obscure them, disappearing in the space above the black page in his mind with the letters of yellow flame, and Feuerbach began to weep and turned suddenly on his heel away from the students to wipe his eyes on his sleeve, he was becoming a bad example, to give them to think that geometry is a cause for weeping, "You must understand, gentlemen, you must forgive, we must all learn to understand and to forgive," and so he cut the veins in his feet, slowly, painfully with a bit of dull metal he had got, and then it began to disturb him that he could not remember where he had got that little bit of metal and he began to weep afresh and turned again away from his students, he could not bear for high-spirited Klaus Hörnli cheerfully smiling in the back of the classroom to see him weeping when he Feuerbach had so much less reason for tears than Klaus who was after all dead, Feuerbach must keep it in mind that Klaus had died, accepted into the Nothing triangle while he Feuerbach had been rejected, it was the medal with the portrait of Euclid he had won as a school prize and kept on a little chain round his neck, the mathematics prize he had won in fifth form, a medal whose edges he had kept honing honing against the stone wall of his cell until he had achieved a sort of keenness not very satisfactory, and so had managed to cut or to saw through the veins in his feet and lay back to die, now they would free the others, Feuerbach's death a surety for their innocence their youthful harmlessness, now he remembered and his feet began to hurt and he hopped up on the desk and held his left foot in both hands, cooing to it as a mother to her child, gentlemen gentlemen gentlemen, but as the snow of sleep began to settle on the letters in his mind and now at last not melting away but covering over the letters he closed his eyes, he tried not to sleep but the heavy inevitable snow kept falling on the yellow-flame letters, gray snow like greasy ash, snow as warm and sleepy as it was cold, and finally the burning letters could be seen no longer though they must be burning somewhere still, and then he awoke, awoke oh God, in the infirmary and a white pure snow was falling outside the window on the sharp angles of the roofs, on the triangles of the gables, on the curves in space of bare oak limbs, a pure white cold snow and in a little while he knew he was alive, he had not died, and when he knew that fact the sound of shuffling feet returned into the falling snow and no clean geometric constructions would appear on black paper in his mind any more, and his friends and colleagues were still miserable in their cells, and now the greasy ash of snow began to melt off the black paper and the letters appeared burning once again IF ONE MAN DIE THE OTHERS SHALL BE FREED the characters of yellow fire hotter and brighter than before, and he turned in the narrow infirmary bed to face the wall though the turning made his feet hurt as if scalded and begin to bleed again, and he wept copiously and bitterly because he had not managed to die, he had failed, "Gentlemen gentlemen gentlemen, did Plato and Euclid and Aristotle fail the intuitions that were so clearly delivered unto them, appearing in their minds as sharp as flame? Gentlemen, they did not, ours is an age of pygmy cowards with tedious little secrets and we are called upon to solve problems that are not problems, anarchical geometry, that is no problem, it is a whim of unlettered tyrants who cannot know the proper use of words, do not be taken in, gentlemen, by the spurious fancies of our own puny century," and he let go his foot as if it were a burning thing and let it swing like a pendulum back and forth under the open desk, the directive still imperative in his mind, *if one man die*, and he Feuerbach still determined to carry it out but stricken breathless on the paradox that in order to die he must a little at least regain his health, and turned again in his infirmary bed to stare out the window at the shuffling snow which had begun to cough quietly, falling on roof-ridge and gable-angle, if he could not produce clear geometric constructions in his mind there were yet these angles in nature to be looked at through the window, and the coughing snow could not obliterate them, that much was clear, could soften but not obliterate, and so he began to grow cunning, oh he was very crafty he was, not speaking unless spoken to, and obeying all the instructions of the doctor and the guards, though they persisted of course in asking those moronic questions that were not questions, he had no answers to the questions not questions but began to smile at them, gently wisely forgivingly smiling whenever they started with those propositions of anarchical geometry, and little by little the season turned into deep winter, the snow kept falling and its shuffling-coughing sound always grew louder, "Gentlemen, it is hard to think with so much noise in this classroom, can you not keep your feet quiet, must you always?" and he had formed a plan while smiling to win their confidence so that one day he might casually stroll to the window and open it as if without thinking and leap out and be killed, IF ONE MAN, and kept smilingly to his plan and did just that, opened the window just so, gracefully, while humming a tune, and hopped up on the ledge and plunged three stories to his death   no   for as it happened, in his descent through the icy air, his bed robe flapping about him like broken wings, he saw the triangle of infirmary wall as base and the two courtyard walls as sides, the triangle rising to meet him, a triangle without architectural reason here, cramped out of the way behind the infirmary, "Gentlemen it is important, it is imperative gentlemen that we teach our workmen and the designers of our buildings proper appreciation and knowledge of geometry so that we may prevent such pervasive ugly and expensive public construction," and the cruel useless triangle that rose to meet Feuerbach had filled up completely with snow during this strange long winter and he plummeted into it, plummeted into a burning pain that was not death and which collapsed his youthful scholarly body like a field telescope, now finally the letters of yellow fire on the black paper in his mind were obliterated not by the snow which was Nothing but by the towering hotter white fire of pain, he died but did not die in that triangle, the snow that was a Substantive Nothing had held him back from death and held him back from giving his comrades freedom, for when he came to himself again they told him it was many weeks later but he was not certain of that there in the same infirmary room in the same bed, disbelieving them because outside the window the same snow was still falling, and told him that Klaus Hörnli had died while he Feuerbach was unconscious, drifting back to the world of men again out of the triangle of Substantive Nothing, he Klaus Hörnli had died, his health broken in the cold and horrible cell, and of course they were to be freed, the death had brought the anarchical geometers and even King Maximilian Joseph to good sense, IF ONE MAN, Feuerbach thought, but he could not remember the rest, the fire of pain had burned off the letters of fire, he must attempt to, it was imperative that, what was the

He snapped his fingers repeatedly. "You must forgive me, gentlemen. I fear that I have been digressing. You must help me to recall the topic under discussion."

He looked at them imploringly. But how could they help him? They were strangers to him, and senile, these eleven old men who sat in the students' desks, their stringy white hair unclean on their shoulders and their unclean fingernails long and horny.

"Gentlemen, please!" Feuerbach said, but they would not answer. They began to shuffle their feet, a whispery sound at first but growing louder; and this noise caused an ashy gray snow to begin falling inside the classroom. It fell furiously and covered the floor and the desks and Feuerbach's hands.

PAM DURBAN

This Heat

IN AUGUST, BEAU CLINTON DIED. HE WAS PLAYING BASKETBALL IN THE
high school gym when his bad heart finally set him free, and he staggered
and fell and blew one bloody bubble that lingered, rising and shimmering, then burst, leaving a shower of blood like rust spots on his pale skin.
The school phoned Ruby Clinton but they wouldn't say what the trouble
was, just that Beau was sick, in trouble, something—it was all the same
trouble—and could Ruby or Mr. Clinton come right down. "Isn't any Mr.
Clinton," Ruby snapped, but the woman had already hung up the phone.
So she figured she'd best go down to see what he'd done this time, her son
with his long slanted eyes exactly like his father's.

Ruby walked down the hall working herself up for the next showdown
with Beau or the principal or whoever crossed her. No one made her
angrier than Beau. She could get so angry that bright points of light danced
in front of her eyes. Of course it didn't matter, not at all; she might as well
rave at the kudzu, tell it to stop suffocating everything under its deadly
green. A woman with a worried face directed Ruby toward the clinic room
and Ruby quickened her step. But when she got there, a man blocked
the doorway. "You can't go in there," he said. Ruby didn't answer and she
didn't stop. She was used to plowing past men such as he, and she knew
her strength in these matters. There were things that wouldn't give but
you put your shoulder against them and you shoved.

"The hell you say," Ruby said. "If he's having one of his spells I know
what to do."

"He's not having one of his spells," the man said. "I'm afraid he's dead."

She squinted and watched while the man collapsed into a tiny man and
grew up life-size again. She had a steady mannish face, and when something stunned her that face turned smooth and still, as if everything had
been hoarded in and boarded up back of her eyes somewhere. Younger,
she'd had a bold way of memorizing people, but that look had narrowed
until she looked as if she were squinting to find something off in the
distance. At the time of Beau's death Ruby was thirty-two, but she looked

worn and strong as if she'd been out in the weather all her life. Her face had settled like the straight dense grain of wood. She'd been what they called *hot-blooded*, a fighter, all her people were fierce and strong, good people to have on your side. There was once something of the gypsy in her: a lancing eye and tongue and the gypsy darkness shot with a ruby light. But that seemed like a long time ago.

She'd gone there ready to scream at Beau, to smack him good for whatever he'd done, to drag him back one more time from hurting somebody—he'd heard what the judge had said—or from playing ball—he'd heard the doctor say that he was not to move faster than a walk if he wanted to live through the summer. She'd gone there ready to smack him, breathing harshly through her nose. She still had faith in the habit of hitting him—he came back then for a second from where he lived most of the time—a numb sort of habit that began as pressure behind her eyes and ended with the blunt impact and the sound of the flat of her hand brought hard against his skull.

The words she would have said and the force of the blow she'd gone ready to deliver echoed and died in her head. Words rushed up and died in her throat—panicked words, words to soothe, to tame, to call him back—they rushed on her, but she forgot them halfway to her mouth, and he lay so still. And that's how she learned that Beau Clinton, her only son and the son of Charles Clinton, was dead.

From then on it was just one surprise after another. She was surprised to find herself standing outside on the same day she'd left when she'd gone inside the school building. Everything should have been as new and strange as what had just happened. But the dusty trees stood pinned and silent against the tin sky, and below in the distance Atlanta's mirrored buildings still captured the sun and burned. Then the word *dead* took her by surprise, the way it came out of her mouth as though she said it every day of her life. "Well, that's that," she said to Mae Ruth as her sister sat there, hands gripping the steering wheel, exactly the way she'd been caught when Ruby had dropped the word onto her upturned face. Then she was surprised by her sister's voice, how it boiled on and on shaped like questions, while Ruby breathed easily, lightheaded as a little seed carried on the wind. It was the most natural thing in the world that Beau should be dead; it had never been any other way. She patted her sister's hand:

"That sneaky little thing just slipped right out on me," she said, chuckling to herself and wiping her eyes with the backs of both hands. And her heart gave a surge and pushed the next wave of words at him, as though he were standing right in front of her again: "That sneaky little bastard," she said, "goddamn him."

Mae Ruth drove like a crazy woman—running red lights, laying on the horn, heading back towards Cotton Bottom at sixty miles per hour, gripping Ruby's wrist with one hand. "We got to get you home," she said.

"You do that," Ruby said. It would be nice to be back there among the skinny houses that bunched so close together you could hear your neighbor drop a spoon. She could slip in there like somebody's ghost and nobody'd find her again. That was the comfort of the village—the closeness made people invisible. She could hide there and never come out again, the way old lady Steel did after her kid got run over by a drunk: rocking on her porch day and night and cringing anytime tires squealed and crying out at the sight of children in the street. That was a good use for a life, she thought. She just might take it up like so many of the rest of her neighbors. They saw something once, something horrible, and it stuck to their eyes and the look of it never left them.

When they turned onto Rhineheart Street, Ruby sat up. "This ain't right, Mae Ruth, you took a wrong turn somewhere," she said anxiously. Her eyes never left the road which ran into a lake of white sun, a mirage. In the glare, her street looked like a place she'd seen once, and forgotten. Then there was her house and the neighbors three deep on the narrow porch because somehow the news had gotten loose and run home before them. And she saw that the emptiness was a trick of the light on the windshield and she sat back and said, "Oh, now I get it. Fools you, don't it?" And she chuckled to herself. Someone had played a fine joke, and now it was revealed.

The village where Ruby lives is called Cotton Bottom because of the cotton mill and because of the fact that the main street is down in a slump in the earth. All the streets above and below the main street run straight between the mill on one end of the village and the vacated company store on the other. In February when the weather settles in and the rain falls straight down, the air turns gray and thin and there's silence as though the air had all been sucked into the big whistle on top of the mill and scattered again to the four corners of the earth. But in the summer, this place comes alive: the kids all go around beating on garbage-can lids, the air is so full of the noise you couldn't lose them if you tried, and the heat is heavy so you drag it with you from place to place.

The other border of this place is an old city cemetery with a pauper's field of unmarked graves down in a low meadow. Ruby used to go there between shifts or after work if it was still light and sit and listen to the wind roughing up the tops of the trees. Sometimes she thought of the roots of the trees, and it gave her a funny cold knot in the pit of her stomach to think of the way the roots were all tangled up with the bodies and of how people's bones fertilized the trees. She sat very quietly then, listening, as if she might catch that long faithful story as it's told from the ground up, as it ends in the wind, in the tossing crowns of the oaks, in the way they bend and sigh and rise and lash the air again.

By eight o'clock the morning after Beau's death the sun looked brassy, as though it had burned all day. You had to breathe shallow for fear you'd suck in the heavy heat and choke on it. Ruby didn't question how the night had passed; she watched while the sweating men struggled and pushed Beau's coffin up the narrow steps. And as she watched them coming closer she had one of her thoughts that seemed to come out of nowhere: Who is that stranger coming here? And she must have mumbled it to herself because Dan Malvern and Mae Ruth both leaned over at the same time to catch what she'd said. "You'd think that'd be the easy part," she said, nodding towards the men with the coffin. Her arms hung at her sides; her face was slack, red, and chafed looking; her feet were planted wide to keep her upright. When they passed with Beau's coffin, her mouth went dry and her knees gave a little and Dan squeezed her arm and whispered: "Ruby you hold on now." His warm breath on her ear annoyed her.

She tried not to listen to the rustling of the undertakers, the whispers as they arranged the casket. They opened the casket and draped an organdy net from the lid to the floor and arranged it in a pool around the legs of the coffin stand and it all seemed to be happening beyond glass somewhere in front of her face. The open lid was lined with shirred satin gathered into a sunburst and below it her son floated on his cushions with the stubborn look stuck to his face as though he were about to say *no* the way he did:

PAM DURBAN

105

jutting out his chin and freezing his eyes and defying the world to say him *yes*. "I never believed it," she said, and the words were cold drops in her ears, "not for a minute, and now look." And with that, a heaviness in her chest dragged on her, and she turned on them and said: "What was the way he should've come, tell me that. What other road could he have gone, why don't you tell me?" She grabbed Mae Ruth's arm.

It seemed that she'd been strong forever and in everything. Just after Beau was born sick she'd been strong in her faith. Her religion had leapt on her one day like something that had been lying in wait, preparing itself. Afterwards, she'd gone about preaching the word to anyone who'd stand still long enough to hear. That's when Charles Clinton had left for the first time. She'd worked herself into raptures: down on her knees, voice about to break with the joy of it, the joy dilating, pressing against the walls of her chest, the walls of her skull, till the spirit was so restless it threatened to tear her open. She swooped down on her neighbors' houses then, praying, singing, weeping for all who lived inside sunk in the sin and error of their ways, all their sin a pressure inside her as though she lived inside their lives too. She sang the hymns with the force and flatness of a hammer hitting a rock, and she beat the tambourine so loudly that no one could stand close to her, and her face looked angry as if she were defying something.

Then she'd been strong at work in the mill. First, she wielded the sharp razor, slashed open the bales so the cotton tumbled out. She roughed up the cotton and set it going toward the other room to be wooed and combed straight into fiber. They took note of how she worked and she was promoted to spooler. She stood beside the machines until she thought the veins in her legs might burst. She worked there yanking levers, guiding the threads as they sped along from one spool to the next. You had to yank the levers because the machines were old and balky, but the habit of it became the same as its action, and the habit felt like anger after a while. The threads flew by never slowing, drawing tighter, flying from one spool to the next, the separate strands twisting, making miles of continuous threads for the big looms in the room beyond. The noise could deafen a person. The machines reared up and fell forward in unison and grabbed the fiber with witchfingers and twisted the strands and rose and grabbed and fell again in rhythm all day and all night. The machines crashed like sacks full of silver being dropped again and again until she couldn't think, she could only watch the threads as they came flying out of the dark door and caught and flashed around the spools and flew out the other door.

At night she used to go to prayer meetings or to church singings. And once when they'd prayed, and something ugly had come into their presence, something with the smell of burning hair, she'd known what to do. She'd been strong for them all and had led them in raising their voices louder in praise till the smell had ebbed. She felt so strong then, every fiber set against the thing that had entered and filled the room so completely, the thing that had swamped them in the middle of prayer. She'd known right away that whatever it might be, it was between this thing and Beau that she needed to stand. She already knew that much. "Don't be afraid," she said, "that's what it wants." She made *quiet down* motions with her hands and she said: "You know ladies, it comes to me to say there isn't nothing strange under the sun. There is this thing—we don't want to call it the devil, because once you give it a name it's got half of what it wants—and it turns things inside out and upside down just that quick, and what you've got there staring you in the face is an empty lining, ain't that right?" That is where the work begins, she told them.

But it didn't stop there, oh no. The work went on working and people began to mistake the lining for the whole cloth, and it made them bitter and sad, and it made them call themselves shameful and monstrous before God. You could see it all the time, she told them, in the sad empty eyes around you. And the worst of the work, the end of the work came when people's lives were x'd out—not by death, but by life. When people turned into living tombstones over their own lives, when people hid their faces from each other, when human life turned foreign, then the work was finished, she told them. "Now you've all seen it happen," she said. "Every single one of us in this room's seen it happen. But the way I figure it, we got to go one better than that. We got to stand up and say 'All right then, I got something for you better than what you got for me.' That's what we're all put here to do on this earth, and we can't ever let each other forget."

But that all seemed to have happened in another lifetime, in another country, a long time ago. Now there was this: the undertakers finished their business and left the house. Ruby dragged the reclining chair right next to the steel-gray coffin and eased herself down, feeling like a bag of flesh with a cold stone at the center. The coffin looked cold and shiny as coins and her mind wandered there, counting the coins.

The green vinyl of the chair arms sucked to the back of her arms and she saw the looks go around the room from Mae Ruth to her aunts, to Granny Brassler and the rest of them. Looks and sighs that flew around the room, passed from one to the other, but she didn't care. She knew what they were thinking; she'd thought the same herself many a time about someone else: they were worrying that all the fight had gone out of her and wondering what they would do with another one to feed and wipe clean. In the village, that's the worst that can happen. "I'm here to stay," she said, "don't want no bath, don't want no supper, so don't start on me about it, just tend to your business and let me tend to mine."

She thought of that business and how she'd learned it well. To work, to live, you had to be angry, you had to fight—that much she remembered. Her father had fought for his life, for all their lives, the time half the mill walked out and the mill police came muscling into their house on fat horses. She could still see the door frame give, see her father's arm raised, all the veins standing up before he brought the stick of stove wood down hard across the horse's nose. That was what life was for—fighting to keep it. That's how she'd been raised. All the good sweet passion and flavor of life soured if you just let it sit. Like milk left out, it could spoil. You had to be strong.

She smelled her own exhausted smell, like old iron, leaving her. Someone had drawn the curtains across the front window. Someone wiped her face with a cloth. They bent over her one after the other. "Ruby, trust in the Lord," someone said. The thought rolled over her.

"I do," she said automatically, because the Lord was still a fact, more or less, "but that's all there is to it and it's got nothing to do with him." She nodded toward her son. There. She was afraid to say it, but that was the truth. She snapped up straight, defying any of them to say differently. And just then she was taken by grief that pushed up in waves from the dead center of her. Each wave lifted her out of the chair and wrenched her voice from her throat, and that voice warned them: "I can't bear it." She couldn't open her eyes and inside the darkness there was a darker darkness, a weight like a ball, rolling against the back of her eyes. "I can't support it," she said, and everything obliged inside her and fell in, and there was a quick glimpse of Beau the way he'd come home one time after a fight: the tatters of blood in the sink, too much blood to be coming out of his nose and no way to stop it, and she was falling, tumbling over and over. Someone shouted her name; hands held her face, her hands. They bobbed all around her, corks on a dark water.

And when finally she could open her eyes, she glared at them as if they'd waked her from a deep sleep. She looked at Beau's face: it was rosier than in life, and dusted with a chilly-looking powder. The blue-gray lips were likewise frosted. The hair looked washed straight back by a wave, so silky and fine. He'd taken to dyeing his hair—the roots were dark and a soapy cloying smell rose through the organdy—and she said on the last receding wave of grief: "Lord, don't I wonder what's keeping him company right now."

"Now don't you go wandering off there all by yourself," Mae Ruth said. Her eyes were inches from Ruby's own. She looked at her sister and almost laughed in spite of herself at that funny veiny nose, more like a beak than a nose, the eyes like her own, two flat dark buttons. Now Mae Ruth's life was hard too, but there seemed to be more room for it. She made more room. She could tell funny stories, then turn around and tell somebody off just as neat and they'd stay told off. Once they'd both gone to a palm reader out by Doraville and the woman had scared Ruby, and Mae Ruth had said, "Lady, far's I'm concerned you get your jollies out of scaring people half to death." That was Mae Ruth for you. Just then, her face looked like she was about to imitate the way the woman had looked. Mae Ruth could pull her face down long as a hound's and say "Doom" in this deep funny voice and you'd have to laugh.

"You know Mae Ruth, you're right," Ruby said. They had a way of picking up pieces of conversation and weaving them together again. "I can't remember a time when anything was much different than it is now, but I know it must have been. Because sometimes I get a thought and it seems like it's not a new thought at all, it's something I can almost remember, like I've thought the same thought before, you know? The way you turn a corner and think you've been there before or hear a noise or catch something off the corner of your eye?"

Someone new had come into the room. She felt it in the stirring among the crowd around her chair, the way they coughed and got quiet. "Dan?"

she said. He'd left after the coffin was carried inside and had gone to stand with the men on the porch. She looked up, expecting to find Dan's narrow brown face, and there stood Charles Clinton and his new wife, looking cool and pastel in spite of the heat. She said: "Well, look who's here, everybody, look who's showing his face around here again." The welcome in her voice would have chilled you to the bone. "Look who's come back to the well," she said. "Well's all dried up, Charles Clinton," she said. Her breathing turned down like a low gas flame. His new wife tried to get in her line of vision, but Ruby kept ducking around her in order to keep an eye fixed on Charles. And doesn't it always happen this way? When she was most in need of the blessing of forgetfulness—just then, she remembered everything.

She was sixteen, up from Atlanta to Gainesville for the Chicopee Mill picnic. He stood apart from everybody, working a stick of gum. The lights inside the mill had come winging out through the hundreds of small windows. Like stars, they'd winked on the water of the millpond. And the roaring of the mill barely reached them across the mild night, and it was no longer noise that could make you deaf. The air was clean of cotton lint and clear, and the mill glittered. Everything glittered that way. Oh yes, she remembered that glittering very well. He had eyes like dry ice. She should have known; she should have turned and run with what she knew instead of thinking she could sass and sharp-tongue her way out of everything. He said: "You're Ruby Nelson from Atlanta, aren't you?"

"How'd you know?" she said.

"I have my ways," he said. And thinking about those ways had thrilled her down to the soles of her feet.

She should have bolted for sure. She was supposed to have married Hudger Collins, and she had no business forgetting that. But Hudger was dull next to this one who had hair like corn silk, a sloped and angled face, and tilted eyes that watched and watched.

"I take you for a soldier," she said. And he smiled that smile that rippled out across his face and was gone so fast you couldn't catch it.

"Now you're a right smart girl," he said, wrapping one hand around the top of her arm. "I was in the Navy. You're real smart. I bet you could teach me a lot."

Later that night he said the word *love* over and over, as if he would drive it into her. Now when she saw him again a pit opened and all the fiends let fly. She looked at Beau jealously, as if he might rise up and join his father and together they'd waltz away into the night. "Why doesn't he come closer?" she said. "I'm not a rattlesnake." She hated her voice when it got quavery like that. She said: "Charles Clinton, who's going to hurt you now? Why don't you come here and look at your boy? He's dead, he isn't going to get up and bother you anymore. You don't even have to be ashamed anymore." And she heard a dry crackling sob burst out of his throat and nose, and she leaned her head back and smiled at the ceiling.

"Ruby," Mae Ruth rasped in her ear, "everyone's suffering, let him be."

Ruby hooted and smacked the arm of the chair. "Who's suffering?" she said. "How can you tell he's suffering?"

"Oh Lord," someone said from the corner of the room, "there's just no end to it."

He stepped closer then, and for the first time she looked directly into his eyes. She was afraid to do it because she believed in what she saw in people's eyes. When she saw his eyes she bit her lip halfway into another bitter word. His eyes were washed out, drained, the color broken. And his mouth turned down, and something elastic was gone from under his skin. He'd lost a tooth and in spite of the powder-blue leisure suit, the backs of his knuckles looked permanently grimy. And those were the very eyes I searched and searched, she thought, the ones where I tried to see myself for so long. And those eyes stared at her, void of anything but a steady pain that threatened to break from him. And it scared her so much she couldn't speak, and she leaned over and fussed with the net over Beau's coffin.

She didn't love Charles, never had; she'd known that from the start, and that was the crime. But it acted like love; it kicked like a horse colt inside. And it was time: Ruby saw that in the eyes of the men on the streets of the village when she passed them by, and she saw it in her mother's eyes. And love was something that grew: that's what she'd been taught. That's what she'd believed.

She wore a tight dress of lilac-colored imitation linen all the way to Jacksonville on the bus. It was their honeymoon trip, but all the while she had the sense that she was riding along beside herself. Away over there was the girl who was wild crazy in love, but she, Ruby, couldn't get to her.

PAM DURBAN

111

All the while she waited for that special feeling to come up in her throat, the way a spring starts up out of the ground. She wanted that feeling, but it didn't come. She didn't love him, but she shut that feeling away. That was her secret. She always believed it would be different, and that was her secret. And her faith, and her shame.

So, love or no love and faithful to another law, Beau was born barely moving, hardly breathing through his blue lips. And both times—after the birth when the doctor had come in peeling off his rubber gloves, and now—Charles had stood there looking like something broken, his face taking on no more expression than the dead boy's. Only his eyes still spoke, and his hand that trembled like an old man's hand as he lifted it to wipe his mouth. Why I'm better off than he is, she thought. For all this, I'm better off. It was cold, proud comfort. The sweet vengeful cry she'd hoped for, the hot bass wire she'd hoped to hear sing at the sight of him broken by the death of his only son, wouldn't sound. She grabbed for Mae Ruth's hand because the falling sensation was creeping in behind her eyes again.

The fact of the boy had stuck in Charles like a bone in his throat. She spent her days sitting in clinics with Beau's heavy head lolling over one arm, because there had to be an answer. You'd have thought the boy was contaminated the way Charles' hands had stiffened when he picked up the baby. You'd have thought the boy was permanently crippled or contagious the way Charles had held him away from his body. "Lots and lots of people's born with something just a little off," she said. "Lord, some of them never even know it," she told Charles pointedly. Of course, as things had gone on, the depth of the damage had been revealed as it always is. By the time Beau had surgery on his heart at the age of five, Charles wouldn't even come up to sit with him. He said it was too humiliating to sit in the charity ward, where people treated you like you were something to be mopped off the floor.

And after Beau had managed to grow up and after he started coming home with pockets full of dollar bills, Charles could only say "What's going on?" She could almost see the words forming on his lips as he looked at his son in the coffin. Charles never understood a thing; that was his sorrow. She didn't want him near her.

She remembered her own sorrow, how it had struck so deep it had seemed to disappear inside her the first time Beau got caught in Grant Park in a car with a rich man from the north side of town. He was nothing but a baby, twelve years old. The police cruiser brought him home—because the other man was not only rich, he was also important, and he didn't want trouble on account of Beau. Her son smelled like baby powder and dirty clothes. He was growing a face to hide behind. His lips were swollen as though someone had been kissing them too hard, and she stared and wondered whether that brand was put on his mouth by love or hate or by some other force too strange to be named. She had to drag Charles into the room. "It's not the money," Charles had shrieked at his son. "I know it isn't the money." That's as much of the discovery as he could force out of his mouth; the rest was too terrifying.

"Why?" she asked her son. Her voice was a tool, boring into him. She held onto his skinny arm and watched the skin blanch under her fingers.

"They talk nice to me," Beau said.

"Honey, those men don't care about you," she said, watching Charles turn away; watching Beau watch him turn away.

When Charles left, he said their life wasn't fit for human beings and he moved to Marietta. He'd never lifted a hand against her. By village standards, he was a good man. But she felt that violence had been done to her; there was a hardness and a deadness inside that made her swerve away from people as though she might catch something from them.

During that time, she went to Dan Malvern. It was right: he was her pastor as well as her friend, and together they'd puzzled over that deadness and prayed endlessly for forgiveness for her. She was never quite sure for what sin she needed to be forgiven, but she'd kept quiet and prayed anyway.

Now, sitting beside Beau's coffin, she'd come a whole revolution: she felt like asking for forgiveness about as much as she felt like getting up and walking to New York City. Forgiveness belonged to another lifetime, to people like Dan who had a vision left to guide them. Once Dan had seen armies of souls pouring toward heaven or hell while he stood at the crossroads, and he was still standing there, frantically directing traffic. Dan stood just outside the door with his big black shoes sticking out of his too-short pants. You had to be gentle with Dan; he always had to be invited so she said: "Dan'l, you're always welcome here." He crossed the room with one long country stride and grabbed her hand and rubbed it and said: "Are you holding up all right in the care of the Lord?"

"Getting by," she said. His eyes looked old and sad. She took his hand more warmly and said: "Dan, bless you." But when she took her hand away, it hung in front of her, bare and powerless. And there was Beau, dead, his life full of violence in spite of that hand, and she said "Oh," and bit her knuckle, and Dan hauled her up and pulled her into the kitchen and shut the door behind him. He rested a hand on her shoulder and threw back his head, and the tears squeezed out through the lashes like beads. She moved to embrace him but he stopped her. He was maneuvering into the current, she saw that, setting his back to the wind. He shifted and hunched his shoulders: "Kneel down with me, sister," he said.

"Oh, all right, Dan," she said, sighing. She knew this part of the ritual, when they had to forget each other's names in order that God might hear their prayers. She knelt down facing him. She had to endure this, because when Dan wasn't busy acting like God's own special riding mule, he was one who shed a steady light onto her life, a light in which she could stand holding all her shame and be known without shame. Mae Ruth was another, only her light was barer and warmer. Dan remembered her and could remind her sometimes of ways she'd been that she could barely recall. He knew her practically all the way back. She could go to him feeling small and cold, the way lights look in winter, and come away after talking about nothing for a few hours, with her feet set squarely on this earth again.

But something happened when he talked about God, when he started to pray. They didn't have much in common then. He became hard then, he saw things in black and white and spoke of them harshly through his teeth. His jawbone tried to pop through the skin, and his black hair began to tremble with indignation, and he jerked at the words as if he were chewing stringy meat. He strained after the words as though he could pull them from the air: "Lord, help her to see that sin is there," he began, "that sin has taken away her son. Help her to see the sin, to look on the *wages* of sin and to ask forgiveness, and help this woman, your servant, to know in her HEART the sin and to call OUT to the Lord in her hour of need."

She would have laughed had she not felt so lonely. Dan could let himself down into it any time and drink of the stern comfort there. She envied him that plunge. She imagined the relief must taste hard and clean. She closed her eyes and tried to pray, to sink into that place. It would be so good to believe again in the laws, she thought, because those laws named the exile and the means of coming home in such clear ringing tones. First there was sin, a person drifting in some foreign land, then confessing the sin, then redemption, then hallelujah sister and welcome home. She felt for her heart, for its secret shame, and found only a sort of homesickness, a notion that there was someplace else that she'd forgotten, a place where there were no such people as foreigners, a place big enough to hold sin, grief, ugliness, all of it.

But forgetfulness, that was the sickness, the worm in the heart. Words like good and evil and death simplified things and rocked you and lulled you and split things apart. There was something else moving back there; she could barely feel it but it was there.

She watched his face move through the prayer, laboring against a current. "The grave," Dan said with a shiver, and when he came back to himself with a great bass "Amen" she said Amen too, and a sob broke from her at the sound of that blank word. Her shoulders shook and her head wagged from side to side and she said: "Dan, where'd you learn all that? It must tire out the Lord himself to listen to all that talk about sin all the time. There must be some wages due to you for that, wouldn't you say?"

"Ruby," he said, "don't blaspheme now, don't go piling sin on sin."

And at that she labored to her feet and shook herself. "The way I understand it," she said, "we're all born fools, ain't that right? Nothing we can do about that. What's the sin in that? Seems like everything we do has got wages." The man of God with thunder and sword faded, his face was restored to him, and the Daniel she knew came back, looking sheepish, pulling on his bottom lip. "So where are you going to look for better wages is what I want to know?"

"I know you're under a terrible strain," he said, "but I don't know where you get such talk." But by then she was halfway into the other room. And seeing her son in his coffin again, she felt she was coming on him fresh, and she saw how much Beau's face looked like her own—much more like her own than like Charles' face—and it scared her. The hard life he'd led showed in the set defiance of the chin, in the squint marks around the eyes that the mortician's powder puff couldn't erase. That look was stuck there for all eternity, and he was only sixteen years old.

It was the same look he'd given her any time she'd asked him about those men and why he went with them. She'd fought for him for so long, and the fatigue of that fight caught up with her again and she was tossed up on a fresh wave of grief. She began to sob and twist, turning this way and that, trying to escape from the people who pressed in from all sides, suffocating her. Strong hands gripped her and shook her, and she recognized Dan and Mae Ruth though neither of them spoke and her eyes were squeezed tight. "Get it out," Mae Ruth said. "You go on and get it all out, then you come on back here with us."

"I think I want to sleep for a while now," she said, opening her eyes.

"You want a nerve pill?" Mae Ruth asked. She shook her head no. She stopped beside the coffin.

"Well now," she said softly, "don't he look sweeter without that harsh light on him?" During the minute that she'd had her spell of grief, the light had shifted and softened and turned gray and round as a belly pressing back against the dark outside. As the light softened in the room, her son's face softened too; he looked younger and not so angry at the air. He hadn't looked that way since he was a baby, and she loved him with a sweetness so sharp she felt she might be opened by it.

And what became of that sweetness, she thought, as she pushed through the curtains into her bedroom. By what devilish sly paths did it run away, leaving the harsh light that never ceased burning on him? It took too much effort to remember that he was not just that strange being who'd thrashed his way through her life and out, leaving wreckage in his path. He was also another thing, but it made her head hurt to think of it. She pulled off her slippers and unhooked her slacks at the waist. It was easier to think that the march he'd made straight to his grave was the sin. To call that life ugly and be done with it. But the changing of the sweet to the ugly was the most obvious trick in the book. Anyone with eyes could see through that one. There was a better trick. She thought how much she wished she could still believe that the devil dreamed up the tricks. That would explain the ashes around her heart.

But never mind: the better trick was that the soft curtains of forgetfulness dropped so quietly you did not hear them fall. It was forgetfulness that made things and people seem strange: that was sin if ever there was sin. Still, remembering things made you so tired. Better to live blind, she thought.

Once she'd begged Beau to remember who he was. She'd meant *her* people, the Nelson side, dignity and decency deep enough to last through two or three lifetimes. But they were as strange to him as the whole rest of the wide world. "Sure," he'd said, "I know who I am. I'm a Nelson from the cotton patch and a Clinton straight from hell." Seeing her shocked, hand pressed to her throat the way she did, he'd laughed and said: "Well ain't I? You're always saying 'goddamn your daddy to hell.'" The way he'd imitated her, his mouth drawn back like a wild animal's, had terrified her. "That means I come from hell, don't it, mama?"

She shook her head in frustration and eased herself down onto her bed. She wished that he were there, given back to her for just one minute, so that she could collect, finally, all that she'd needed to tell him, so that she could tell him in words he'd have to understand: that if one person loved you, you were not a chunk of dead rock spinning in space. That was what she'd tried to tell him all during the long winter just past.

That was the winter when the mill had stepped up production again and had taken on everyone they'd laid off. She'd gotten a job in the sewing room. All day she sat there sewing, while her mind worked to find an end to the business with Beau. Last winter he was gone more than he was home, and his face was pale and sunken around the cheekbones. Every so often she'd start way back at the beginning and come forward with him step by step, puzzling out the way and ending always in the same spot: the place she'd seen him staring into. She turned it over and over like the piecework in front of her, looking for the bunched thread, the too-long stitch that would give, the place where her mind had wandered and the machine had wandered off the seam.

Once she'd taken half a sick-day and had gone home to find him staring at nothing. She'd barely been able to rouse him, and when she'd bent over him she'd been repelled by his sweet sick odor. But it was the way he'd looked that stuck in her mind: tight blue jeans, a black shirt, a red bandanna wound tightly around his neck. And his face, when he'd finally turned it up to her and smiled dreamily into her screaming, had looked serene and sly as the face of a wrecked angel. It was the smile that made her blood shut off. When he smiled that way, there was a shudder in the room like the sound that lingered in the air if the looms shut down, and she knew that he was bound to die, that he was already looking into that place. She saw it in his eyes all winter.

The cotton came in baled through enormous doors and was pulped, twisted, spun, woven, mixed with polyester and squeezed and pressed and dyed, printed with tulips, irises, gardens of blowing green, and made into sheets and blouses.

It wasn't right that she should worry herself the way she did all winter. She was up all hours of the night waiting for him, but half the time he never came home. And then one day she went to his room and nailed the window shut and when he went into his room that night, she locked him in and sat in the living room with arms folded and cried as he bumped and crashed around and screamed awful names at her. It was for his own good and because she loved him. And if you loved somebody, she told herself, you had to make a stand and this was her stand, and in the morning she'd explain to him that she did it out of love in words he'd have to understand.

Afterwards she was ashamed, and she never told anyone—not even Mae Ruth. She felt that she'd been in a dream, a fever dream, where crazy things made perfect sense and everything hung suspended way up high in clear air. But it didn't matter anyway, because when she unlocked the door to set him free in the morning, he was gone. There was glass all over the floor and the window was kicked out.

She woke up after dark, groping around with one hand, looking for something on the bedspread. She'd been dreaming of black rocks looming over her, while at the base of the rocks hundreds of people scrambled around picking up busted-off pieces of the largest rock and holding them up in the moonlight. She groped her way out into the living room, and people patted her and helped ease her down into her chair again.

All night she slept and woke, and whenever she woke, one pair of hands or another reached for her, and once she tried to say: "I want to thank you all for being so good." But her voice broke when she said "good," and someone said: "Hush, you'd do the same."

The voices went around and around her, a soothing drone that filled the room. And then the sun was up, the day was up bright and blazing, and she looked at her son beside her in his coffin and the thought of his going was borne fully onto her. And as the day rushed back at her, so did her memory of Beau, which was as sharp as if he were still alive. In fact, they were hardly memories at all, they were more like the smaller sightings we keep of someone's day-to-day life.

This is how he came in: her body had threshed with him for two days and a night. Then his sickness: she walked him day and night, while over on Tye Street, Granny Brassler and the others went down almost to their knees, taken by the spirit, shouting: "Devil, take your hands off that baby."

He was never full of milk and quiet; he was long and gangly and he never fleshed out. And all the while he was growing a man's mind. By the time he was twelve, right after Charles left, he'd stay gone for days without even a change of clothes. Until the June just past, when he and his friends had started sticking closer to home and robbing the men in the park nearby. Then she'd set herself against him in earnest. The last time she'd smacked him good was for calling somebody a nigger motherfucker. She'd grabbed his face and squeezed and said: "Don't you never let me hear you talking like trash again. You are not and never will be trash, and don't you forget it."

"Everybody calls me trash," he said. "What makes you any different?"

"Cause I'm your people," she said. "Cause you're mine."

"Ain't that funny?" he said. "That's what they say too."

Every time, somebody else was holding the gun, but the next time or the time after that she knew it would be Beau, and then he would be tried as an adult and sent away to the real prison and that would be that. But last June they'd only taken him as far as the jumping-off place—the juvenile evaluation center, they called it. But it was a prison as surely as the other place where he'd end up someday.

She wasn't like the other mothers, the ones who wept or pleaded or shouted. That time was long gone and she knew it. She was there for another reason but it had no name, only a glare, like the harsh sunlight on the white white walls of his room. She listened. He beat time on his thigh with the heel of one hand and talked, and sometimes he looked up and said: "Ain't that right?" And with knees spread, elbows resting on her knees, hands loosely knotted and fallen between her knees, she looked back at him and said: "Yes, it is," in the strongest voice she could muster.

But staying, listening and staying, was a habit she'd had to learn. The first visit had ended with her reeling out of the room, driven back by his words that were so ugly they seemed to coil like tar snakes out of his mouth. But she went back, *she did go back*, and she knew she must never let herself forget that. She went back and she listened to every word, and she had never felt so empty, so silent. The city and the room turned strange around her, and the only familiar face was the one just in front of her—the one with the mouth that opened and said: "You ought to see their faces when Roy shows them the gun."

She looked up quickly, hearing that voice again just as clear as if it were still ringing off the walls of the jail. She looked at his dead face, and her head began to tug with it, and she stood and bore down on him while all around her the dark closed in as it does when a person's about to faint. Only she was far from fainting. The dark narrowed around her until she stood inside a dark egg looking down at her son, the stranger made up for his grave, who rested in a wash of light that lingered at the core of the outer dark shell. And as she watched and listened—watching and listening with every cell—the stranger's face dropped away and below it there was another, older face, and the whole harsh chorus of his life tangled in her and sang again, and she remembered what she'd seen in the jail, what she'd seen a long time before the jail and had forgotten and carried with her the whole stubborn way and had never wanted to believe, and had believed: he was lost, and she loved him.

She sat down in her chair with a moan and began to rock herself and to pat the edge of the coffin in time with her rocking. She saw the panic start up on every face, and she pressed a hand to her chest to quiet herself. "Things should slow down," she said, "so that a person can have time to study them."

As though they'd been held back, people crowded into the room again. The air got sticky and close, and the smell of flowers and sweat and not quite clean clothes and the soapy smell over Beau's coffin began to make her dizzy. So she focused on Charles and a prickly rash began to spread over her neck and arms and her vision began to clear. Finally she said, in a lazy kind of voice—lazy like a cottonmouth moccasin stirring the water—"Charles, you and your wife's taking up more than your share of the air in here. Why don't you just step out onto the porch?" They ignored her. But Mae Ruth clucked her tongue.

"Ruby, shame, he's still the boy's father; you can't deny him that," she said.

"I know that," Ruby snapped. "Don't I wish I didn't."

She closed her eyes and wished for the old way, the old law that said *such as gives, gets hack in kind*. She wished that the weight of that law might lie in her hand like a rock. She wished for some revenge sweet enough to fit his crimes, the kind of revenge that came from a time before people were condemned to stand linked to one another. She could make him order the tombstone and have Beau's name drilled there, yes, and be gone before the funeral started. She tried it out on herself but the little cold thrill the thought gave her wasn't enough to satisfy. Oh me, she said to herself, there isn't no country far enough away where I could send him. She opened her eyes and searched the room for a single unfamiliar face on which to rest her eyes, and found not a one. And she felt the whole dense web of love and grief descending, settling over her shoulders as it had before, in the prison. "This don't ever stop," she said out loud. And she thought of how she had never loved Charles, not in the way that a woman loves a man, and how, still, he was part of the law that turned and turned and bound them all together, on each turn, more deeply than before.

And then there was the vault out under the strong sun without a tent to cover it, and the flowers were wilting under the sun, and Mae Ruth's strong voice led off a song. Then Daniel spoke of heaven and hell for a long time. They were in a new cemetery and the lots were parceled out of a flat field. Through the thin soles of her shoes, Ruby could feel the rucks and ripples of once-plowed ground. She wore a dress of hard black cloth that trapped the heat inside and made the sweat trickle down her sides. Charles stood on the edge of the crowd, his chin sunk onto his chest, and he looked faded under the light that seemed to gather into a center that was made of even whiter and hotter light.

Ruby barely listened to the resurrection or the life. She saw her son's face: that fierce look into the darkness which now rolled around him. Those words Dan said, they weren't the prayers, she thought, not the real prayers. The prayer rested in the squat coffin, in the dark there. Her eyes followed its deaf, dumb lines. The prayer was his life that she couldn't save, and the prayer was her own life and how it continued. And the prayer never stopped; lives began and ended, but the prayer never stopped. She looked at the ground and had the sensation that she'd been standing there for a very long time, trying to memorize each one of the scrappy weeds that had begun to grow again out of the plowed-over land. Those weeds were like the threads, she thought; she watched them in the same way. The threads flew towards her like slender rays of light and twisted spool to spool and disappeared through another door toward the looms beyond. The sound of their coming and going made one continuous roar.

Because she wanted it that way, they all stayed as the coffin was lowered into the hole. She stepped up to the side of the grave and saw her own shadow, thrown huge, on the lid of the vault. It startled her so much she stepped forward instead of back and the edges crumbled under her shoes. Then there were hands on her arms, and she looked down again and saw Mae Ruth's shadow and Dan's beside her. It was as though they were in a boat together, looking over the side. And the sun beat down on them all: on the living, and into the grave, and on those who had lived and died.

NAOMI SHIHAB NYE

The Cookies

ON UNION BOULEVARD, ST. LOUIS, IN THE 1950S, THERE WERE WOMEN in their eighties who lived with the shades drawn, who hid like bats in the caves they claimed for home. Neighbors of my grandmother, they could be faintly heard through a ceiling or wall. A drawer opening. The slow thump of a shoe. Who they were and whom they were mourning (someone had always just died) intrigued me. Me, the child who knew where the cookies waited in Grandma's kitchen closet. Who lined five varieties up on the table and bit from each one in succession, knowing my mother would never let me do this at home. Who sold Girl Scout cookies door-to-door in annual tradition, who sold fifty boxes, who won The Prize. My grandmother told me which doors to knock on. Whispered secretly, "She'll take three boxes—wait and see."

Hand-in-hand we climbed the dark stairs, knocked on the doors. I shivered, held Grandma tighter, remember still the smell which was curiously fragrant, a sweet soup of talcum powder, folded curtains, roses pressed in a book. Was that what years smelled like? The door would miraculously open and a withered face framed there would peer oddly at me as if I had come from another world. Maybe I had. "Come in," it would say, or "Yes?" and I would mumble something about cookies, feeling foolish, feeling like the one who places a can of beans next to an altar marked *For the Poor* and then has to stare at it—the beans next to the cross—all through the worship. Feeling I should have brought more, as if I shouldn't be selling something to these women, but giving them a gift, some new breath, assurance that there was still a child's world out there, green grass, scabby knees, a playground where you could stretch your legs higher than your head. There were still Easter eggs lodged in the mouths of drainpipes and sleds on frozen hills, that joyous scream of flying toward yourself in the snow. Squirrels storing nuts, kittens being born with eyes closed; there was still everything tiny, unformed, flung wide open into the air!

But how did you carry such an assurance? In those hallways, standing before those thin gray wisps of women, with Grandma slinking back and pushing me forward to go in alone, I didn't know. There was something here which also smelled like life. But it was a life I hadn't learned yet. I had never outlived anything I knew of, except one yellow cat. I had never saved a photograph. For me life was a bounce, an unending burst of pleasures. Vaguely I imagined what a life of recollection could be, as already I was haunted by a sense of my own lost baby years, golden rings I slipped on and off my heart, Would I be one of those women?

Their rooms were shrines of upholstery and lace. Silent radios standing under stacks of magazines. Did they work? Could I turn the knobs? Questions I wouldn't ask here. Windows with shades pulled low, so the light peeping through took on a changed quality, as if it were brighter or dimmer than I remembered. And portraits, photographs, on walls, on tables, faces strangely familiar, as if I were destined to know them. I asked no questions and the women never questioned me. Never asked where the money went, had the price gone up since last year, were there any additional flavors. They bought what they remembered—if it was peanut-butter last year, peanut-butter this year would be fine. They brought the coins from jars, from pocketbooks without handles, counted them carefully before me, while I stared at their thin crops of knotted hair. A Sunday brooch pinned loosely to the shoulder of an everyday dress. What were these women thinking of?

And the door would close softly behind me, transaction complete, the closing click like a drawer sliding back, a world slid quietly out of sight, and I was free to return to my own universe, to Grandma standing with arms folded in the courtyard, staring peacefully up at a bluejay or sprouting leaf. Suddenly I'd see Grandma in her dress of tiny flowers, curly gray permanent, tightly laced shoes, as one of *them*—but then she'd turn, laugh, "Did she buy?" and again belong to me.

Gray women in rooms with the shades drawn . . . weeks later the cookies would come. I would stack the boxes, make my delivery rounds to the sleeping doors. This time I would be businesslike, I would rap firmly. "Hello Ma'am, here are the cookies you ordered." And the face would peer up, uncertain . . . cookies? . . . as if for a moment we were floating in the space between us. What I did (carefully balancing boxes in both my arms, wondering who would eat the cookies—I was the only child ever seen in that building) or what she did (reaching out with floating hands to touch what she had bought) had little to do with who we were, had been, or ever would be.

ERNEST J. GAINES

Robert Louis Stevenson Banks, a.k.a. Chimley

ME AND MAT WAS DOWN THERE FISHING. WE GOES FISHING EVERY Tuesday and every Thursday. We got just one little spot now. Ain't like it used to be when you had the whole river to fish on. The white people, they done bought up the river now, and you got nowhere to go but that one little spot. Me and Mat goes there every Tuesday and Thursday. Other people use it other days, but on Tuesday and Thursday they leaves it for us. We been going to that one little spot like that every Tuesday and Thursday the last ten, 'leven years. That one little spot. Just ain't got nowhere else to go no more.

We had been down there—oh, 'bout a hour. Mat had caught eight or nine good-size perches, and me about six—throw in a couple of sackalees there with the bunch. Me and Mat was just sitting there taking life easy, talking low. Mat was sitting on his croker sack, I was sitting on my bucket. The fishes we had caught, we had them on a string in the water, keeping them fresh. We was just sitting there talking low, talking about the old days.

Then that oldest boy of Berto, that sissy one they called Fue, come running down the riverbank and said Clatoo said Miss Merle said that young woman at Marshall, Candy, wanted us on the place right away. She wanted us to get twelve-gauge shotguns and number five shells, and she wanted us to shoot, but keep the empty shells and get there right away.

Me and Mat looked at him standing there sweating—a great big old round-face sissy-looking boy, in blue jeans and a blue gingham shirt, the shirt wet from him running.

Mat said, "All that for what?"

The boy looked like he was ready to run some more, sweat just pouring down the side of his round, smooth, sissy-looking face. He said: "Something to do with Mathu, and something to do with Beau Boutan dead in his yard. That's all I know, all I want to know. Up to y'all now, I done done my part. Y'all can go and do like she say or y'all can go home, lock y'all doors and crawl under the bed like y'all used to. Me, I'm leaving."

He turned.

"Where you going?" Mat called to him.

"You and no Boutan'll ever know," he called back.

"You better run out of Louisiana," Mat said to himself.

The boy had already got out of hearing reach—one of them great big old sissy boys, running hard as he could go up the riverbank.

Me and Mat didn't look at each other for a while. Pretending we was more interested in the fishing lines. But it wasn't fishing we was thinking about now. We was thinking about what happened to us, after something like this did happen. Not a killing like this. I had never knowed in all my life where a black man had killed a white man in this parish. I had knowed about fights, about threats, but not killings. And now I was thinking about what happened after these fights, these threats, how the white folks rode. This was what I was thinking; and I was sure Mat was doing the same. That's why we didn't look at each other for a while. We didn't want to see what the other one was thinking. We didn't want to see the fear in the other one's face.

"He works in mysterious ways, don't He?" Mat said. It wasn't loud, more like he was talking to himself, not to me. But I knowed he was talking to me. He didn't look at me when he said it, but I knowed he was talking to me. I went on looking at my line.

"That's what they say," I said.

Mat went on looking at his line a while. I didn't have to look and see if he was looking at his line, we had been together so much, me and him, I knowed what he was doing without looking at him.

"You don't have to answer this 'less you want to, Chimley," he said. He didn't say that loud, neither. He had just jerked on the line, 'cause I could hear the line cut through the water.

"Yeah, Mat?" I said.

He jerked on the line again. Maybe it was a turtle trying to get at the bait. Maybe he just jerked on the line to do something 'stead of looking at me.

"Scared?" he asked. It was still low. And he still wasn't looking at me.

"Yeah," I said.

He jerked on the line again. Then he pulled in a sackalee 'bout long and wide as my hand. He rebaited the hook and spit on the bait for luck and throwed the line back out in the water. He didn't look at me all this time. I didn't look at him, neither. Just seen all this out the corner of my eyes.

"I'm seventy-one, Chimley," he said, after the line had settled again. "Seventy-one and a half. I ain't got too much strength left to go crawling under that bed like Fue said."

"I'm seventy-two," I said. But I didn't look at him when I said it.

We sat there a while looking out at the lines. The water was so clean and blue, peaceful and calm. I coulda sat thére all day long looking out there at my line.

"Think he did it?" Mat asked.

I hunched my shouders. "I don't know, Mat."

"If he did it, you know we ought to be there, Chimley," Mat said.

I didn't answer him, but I knowed what he was talking about. I remembered the fight Mathu and Fix had out there at Marshall store. It started over a Coke bottle. After Fix had drunk his Coke, he wanted Mathu to take the empty bottle back in the store. Mathu told him he wasn't nobody's servant. Fix told him he had to take the bottle back in the store or fight.

A bunch of us was out there, white and black, sitting on the garry eating gingerbread and drinking pop. The sheriff, Guidry, was there, too. Mathu told Guidry if Fix started anything, he was go'n protect himself. Guidry went on eating his gingerbread and drinking pop like he didn't even hear him.

When Fix told Mathu to take the bottle back in the store again, and Mathu didn't, Fix hit him—and the fight was on. Worst fight I ever seen in my life. For a hour it was toe to toe. But when it was over, Mathu was up, and Fix was down. The white folks wanted to lynch Mathu, but Guidry stopped them. Then he walked up to Mathu, cracked him 'side the jaw, and Mathu hit the ground. He turned to Fix, hit him in the mouth, and Fix went down again. Then Guidry came back to the garry to finish his gingerbread and pop. That was the end of that fight. But that wasn't the last fight Mathu had on that river with them white people. And that's what Mat was talking about. That's what he meant when he said if Mathu did it we ought to be there. Mathu was the only one we knowed had ever stood up.

I looked at Mat sitting on the croker sack. He was holding the fishing pole with both hands, gazing out at the line. We had been together so much I just about knowed what he was thinking. But I asked him anyhow.

"'Bout that bed," he said. "I'm too old to go crawling under that bed. I just don't have the strength for it no more. It's too low, Chimley."

"Mine ain't no higher," I said.

He looked at me now. A fine featured, brown skin man. I had knowed him all my life. Had been young men together. Had done our little running around together. Had been in a little trouble now and then, but nothing serious. Had never done what we was thinking about doing now. Maybe we had thought about it—sure, we had thought about it—but we had never done it.

"What you say, Chimley?" he said.

I nodded to him.

We pulled in the lines and went up the bank. Mat had his fishes in the sack; mine was in the bucket.

"She want us to shoot first," I said. "I wonder why."

"I don't know," Mat said. "How's that old gun of yours working?"

"Shot good last time," I said. "That's been a while, though."

"You got any number five shells?" Mat asked.

"Might have a couple 'round there," I said. "I ain't looked in a long time."

"Save me one or two if you got them," Mat said. "Guess I'll have to borrow a gun, too. Nothing 'round my house work but that twenty-gauge and that old rifle."

"How you figuring on getting over there?" I asked him.

"Clatoo, I reckon," Mat said. "Try to hitch a ride with him on the truck."

"Have him pick me up too," I said.

When we came up to my gate, Mat looked at me again. He was quite a bit taller than me, and I had to kinda hold my head back to look at him.

"You sure now, Chimley?" he said.

"If you go, Mat."

"I have to go, Chimley," he said. "This can be my last chance."

I looked him in the eyes. Lightish brown eyes. They was saying much more than he had said. They was speaking for both of us, though, me and him.

"I'm going, too," I said.

Mat still looked at me. His eyes was still saying more than he had said.

His eyes was saying: We wait till now? Now, when we're old men, we get to be brave?

I didn't know how to answer him. All I knowed, I had to go if he went.

Mat started toward his house, and I went on in the yard. Now, I ain't even stepped in the house good 'fore that old woman started fussing at me. What I'm doing home so early for? She don't like to be cleaning fishes this time of day. She don't like to clean fishes till evening when it's cool. I didn't answer that old woman. I set my bucket of fishes on the table in the kitchen, then I come back in the front room and got my old shotgun from against the wall. I looked through the shells I kept in a cigar box on top the armoire till I found me a number five. I blowed the dust off, loaded the old gun, stuck it out the window, turnt my head just in case the old gun decided to blow up, and I shot. Here come that old woman starting right back on me again.

"What's the matter with you, old man? What you doing shooting out that window, raising all that racket for?"

"Right now, I don't know what I'm doing all this for," I told her. "But, see, if I come back from Marshall, and them fishes ain't done and ready for me to eat, I'm go'n do me some more shooting 'round this house. Do you hear what I'm saying?"

She tightened her mouth and rolled her eyes at me, but she had enough sense not to get too cute. I got me two or three more number five shells, blowed the dust off them, and went out to the road to wait for Clatoo.

DONALD HALL

The World Is a Bed

1.

It was not until his early thirties that William Bolter understood what the
world was. Thereafter he remained secure in his understanding for twenty
years, with a confidence approaching complacency, until one afternoon it
fell away from him like leaves in a windstorm from a dying tree.

He was thirty-two when he discovered that the world was a bed. If we
lead a life of sexual adventure, he decided, we move in a great dance, for
our lovers have had lovers and their lovers have had lovers also. Going
to a revival of *West Side Story*, or to a gathering of the American Society
of Statisticians, we see *her*, and *her*, and *her*. He resolved that we are all
episodes in the lives of each other; we are a directory of flesh, and though
we have not reclined with X or Y or Z we have touched women who have
had affairs with men who have had affairs with X and Y and Z: the world
is a bed.

When an affair began, William liked to tell the story of the summer he
was sixteen, and the first woman. Of course it did not do to blurt it out;
no one enjoyed the notion that she was one of a series. Yet on such occasions he always wanted to tell the new woman about her predecessors—he
reminded himself of obese people who spend dinner time in anecdotes
of famous meals—and he learned how to go about it: when the alert skin
subsided into dampness, when each leaned back to smoke, he would ask
her, as if he stumbled on the thought, about the first time she had made
love. Usually it was far enough back to be made light of. When she finished
her story he had license to tell his own.

2.

In June of 1945 Bill Bolter turned sixteen, a promising student of mathematics on a scholarship at Cranbrook Academy outside Detroit, and
living with his parents. Besides mathematics there was the violin, dreams
of composing and conducting, of becoming another Baumgartner to

conduct his own compositions. He would have concentrated more on his music if he had not worried about the opinions of his classmates. With a diffidence common among adolescents—he told himself, when his old teacher sighed over his apostasy—he cared for the opinions of people dumber than he was; they accepted his presence when he swam a leg in a medley, but addressed him *Hey, fruit* when he walked with his violin past the Arts Academy, the Milles fountain, and the staid oaks, over the bright lawns to his teacher's quarters. It was this diffidence that kept him from returning to the music camp at Interlochen in 1945, where he had spent the previous two summers on a scholarship. This summer he practiced at home, continued his lessons, studied the calculus in a desultory fashion, took a girl named Beverly to the movies, and read mystery stories. He was bored. When his mother told him about the chance to visit the Balfour Festival on Cape Cod, he was quick to take it.

Mrs. Hugh Fitzroberts was a large lady in her late forties who had befriended his mother, in the thrift shop where his mother worked, and had heard about William's musical abilities. Mrs. Fitzroberts was wealthy, his mother told him, and a patron of the Detroit Symphony, some of whose members spent their summers in the blue air of Balfour. Her husband, on the other hand, was known to care more for balance sheets than for the finer things, and would remain in Detroit aiding the war effort while Mrs. Fitzroberts rented a cabin with two bedrooms near the concert shell, for the two weeks at the beginning of August, and it would be nice to have the boy for company.

They sat up all night on the coach to New York, the Wolverine, when not even the Fitzroberts name could swing a berth. At first the tall older lady attempted to interest him with intelligent questions, but when they had both slept a few hours and awakened disheveled and grubby, their dignities fell away; Mrs. Fitzroberts became "Anne" and William "Bill," and they ate cheese sandwiches as dry as newsprint. At New York they made their connection for Boston where they transferred to a local, and as they approached the Cape her nervousness started. She became suddenly silly, he thought, skittish as a girl, reminding him of middle-aged men around soldiers—falsely friendly, laughing too much, guilty.

He discovered why. Waiting at the station was a ponderous man, older than she was, who occupied a chair in the Detroit Symphony hidden among woodwinds. They took each other's hands, and Mrs. Fitzroberts glanced back at her companion—her *cover*, he realized—with something like panic: there was something she had neglected to mention.

For the next fortnight, Bill saw little of Mrs. Fitzroberts, who never explained herself and never appeared at the cabin, and although he was shocked he was also pleased. It made him feel sophisticated; he found it a relief to be left alone in a new and handsome place with his music. In the mornings he practiced Beethoven, usually on a quiet patch of beach too rocky for bathing and out of range of sea salt. For a while even the natural world seemed to approve; the salt grass waved in his honor, and the cat-tails kept time like the batons of a thousand conductors. Afternoons he attended rehearsals of the visiting quartet—they were working through Beethoven, as it happened—and daydreamed himself a great performer. At night there were concerts in the shell near his cabin.

And there were girls—dozens of young women and few young men. Girls waited on table, flocked together in boarding houses, played flutes and violas, took notes during rehearsals. Most of them were older than he was—eighteen, twenty, twenty-three. He walked in a grove of young women, lush and warm and possible. He had lunch with one girl, went to a rehearsal with another, ate supper with another, took a fourth to the concert and afterwards walked the beach with her and kissed. To each of the girls he pleaded his plea of bed. A few of them confessed to being virgins like him; others warded him off lightly. He suspected that they felt awkward about taking a sixteen-year-old seriously. And when each of them refused his proposal, Bill was quick to abandon her, for it meant he could pay suit to another. Every night he went home feeling rejected and relieved.

There was no competition at all. The only young men at Balfour at the end of the war were crippled or homosexual. (Bill discouraged the attentions of a thirty-year-old piano teacher.) So he dated a girl with a good figure and big teeth who played the cello. He swam on a Sunday with a bank president's daughter and with a Smith graduate he drank illicit beer in a coupe she drove while her brother was in Europe. For a time he lost interest in music: he was too tired in the mornings to practice. Yet after ten days of frantic dating he had not gone to bed with anyone. When he caught sight of Mrs. Fitzroberts, looking younger every day, irony saturated him.

Slowly he became aware of the girl in the red MG. Not many students had brought cars to Balfour, because of gas rationing. On the one night in the coupe, he and the Smith girl counted the miles that they drove. But the tall black-haired young woman whirled in her red MG through the small streets, parking beside the only expensive restaurant in town. Several of the girls mentioned her, annoyed at the ubiquity of the red MG. Then late one morning—Balfour almost done—he paused when the MG parked at tennis courts in front of him. The tall girl leapt out and took up singles with an older woman who clerked at the hotel. The girl wore a short tennis dress, the skirt fluted like a Greek column, and her legs were long, smooth, strong, luxurious. She leaned forward to wait for service with an intensity that looked omnivorous.

The next day, he came to the tennis court at the same time, and brought a racquet, and hit balls against the backboard while the girl with the red MG played tennis with the older woman. When they finished, and her companion walked away toward the hotel, he approached the tall girl. She smiled at him, and he noticed the wedding ring, and he asked her if she would like to practice with him; when they were tired she drove him back to his room. He asked her if she would play again tomorrow, and she asked him about his music, and she told him that her name was Margaret Adams Olson but everyone called her Mitsy. Her husband, Allen, was an army captain in the Pacific, Intelligence, and she was twenty-four. She came from Seattle, and after the war she and Allen would settle nearby in Allison—"like June Allyson with an i"—where the Olsons owned the bank, which was like owning the town. Her music was strictly amateur, she said. She was here because she was bored.

The next day they played and had lunch and met for the Mozart at night, and afterwards walked on the beach and talked. He asked her how she had gas for her car and she laughed and showed him a wad of A coupons clutched in an elastic band; her father took care of that. If your husband was overseas, Mitsy said, and there was nothing to do, why not have some fun? Last year had been rotten, really rotten, she said, because her great-aunt was sick with cancer, right in their house, and they had to take care of her until she died. Then she told him about her husband, and their courtship in college, and how her husband was a dilettante at the piano, and they had met at a concert, a soprano visiting Seattle, she couldn't remember which one. And all the time she talked, animated and charming, he thought only of thighs blooming beneath a white linen skirt.

Gulls flew in circles over their heads; he squinted to watch them as they circled, and imagined for the moment that the gulls were spying on them.

Bill asked her if there had been other boyfriends, wanting to keep her close to the subject, and Mitsy laughed as she told him: yes, yes, that was what she had lived for at college—because her father had always been too busy to pay attention to her—and really she had been terrible. She had been cheerleader her freshman year, because it was a way to meet upperclassmen and football players, and for her first three years she had dated every night, somebody different every night. She was booked for dates three weeks ahead—she told him, and her eyes were brilliant—and on weekends she had two dates a day. Sometimes three.

He felt embarrassed that she might see the effect her words had.

The day before the festival ended, they played tennis again, the third day in a row. For two nights he had slept irregularly, but conjured up her strong, firm, welcoming body, and then drifted off into small patches of sleep, only to wake dreaming erotic dreams. Today again Mitsy wore the fluted white tennis dress, and Bill was so full of her he could not play at all. He was lovesick, he told himself, "sick with longing." After a set which he lost 6—0, she asked him if he was not feeling well, and he agreed that he was not, and they drove together in the red MG back to her hotel. In the lobby everyone scurried about, looking serious and giddy at the same time. They would have lunch after Mitsy changed her clothes. As they waited for the elevator, they heard the hotel's P.A. system telling them that, on account of the surrender of the Japanese, the evening Shostakovich and Prokofiev had been canceled, replaced by a ceremony of memorial and celebration.

He felt shocked—as if Captain Olson might walk through the door and take her away from him. She was jumping beside him, saying "Allen! Allen!," and then she dropped her tennis racquet, hugged him, and kissed him on the mouth. And before she let him go and fell back laughing, he felt with astonishment her tongue push through his lips and twist for a moment against his tongue. Then the elevator took her away.

At lunch they decided that the memorial service was not for them. They listened to the gaiety around them and felt separate from it. "They don't really mean it," Mitsy said.

He was scornful. "They've seen movies of Armistice Day."

She suggested they have a picnic on the beach, in celebration. She would collect a basket of food, and tonight while the other people were at their service, they would sit on the beach and drink wine.

She picked him up at five. His heart pounded as he sat beside her, sneaking looks downward where her gray slacks tucked inside her thighs and made a V. She had visited the delicatessen, bought cold chicken, paté, tomatoes, cole slaw, potato salad, and wine—two bottles of prewar French wine; he tried to memorize the label, but the French dissolved when he looked away from it.

Bill sat near her on the blanket, and in a moment her knee was touching his thigh, and he could feel nothing else. She opened the wine, and out of Dixie Cups they toasted the end of the war. They nibbled at this and that, then confessed that neither of them felt hungry. After a pause in the conversation, after a drink which inaugurated their second bottle, he said, "You know all those dates, all those boys at college . . ."

He waited so long without continuing his question that she said, "Yes?"

". . . did you sleep with them?" he asked. When he heard himself he felt how naïve he sounded.

Mitsy laughed. "Not with all of them, Bill," she said. "Not even with many of them. Some. A few."

He felt jealousy rise in him. "Didn't your husband mind?"

"He was one of them," she said. "He went with other girls too. Why are you asking me?" she said. She sounded friendly.

"Because I want to go to bed with you, too," he said.

She patted his shoulder and smiled pleasantly. "But I can't," she said, "because I'm married and I love my husband."

"I'm a virgin," he said. He felt himself looking depressed. "I'll get a whore."

"Don't do that," she said. "Don't be silly. There are lots of girls who would sleep with you. I'd love to, except for being married, I mean happily married."

Bill fell silent then, with anguish; and alongside the anguish he felt something like cunning. He dropped his head on his chest. He heard her take another swallow from her Dixie Cup. Then Mitsy swiveled toward him on the blanket. He felt her arm extend around his shoulders, squeezing. He still looked down, keeping his eyes closed. Then her finger lifted his chin, and he felt her lips on his. This time her tongue went in his mouth right away, and stayed there, and he felt his penis rise rigid against his tight underpants and his khaki trousers. With his hand he touched her breast, or the sweater over her breast, and she moaned and moved so that their thighs pressed against each other.

"I can't," she said. "I can't. Not now."

He said nothing but put his tongue in her mouth.

As they kissed, her hand swept slowly from his knees to his shoulder, pausing near his waist. Then her hand squeezed him through his clothing.

"Oh, God," she said. "I give up. Come on. Come back to the room."

That was all there was, when William told the story later, except for things that she said, lying with him on top of the sheets in her room. "It's all right," Mitsy said, "because I love Allen so much." And when they first touched, naked, leg to leg, thigh to thigh, breast to breast, her long hair dangling against his shoulder she said, "This is your first time. Feel it—the *skin.*"

The next day Mrs. Fitzroberts appeared again, looking slimmer and younger and not formidable at all, and wept, packing her bags. He should be weeping also—he thought to himself—but when he tried looking morose he felt silly and broke out in a grin. He hinted to Mrs. Fitzroberts about what had happened, and she patted his shoulder. She said that love was the most important thing in the world—the only thing. As they waited on the porch for the taxi that would take them to the station, among crowds of other visitors standing in front of cabins with suitcases, he wondered how many of them had risen from quick beds. Then a red MG swooped down the road, as he had expected it to do, and Mitsy leapt out, shining and untouched, and kissed him long and hard, in front of all the people, then drove away, and he did not see her again for thirty-five years.

3.

In 1965, in early autumn, William went to a cocktail party in Manhattan. He had lived there a dozen years, teaching mathematics to graduate engineers, with a specialty that earned him consultancy fees. His host introduced him to a Mrs. Dodge, the host's sister, and Mrs. Dodge answered his routine question by saying that she lived in Allison, Washington.

He asked her if she was acquainted with a Mrs. Allen Olson.

Mrs. Dodge's smile turned artificial. "Yes," she said, "but I'm afraid she's too grand for me." They both laughed, and his host interrupted and introduced Mrs. Dodge to someone else.

So Mrs. Dodge was jealous of her. On the twenty-year-old snapshot of Mitsy Olson, clear in memory, he tried to impose various "too grand" enlargements, a gallery of Helen Hokinson ladies. None of the images endured. From time to time, over twenty years, he had been curious to see her; now he felt the curiosity again. How strange to hear of her a continent away twenty years later. But the world is a bed, he reminded himself. He had encountered again a woman of the past; it made a connection even with Mrs. Dodge.

At this time in his life, everything that happened seemed to make such a connection. William had married in his senior year at Michigan, too young, and had remained faithful for five years, doing his Ph.D. and beginning to teach. Then there was an episode with a graduate student, and another with a colleague's wife met at a conference. For a year or two he hurtled from affair to affair—inventing late department meetings, conference weekends, Saturday committees—and gradually realized the grandeur of sexual association. He shuffled in the giant dance, and mathematics suffered, but he had known for some years that he would never be more than competent. And music, which his wife did not enjoy, dwindled to an excuse for absence: he went so far as to invent a string quartet in Detroit which practiced Wednesday evenings, often until two or three in the morning.

This extravagance was interrupted when he fell in love, divorced his wife, and married again for six months a young woman he loved and could not abide. When he divorced again he took his job in New York. Cautious of love, finding comfort in variety, he lived in his flat on Ninth Street a life of promiscuous harmony—revisiting old girls sometimes, always with two or three to telephone if he was lonesome—and he searched continually at parties, in bars, at concerts, at the Museum of Modern Art, for the faces of women he would add to his long encounter, as they added him to their own. And many times, as he lay in bed with a new woman, the light from Fifth Avenue faint through the curtains, he told them stories of his sexual life and sought from them stories of their own. He told about his initiation at Balfour, and the first woman whose skin he had touched.

Tonight he glanced over the party to assess the crowd, then moved from group to group with his glass, drinking little, listening to conversations. There was a pretty blonde woman, early thirties, with the animation of the newly divorced. He passed her over; he wanted no tears. There was a young woman, beautiful if overly made-up, surrounded by a shifting group of males and no women at all. Someone identified her vaguely familiar face; she reported local television news, and was supposed to graduate to a network. There would be no tears with that one! . . . but there would be nothing else either. The men would mill about her all night, making little jousts of jokes and attention, and at some point she would glance at her watch, speak of a morning deadline, and disappear leaving the men to each other. William found himself seeking out a tall and pleasant young woman, long legs and large glasses, pretty hair, who was eager to laugh with him. After half an hour of talk, he suggested that she find her purse. She did not protest.

As they were leaving he looked for his host and found him standing with Mrs. Dodge who was very drunk. "Your banker's bitch," — she said to William, twisting the word — "no one is good enough for her. Holier than thou. I wish she'd fall off that deck and break her goddamned neck."

4.

In 1980 at fifty-one he looked forty, they told him, and when he shaved each morning he tested the flattery out. Although his hair was thin, it was black, and he had grown a burly moustache; with handball and diet his waistline remained what it had been at sixteen. His life had not noticeably altered for twenty years, and he took pride in his life, especially as he saw his friends turn fat, alcoholic, diabetic, frightened, and old; one or two had the bad luck to die. It was true that sometimes he was bored. It was true that the prospect of old age depressed him, and when he allowed it to surface, loneliness felt heavy in his chest. It was true that his love affairs, which he continued to enjoy, had become repetitious. William boasted to his male acquaintances that he had discovered a three-part solution, a relationship partaking of music at its most mathematical. In this solution he kept one love affair beginning, one at a summery peak of attention, and one diminishing into silence. The trick was never to allow two to occupy the same phase, or to allow any moment without resource.

It was boredom, not need for money, that led him impulsively to accept a summer teaching job at the University of Washington. Within a week he had found a young woman who moved in with him for the summer, perhaps a dangerous departure from his three-part invention, but undertaken with forethought. He had begun to suspect that he would marry again—perhaps at sixty, perhaps even closer to retirement. And he had not lived with a woman for twenty-odd years.

Two weeks after his arrival, he found Allison on the map, and on a free Friday morning drove for an hour past hills and rivers and waterfalls through great stands of timber. For the first time in years he felt dazzled by the natural world, almost elated with the grandeur of vista and swoop. Maybe this joy was a good omen for his journey. He reminded himself that returns were always foolish—Mitsy might not be there, might not even be alive—but he *was* curious. The girl in the red MG, the first woman of his life, the social snob of 1965—he speculated on what he would find. He would find a woman fifty-nine years old! Then he remembered his own age, and the boredom of his present life made him shudder as he drove. Perhaps he was coming to the end of a thirty-five-year adventure; how appropriate, then, to revisit the first woman.

He entered the streets of the small town, *Class of 80* spray-painted on the water tower, and found the name listed in the phone book. When he telephoned from the drugstore, a maid's voice told him that Mrs. Olson was out but expected home soon. William represented himself as an old friend who preferred not to leave his name because he wanted to surprise Mrs. Olson. He took directions, parked beside a redwood carport, and walked past a border of irises toward the low modern house. His heart pounded as he rang the bell in the bright morning. Mrs. Olson was changing her clothes, and he waited in a large Japanese living room. Long windows gave onto a deck that looked down a gully to a stream. There was money in the room, well-employed and inconspicuous. Three paintings on the wall were signed with a name he could not read.

When she walked in, he entertained for a moment the illusion that she had not changed at all. She stood straight and firm, her black hair tied back. Then he saw, as if a film pulled away and he looked behind it, that her face was everywhere finely wrinkled, with dark creases under her eyes and at the sides of her mouth and a trembling looseness under her chin. She was fifty-nine—and remarkable. Her hair was dyed and her figure was trim, her legs a little knobbed with veins faintly blue under her tan. She reminded him, in fact, of Mrs. Fitzroberts.

"Yes?" she was saying. She looked at him firmly, *grand*.

"William Bolter," he mumbled, and gave her his hand. "We knew each other in 1945," he said. "At Balfour. When you had the red MG . . . We played tennis." She looked as if she were trying to remember. He kept on: "V-J Day, Mitsy."

"Oh," she said, and looked pleased, and then flushed lightly with a look that he remembered. "No one calls me that now," she laughed. "*Margaret*," she pronounced, mocking her own dignity. "I've thought about you. I've wondered so often what . . . My goodness!" She laughed, and again thirty-five years disappeared for a moment. "Really," she said, "I didn't think you would remember me."

He laughed. "Of course I remember you, and I remember June Allyson."

He told her what he was doing in Seattle, and that he had abandoned the violin because you could not serve two masters, and he told her how remarkably unchanged she was. She told him about her life in Allison, about her two grown children, a granddaughter. There was a child who had died. She told about a return to Balfour, the changes there, not for the better. . . . She gave him sherry. She would like him to meet her husband, she said, but he would not be home until late; would he please stay for lunch? She left the room to speak with the cook.

When she returned he asked her, "Who did the paintings?"

She looked pleased again. "Gilbert Honiger," she said. "He's a friend of ours. He lives on a farm west of here." She refilled their sherry glasses. He told her about meeting the woman from Allison at the New York party, without repeating the conversation, and she wrinkled her nose faintly when he pronounced Mrs. Dodge's name. Fair's fair, he thought. He liked her style better than Mrs. Dodge's.

Then he began to reminisce about the old summer, and she seemed happy to join in. He remarked that, over the years, he had come to think that artistic festivals had as much to do with art as checker tournaments did. He was going to tell an anecdote about a Balfour conductor, but she interrupted. "That's what Gilbert says," she said, and made a gesture toward the paintings. "He went to Santa Cruz one summer for something and walked out the second day." The delighted look was on her face again—and he knew that Gilbert was her lover, and felt a regret he could not justify.

Lunch was an omelette with Wente Brothers Grey Riesling and a salad. They talked lightly and it was pleasant but he began to feel irritation and loss. He mocked himself for expecting grand opera. They emptied a bottle of wine and she pressed a buzzer on the floor and the maid brought another. He drank several glasses. He spoke lightly of his two marriages. Feeling mildly flirtatious, he let her know that he had not lost interest in young women; he mentioned the girl in Seattle, who was twenty-four.

He noticed that she had stopped drinking; he kept on. Annoyed that she revealed less than he did, he talked without pausing. He had kept up with contemporary music, and liked it; she had followed it less, she said, and didn't like what she heard. He found himself lecturing, as if he were in a classroom, and the more pompous he knew he sounded, the less he could stop, while her smile grew fainter and more distant. He began to feel angry with her, this smooth social creature, Margaret not Mitsy, who had once clutched him on a beach in Massachusetts. Irritated, he began to be insulting about people who were unable to hear anything later than Stravinsky, and he watched her smile turn cold.

Then again he saw through her dyed hair, back to the luxurious twenty-four-year-old hair of 1945, spread on the pillow of her hotel room the night they stayed together. He wanted urgently to be closer to her, to force her to acknowledge that old closeness, to break through the light graceful surface that she wore to protect herself. Yes, he wanted to make love to her again, and he thought of pulling her up from her relaxed chair and kissing her. Instead, he said, "Gilbert is your lover."

"What?" she said. He watched her cheeks grow red.

"Gilbert is your lover," he said. "The world is a bed. Everybody is everybody's lover. What does it matter? It doesn't matter." When he saw her flush he realized that he was drunk and babbling. "I mean"—he stumbled on—"it's none of my business what you do; I mean I understand . . . The world is a bed."

She was looking down at her plate. After a pause she said, "If Betty Dodge told you that she is a liar . . ."

He shook his head. "She didn't say. I understand about these things."

She laughed. "You understand . . . Why do you say something so stupid? I haven't seen you for thirty-five years and I've been perfectly decent to you. Gilbert is homosexual and has lived with someone named Harold for twenty years. Harold is dying now. I spent the morning with him . . . It was such a beautiful morning. Maybe you noticed . . . if you notice anything. I sat in the bedroom with Harold who didn't even know I was there and watched the sunlight coming through an oak Gilbert transplanted there twenty years ago. The sunlight kept getting into Harold's eyes and bothering him until I pulled the shade. What do you *understand*?"

A sense of his own ridiculousness rose to his cheeks and burned below his eyes. "Oh," he said. "Oh . . . I'm sorry . . . It was foolish . . . I was trying . . ." He could not think how to explain.

"*The world is a bed*," she quoted. "That's what you like to say, isn't it? Of course it is. The world is a bed and someone is always dying in it. Have you ever sat with someone dying? My daughter died when she was sixteen."

"I'm sorry," he said. He stood up. "I'm very sorry. I hate to be stupid . . ."

"I suppose that changed my life more than anything else did." She stood up also. "But most people turn more serious when they are older . . ." She looked past him out the windows where the deck hung over the gully. He understood that she was no longer addressing him. "But some people stay children and when they die they are still children. Harold was like that."

"I'm sorry," he said again, "I'm sorry." Then, as if it would explain things, he blurted, "You were the first woman I ever made love to."

"And you were the last man I went to bed with," she said, "except for my husband. Oh, you idiot. You were a sixteen-year-old boy named Bill, sweet, and I was lonesome. I suppose I used you to make myself feel powerful, the way I did at college . . . and for you of course I was a prize to bring back to school, like a trophy you won swimming. But you were decent enough back then. Now you are an old fool full of self-importance because you still take young women to bed with you. What a life."

He went away quickly, then. Driving back to Seattle, he was arrested for speeding and charged with driving under the influence of alcohol. Later his colleagues wondered why it upset him quite so much.

LEE K. ABBOTT

The Final Proof of Fate and Circumstance

HE LIKED TO BEGIN HIS STORY WITH DEATH, SAYING IT WAS AN uncommonly dark night near El Paso with an uncommon fog, thick and all the more frightful because it was unexpected, like ice or a parade of gray elephants tramping across the desert from horizon to horizon, each moody and terribly violent. He was driving on the War Road, two lanes that came up on the south side of what was then the Proving Grounds, narrow and without shoulders, barbed-wire fences alongside, an Emergency Call Box every two miles, on one side the Franklin Mountains, on the other an endless spectacle of waste; his car, as I now imagine it, must have been a DeSoto or a Chrysler, heavy with chrome and a grill like a ten-thousand-pound smile, a car carefully polished to a high shine, free of road dirt and bug filth, its inside a statement about what a person can do with cheesecloth and patience and affection. "A kind of palace in there," he'd always say. "Hell, I could live out of the back seat." He was twenty-eight then, he said, and he came around that corner, taking that long, stomach-settling dip with authority, driving the next several yards like a man free of fret or second thought, gripping that large black steering wheel like a man with purpose and the means to achieve it, like a man intimate with his several selves, scared of little and tolerant of much. I imagine him sitting high, chin upturned, eyes squinty with attentiveness, face alight with a dozen gleams from the dashboard, humming a measure of, say, "Tonight We Love" by Bobby Worth, singing a word of romance now and then, the merry parts of the music as familiar to him as a certain road sign or oncoming dry arroyo. "I'd just come from Fort Bliss," he said. "I'd played in a golf tournament that day. Whipped Mr. Tommy Bolt, Jr.; Old Automatic, that's me. Show up, take home the big one." He was full of a thousand human satisfactions, he said—namely, worth and comforts and renewals. He could hear his clubs rattling in the trunk; he could hear the wind rushing past, warm and dry, and the tires hissing; and he was thinking to himself that it was a fine world to be from, a world of many rewards and light pleasures; a world (from the vantage point of a victory on the golf course) with heft and sense to it, a world in which a person such as himself—an Army lieutenant such as himself, lean and leaderly—could look forward to the lofty and the utmost, the hindmost for those without muscle or brain enough to spot the gladsome among the smuts; yes, it was a fine world, sure and large enough for a man with finer features than most, a grown-up man with old but now lost Fort Worth money behind him, and a daddy with political knowledge, and a momma of substance and high habit, and a youth that had in it such things as regular vacations to Miami Beach, plus a six-week course in the correct carving of fowl and fish, plus a boarding school, and even enough tragedy, like a sister drowning and never being recovered, to give a glimpse of, say, woe—which is surely the kind of shape you'd like your own daddy's character to have when he's about to round a no-account corner in the desert, a Ray Austin lyric on his lips, and kill a man.

It was an accident, of course, the state police saying it was a combination of bad luck—what with the victim standing so that his taillight was obscured—and the elements (meaning, mostly, the fog, but including as well, my daddy said, time and crossed paths and human error and bad judgment and a certain fundamental untidiness). But then, shaken and offended and partly remorseful, my daddy was angry, his ears still ringing with crash noises and the body's private alarms. "God damn," he said, wrestling open a door of his automobile, its interior dusty and strewn with stuffings from the glove box, a Texaco road map still floating in the air like a kite, a rear floormat folded like a tea towel over the front seat, a thump-thump-thump coming from here and there and there and there. It was light enough for him to see the other vehicle, the quarter moon a dim milky spot, the fog itself swirling and seemingly lit from a thousand directions—half dreamland, half spook-house. "There was a smell, too," he told me, his hands fluttering near his face. A smell like scorched rubber and industrial oils, plus grease and disturbed soils. His trunk had flown open, his clubs—"Spaldings, Taylor, the finest!"—flung about like pick-up sticks. His thoughts, airy and affirming an instant before, were full of soreness and ache; for a moment before he climbed back to the road he watched one of his wheels spinning, on his face the twitches and lines real sorrow makes, that wheel, though useless, still going round and round, its hubcap scratched and dented. He was aware, he'd say every time he came to this part, of everything—splintered glass and ordinary night sounds and a stiffness deep in his back and a trouser leg torn at the knee and a fruit-like tenderness to his own cheek pulp. "I felt myself good," he said, showing me again how he'd probed and prodded and squeezed, muttering to himself, "Ribs and necks and hips," that old thighbone-hipbone song the foremost thing on his mind. He said his brain was mostly in his ears and his heart beat like someone was banging at it with a claw hammer, and there was a weakness in the belly, he remembered, which in another less stalwart sort might have been called nausea but which in this man, he told himself as he struggled to the roadway, was nothing less than the true discomfort that comes when Good Feeling is so swiftly overcome by Bad.

At first he couldn't find the body. He said he walked up and down the road, both sides, yelling and peering into the fog, all the time growing angrier with himself, remembering the sudden appearance of that other automobile stopped more on the road than off, the panic that mashed him in the chest, the thud, the heart-flop. "I found the car about fifty yards away," he said, his voice full of miracle and distance as if every time he told the story—and, in particular, the parts that go from bad to worse—it was not he who approached the smashed Chevrolet coupe, but another, an alien, a thing of curiosity and alert eyeballs, somebody innocent of the heartbreak human kind could make for itself. The rear of that Chevy, my daddy said, was well and thoroughly crunched, trunk lid twisted, fenders crumpled, its glowing brake light dangling, both doors sprung open as if whatever had been inside had left in a flurry of arm and legwork. My daddy paced around that automobile many times, looking inside and underneath and on top and nearabout, impatient and anxious, then cold and sweaty both. "I was a mess," he said. "I was thinking about Mr. Tommy Bolt and the duty officer at the BOQ and my mother and just every little thing." He was crying, too, he said, not sniveling and whimpering, but important adult tears that he kept wiping away as he widened his circle around the Chevy, snot dribbling down his chin, because he was wholly afraid that, scurrying through the scrub-growth and mesquite and prickly cactus and tanglesome weeds, he was going to find that body, itself crumpled, hurled into some unlikely and unwelcome position—sitting, say, or doing a handstand against a bush—or that he was going to step on it, find himself frozen with dread, his new GI shoes smack in the middle of an ooze that used to be chest or happy man's brain. "I kept telling myself Army things," he said one time. "Buck up. Don't be afraid. Do your duty. I told myself to be calm, methodical. Hope for the best, I said." And so, of course, when he was hoping so hard his teeth hurt and his neck throbbed and his lungs felt like fire, he found it, bounced against a concrete culvert, legs crossed at the ankles, arms folded at the belt, with neither scratch nor bump nor knot nor runny wound, its face a long and quiet discourse on peace or sleep.

"At first, I didn't think he was dead," my daddy told me. He scrambled over to the body, said *get up*, said *are you hurt*, said *can you talk, wake up, mister*. His name was Valentine ("Can you believe that name, Taylor?" Daddy would say. "Morris E. Valentine!") and my daddy put his mouth next to the man's earhole and hollered and grabbed a hand — "It wasn't at all cold" — and shook it and listened against the man's nose for breaths or a gurgle and felt the neck for a pulse. Then, he said, there wasn't anything to do next but look at Mr. Valentine's eyes, which were open in something like surprise or marvel and which were as inert and blank and glassy, my daddy said, as two lumps of coal that had lain for ten million years in darkness. It was then, my daddy said, that he felt the peacefulness come over him like a shadow on a sunny day — a tranquility, huge and fitting, like (he said) the sort you feel at the end of fine drama when, with all the deeds done and the ruin dealt out fairly, you go off to eat and drink some; yup, he said one night, like the end of the War Road itself, a place of dust and fog and uprooted flora and fuzzy lights where you discover, as the state police did, a live man and a dead one, the first laughing in a frenzy of horror, the second still and as removed from life as you are from your ancestral fishes, his last thought — evidently a serious one — still plain on his dumb, awful face.

He told me this story again today, the two of us sitting in his backyard, partly in the shade of an upright willow, him in a racy Florida shirt and baggy Bermudas, me in a Slammin' Sammy Snead golf hat and swim trunks. It was hooch, he said, that brought out the raconteur in him, Oso Negro being the fittest of liquors for picking over the past. Lord, he must've gone through a hundred stories this afternoon, all the edge out of his voice, his eyes fixed on the country club's fourteenth fairway which runs behind the house. He told one about my mother meeting Fidel Castro. It was a story, he said, that featured comedy in large doses and not a little wistfulness. It had oompphh and running hither and hoopla when none was expected. "Far as I could tell," he said, "he was just a hairy man with a gun. Plus rabble-rousers." He told another about Panama and the officers' club and the Geists, Maizie and Al, and a Memphis industrialist named T. Moncure Youtees. It was a story that started bad, went some distance in the company of foolishness and youthful hugger-mugger and ended, not with sadness but with mirth. He told about Korea and moosey-maids and sloth and whole families of yellow folk living in squalor and supply problems and peril and cold and, a time later, of having Mr. Sam Jones of the Boston Celtics in his platoon. "You haven't known beauty," he said, smiling, "till you see that man dribble. Jesus, it was superior, Taylor." He told one about some reservists in Montana or Idaho—one of those barren, ascetic places—and a training exercise called Operation Hot Foot which involved, as I recall, scrambling this way and that, eyes peeled for the Red Team, a thousand accountants and farmboys and family men in nighttime camouflage, and a nearsighted colonel named Krebs who took my daddy bird watching. My daddy said that from his position on a bluff he could see people in green scampering and diving and waving in something approaching terror, but that he and Krebs were looking through binoculars for nest or telltale feather, listening intently for warble or tweet or chirp, the colonel doing his best, with nose and lipwork, to imitate that sort of fear or hunger or passion a rare flying thing might find appealing. "It was lovely," my daddy said, the two of them putting over two hundred miles on the jeep in search of Gray's Wing-Notch Swallow or something that had been absent from the planet, Daddy suspected, for an eon. There were trees and buttes and colors from Mr. Disney and a kind of austerity, extreme and eternal, that naturally put you in mind of the Higher Plane.

For another hour he went on, his stories addressing what he called the fine—events in which the hero, using luck and ignorance, managed to avoid the base and its slick companion, the wanton. I heard about a cousin, A. T. LeDuc, who had it, let it slip away, and got it back when least deserved. I learned the two things any dog knows: Can I eat it, or will it eat me? I learned something about people called the Duke and the Earl and the

LEE K. ABBOTT

147

Count and how Mr. Tommy Dorsey looked close up. I was touched—not weepy, like my wife Nadine gets when I tell her a little about my Kappa Alpha days at TCU or how I came out looking like a dope when I had gone in imagining myself a prince. To be true, I was in that warm place few get to these days, that place where your own daddy—that figure who whomped you and scolded you and who had nothing civil to say about the New York Yankees or General Eisenhower, and who expressed himself at length on the subjects of hair and fit reading matter and how a gentleman shines his shoes—yes, that place where your own daddy admits to being a whole hell of a lot like you, which is sometimes confused and often weak; that place, made habitable by age and self-absorption and fatigue, that says much about those heretofore pantywaist emotions like pity and fear.

Then, about four o'clock, while the two of us stood against his cinder-block fence, watching a fivesome of country-club ladies drag their carts up the fairway, the sun hot enough to satisfy even Mr. Wordsworth, my daddy said he had a new story, one which he'd fussed over in his brain a million times but one which, on account of this or that or another thing, he'd never told anyone. Not my momma Elaine. Not my Uncle Lyman. Not his sisters, Faith and Caroline. His hand was on my forearm, squeezing hard, and I could see by his eyes, which were watery and inflamed by something I now know as purpose, and by his wrinkled, dark forehead and by his knotted neck muscles—by all these things, I knew this story would not feature the fanciful or foreign—not bird, nor military mess-up, nor escapade, nor enterprise in melancholy; it would be, I suspected while he stared at me as though I were no more related to him than that brick or that rabbit-shaped cloud, about mystery, about the odd union of innocence and loss which sometimes passes for wisdom, and about the downward trend of human desires. There was to be a moral, too; and it was to be, like most morals, modern and brave and tragic.

This was to be, I should know, another death story, this one related to Valentine's the way one flower—a jonquil, say—is related to another, like a morning glory, the differences between them obvious, certain, and important; and it was to feature a man named X, my daddy said; a man, I realized instantly, who was my father himself, slipped free of the story now by time and memory and fortunate circumstance. X was married now, my daddy said, to a fine woman and he had equally fine children, among them a youth about my own age, but X had been married before and it would serve no purpose, I was to know, for the current to know about the former, the past being a thing of regret and error. I understood, I said, understanding further that this woman—my daddy's first wife!—was going to die again as she had died before.

She was a French woman, my daddy said, name of Annette D'Kopman, and X met her in September 1952 at the 4th Army Golf Tournament in San Antonio, their meeting being the product of happenstance and X's first-round victory over the professional you now know as Mr. Orville Moody. "X was thirty-one then," my daddy said, filling his glass with more rum, "the kind of guy who took his celebrating seriously." I listened closely, trying to pick out those notes in his voice you might call mournful or misty. There were none, I'm pleased to say, just a voice heavy with curiosity and puzzlement. "This Annette person was a guest of some mucky-muck," my daddy was saying, and when X saw her, he suspected it was love. I knew that emotion, I thought, it having been produced in me the first time I saw Nadine. I recalled it as a steady knocking in the heart-spot and a brain alive with a dozen thoughts. This Annette, my daddy said, was not particularly gorgeous, but she had, according to X, knuckles that he described as wondrous, plus delicate arches and close pores and deep sockets and a method of getting from hither to yon with style enough to make you choke or ache in several body parts. So, X and Annette were married the next week, the attraction being mutual, a Mexican JP saying plenty, for twenty dollars, about protection and trust and parting after a long life of satisfactions, among the latter being health and offspring and daily enjoyments.

As he talked, my daddy's face had hope in it, and some pride, as though he were with her again, thirty years from the present moil, squabbling again (as he said) about food with unlikely and foreign vegetables in it, or ways of tending to the lower needs of the flesh. X and Annette lived at Fort Sam Houston, him the supply officer for the second detachment, she a reward to come home to. "It wasn't all happy times," Daddy was saying, there being shares of blue spirits and hurt feelings and misunderstandings as nasty as any X had since had with his present wife. "There was drinking," he said, "and once X smacked her. Plus, there was hugging and driving to Corpus Christi and evenings with folks at the officers' club and swimming." I imagined them together and—watching him now slumped in his chair, the sun a burning disc over his shoulder—I saw them as an earlier version of Nadine and me: ordinary and doing very well to keep a healthful distance from things mean and hurtful. The lust part, he said, wore off, of course, the thing left behind being close enough to please even the picky and stupid. Then she died.

I remember thinking that this was the hard part, the part wherein X was entitled to go crazy and do a hundred destructive acts, maybe grow moody and sullen, utter an insulting phrase or two, certainly drink immoderately. I was wrong, my daddy said. For it was a death so unexpected, like one in a fairy tale, that there was only time for an "Aaaarrrggghhh!" and seventy hours of sweaty, dreamless sleep. "X didn't feel rack or nothing," my daddy said. "Not empty, not needful, nor abused by any dark forces." X was a blank—shock, a physician called it—more rock than mortal beset with any of the familiar hardships. "X did his job," Daddy said, "gave his orders, went and came, went and came." X watched TV, his favorite being Mr. Garry Moore's "I've Got a Secret," read a little in the lives of others, ate at normal hours, looked as steadfast as your ordinary citizen, one in whom there was now a scorched and tender spot commonly associated with sentiment and hope. Colonel Buck Wade made the funeral arrangements—civilian, of course—talking patiently with X, offering a shoulder and experience and such. "X kept wondering when he'd grieve," Daddy said. Everyone looked for the signs: outburst of the shameful sort, tactless remark, weariness in the eyes and carriage, etc. But there was only numbness, as if X were no more sentient than a clock or Annette herself.

"Now comes the sad part," my daddy said, which was not the ceremony, X having been an Episcopalian, or the burial because X never got that far. Oh, there was a service, X in his pressed blues, brass catching the light like sparkles, the minister, a Dr. Hammond Ellis, trying through the sweep and purl of learnedness itself to put the finest face on a vulgar event, reading one phrase about deeds and forgiveness and another about the afterworld and its light comforts, each statement swollen with a succor or a joy, yet words so foreign with knowledge and acceptance that X sat rigid, his back braced against a pew, his pals unable to see anything in his eyes except emptiness. No, the sadness didn't come then—not with prayer, not with the sniffling of someone to X's left, not at the sight of the casket itself being toted outside. The sadness came, my daddy said, in the company of the driver of the family car in which X rode alone. "The driver was a kid," my daddy said, "twenty, maybe younger, name of Monroe." Whose face, Daddy said, reflected a thousand conflicting thoughts—of delight and of money and of nookie and of swelter like today's. Monroe, I was to know, was the squatty sort, the kind who's always touchy about his height, with eyeballs that didn't say anything about his inner life, and chewed nails and a thin tie and the wrong brown shoes for a business otherwise associated with black, and an inflamed spot on his neck that could have been a pimple or ingrown hair. "Stop," X said, and Monroe stared at him in the mirror. "What—?" Monroe was startled. "I said stop." They were about halfway to the gravesite, funeral coach in front, a line of cars with their lights on in back. "Stop here. Do it now." X was pointing to a row of storefronts in Picacho Street—laundry, a barber's, a Zale's jewelry.

My daddy said he didn't know why Monroe so quickly obeyed X, but I know now that Monroe was just responding to that note in my daddy's voice that tells you to leave off what you're doing—be it playing Canasta, eating Oreos with your mouth open, or mumbling in the favorite parts of "Gunsmoke"—and take up politeness and order and respectfulness. It's a note that encourages you toward the best and most responsible in yourself, and it had in it a hint of the awful things that await if you do not. So the Cadillac pulled over, Monroe babbling "Uh-uh-uh," and X jumped out, saying, "Thank you, Monroe, you may go on now." It was here that I got stuck trying to explain it to Nadine, trying to show that funeral coach already well up the street, Monroe having a difficult time getting his car in gear while behind him, stopped, a line of headlamps stretching well back, a few doors opening, the folks nearest startled and wild-eyed and looking to each other for help, and X, his hat set aright, already beginning a march down the sidewalk, heels clicking, shoulders squared, a figure of precision and care and true strength. I told Nadine, as my daddy told me, about the cars creeping past, someone calling out, Colonel Buck Wade stopping and ordering, then shouting for X to get in. X didn't hear, my daddy said. Wade was laughable, his mouth working in panic, an arm waving, his wife tugging at his sleeve, himself almost as improbable as that odd bird my daddy and another colonel had spent a day hunting years ago.

"X didn't know where he was going," my daddy said. To be true, he was feeling the sunlight and the heavy air and hearing, as if with another's ears, honks and shouts, but X said he felt moved and, yes, driven, being drawn away from something, not forward to another. The sadness was on him then, my daddy said, and this afternoon I saw it again in his face, a thing as permanent as the shape of your lips or your natural tendency to be silly. X went into an ice-cream parlor, and here I see him facing a glass-fronted counter of tutti-frutti and chocolate chip and daiquiri ice, and behind it a teen-age girl with no more on her mind than how to serve this one then another and another until she could go home. X ordered vanilla, my daddy said, eating by the spoonful, deliberately and slowly, as if the rest of his life—a long thing he felt he deserved—depended on this moment. It was the best ice cream X ever ate, my daddy said, and for three cones he thought of nothing, not bleakness, not happiness, not shape, nor beauty, nor thwarts, nor common distress—not anything the brain turns toward out of tribulation. It was then, my daddy said, that X realized something—about the counter girl, the ice cream itself, Colonel Buck Wade, even the children and the new wife he would have one day, and the hundreds of years still to pass—and this insight came to X with such force and speed that he felt lightheaded and partially blind, the walls tipping and closing on him, the floor rising and spinning, that mountain of sundae crashing over his shoulders and neck; he was going to pass out, X knew, and he wondered what others might say, knowing that his last thought—like Mr. Valentine's in one story—was long and complex and featured, among its parts, a scene of hope followed by misfortune and doom.

When Nadine asked me an hour ago what the moral was, I said, "Everything is fragile." We were in the kitchen, drinking Buckhorn, she in her pj's; and I tried, though somewhat afflicted by drink and a little breathless, to explain, setting the scene and rambling, mentioning ancient times and sorrows and pride in another. It was bad. I put everything in—the way of sitting, how the air smelled when my daddy went inside, gestures that had significance, what my own flesh was doing. But I was wrong. Completely wrong. For I left out the part where I, sunburned but shivering, wandered through X's house, one time feeling weepy, another feeling foolish and much aged.

The part I left out shows me going into his kitchen, reading the note my momma wrote when she went to Dallas to visit my Aunt Dolly; and it shows me standing in every room, as alien in that place as a sneak thief, touching their bric-a-brac and my daddy's tarnished golf trophies, sitting on the edge of the sofa or the green, shiny lounger, opening the medicine cabinet in the guest bathroom, curiosity in me as strong as the lesser states of mind. It's the part that has all the truth in it—and what I'll tell Nadine in the morning. I'll describe how I finally entered my daddy's room and stood over his bed, listening to him snore, the covers clenched at his chest, saying to myself, as he did long ago, headbone and chinbone and legbone and armbone. Yes, when I tell it I'll put in the part wherein a fellow such as me invites a fellow such as him out to do a thing—I'm not sure what—that involves effort and sacrifice and leads, in an hour or a day, to that throb and swell fellows such as you call triumph.

T. E. HOLT

Apocalypse

Thou canst understand, therefore, that all our knowledge will be dead
from the moment the door of the future is closed.
—*Inferno* x: 106–8

IN THE GORGE THE ECHOES FADED. I FOUND MYSELF LISTENING, HOPING
there would be no voices. For a minute or so—it may have been ten—we
waited. I could hear the kitchen clock tick.

When the silence in the room became intolerable, we both stood to go.

The slate steps down into the gorge were buried in snow, and we stepped
carefully, taking turns. The cold dimmed our flashlights, leaving us only
the light of the sky to tell wet slate from ice. When we reached bottom and
walked out onto the frozen stream, the light lay pale around us. Tonight's
wreck had joined the others without a sign. There was no fire. Through
the sound of water under ice, we listened, and heard nothing.

I could feel Ellen shiver. She told me once, after we had climbed back
home, that she is afraid to let me come down here alone. She worries that
another car will fall. As I put an arm around her—tried to, but in our
parkas the gesture turned into a clumsy shove—I looked up to the rim
of the gorge, where our house stands. There the road turns sharply down
toward the bridge, and the safety barrier has long since broken down.

It was a mistake to look. No cars (the night was soundless): only the
hard angles of the rocks, and the bare trees threading the sky. The night
was bitter cold, clear and moonless. Before, a night like this would have
burned with stars, and the sky seemed infinitely far away. This night, I
saw four, six, seven stars swimming, awash in a faintly luminous haze that
lowers, night by night.

Ell caught me staring and pulled at my ann. She dragged us stumbling
over rocks hidden in the snow to where the new wreck lay, broken-backed
on the stream side. Its engine had spilled out in a single piece, hissing into
the ice. Glass glittered everywhere. We bent to a place where a window

had been. Inside were six bodies, all fallen on their heads. Their arms were tangled, as if still gesturing.

Last night was Sunday. I had lost track of the day until, as we were halfway up the stairs, Ell asked if I had remembered to wind the clock. She has asked me this every Sunday night for seven years. It used to irritate me.

It is an heirloom, the clock. It was my father's, and his father's, and the story goes that it has been around the world ten times: a great, gleaming ship's chronometer. When I was young, my father would—rarely—consent to show me its works. I would dream about them, sometimes, in the conscious dreams that come before sleep. The gleam and the motion, and the oddly susurrant ticking merged with my pulse and my own breathing to whirr me into sleep.

At an early age I conceived the notion that the clock was responsible for time. I remain superstitious about keeping it wound, and have never let it stop since the day I inherited it, still ticking. When I opened its back that day, I was surprised how my memory had magnified its works: the springs and cogs occupy no more than a quarter of the massive, largely empty casing. I use it to hide spare keys.

Last night, when Ellen asked if I had remembered to wind the clock, I stopped on the stairs, and without a word turned back down. I felt her eyes on my back, and felt ashamed at my own carelessness.

In life I was the editor of a small science quarterly. I read widely in the literature, and so for ten years or more I was forewarned. But some part of me always believed that the world written up in the journals was imaginary. It never touched me: there were no people in it. It was an elegant entertainment, nothing more. This world—the one we live in—was real, and there could be no connection.

Can I understand what is happening? No, nor can I imagine the hour that launched it, some sixty thousand years ago, from the heart of the Milky Way. I can only tell myself facts: since I began this paragraph, it has moved two million miles closer. The words clatter emptily about the page. I only know that when it emerged last June—a faint gleam, low in the summer sky—the world changed.

Part of me feels certain this cannot be, that all of us are in a dream, a mass psychosis: the second week of January will come after all, and we will waken, grinning at ourselves. The other part of me feels the emptiness in those words.

There is a quiet over the land. We drive often now—gasoline is plentiful once more—in the hills outside the town, past farmsteads that could have been abandoned last week, or ten years ago. The livestock have broken down their fences. Cattle, horses, pigs stand in the road, root in the ditches. I saw a goat standing on a porch, forefeet up in a swing-chair, staring abstractedly into the distance. I wonder where the owners of the animals have gone, if anyone still feeds or waters them. I worry for them, should the snow lie deep this winter, and the ponds ice over.

We stop at the grocery store, and the quiet has penetrated there, too, a chill emitted from the frozen foods, the dearth of certain products. The aisles are quiet, but there is no serenity in this place. Out in the countryside there could be something like serenity. I think when I am out there that my intrusion has shattered the peace, this edginess I feel will depart with me, and the pigs will lie down again in the road and sleep. Here in the supermarket, every selection asks us: This large? How long? For what?

The pet-food aisle is empty. A man had hysterics there this week; we could hear him across the store. Everyone looked up, checked his neighbor, and looked down again.

When we found him, he was standing sobbing by his cart, his face gleaming in the fluorescent lights. I wanted to make him stop, but when I laid a hand on his shoulder, he wheeled.

—Do you have any?

I shook my head and offered a package of cheese.

—No. He sleeved his nose. —Do you have any *cats*?

I tried to move him toward the dairy aisle, but he shrugged my hand away.

—It's not *fair*, he howled. —She's just a *cat*.

The last word made him blubber again. At the end of the aisle I saw Ell, looking diminished, mute—one of the frieze of strangers gathered there. I could not meet her eye.

Suddenly furious at him, I dragged him away, wanting to slap him into silence. Instead I pushed his cart across the back of the store, where he lapsed into a sullen calm. I pulled from the shelves anything I thought a cat might eat: marinated herring, heavy cream, Camembert. With each, I gestured, as if to say—She'll like this; there, that's my favorite; isn't this good?—until his flat stare unstrung me, and I led him to the checkout.

I had been down to the bridge, watching the sun go down across the valley. The lake is icing early this winter; the town was sunk in blue shadow. Below me, the gorge was already dark.

The deck of the bridge is an open steel grid. I hate to look down through it: the trees, foreshortened, look like bushes. I came home and found Ellen gone.

I thought at once of the gorge. In the darkening hall I stood and listened to the kitchen clock, and wondered how long I could wait before going to see. Then the door behind me opened, and she entered, swathed in her old, over-large winter coat. She looked as if she had walked in from an earlier year. She looked so familiar—and everything familiar now looks strange—I could not catch my breath and only nodded. —The roads are getting terrible, she said, bearing down drolly on the last word, balancing on one leg as she took off her boots.

When she caught the expression on my face, she laughed. —Were you worrying about me?

My appetite diminishes each day, as I awake before dawn and pad about the house, too restless to start writing. The time required to toast a slice of bread seems too long. Were it not for Ell, I would no longer cook at all. I am wasting, I know: my face in the mirror shows its bones clearly now in the morning light. But Ellen grows. She eats with an appetite she never had before, and seems taller, broader of hip, and of shoulder and breast as well. It suits her. Her face retains its graceful lines, and somehow her cheeks are still indented beneath the high, Slavic bones. Her eyes, too, are still hooded, guarded above the strong, straight bar of her nose.

She has stopped wearing her glasses. She focuses as best she can on the empty air above her lap. What does she see? I have not asked. I watch her, and try to guess. Sometimes she looks up—suddenly, as if she has seen something marvelous—her mouth opens, and I catch my breath.

The telephone system still works. I hear a tone when I lift the receiver. It sounds mournful now, this fabulously complex network reduced to carrying nothing but this message of no message, this signal that says only that it's ready to send. Our phone has not rung in weeks, nor is there anyone I call: I cannot imagine what there is to say. Some numbers I try no longer respond: the weather, dial-a-joke, dial-a-prayer. The number for the time survives, telling the ten-second intervals in its precise, weary voice.

Tonight I was alone in the kitchen, washing dishes. Something was rotting in the trash. For a long time I failed to recognize the smell (my sinuses are bad this winter), or even that I was smelling anything at all. Something was wrong. What had I done? I worked faster, scrubbed harder, but the feeling grew. What had I done? When I finally recognized the smell, my guilt and anxiety changed abruptly into anger. It had been Ellen's turn to take out the trash. I was certain of it.

When I found her, she was in the small upstairs room that still smells faintly of the coat of paint we gave it in the summer. She was sewing again; the light was bad. She looked up as I entered, her glasses on the table beside her, straining to focus on what I knew she could see only as the pale blur of my face. Her eyes still struggle to see at a distance; the effort gives her the look of a worried child. It is the expression that gazes out of the few early snapshots she still has.

That look stopped me in the doorway. I tried to slow my breathing, reminding myself that, without her glasses, she could not see the expression on my face. I pretended my grimace was a smile, walked over to her, and turned on the lamp. She smiled back and returned to her work, presenting me the part of her hair. I stooped, kissed it, and quickly left.

Out in the cold, the smell from the trash was thinner, almost fragile among the smells of wood smoke and snow as I walked past our stuffed and sealed garbage cans, through the hedge to the neighbors' drive. Their house has been dark three weeks. They left their car, which I use as a temporary dump. I would use their house, if I could bring myself to try the door. Their car is starting to fill, and even in the cold stinks dangerously, but it will be enough.

We fought the next morning instead. I had thrown something away—a magazine, the last number of a subscription that expired in November—before she had finished with it. She complained, I snapped, she turned and left the room. The fight continued as a mutual silence that went on throughout the afternoon. When I could no longer bear the rising tension, I brought her a cup of tea. She was reading in the upstairs room—the light was bad again—and when I set the tea beside her, she did not look up.

As I turned to leave, she cleared her throat. —I was afraid you were going to go through the trash.

I turned, and she was smiling at me over the brim of the cup. —I wouldn't have wanted it, you know. It would have stunk. Her smile broadened as she spoke, but before she could sip the tea, she was crying. I tried to comfort her, and felt ineffectual as I always do, at a loss for words. I patted her back, and wondered at the empty sound.

The same dream has come to me these three nights. It starts in a scene I cannot forget, two faces I still see when I close my eyes. They were the first to fall into the gorge. We found them at first light, the car absurd among the boulders. The twin stars in the windshield told us what we would find inside. Perhaps it was the shock of finding them still so young, so peaceful behind the shattered glass, that reverberates now in my dreams: they looked asleep, their faces almost touching.

In my dream they wake, they speak to us, and as they tell us their story, weep—whether for each other or for us I cannot say. As they speak, their words live, showing us their last moments: the guardrail flying away, the slow, looming tilt of the far wall, and then the rocks uprushing. On the seat beside me, Ellen hovers at the corner of my eye. There is something I must tell her, but before I can speak, there is a noise, and then silence, which continues for a long time.

Ell wakes me. —You were crying.

Sitting up in the cold room, by the pale light the curtains cannot cover entirely, I turn and tell her the words the dream would not let me say. But as I speak, Ellen grows smaller, the room lengthens, the distance between us grows and still she lies only just beyond the farthest stretch of my arm. My voice make no sound. Her lips move. Each object in the room is isolated, meaningless, and I think, this is the end, it has happened, and Ell diminishes still farther, contracting to the one clear point in the deepening gloom.

When I finally awake, the world is still, and Ellen still beside me.

Her face relaxes every night, so that by morning the angles and the lines have vanished, her nose is round and freckled, and her lips are parted. Every morning the urge to clutch her, shake her awake, almost overpowers me. I want to ask her something—just what, I still can't say. But this morning, as every morning, I let her sleep. The aching in my chest ebbs slowly, and the daylight grows around us.

At the neighbors' back door I looked in the curtained window: dishes in the sink, a dinner for four spread on the table. One of the chairs lay on its back, legs up in an expression of helpless surprise. The door swung open as I pressed, and a burst of hot, fetid air swept past me. Dinner had spoiled, filling the kitchen with a high, wild sweetness. The temperature inside was so hot the air seemed gelid: sweat burst out on my face. From the basement I heard the furnace roar. To leave in the middle of dinner seemed unremarkable; but why turn up the heat? I stopped amid the ruins of the meal, stooped and righted the chair. As I bent, I saw in the far doorway another leg stretched out on the floor, and beyond it a room where nothing was right.

I am afraid I understood. I could deduce—I could not stop myself from observing—the tools they had used, and how. Who must have gone first. Him last. But more than that I am afraid I knew exactly how they felt, as the moment came on them over dinner, and they rushed—in some terrible parody of joy—into each others' arms.

I locked the door behind me, and wondered how long I could keep this to myself.

There is a sound that comes at dawn. I have never heard it. I wake in a room full of echoes, holding my breath, and lie beside Ell sleeping, and watch the light change in the room. I cannot escape the sense that I have missed something important. But as the light grows, the room around me is utterly ordinary.

I rise from the bed, the cold floor at my feet telling me again I am awake, the world is real. Through a fragile silence I inspect each room, and everything is as we left it. But in each room, the objects I find—the chair with the book face down upon its arm, my binoculars on the windowsill—seem to be holding a pose, waiting for my back to turn. Only the kitchen clock confesses, filling the room with the catch and release of its cogs. In a distant, unconscious way I hear the sound of water flowing in the gorge, whispering dimly. The falls are almost frozen over.

I wring back the curtains, snap up the shades, flush the rooms with light and nothing moves. In the kitchen I heat the kettle to a scream, bang pots, and overcook the oats. Upstairs, Ell is moving slowly; she showers, the pipes shudder and groan, the wind picks up outside. In the feeders, finches hiss and flutter, fighting for a perch. A dog lopes hip-deep through the yard, barking bright blue clouds of breath at the treetops, where four crows cling to the waving limbs. They flap and caw, caw a senseless monody. Over all of us, gray clouds pour ceaselessly into the cast.

The wind has blown for days. I wonder how much longer it can blow before the country west of us lies in a vacuum, and dogs and crows, finches and clouds freeze solid, and the trees' metallic branches thrill faintly against the stars. I have dreamed this. I have been dreaming of the stars as they once were, as I will never see them again, unless there is after all another life after this one, in a cold and airless west.

I woke again this morning among the booming echoes. Through the window I saw the morning star, failing, dim in the sick gleam that made my hand a skeleton on the curtain. Between my ribs my heart was thunderous in its hollow, ticking off the seconds of the dawn.

A restlessness took me out of the house today, on a final, senseless errand. I took the car downtown to fill its tank, though I have nowhere left to go, no errands left unrun.

As I coasted down the long hill into town, I noticed that the odometer was less than ten miles from turning over. This fact—this string of nines rolling up under the quivering needle—loomed before me much larger than I wanted it to. The windshield hazed, and the large, familiar hands that held the wheel seemed not my own. They are older than I noticed them last—the skin is drier, nicked with scars I don't remember, and a gold band glints at one finger.

As I came down the block I saw a banner over the pumps. FREE GAS it read, in hand-drawn black. The sign sighed and billowed in the breeze, but nothing else moved: the pumps were deserted.

By the time I stopped the car, I was almost laughing, glad to have my mood broken by this sorry joke. I have given over too often to self-pity: it is only a car. Through the glass, still decked with offers of antifreeze, I saw the owner dimly, seated at his desk, and thought I saw him smiling.

Gasoline spilled from the neck of the tank. The trigger gave a dull clunk and went limp.

The door to the office was locked; the knob rattled loudly in my hand, but the figure smiling by the open cash drawer did not move. I stooped to peer through the glass. He sat upright, his mouth and eyes wide open.

I took a winding route back home, through the empty streets. Not everyone is dead: as the sun set, windows lit in many houses. The people at the power station are still at their posts. I drove past every drugstore I could think of, and every one was empty, dark. On some of them, the doors stood open; others had their windows smashed. The street by a liquor store glittered and flashed. I drove home wondering, what are they waiting for?

I could not think of an answer.

At the sound of my key in the lock, Ell pulled open the door, rushed at me, and grabbed my shoulders. As I thought horribly of what could be wrong she was saying—Where have you been? and, I was sure, and, where were you?

I couldn't speak. We did not fight. Normally, in such a case, we would, and eventually would understand. I couldn't. There was something on my tongue, even now I cannot say what, only that a fear of speaking welled up once again and stifled me. When she ran weeping from the room, guilt stabbed me, but I could not explain. I walked upstairs and closed the study door, sat here at my desk for a long rime before turning on the lights.

The morning is bright. Outside the house the icicles are running, and water echoes loudly in the drain. Fresh air stirs the curtains, breathing in at the window opened for the first time in months. The January thaw has come, but a few days past the turning of the year, rushing as if to make the time. The air is piercing, fresh and sweet. It buoys me with an indiscriminate urge to do something—nothing I can name. It speaks tongueless, as varying and monotonous as the water in the drains. The fresh air blows past my ears, whispering promises of spring.

When I came down from my study after our fight, Ell was reading in her accustomed chair, her feet tucked underneath her legs against the cold. She looked up, angry and compact. I knew she would not speak—that it was up to me. But what was there to say? A minute passed, drawn out into a wire that tightened between us. I wanted to flinch—to run away. But where was there to run?

From where I stood in the doorway, her face seemed a shield held out against me. But in the curve of her lower lip, I saw a trace of motion, a sustained, suppressed tremor. It told me something of what she must have felt when I did not come home—and what she must be feeling now. I understood the offering of her face then, the cost it exacted as the minutes wore on and the muscles of her neck grew tired, quivering. I met her eyes, and the intensity of the look that met me seized me out of vagueness into something solid, here and real.

At that moment the lights flickered, and my heart leapt with an animal despair—dumb, and damned so. The lights went yellow, faded slowly to orange, red, and as the darkness closed in around us, I saw in her face—motionless still, and pale—the same mute despair, and then it was dark.

We found candles in the kitchen. By their light we made love upstairs, in a bed piled high with blankets. The clock beside us was stopped at a quarter to, and the candles held at bay the sky's sick light. We were awkward. I could not remember the last time we had broken the unspoken agreement that for months has kept us from each other.

A silence this morning disturbed me as I stood, awash in morning light, at the kitchen sink. Something was missing. I listened, until I realized that what I missed was the sound of birds at the feeders: the crack and scatter of the seeds, the whirr of wings—the ungainly thud of the jays. I wiped steam from the windows. Every feeder hung deserted, full of seed,

T. E. HOLT

163

shuddering gently in the wind. I watch, and no birds come. Hours have passed, and I have not seen or heard them yet.

Perhaps they know. Perhaps some message came to them. I hope so. I hope that, even now, someone in a Southern kitchen is wondering at the chickadees, the juncoes, the titmice, and the nuthatch, upside down, inspecting some unnaturally sweet and tender fruit.

There had been another wreck. Both of us stayed seated long after the booming died away. The falls have frozen over at last; no sound rose to fill the silence. We sat throughout the afternoon, as the light faded and the sun went down for what must have been the last time—a dull, dim, red extinction. It disappeared and left behind a sky as blank as if the constellations had been destroyed. Perhaps they have. The moon rose soon after, waning, gibbous, sick in a sea of spoiled milk, and still we sat.

Ell rose, groaning a little with the effort it takes her now to stand. She shuffled out to the kitchen. I heard her fumbling in the drawer where the candles are, rattling hollow objects for a time that stretched out far too long. I couldn't bear it. When she returned, her face alight, I stood abruptly, unable to look at her.

I think she knew, as I walked out the door, that I was not going to the gorge.

The streets lay deep in snow, and as I drove down the steep and winding road that ends in the bridge across the gorge, I lost control, fishtailed out onto the span sideways for the rail. Someone laughed as I spun, the railing moving wrong-way by the windshield; then I was stopped, turned sideways in the middle of the bridge.

I got out of the car, stepping out onto the steel grid. Wind whistled up at me. I looked down through the deck; a dozen dark shapes lay at the ends of scars scraped in the snow. I walked to the western rail and looked out over the valley where the gorge opens and falls finally into the lake. On the far hill shone a constellation of kerosene and candles, flickering dimly across the miles. Down in the town, a brighter glow grew into a blaze of buildings burning at the center. On the north wind came no sound, no smell of smoke, only the wind.

In the southwest, a dim glow, as the sunset faded into the ashen light of the sky. No evening star.

Then I was driving, fast again, swerving around curves I had never seen before, headlights doused. I remember nothing until three deer stood and faced me in the road.

Then there was light, shining in my eyes. They lifted me by the shoulders, headfirst through the window of my car although I clutched the wheel and cried. I saw a tire turning, spinning slowly in the air.

Then there was light again, and warmth, a chair, and hands rubbing mine and feeling up and down my arms and legs, voices asking—Hurt? Talk?—a voice whispering—Shock.

They put my fingers around a cup, where heat thawed feeling out of numb nothing. Something hot trickled down my throat, buoying me out of myself.

And the first thing I saw was a tree, standing in the corner, shedding its needles on the floor. I thought: I missed Christmas, and: it was all a dream. The room solidified: a kitchen, plank floor, wood stove, iron washstand, water heater in the far corner. Warm light and the smell of kerosene. A man in coveralls, about my age, but the lines in his face had cut more deeply, the hand with which he slid the teacup back across the table was a farmer's hand, old already. As he watched me critically, I reached out to take the cup, and flushed.

—You're not the first, he said.

I nodded, unable to explain.

He nodded back, indicating my hand. —You're married. I nodded again.

—Alive?

Again.

The man paused, looked away from me, and cleared his throat.—Do you want to go back?

I feel tears on my face. My voice makes no sound; the room seems to expand around me, leaving me in darkness. It is too late for words.

I heard a chair move, and felt a hand on my shoulder. —I'll go warm up the truck.

The man did not return. I heard an engine catch, roar, and settle into a rapid idle. A woman, in a faded print, and herself worn thin enough to show the pulse at her temple, a tremor in her jaw, each bone and tendon of her hand, sat around the corner of the table. She reached out to touch the tabletop before me, paused.

—Your wife alone? Her voice was hoarse.

—I wondered what she might mean, and looked around the room. Through an open door I saw three children all alike in dingy pastel pajamas, staring back at me.

—We let them stay up late tonight, she apologized. —When we talk about it, they don't understand. But they like to stay up, We wanted to *do* something for them. She looked at them, and whispered—Do you know what I mean?

I stood abruptly, caught myself with a hand on her shoulder and staggered into her lap. Embarrassed, she gave me her thin arm, and, biting her lower lip, led me to the truck. There she whispered to her husband, and with a shy glance at me, kissed him long and urgently. Then we were gone.

The road was drifted deep where snow had blown across the fields. The clouds had broken before the rising wind. The moon burned bright at our backs, the only thing in the ghostly sky. It shone unnaturally bright. I felt it pushing, as it brightened by the minute, behind us.

The man drove fast, his need for haste twice mine. Deer were everywhere. They stood in silent groups of twos and threes beside the road. Smaller shapes, writhing in the headlights, fled before us. Overhead, darkness dotted the sky, flitting from horizon to horizon as if the graves gave up their dead. The face of the man beside me was taut in the dim green light of the speedometer. He swerved to miss something that froze before us—a skunk—and silently drove on.

He turned on the radio, tuned from static to a voice beseeching to the sound of running water, then fire, then large masses breaking, waves upon a shore, marching feet, applause, a voice explaining, violins, a chorus shouting, a man singing

Froh, wie seine Sonnen fliegen
Durch des Himmels prächtgen Plan.

He switched it off. —Last night there was hymns, down from Canada. You could tell it was hymns, even in French.

One road to the city was blocked by fire: black against the flames, men and women were dancing, singing, in tuxedos and gowns, diamonds flaming like stars.

The bridge from the north was destroyed.

The way from the south was blocked by a creature I cannot describe.

The door was unlocked. It opened into the dark hall, and I stepped in. I stood in the doorway, seeing no reason to shut the door behind me. The house was as cold as a crypt, and—I knew without having to ask—as empty. I wondered where she had gone, where she would be when the time caught her. I hoped the time would find her ready. I would never be, and saw no reason to wait, not any longer.

I went to the kitchen and pulled the stool up to the sink, and fumbling open the casing of the clock, I found the vial that I had hidden the night we fought. Not all of the drugstores had been closed that evening. I am more coward than I seem. I stood on the stool, the vial warming in my palm, and tried to remember something I had forgotten. The silence in the room was complete: my pulse seemed to surge out to the walls and return. The clock at my ear was silent.

She reached up and took the vial away. —I poured it out. It's just food coloring now.

How foolish I was to think anything would remain hidden. She helped me from the stool, stopping me as I started to fall. Her hair was cold, smelling of the outdoors. For a long time we were silent. For the space of half an hour, nothing mattered.

Then she moved, reached up a hand to touch my face. The light of the moon had brightened abruptly, as if a window shade had snapped up. As the light and silence grew, I felt the spell that has kept me speechless breaking. But when I bent to her ear and started to whisper, she placed her hand gently over my mouth and held it. I understood: there is nothing to say.

We stood together in the growing light, the thunder rumbling in the distance, drawing nearer, and I shrugged away impulses that no longer had meaning—to speech, to fear, to sorrow. I felt laughter growing inside me. Certainly she was laughing. At the window, moonlight poured in.

Ellen spoke. —Is there anything you want?

—Yes. The words came easily. —I want to finish something.

And at the door of this room, she left me. —I'll call if I need you.

Little remains. She is calling. The moon burns still brighter with each passing second, leaves my hand too slow to record, to report. I must end now.

But before the end we will speak once more, of everything that matters: of the brightness of the moon; of the birds still flying dark against the sky; of the man who brought me here; of the hours that she waited; of what we would name the child; of the grace of everything that dies; of the love that moves the sun and other stars.

MARY HOOD

Manly Conclusions

HIS WIFE, VALJEAN, ADMITTED THAT CARPENTER PETTY HAD A TREE-topping temper, but he was slow to lose it; that was in his favor. Still, he had a long memory, and that way of saving things up, until by process of accumulation he had enough evidence to convict. "I don't get mad, I get even," his bumper sticker vaunted. Fair warning. When he was angry he burned like frost, not flame.

Now Valjean stood on the trodden path in the year's first growth of grass, her tablecloth in her arms, and acknowledged an undercurrent in her husband, spoke of it to the greening forsythia with its yellow flowers rain-fallen beneath it, confided it to God and nature. Let God and nature judge. A crow passed between her and the sun, dragging its slow shadow. She glanced up. On Carpenter's behalf she said, "He's always been intense. It wasn't just the war. If you're born a certain way, where's the mending?"

She shook the tablecloth free of the breakfast crumbs and pinned it to the line. Carpenter liked her biscuits—praised them to all their acquaintances—as well as her old-fashioned willingness to rise before good day and bake for him. Sometimes he woke early too; then he would join her in the kitchen. They would visit as she worked the shortening into the flour, left-handed (as was her mother, whose recipe it was), and pinch off the rounds, laying them as gently in the blackened pan as though she were laying a baby down for its nap. The dough was very quick, very tender. It took a light hand. Valjean knew the value of a light hand.

This morning Carpenter had slept late, beyond his time, and catching up he ate in a rush, his hair damp from the shower, his shirt unbuttoned. He raised neither his eyes nor his voice to praise or complain.

"You'll be better at telling Dennis than I would," he said, finally, leaving it to her.

She had known a long time that there was more to loving a man than marrying him, and more to marriage than love. When they were newly wed, there had been that sudden quarrel, quick and furious as a summer squall, between Carpenter and a neighbor over the property line. A vivid memory and a lesson—the two men silhouetted against the setting sun, defending the territory and honor of rental property. Valjean stood by his side, silent, sensing even then that to speak out, to beg, to order, to quake would be to shame him. Nor would it avail. Better to shout Stay! to Niagara. Prayer and prevention was the course she decided on, learning how to laugh things off, to make jokes and diversions. If a car cut ahead of them in the parking lot and took the space he had been headed for, before Carpenter could get his window down to berate women drivers, Valjean would say, "I can see why she's in a hurry, just look at her!" as the offender trotted determinedly up the sidewalk and into a beauty salon.

She was subtle enough most times, but maybe he caught on after a while. At any rate, his emotional weather began to moderate. Folks said he had changed, and not for the worse. They gave proper credit to his wife, but the war had a hand in it too. When he got back, most of what he thought and felt had gone underground, and it was his quietness and shrewd good nature that you noticed now. Valjean kept on praying and preventing.

But there are some things you can't prevent, and he had left it to Valjean to break the news to Dennis. Dennis so much like Carpenter that the two of them turned heads in town, father and son, spirit and image. People seemed proud of them from afar as though their striking resemblance reflected credit on all mankind, affirming faith in the continuity of generations. He was like his mama, too, the best of both of them, and try as she might, she couldn't find the words to tell him that his dog was dead, to send him off to school with a broken heart. The school bus came early, and in the last-minute flurry of gathering books and lunch money, his poster on medieval armor and his windbreaker, she chose to let the news wait.

She had the whole day then, after he was gone, to find the best words. Musing, she sat on the top step and began cleaning Carpenter's boots—not that he had left them for her to do; he had just left them. She scrubbed and gouged and sluiced away the sticky mud, dipping her rag in a rain puddle. After a moment's deliberation she rinsed the cloth in Lady's water dish. Lady would not mind now; she was beyond thirst. It was burying her that had got Carpenter's boots so muddy.

"Dead," Valjean murmured. For a moment she was overcome, disoriented as one is the instant after cataclysm, while there is yet room for disbelief, before the eyes admit the evidence into the heart. The rag dripped muddy water dark as blood onto the grass.

They had found Lady halfway between the toolshed and the back porch, as near home as she had been able to drag herself. The fine old collie lay dying in their torchlight, bewildered, astonished, trusting them to heal her, to cancel whatever evil this was that had befallen.

Carpenter knelt to investigate. "She's been shot." The meaning of the words and their reverberations brought Valjean to her knees. No way to laugh this off.

"It would have been an accident," she reasoned.

Carpenter gave the road a despairing glance. "If it could have stayed the way it was when we first bought out here. . . . You don't keep a dog like this on a chain!"

It had been wonderful those early years, before the developers came with their transits and plat-books and plans for summer cottages in the uplands. The deer had lingered a year or so longer, then had fled across the lake with the moon on their backs. The fields of wild blueberries were fenced off now; what the roadscrapers missed, wildfire got. Lawn crept from acre to acre like a plague. What trees were spared sprouted POSTED and KEEP and TRESPASSERS WILL BE signs. Gone were the tangles of briar and drifted meadow beauty, seedbox and primrose. The ferns retreated yearly deeper into the ravines.

"Goddamn weekenders," Carpenter said.

They had lodged official complaint the day three bikers roared through the back lot, scattering the hens, tearing down five lines of wash, and leaving a gap through the grape arbor. The Law came out and made bootless inquiry, stirring things up a little more. The next morning Valjean found their garbage cans overturned. Toilet tissue wrapped every tree in the orchard, a dead rat floated in the well, and their mailbox was battered to earth—that sort of mischief. Wild kids. "Let the Law handle it," Valjean suggested, white-lipped.

"They can do their job and I'll do mine," Carpenter told her. So that time Valjean prayed the Law would be fast and Carpenter slow, and that was how it went. A deputy came out the next day with a carload of joyriders he had run to earth. "Now I think the worst thing that could happen," the deputy drawled, "is to call their folks, wha' d'ya say?" So it had been resolved that way, with reparations paid and handshakes. That had been several years back; things had settled down some now. Of late there were only the litter and loudness associated with careless vacationers. No lingering hard feelings. In the market, when Valjean met a neighbor's wife, they found pleasant things to speak about; the awkwardness was past. In time they might be friends.

"An accident," Valjean had asserted, her voice odd to her own ears, as though she were surfacing from a deep dive. Around them night was closing in. She shivered. It took her entire will to keep from glancing over her shoulder into the tanglewood through which Lady had plunged, wounded, to reach home.

"Bleeding like this she must have laid a plain track." Carpenter paced across the yard, probing at spots with the dimming light of the lantern. He tapped it against his thigh to encourage the weak batteries.

"She's been gone all afternoon," Valjean said. "She could have come miles."

"Not hurt this bad," Carpenter said.

"What are you saying? No. No!" She forced confidence into her voice. "No one around here would do something like this." Fear for him stung her hands and feet like frost. She stood for peace. She stood too suddenly; dizzy, she put out her hand to steady herself. He could feel her trembling.

"It could have been an accident, yeah, like you say." He spoke quietly for her sake. He had learned to do that.

"You see?" she said, her heart lifting a little.

"Yeah." Kneeling again, he shook his head over the dog's labored breathing. "Too bad, old girl; they've done for you."

When the amber light failed from Lady's eyes, Valjean said, breathless, "She was probably trespassing," thinking of all those signs, neon-vivid, warning. He always teased her that she could make excuses for the devil.

"Dogs can't read," he pointed out. "She lived all her life here, eleven, twelve years. . . . And she knew this place by heart, every rabbit run, toad hole, and squirrel knot. She was better at weather than the almanac, and there was never a thing she feared except losing us. She kept watch on Dennis like he was her own pup."

"I know . . ." She struggled to choke back the grief. It stuck like a pine cone in her throat. But she wouldn't let it be *her* tears that watered the ground and made the seed of vengeance sprout. For all their sakes she kept her nerve . . .

"And whoever shot her," Carpenter was saying, "can't tell the difference in broad day between ragweed and rainbow. Goddamn weekenders!"

They wrapped the dog in Dennis' cradle quilt and set about making a grave. Twilight seeped away into night. The shovel struck fire from the rocks as Carpenter dug. Dennis was at scout meeting; they wanted to be done before he got home. "There's nothing deader than a dead dog," Carpenter reasoned. "The boy doesn't need to remember her that way."

In their haste, in their weariness, Carpenter shed his boots on the back stoop and left the shovel leaning against the wall. The wind rose in the night and blew the shovel handle along the shingles with a dry-bones rattle. Waking, alarmed, Valjean put out her hand: Carpenter was there.

Now Valjean resumed work on the boots, concentrating on the task at hand. She cleaned carefully, as though diligence would perfect not only the leather but Carpenter also, cleaning away the mire, anything that might make him lose his balance. From habit, she set the shoes atop the well-house to dry, out of reach of the dog. Then she realized, Lady was gone. All her held-back tears came now; she mourned as for a child.

She told Dennis that afternoon. He walked all around the grave, disbelieving. No tears, too old for that; silent, like his father. He gathered straw to lay on the raw earth to keep it from washing. Finally he buried his head in Valjean's shoulder and groaned, "Why?" Hearing that, Valjean thanked God, for hadn't Carpenter asked *Who?* and not *Why?*—as though he had some plan, eye for eye, and needed only to discover upon whom to visit it? Dennis must not learn those ways, Valjean prayed; let my son be in some ways like me . . .

At supper Carpenter waited till she brought dessert before he asked, "Did you tell him?"

Dennis laid his fork down to speak for himself. "I know."

Carpenter beheld his son. "She was shot twice. Once point-blank. Once as she tried to get away."

Valjean's cup wrecked against her saucer. He hadn't told her that! He had held that back, steeping the bitter truth from it all day to serve to the boy. There was no possible antidote. It sank in, like slow poison.

"It's going to be all right," she murmured automatically, her peace of mind spinning away like a chip in strong current. Her eyes sightlessly explored the sampler on the opposite wall whose motto she had worked during the long winter she sat at her mother's deathbed: *Perfect Love Casts Out Fear.*

"You mean Lady knew them? Trusted them? Then they shot her?" Dennis spoke eagerly, proud of his ability to draw manly conclusions. Valjean watched as the boy realized what he was saying. "It's someone we know," Dennis whispered, the color rising from his throat to his face, his hands slowly closing into tender fists. "What—what are we going to do about it?" He pushed back his chair, ready.

"No," Valjean said, drawing a firm line, then smudging it a little with a laugh and a headshake. "Not you." She gathered their plates and carried them into the kitchen. She could hear Carpenter telling Dennis, "Someone saw Gannett's boys on the logging road yesterday afternoon. I'll step on down that way and see what they know."

"But Carpenter—" She returned with sudsy hands to prevent.

He pulled Valjean to him, muting all outcry with his brandied breath. He pleased himself with a kiss, taking his time, winking a galvanized-gray eye at Dennis. "I'm just going to talk to them. About time they knew me better."

She looked so miserable standing there that he caught her to him again, boyish, lean; the years had rolled off of him, leaving him uncreased, and no scars that showed. He had always been lucky, folks said. Wild lucky.

"Listen here now," he warned. "Trust me?"

What answer would serve but yes? She spoke it after a moment, for his sake, with all her heart, like a charm to cast out fear. "Of course."

Dennis, wheeling his bike out to head down to Mrs. Cobb's for his music lesson, knelt to make some minor adjustment on the chain.

"I won't be long," Carpenter said. "Take care of yourselves."

"You too," Dennis called, and pedaled off.

Carpenter crouched and pulled on his stiff, cleaned boots, then hefted one foot gaily into a shaft of sunset, admiring the shine. "Good work, ma'am." He tipped an imaginary hat and strode off into the shadows of the tall pines.

A whippoorwill startled awake and shouted once, then sleepily subsided. Overhead the little brown bats tottered and strove through the first starlight, their high twittering falling like tiny blown kisses onto the wind-scoured woods. It was very peaceful there in the deep heart of the April evening, and it had to be a vagrant, unworthy, warning impulse that sent Valjean prowling to the cabinet in the den where they kept their tax records, warranties, brandy, and sidearms. Trembling, she reached again and again, but couldn't find the pistol. Carpenter's pistol was not there.

Not there.

For a moment she would not believe it, just rested her head against the cool shelf; then she turned and ran, leaving lights on and doors open behind her, tables and rugs askew in her wake. She ran sock-footed toward trouble as straight as she could, praying *Carpenter! Carpenter!* with every step. And then, like answered prayer, he was there, sudden as something conjured up from the dark. He caught her by the shoulders and shook her into sense.

"What's happened? Babe? What is it?"

But she could not answer for laughing and crying both at once, to see him there safe, to meet him halfway. When she caught her breath she said, "I was afraid something awful—I thought—I didn't know if I'd ever—"

"I told you I was just going to talk with them," he chided, amused. She gave a skip to get in step beside him. He caught her hand up and pointed her own finger at her. "I thought you said you trusted me."

"But I didn't know you were taking the gun with you . . ."

Angry, he drew away. Outcast, she felt the night chill raise the hair on the back of her neck.

"I didn't take the damn gun! What makes you say things like that? You think I'm some kind of nut?"

"But it's gone," she protested. "I looked."

And then a new specter rose between them, unspeakable, contagious. For a moment they neither moved nor spoke, then Carpenter started for home, fast, outdistancing her in a few strides. Over his shoulder he called back, edgy, unconvinced, "You missed it, that's all. It's there." He would make sure.

She ran but could not quite catch up. "Dennis has it," she accused Carpenter's back.

"Nah," he shouted. "Don't borrow trouble. It's home."

When he loped across the lawn and up the kitchen steps three at a time he was a full minute ahead of her. And when she got there, Carpenter was standing in the doorway of the den empty-handed, with the rapt, calculating, baffled expression of a baby left holding a suddenly limp string when the balloon has burst and vanished. The phone was ringing, ringing.

"Answer it," he said into the dark, avoiding her eyes.

JIM HEYNEN

Stories about the Boys

EYE TO EYE

The boys liked to watch pigs being born. Drying them off in the straw.

Putting them next to the sow's teats. Watching them discover the little world of the farrowing pen. But after a while the boys would get tired of this and go off to do something else.

Except for the youngest boy. He liked to stick around by himself. When the other boys left, he leaned down and put his face close to the sow. Now that there was no one there to laugh at him. This way he could hear the pig coming, and when it was born his face was right over the newborn. He quickly put his eye over the eye of the little pig. When it opened its eye, the first thing it saw was the boy's eye, only an inch or two away from its own.

The boy stared into the pig's eye and the pig stared into the boy's. What the boy liked to see was the expression on the pig's face. It was a look of surprise. But not a big surprise. Not the startled look of seeing something you didn't expect to see—like a ghost or a creature from Mars. More like the look of somebody waking up in the back seat of a car who doesn't realize how far he's gone since he fell asleep. The look that says, *Oh, I didn't know we'd gone this far, but okay.*

Then the boy lifted his head so the pig could notice everything else. The pig knew what to do. Stand up, breathe, look around for a nipple. The boy didn't try to keep the pig from its business. He knew they both had their own worlds to live in. That didn't change the fact that for a few seconds they had been somewhere that nobody else would have to know about.

YELLOW GIRL

When drainage tile was put in the bottom lands, corn could be planted where only slough grass grew before. But the tile drained the pond too. The boys couldn't remember when ducks and bullheads swam there, but the pond was still surrounded by willow trees and made a good place to get away from everything. They'd go down to the pond and look for old bottles and badger holes, or they'd make dust castles out of the pond bed.

Then one year there was a big flood and the pond was back in spite of the drainage tile. When the waters went down, the boys went to the pond to see what it looked like with water in it. They brought fishing poles, figuring that where there was water there would be fish. Corn stalks and debris from all over the county were hanging in the willow trees around the pond and the pond was brimming with muddy water. They fished for an hour and now and then saw ripples in the water that told them something alive was in there. But they couldn't tell what.

Then one of the boys hooked something. It didn't fight much but it was big. His pole bent like a horseshoe. The boy managed to pull it toward the shore slowly. They were expecting a big mud turtle, and they had sticks ready. Then part of the catch showed itself on the surface, a large rolling motion, like a big fish turning over on its back as it swam.

"I saw its yellow belly!" shouted one of the boys. "It's a giant catfish!"

But it wasn't a catfish. It wasn't anything alive at all. It was a dirty dress the flood had brought from somewhere. The boys took it off the hook and laid it out on the shore. It was a girl's dress. When they squeezed the water out, they could see that it was yellow, with small red flowers. It had two pockets and white buttons at the neck. The boys fastened the buttons and checked the pockets. They were empty.

The dress lay on the shore and the breeze started to dry it. The colors became clearer and brighter as it dried and the hem ruffled a little in the breeze.

As a joke one of the boys drew a head over the dress. The other boys joined in, scratching legs and arms in the soft dirt. "There," one of them said. "There is our yellow girl."

The boys left her lying there, knowing there was little chance that such a flood as the last one would come and wash her away. They went down to the pond often that summer, always saying they were going fishing. And they did catch a few small bullheads. The yellow girl stayed in place through the summer and when the weather changed her at all the boys fixed her up again by retracing her head, arms, and legs in the dirt. They came to think of her as their sleeping beauty, though none of them stooped to kiss her.

He stopped chewing on his cigar and laid it down next to the lantern. It simmered there on the burnt spot where he had laid other cigars. He picked out an egg from the bucket and rubbed at a spot with the damp dishcloth. He would start talking now. The boys sat at the edge of the hoop of lantern light and looked up at his face.

"Well, I'm a pretty old farmer," he said. "I can remember the days before rat poison. There was as many rats back then as good stories. Good talkers and good workers. In those days you could tell the speed of a man's hands by checking the scar tissue on his legs."

He held an egg up to the lantern light, as if he could tell this way which ones would be culled out at the hatchery.

"One time we was shelling corn. Corn shelling. Five or six of us shoving corn in the hopper. We was going for a thousand bushels. Big crib. And big rats. I don't know how many. Lots of them. They was legion. We seen their tails slickering in the corn. They was digging right ahead of our scoops."

He laid an egg down and wiggled his short forefinger as if he could make it look like a rat's tail. He picked up his cigar, chewed on it, and laid it down on the burnt spot again.

"First thing you gotta know about rats is they're dumb, but they know when they're in trouble. The second thing you gotta know is that when they're in trouble, they don't run for light—they run for dark."

He adjusted the wick on the lantern. The egg bucket was not quite half empty. The boys leaned back on their hands.

"So we was almost to the bottom of this corn when we run into them rats. First one trickles out. Then the whole works. Like when one ear of corn falls out of the pile and then it all comes down. So we start stomping. I must of stomped a dozen of them when the fella next to me misses one when he stomps. And that rat swickers around real quick and comes at me from the side where I can't see him. He is looking for a dark tunnel. And he finds it. My pants leg! He saw that little tunnel over my shoe and up he comes. I had on wool socks, the thick kind that gives rat claws something good to dig into. Good footing. So he gets his claws in my wool socks, looks up the tunnel, and don't see daylight. He must of thought he was home free for sure."

He paused and rubbed his chin while the boys squirmed.

"Well, you know, in those days, rats was always running up somebody's leg. Specially during corn shelling. I guess it was just my turn. You just had to figure on it a little bit during corn shelling. Like getting stung when you're going after honey. You was always hearing somebody yelling and seeing him kick his leg like crazy in a corn crib or pulling his pants off so fast you'd think he got the instant diarrhea.

"Now let me show you the scar that critter give me."

He pulled up his overalls. His leg was white and hairless. Just below the knee, on the inside calf, was a set of jagged scars.

"That's how fast my hands was," he said. "I grabbed that sucker before he could clear my shoestrings." He rubbed the scars with the tip of his finger, gently, as if they were still tender.

"There's the top teeth. And there's the bottom," he said. "I grabbed and I squeezed. And I squeezed. And the rat bites. And he bites. I felt his rib cage crack, but his teeth stayed in me like they was hog rings. I guess we both got our way. Now he's still hanging there dead inside my pants while we killed the rest of them rats. Then I pried him loose with my pocketknife. Stubborn sucker. But he knew a dark tunnel when he seen one."

There were only two eggs left in the bucket. He rinsed the washcloth and took one more chew on his cigar. He picked up an egg and rolled it over in his hand looking for spots.

"Now almost any old farmer can tell you his rat story. They've all had a rat or two up their pants. But just ask him to show you his scar tissue. I can wager you this—the ones with slow hands won't show you where they got theirs."

The boys giggled a little as he put the last egg into the crate with his careful hands. It was time to make their escape. The door to the shed was open.

"Watch out for the dark now," he said as the boys filed out, their shirt-tails fluttering behind them into the night.

ELECTRICITY

The boys remembered the night electricity came to the farm. At least the oldest did, and the others pretended to. Or they'd heard the story so often they thought they remembered it. After a while, it didn't matter who really remembered it and who didn't. They all knew the story.

It was the night the big switch was thrown somewhere at some big dam. This was long after the electrician had spent weeks wiring all the buildings, putting switches on walls where only wallpaper had been, putting a long fluorescent light like the ones they'd seen in town right in the middle of their kitchen ceiling, so that the old lantern had to hang on a new hook until the big switch was thrown.

The night of the big switch: that's when all these dead wires and gray light bulbs were supposed to come to life. Could it really work? Could electricity get all the way out here from that big switch at that big dam hundreds of miles away?

A letter had come telling how to get ready for the big night. Five o'clock PM on such and such a day the big switch would be thrown. *Have all switches turned off*, the letter said, *and turn them on one at a time.* As if the big dam couldn't stand to have all of its electricity sucked out at once. Which made sense to the boys. Cows kicked if you tried to milk all four teats at once. And a horse would take more easily to four riders if they didn't all get on at the same time. Imagine a chicken laying ten eggs in one shot. It made sense.

So the night of the big switch they sat around the kitchen table waiting, switches turned off. Waiting for five o'clock. Then they saw it happen—a light on the horizon where there hadn't been a light before. Then a light in the neighbor's window, about a half-mile away. Then lights popping on everywhere. It looked as if the whole world was covered with fireflies. The new light was not the yellow light of lanterns, but the white clear light of electricity. Light clear as water from the big dam, wherever it was.

One of the boys flicked the kitchen switch. And it happened right there. The big switch worked, even here. It was as if the ceiling opened with light: a fluttering fluorescent angel. A splash, a *woof*, a clatter of light. Light brighter than high noon on the Fourth of July. They looked at each other in this new light—every freckle, every smudge, every stringy hair, every ring around the collar, clearer than ever. Then they looked around the room—the cupboards, the wainscoting, the wallpaper, the ceiling where the old lantern dangled like a hanged man.

And out of the throat of one of the horrified light-stricken grown-ups came the words, *My goodness! Look how dirty this place is!*

So the first night of that great fluorescent light they spent washing the walls. Every one of them. Every inch. That was the story the boys knew. That was the story they would always be able to tell, whether they remembered it or not.

ONE DEAD CHICKEN

In the neighborhood where the boys lived, people went to a very strict church. It was a church that taught that people are evil, and that if they were left to themselves, the whole world would turn into a cesspool. If left to themselves, they would eat each other like dogs. Or worse. As the boys understood it, rules kept people from going all out in their naturally bad ways. Rules and punishment. Maybe the punishment even more than the rules.

But obeying rules was sort of like holding your breath. You could do it for a while if you really kept your mind on it, but sooner or later *Poof!* and you'd be back to your bad old self. There didn't seem to be much middle ground. What you were doing was either good, like holding your breath, or bad, like letting it all out. A few games might be in the good category if they weren't being played on Sunday and so long as everybody was being a good sport. Which, they supposed, meant not feeling bad if you were losing and not feeling good if you were winning. Almost all work was probably all good because it almost always felt bad in the doing. What was hardest to understand was why things that felt so good in the doing could be so bad when looked at from the point of view of having been done.

I am so disappointed that you did that.

How could anybody be disappointed in a boy doing what made him feel good? He was just being his naturally bad self. Was he supposed to hold his breath and believe some kind of rule that was the opposite of what he really was?

One day a boy who was thinking too much about good and bad caught a chicken and stuck it head first into a gallon syrup can full of water. When the chicken was dead, the boy didn't ask himself, Now, why did I do that? He asked himself, What can I do with this dead wet chicken? Which meant, Where should I hide it? He buried it in the grove and then came back out into the ordinary world where nothing looked particularly good or bad.

He was supposed to feel guilty for doing something terrible like that. He didn't. He was supposed to be punished for doing something so awful. He wasn't. When he looked around, he couldn't see that he was any better or worse than anything or anybody around him. Only one thing was different now, and that was this one dead chicken. And that didn't seem to make things better or worse. It pretty much left him back where he started.

HOUSE VISITATION

Once a year the minister and an elder from the consistory visited every family in the church. The house visitation day was so important that the house had to be cleaned spotless, and all the dandelions had to be dug out of the lawn. House visitation meant taking off overalls and putting on suits and ties right in the middle of the day in the middle of the week. House visitation was serious business, and the boys knew it.

Visitors and hired hands left when the minister and elder drove into the yard. These men in black suits weren't coming to look at the crops or to talk seed corn, that was for sure. They were more like the IRS coming to check out the bottom line of everybody's hidden lives.

And how is your spiritual life? the minister was likely to ask, after opening the meeting with a prayer that told more than it asked about how everyone was guilty even of sins they didn't know they had committed because they were born guilty. He would ask questions about family devotions, about taking the name of the Lord in vain, and about Sabbath Day observance. He would ask if there was anything that anybody knew in his heart that should be talked about. The elder would listen to the minister and then add a question of his own. Sometimes the elder asked the hardest question, like *In what ways do you feel you have grown closer to God during the last year?* The boys would sit nervously on the sofa, hoping the grown-ups would answer all the questions so that there wouldn't be any left for them.

But one year the youngest elder who had ever been selected in the church came with the minister. He believed in making people comfortable before the serious talk started. He chatted with the boys about baseball and 4-H. He asked them if there were any new pigs on the farm. He asked them about their new dog Fritzy. He asked if Fritzy did any farm work.

Oh, yes! said one of the boys. He chases the pigs. He barks and chases them if one gets out!

Now all the boys were excited about telling the young elder about Fritzy's escapades. They interrupted each other in their excitement, each trying to add new dimensions to Fritzy's barnyard achievements. And in all this excitement, like passing gas in Sunday School by mistake, one boy blurted out, Yes! And Fritzy bit the boar in the nuts!

House visitation didn't turn out as bad as the boys thought it would that year. They never did stop blushing as they sat quietly on the couch, but the grown-ups answered all the minister's questions before he could even think of turning to the boys. The young elder sat quietly with his eyes wide and his lips tight. He looked as if he had been stunned by an electric cattle prod. Of everyone in the parlor, he looked like the one to whom God had spoken most directly that day.

THE DREAM

One night the youngest boy dreamed that someone in his family would have to die. It was a law or something. He was not scared in the dream because there were many people in his family, and he, the quiet one, seemed least likely. He figured he would be the last to go.

Then the whole family decided that he was the one who should die. He ran away through the cornfields with everybody chasing him. They had buckets of gasoline they were going to throw on him and burn him.

His oldest brother caught him in the cornfield and was laughing. The rest of the family came running up behind, with gasoline spilling all over.

Then he woke up.

The next day the boy took a closer look at everyone around him. They did not look like people who would kill him now. They did not even look quite like the family in the dream. It was just a dream, he thought. But he did not say, Pass the potatoes. He did not ask them for anything.

WHAT IF

What would happen if you lit a fire in the haymow, took one of these matches and lit the hay here by the door, then sat in the door and yelled Fire! Or you could yell Help! and see who came running.

But what if you couldn't get the fire put out?

You could put it out. You just stamp on it with your foot, and it goes right out.

Nothing came of the talk that morning. It was just an idea. But a week later the boys found some twelve-gauge shotgun shells in the toolshed. If you give it a shake, one of them said, you can hear the BBs inside.

So they decided to get the BBs out. They peeled open the end, and out came the little black BBs. Then they noticed the shell was still not empty.

How do you get the rest of that stuff out? one of them asked. He stuck a nail inside the shell and got the little paper wadding out, but the dark, packed gunpowder was still inside the shell. They put the shell in the vice, then hammered with a nail, trying to chip the gunpowder out. It wouldn't chip out, but at least it didn't explode. They didn't know that the little cap on the other side, where the firing pin hits, is what made the shell explode.

Something distracted them—maybe a rat, or hunger, or boredom. They left the shotgun shell locked in the vice where the men found it later, along with the hammer and nail. The men figured out what the boys had been up to right away. They released the shell slowly, trying not to squeeze the firing cap. Their hands shook. They knew what might have happened, and they relived for an instant their own boyhoods, remembering the tree that fell the wrong way, the rope they almost didn't get loose from a friend's neck, the ice that was just as thin as they were told it was—all those moments of curiosity or ignorance that might have killed them. They chatted with each other about their own adventures, dropped in a few nervous chuckles, then coached each other toward anger and the work to be done.

THE HARVEST

At harvest time, things didn't go on in their usual way. The women came out of the houses and gardens wearing gloves, overalls, and shoes that were too big for them. But they were ready for work, ready to bring in what everyone had been waiting for.

Where did they learn to do all of these things? You never saw them on the tractors at other times. And now here they were, even driving catty-cornered across the picked corn rows at just the right angle so they wouldn't bounce off the seat—where'd they learn that trick? And for the oats harvest, somehow they knew how to shock bundles in perfect little tepees all over the stubble. They didn't try setting up four bundles at a time, but the bundles got set up—and set up so they didn't tip over in a wind. Some of them even pitched bundles—maybe not as fast as the men, but the women were fussier about getting the oats heads pointed into the threshing machine in a straight line. And who taught them to keep the cattle from sneaking out when a load of grain was being drawn through an open gate? As strange as they looked in those big clothes, they didn't waste any steps.

The men joked about how funny the women looked getting on a tractor or bending over in the field, and the boys laughed along with them.

But at night, when the women had to quit early to cook supper and clean up the houses, the boys moved in to take their places, figuring that at harvest time the fields would be as friendly to one hand as another. They couldn't throw bundles with the kind of muscle the men had, but they got some work done by trying to remember the way the women did it.

THAT COULD HAVE BEEN YOU

The boys knew that on the farm danger was everywhere, sometimes in the teeth of a spinning gear, other times in the jaws of a growling boar. Danger could plunge from the sky in jagged-edged hailstones or collapse beneath them in weak timbers over a well. Hay balers didn't care what they baled, and silage choppers didn't care what they chopped. But mostly the danger the boys knew was in stories about what happened somewhere, someplace, just out of sight, in the next county, down the road six miles, somewhere else. The bull that crushed a man against a gate. The woman who drowned trying to save her child from rushing spring floods. The man who broke his neck falling from the haymow. The tornado that killed a whole family except the two-month-old baby, who was found in a lilac bush without a scratch on her.

The boys listened to the stories, and they didn't argue with the truth of them. They'd had their own fair share of close calls. There was the eighty-pound hay bale that fell thirty feet and exploded in a green spray around them, and the lightning that splintered a huge box elder right after they decided to run out from under that very tree and play in the rain. Once a steel splinter from the corn sheller flywheel whirred like a table saw past their heads.

And they had their cuts and bruises. Knuckles that looked as if they'd been gnawed on by meat grinders. Sprained ankles and wrists. Blood blisters that took toenails and fingernails off as they healed. Small concussions that were good for weeklong headaches. Wood slivers of all sizes that had punctured every part of their bodies. And that's not even counting all the skinned knees and nose bleeds. The boys had plenty of bangings-around, but nothing so bad that they weren't able to talk about it, maybe even boast about it, the next week.

In town on Saturday nights, the grown-ups would point out what terrible things had happened to other people:

See those farmers with all those missing fingers? Cornpickers did that.

See that boy who doesn't have an arm in his sleeve? Power takeoff did that.

The evidence was everywhere: missing thises and missing thats. Hobblers and limpers and a scar-face or two. Farms tore lots of people up, no doubt about it.

Then the grown-ups would always come up with the clincher: That could have been you, they'd say. That could have been you.

Of course it could have been them. The boys knew that. They also knew that it was impossible to explain that they still lived without fear, lived as if every day held the promise of adventures in the sunlight, even if the sky was dark, even if the icicles hanging from the eaves on the barns could drop at any moment like dazzling swords and impale them, pinning them to the snow—the way one did to this twelve-year-old not so far away, just far enough away that the boys didn't know his name.

THE ROBIN'S NEST

Their grandfather was going to show them where a robin had built a new nest in the grove. They walked along, staring up into the leafy branches, when one of the boys tripped on something. His *ouch!* made everyone's eyes look down instead of up.

Until now it had been such a quiet and easy day, with the sun and breeze mixing together like whipped cream and sugar and spreading a sweetness over everything and everybody. Seeing the robin's nest with its pale blue eggs would have been what this day was all about. And now this.

The boy who tripped sat down and grabbed his foot.

Something sharp stuck out of the ground, a rusty pointed thing.

This is where we used to bury old equipment we didn't need anymore, said their grandfather. That's the tooth of an old dump rake trying to sneak back into the world.

The boy who had tripped saw that the others were finding the metal tooth more interesting than his misery. He got up and helped them pull on the tooth, which was curved like a sliver of moon—and when they pulled, it was as if they were unzipping the earth, which split open, and plant roots frayed out from the wound like tiny threads.

Look at that, said their grandfather. He kicked at the dirt they had loosened. He knelt down and started into the dirt. Look, he said, and held up what looked like a bent horseshoe. This is called a twisted clevis, he said.

He went back to digging. *This* is part of the knotter for the binder back in the days of threshing machines. And here's a piece of a corn shucker glove. See that little hook that would pull the husk back? And here's the sediment bulb off an old tractor.

The grandfather was acting like a dog going after a hidden bone, scratching away with his strong old hands as if digging up and naming this useless junk was good for something.

This here is from an old harrow, he said. Those there from a cream separator. Here's part of a stanchion lock. That's from a doubletree. See this? It's a gear from a derrick for lifting the fronts of wagons off the ground.

The boys watched and listened. What their grandfather was doing didn't make much sense. If you're going to throw things away and bury them, why not forget about them and do what you were going to do—which was find that robin's nest? But they waited, and after a while they could see that their grandfather must have gotten what he needed. He shoved dirt back over what he had dug up, brushed off his dirty hands, and looked up into the tree branches with them.

It sure is a nice day, he said. Perfect for finding a robin's nest. Now be quiet. We don't want to scare her away.

It occurred to the youngest boy, early in the morning when his mind was still swimming in daydreams, that there were two kinds of people in the world. It came to him very clearly: there are people who are always trying to give something, and there are people who are always trying to get something. Givers and getters, he called them in his daydreaming mind. His grandfather was a giver. If you saw him coming, you knew he had something to give, maybe some advice, maybe something he had made for you. A neighbor across the section was just the opposite. He was a getter. He was the one who mowed the grass along the railroad track because he could get that hay free. No wonder people called him a go-getter.

The youngest boy talked about his giver and getter ideas over breakfast.

The other boys laughed at him. There are two kinds of people in the world, said one, people who can find their socks and people who can't. The youngest boy knew which kind he was.

No, said another, there are two kinds of people in the world, people who are so stupid that they think there are only two kinds of people in the world, and people who aren't that stupid.

Maybe there was another set of two kinds of people, the youngest boy thought: the ones who make fun of and the ones who get made fun of.

The grown-ups put a stop to the talking. You want to talk about getting and giving? All of you *get* ready for church or we'll *give* you something to think about.

Good thing it was a Sunday, so the youngest boy could have plenty of time to be by himself, inside his own mind, while the preacher preached.

But the preacher said something so loud that the youngest boy couldn't daydream himself away from it: Go to the ant, thou sluggard, consider her ways and be wise.

That probably meant there were two kinds of people in the world: lazy people and workers. But would the workers be the givers or the getters? the youngest boy wondered.

There was an anthill in the grove, so the youngest boy went to the ant that afternoon to consider her ways. All the ants looked like real go-getters, just like the neighbor who tried to get his hands on everything he could get. But the ants didn't seem to be getting anything for themselves; they were hurrying back home to give what they had got, maybe even to the sluggards somewhere deep inside the little world of their anthill.

There are three kinds of people in the world, the youngest boy announced over supper: people who get, and people who give, and people who get to give.

One of the grown-ups said, Where did he pick *that* up?

THE PARROT

You didn't see something like this every day—a green and red parrot flying across the hog yards and landing on the pointy-topped metal grain bin. Just perching there and squawking as if it owned the place, as if it thought it could carry on like a noisy angel on top of a Christmas tree or something.

All the boys saw it. All the boys heard it. Look at that thing! they yelled. Then they ran to the house where the grown-ups were having afternoon coffee. Everyone ran outside to see and hear what the boys saw and heard. The parrot was gone.

It was big and green and yellow and red! shouted one of the boys.

And it went like *squawk squawk!* said another. It was right there on top of that metal grain bin.

But the parrot wasn't right there, or anywhere, and the grown-ups didn't have much patience with the idea of a parrot flying around the hog yards or perching on a grain bin. It wasn't even close to April Fools' Day, so this kind of nonsense, making everybody run outside for nothing, wasn't something they wanted any more of, did the boys understand that?

The grown-ups went back to the house to finish their coffee, but the boys set off to find the parrot which, so far, had done nothing but get them in trouble. They figured anything that big, with so many colors on it and with such a loud squawk, should be easy enough to find. When they first saw it flying over the hog yard, it hadn't really flown all that fast, and it flapped its wings so hard that it probably couldn't have gone very far without needing to stop to catch its breath.

They started by looking in the grove. Then they checked every barn and shed. Sometimes they stood and listened, waiting for the parrot to give itself away. Nothing. No red, green, or yellow feathers. And not a sound except the ordinary sounds of the sparrows chirping and the pigeons *ooo-googling* and the pigs scruffing around and the electrical transformer humming a little.

At supper nobody talked about the parrot. The next day the boys went looking for it again. Not a flutter. Not a squawk. They talked about the parrot among themselves—how big it was, how bright the colors were. They wondered if the hogs had seen it, and what they might have thought of it. They wondered if the parrot had flown over the cows, and what the cows would make of seeing a parrot in the pasture. And what would a pigeon or sparrow think? Would something as strange as a parrot on the farm be able to make friends with any of the animals?

A few days later, when they still hadn't seen any sign of the parrot, they started wondering what else it might have been. Could it have been a crow or something with some sort of colorful cloth it had picked up somewhere? Maybe a little girl's bright sweater? But what about the squawking? No birds around there made that kind of noise. When they weren't talking to each other about the parrot or whatever it was, they started wondering if they had seen or heard anything at all.

JACK DRISCOLL

Wanting Only to Be Heard

ASHELBY JUDGE WAS AN ODD NAME FOR A KID GROWING UP IN
northern Michigan, so we just called him by his last name, Judge. Everyone
did. In a way he always was holding court, pronouncing sentence: Kevin
Moriarty was a first-class cockroach, Jake Reardon a homo from the word
"go." He had once called me a dicksqueeze, but later he took it back, gladly,
he said, having indicted me prematurely. I was okay, he said, I really was,
that being the final verdict.

Judge was not easy sometimes, but I liked him. I liked his impatience
with boredom and the way he gathered all the pertinent information in
the end, the evidence to prove or discredit a story. He always proceeded
step by step, building an air-tight case for whatever he was defending or
attacking, whatever he was attempting to pin down. It wouldn't have surprised me, forty years later, to read he'd been appointed to the Supreme
Court. Judge Ashelby Judge. Or, for the sake of a joke, Judge Judge. I liked
famous names that repeated or almost did, names like Robin Roberts or
Ricky Ricardo, or even slant combos like Jack Johnson. The duplication
had a friendly ring, a sense of conviction and rectitude, the feeling that
they really knew who they were and liked it and would never entirely grow
up, grow old.

It was a Friday night, no wind for a change, and we were fishing smelt,
three of us inside my father's shanty, when Judge told me and Timmy
Murphy about the claustrophobic Irish setter who, after being locked
all afternoon in a fishing hut on Torch Lake, jumped right through the
spearing hole just after dark and, ten or twelve feet under the ice, swam
toward the faint, opalescent glow of another shanty almost fifty yards away
(someone later measured it) and came bursting up there from the muck
like some monster awakened, the water swelling, convulsing up over the
wooden floor. That one simile, "like a monster," was the only embellish-
ment, Judge's single artistic touch.

He was not a natural storyteller who teased his listeners by saying,
"imagine this," or "pretend that," or "just think if," and on and on, suspend-

ing their willingness to imprint the local tales into myth. He despised the "what then, what next" demands made on every story. Which was exactly what Timmy was doing, all excited and ahead of himself as usual: "What'd the guy do? Holy shit, I bet he croaked right there. I can't believe it, a dog under the ice. That's great!" Judge, calculatedly slow and flat, said the guy was plenty scared, who wouldn't be, but not berserk scared the way you might expect. He was old, Judge said—a simple observation of fact, like what day it was or how cold. He never speculated that age buffered the body's reaction to shock or trauma, but I translated it that way anyhow, without thinking. "Who cares?" Timmy asked. "Twenty, fifty-seven, a hundred-and-two years old. It doesn't matter." But it did, the way it mattered that the dog was an Irish setter and male and was abandoned by his owner who loved him but hadn't gotten any fish, and instead of a quick trip to the 7-Eleven for a six-pack of Stroh's, he drank away the afternoon, alone in a bar that said just that in red neon, BAR, just outside Bellaire, forgetting the dog, and playing, over and over on the free jukebox, Patsy Cline's "Walking After Midnight." Which was about the time he left the bar, broke and drunk, and halfway home remembered the dog and right there, on I-37, opened his window full for the few seconds it took him to slow down and power slide into the other lane, the pickup fishtailing back up the gradual incline beneath the stars, the hook of the moon. And it mattered that he honked his horn a couple of times from the lake's edge, his shanty invisible somewhere beyond the white perimeter of his high beams. That was the *real* story, that sadness, and the way the guy, on both knees, fiddled with the combination lock until his fingers went numb, the whole time talking to the dog who wasn't even there. When he finally opened the door and lit the lantern, the white flame hissing in the mantle, he stepped back outside and screamed the dog's name a single time across the emptiness.

Judge said you could measure a story by its private disclosures, by how far a person came forward to confess a part of himself, asking forgiveness. The dramatics meant nothing, those exaggerations that served only to engage our obvious and temporary fascinations. And he continued, refining the art of meticulous detachment from such a rare and bizarre event, saying he didn't care what the Irish setter looked like emerging—a giant muskie or sturgeon or a red, freshwater seal. "The fact is," he repeated, "it was a hundred-pound dog. That's it, cut and dried!" I thought maybe the "cut and dried" part was a pun, and I smiled until Timmy, really miffed, said, "You take away all the magic. You make everything too real, too damn ordinary." But Timmy was at least partly wrong. There was something principled about facts, something stark and real that required nothing but itself to survive. Maybe that's why I liked *Dragnet* so much, the claim that it was a true story, that the sentence handed down after the last TV commercial was really being served. I thought of that while leaving the shanty, to pee and to check the tip-ups set for browns behind us in the dark. My father let me and my buddies use the shanty on weeknights while he worked at the Fisk. Usually he'd drop us off at the state park, and we'd take turns dragging the sled with the minnow bucket and spud and the gallon can of stove gas straight toward the village of fifty or sixty tiny structures in a cluster set over the deep water. It was easy to find my father's shanty because it was separated a little ways from the others, and because of the spoked hubcap from a Cadillac Eldorado he'd nailed to the door. His house sign, he called it. Other guys had other things, and it was fun to traipse around at night out there, just looking around, the world glaciated, frozen so tight you could feel your breath clinging to the fine hairs on your face. The name of each owner and town he was from was painted on every shanty—that was the law—some from as far south as Clare, though those were the ones that were not used very much. Sometimes as you passed you could hear talking from inside, or good laughter, or country music on the radio, and when you returned to the heat of your own hut, maybe you'd be humming a certain song, surprised by how happy you were, how peaceful, knowing that you belonged. I figured that was why my father decided to fish again after all these years, why he spent most of every weekend out here, calm and without worries.

That wasn't the feeling, however, when I stepped back inside and Judge and Timmy were both just staring into the rectangular hole, staring at the blue rubber-band bobbers and saying nothing. The smelt pail was still empty and half the minnows in the other bucket had turned belly up. My father would have said no big deal, that smelt would go for the dead bait just as good if they were feeding, but either Judge or Timmy, having already given up, had entered a big *O*, a goose egg, in the calendar square for February 12th. On good nights you loaded up fast, constant action, and on the homemade speed reels you could bring in two or three smelt at a time, every few minutes without a break. Just three nights earlier my father had recorded 268, and that was by himself. That's how it happened, streaky and unpredictable, and you simply had to like being out there, maybe sharing a Pall Mall around or talking girls if that's what mystery happened to be biting. But on this night of the Irish setter story, everything had gone closemouthed.

"No flags," I said, latching the door and hanging the gaff on a hook above the stove. This was Judge's first time ice fishing, and I knew he was bored—knew it even better when he said to Timmy, "Why not?" responding to whether a person (forget the dog) could survive the thirty-three-degree water long enough to swim from this shanty to the one closest by, the one that said M. KULANDA, KALKASKA, MI, the largest one on the ice. I'd never seen anybody there, not once.

"Houdini stayed under twenty minutes," Judge said, "under the Detroit River. No wetsuit. Nothing but a pair of pants."

"What was he doing there? A trick?" Timmy asked.

"An escape," Judge corrected, and although Timmy argued, "Trick, escape, whatever he did . . . ," I understood the difference, the dangerous mishandling of a single word so that a story softened, collapsed like a fragile set of lungs.

"Houdini said later he sucked the air pockets, bubbles trapped between the water and ice, and with the current, followed his dead mother's voice until he emerged, a quarter mile downriver." Judge was still staring into the thick, dark water while he talked, until Timmy, excited, just like at first with the Irish setter story, said, "You're shitting me!" Judge, looking up finally, straight-faced and serious, said, "I shit you not," as if under oath, and they both went silent as if the naked truth of Houdini and the Irish setter were tempting them to find out.

It started simple as that, and next thing I knew we were pacing off the distance between the shanties. About thirty yards. I had once stayed underwater in the bathtub for as long as I could, just sliding back holding my nose. I counted a minute and forty-four seconds, long seconds—one, one thousand two, one thousand three, the facecloth kind of floating back and forth across my stomach. And sneaking into the Camp Ketch-A-Tonk swimgrounds one night last summer, I breast stroked real close to the sandy bottom, from the Great Raft all the way up to shore. My father did it too, swimming behind me, and without coming up for air he turned and swam halfway back. I was scared, the way you get when someone's been down a long time, maybe just monkeying around, but scaring you just the same. I remembered whispering, "Come up, please come up," and he did, beyond the blue lifeline, gracefully rolling onto his back in a single motion and kicking, eyes closed I imagined, straight out toward whatever secret had surfaced in his memory. That's how it is with the mind, always buoyant, bobbing up and down on that complex sea of recollection.

Judge knocked on Kulanda's door, but nobody was there. "Nobody has been," Timmy said, trying to take charge. "Look around. No footprints anywhere." And I noticed there were no bloodstains from trout or pike tossed into the snow, no frozen minnows. Nothing. The shanty was un-locked, a lousy idea, my father always lectured, every time he'd see a door blown open, slapping backwards hard against its hinges. He said that only invited trouble, people snooping around, poking their heads in where they didn't belong, which was exactly what we were doing and I didn't like it and said, "Come on you guys, let's go. Let's get out of here." But when Timmy stepped inside with the lantern, the hut was nearly empty, unused, the kind that just got left sitting there until the ice softened toward spring, and one morning it would be gone forever. Who knows, maybe the owner died or got sick or one Sunday started watching the Pistons on TV with his son-in-law and thought, "Screw the fishing," and that was that for the whole season.

Timmy said, "The guy's got a couch in here," and when he sat down he was staring at a calendar hanging on the opposite wall. It was the kind of calendar I first saw in a gas station in Germfask when my father's station wagon broke down. We were there a good part of the afternoon while the garage owner phoned around until he finally located a water pump at a junkyard in Greighton. The owner's kid drove over to pick it up, and while our fathers small-talked engines and horsepower and cubic inches, I snuck into the men's room three or four times to examine, close-up, this woman who was showing me everything, her lips parted just enough to show the pink edge of her tongue. The last time I stepped out my father was waiting by the door and he told me, "Pee out back. I don't want you in there anymore." And that was the feeling I had again in Kulanda's abandoned shanty, of wanting to be there and not, both at the same time. Timmy lowered the lantern to the ice, right under the calendar where the fishing hole should have been, really lighting up the glossy nude, and he said, acting the big shot for this lucky find, "I'd swim anywhere if I could surface between legs like that!"

But it was Judge who decided to really do it, and when my father dropped us off again the next night, we brought, along with the fishing gear, a book on Houdini and a *National Geographic* that showed people in swimsuits running toward the Atlantic Ocean from a snowy beach, in Rhode Island, I think. And Judge talked on and on about some Mr. Maslowski who chopped a large, round hole in the ice of his man-made pond, and letting the same red towel drop behind him, he'd hold his hands flat to the sides of his thighs, and each morning, without hesitation, he'd step right through over his head. "For his rheumatism," Judge said. "He worshiped what he called 'certitude,' the ancient and natural cure taking place under the world." Judge had done his homework, covering the Polar Bear Club and U.S. Navy ice divers, the whole time spouting off dates and temperatures and distances, building his case until I believed there was hardly any danger after the initial shock of entering, and he said, staring at me, "You'll be my key witness." And to Timmy, "Who knows what you'll see."

Of course we wanted to see everything: the entry, the look of his eyes behind the mask the instant he surfaced in Kulanda's shanty. But most of all we wanted desperately to watch him moving under the ice, so later that week Judge waterproofed a flashlight with candle wax and electrician's tape, and tested it by lowering the light about twenty feet under the ice. Then Timmy turned off the Coleman lantern and we just stared, all three of us in complete darkness, at that dim glimmer wavering back and forth below us, slow motion, soporific. Judge was the first to speak, his unquestionable right now, presiding and authoritative, factitious as always, but Timmy was making no objections anymore. Judge said, "It works," and we just nodded, accomplices who had learned to listen closely, to rehearse every detail at night in our dreams. "We'll fasten the light to my back," Judge said, "and you guys can walk right above me."

Although we didn't actually fish anymore that week, we'd make up numbers and jot them down each night on my father's calendar, keeping the records current: 114, 226, and—a slow night, Timmy's entry—27. "Just to keep things honest," he said, and we laughed, sitting and clowning around and smoking Pall Malls in what now seemed more like a fort, a refuge—not from the gusting wind, but from the predictable, ordinary things we might have done late after school, like playing ping-pong in Timmy's basement, or being home alone tinkering with science projects, or making up a story for English—something sensational and dangerous and totally unbelievable. And whenever my father asked about the fishing I'd tell him Judge and Timmy were splitting up the smelt, taking them home. "Good," he said, as though it were the proper courtesy, the way to make and keep good friends.

If Judge had moments of panic, he never let on, not even on the night of his dive, the Saturday my father decided to work OT. He dropped us at the State Park as usual and asked, "You got a ride back?"—and Timmy said, "Yep, my father's picking us up," which was true, but he was coming later than usual. He wouldn't be here until eleven. I don't know why we wanted the extra time, I really don't. Maybe to change our minds, or to deny, as Judge would have been the first to point out, that redemption had anything to do with danger, with the spectacular moments in a life. But that didn't happen. We felt transformed, faithful to the careful preparation of an entire week, and when we started across the ice toward the village, we believed those two shanties were ours, and ours to swim between if we wanted, the way you might swim deep under a cliff in order to come up in a secret cave. After the first time, it would be easy. And we felt all set, having already stashed an extra heater and lantern, an army blanket, and towels in Kulanda's, and we'd hung a thermometer on the same nail that held what Judge was calling Timmy's porno queen, but I'd seen him peeking from the couch at those hard nipples, too, or at the red mercury rising slowly between her breasts after we'd fired the heater up. Right now chips of ice were bouncing off her paper flesh as Timmy started to spud the hole, Judge's exit, and Judge and I left him there and headed for the other hut. But Judge stopped halfway and said, "No hurry," and we stood there, watching the lights of houses blink on the far side of the lake. I felt calm as the lights vanished and appeared again, floating, I thought, behind a cold vapor of darkness. And I could hear Timmy in Kulanda's shanty, a strange *thud, thud*, as though coming from a great distance, and already we'd begun walking even farther away.

By the time Timmy got to my father's hut he was breathing heavily, but he laughed real hard at Judge just sitting there in his white boxers, the flashlight already taped to his back like a dorsal fin. "All you need now are scales," Timmy said, taking off his gloves and coat, and Judge, reaching into his knapsack, said, "This will have to do," and pulled out a tub of ball-bearing grease and said, "Cover me real good," scooping the first brown gob himself with his fingers and sculpting it up and down one arm. Then he stood there, arms out, and me and Timmy did the rest, each a skinny side, and Judge, still joking around, said, "Save a little for my dick," and Timmy said, "A little is all you'll need," as I knelt and reached my greasy hand into the freezing water to see if this translucent coating really helped, and for that second I was terrified of falling in, the rectangular hole seeming so much like a grave, calm and so carefully ladled out. And without them seeing me, I crossed myself, as my father had taught me to do every, every time before entering strange water.

When I stood up, Timmy, having taken charge of things in Kulanda's shanty, had left again, and Judge was wiping his hands clean on a rag. Then he knotted the white clothesline around his waist—knotted it a couple of times, nothing fancy, but I knew by the way he tugged it wasn't coming free. Still, I wanted something thicker, stronger, a new length of rope, a boat line maybe. Judge said he just needed something to follow back if he got lost or in trouble. It didn't need to be strong. The other end was already tied off around the single roof brace, the rest of the clothesline coiled in wide loops on the floor. Nobody needed to be there to watch or feed it out. It would uncoil smoothly, trailing behind him, a long umbilical cord. Judge, the literalist, would have hated the metaphor, as he would have hated me telling him he looked a little like the creature in *The Creature from the Black Lagoon*, standing there. But he did, primordial and weedy-green in the bright light of the lantern, breathing hard now, hyperventilating for whatever extra oxygen he could squeeze into his lungs. I thought there would be some talk, a final go-over of the details, maybe even a last-minute pardon from this craziness if my father would unexpectedly burst in. But it was Timmy, back again and out of breath, who said, "All set," and Judge simply reached back without hesitation, snapped on the flashlight, then pushed the mask with both hands to his face for better suction and stepped under. I wasn't even sure it happened—he disappeared that fast, without a single word or even a human splash, as though all that body grease had dissolved his bones, his skull, the entire weight of him so that only a ghost drifted under the ice, a vague iridescence.

When we got outside Judge was moving in the right direction. All winter the winds had blown the snow from the ice, so we could see the blurry light down there, and Timmy had one of his own which he kept blinking on and off to let Judge know we were there, right above him, ready to guide him home. The moon was up too, and suddenly the distance to Kulanda's shanty did not seem so far, not with Judge already halfway there and Timmy, all wound up and hooting, "He's got it made, he's got it now!" It was right then Judge's light conked out, and we both stopped, as if Judge would surface there. Neither of us wanted to move, afraid, I think, that we would step on him in the dark and send him deeper, and when we started running for Kulanda's, I circled wide, way behind where Judge would be, hoping he wouldn't hear the slapping panic of our boots, the fear inside us struggling desperately to break free.

Timmy pumped and pumped the lantern until I thought the glass globe would explode. Then he held it just inches above the black water, and he seemed to be staring at the nude, staring all the way through her as if counting each vertebra, the soft curves of her back, and I knew Judge was not coming up. I didn't have to tell Timmy to stay. He was crying now. He was all done, and I think if Judge had surfaced right then, Timmy would have just dropped the lantern and walked away and would never have spoken of this again.

I slipped and fell hard, almost knocking myself out, and in that moment of dizziness, face down on the ice, I imagined Judge staring back, just ten inches away, his black hair wavering in moonlight, his eyes wide-open behind his mask. And I imagined him pointing and pointing, and I got up and ran, sweating now, into my father's shanty. I believed the rope twitched or pulsed when I picked it up, something like a nibble, but when I yanked back there was nothing there, just the loose arc of slack, and I remembered my father always shouting from the stern of the boat, "Reel hard, keep reeling," when I thought I'd lost a big one, and this time the weight was there, solid and unforgiving. It was the same heavy feeling of a snag that begins to move just when you're sure it will bust your line, and I knew that bulk dragged backwards was enough to snap any line with a nick or fray, and to hurry was to lose it all. I kept it coming, hand over hand, Judge's body drifting sideways, then back again, always rising slowly from the deep water. I shouted for Timmy four or five times, tilting my head backwards and toward the door, but he did not come. And it was during one of those shouts that the flashlight on Judge's back appeared in the center of the hole, then the whole back hunched in a deadman's float. I could not get him up, my arms weak and shaking, and I hauled back one last time and dropped the rope and grabbed, all in the same motion, his thick hair with both my hands, his face finally lifting out of the water.

His mask was gone and I just held him like that for a long time, one arm under his chin, the lantern dimming. I was stretched on my belly, our cheeks touching, and I had never felt anything so cold, so silent. I knew mouth-to-mouth resuscitation would do Judge no good in this position, his lungs full of water, so maybe I was really kissing him, not trying to reclaim a heartbeat, but to confess, as Judge said, a part of myself, and to ask forgiveness. I did not know how long I could hold him there, though I promised over and over I would never let him slide back to that bottom, alone among those tentacles of weeds. I closed my eyes, and in what must have been a kind of shock or sleep, I drifted into a strange current of emptiness, a white vaporous light, the absolute and lovely beginning of nothing.

I did not see the two ice fishermen hoist Judge from the hole, and I did not remember being carried to Kulanda's shanty or being wrapped in the army blanket on the couch. I awakened alone there, still dizzy but very warm. I was wearing Judge's sweatshirt, the one we had waiting for him when he came up. I did not take it off or even move very much, and I could hear my father's voice just outside the door, though it sounded distant, too, and dull, the blunt echo of a voice approaching. I thought, if he entered, the flood of his words would drown me for good. But only silence followed him in. I did not look up and I did not cry when he touched my head, or when he turned away to face the wall. There would be no sermonizing, no interrogation from him or from anyone else. Not that night anyway. And I noticed, eye-level across from me, that the nude was gone, removed like evidence we didn't want found. The cigarette butts on the floor had disappeared too. And it sounded strange to hear someone knock on the door. My father did not say, "Come in," but a man did, an ambulance driver, and he bent down on one knee and said, "How do you feel now?" I didn't know, but I said, "Good," and I wanted more than anything in the world for the three of us just to stay there, maybe all night, making sure the hole did not freeze over.

Next morning, as we walked together toward the shanties, my father said, "Tell them everything exactly like it happened. There's only one story." What he meant was that the options narrowed and narrowed when the ending was already known.

"They won't keep us long," my father said. "We'll get back home." I thought he might add, "For the Pistons-Celtics game," but he didn't.

It was Sunday morning and sunny, and up ahead, off to the left, I saw a red flag go up from the ice, then someone running toward the tip-up, shaking his gloves off. I watched him set the hook, and after a few seconds, with his left hand, move the gaff a little bit away from the hole. "Probably a pike," my father said, and I was glad he did, so natural, without the conviction of disguise.

There were not all that many people gathered at the shanties, not the way I thought it would be with a lot of photographers and sheriff's department deputies. Timmy was already there. I could see his green hat and his arms flailing like an exhausted swimmer, and for that split second I imagined he was yelling, "Help, help me," and I started to run, not toward him, but the other way, back toward the car. My father caught me from behind, caught me first by the collar, then wrapped both his arms around me and turned me back slowly to face Timmy and whatever version he was carving of the story. My father just held me there and released the pressure gradually and then, after a couple minutes, let me go.

His shanty had been moved back, and two divers were adjusting their masks at the side of the hole. I did not know what they were searching for, what more they could possibly find. But they jumped through, one after the other as Judge had, but with black wetsuits and yellow tanks and searchlights sealed with more than candle wax and electrician's tape. The sheriff met us and shook my hand and my father's hand and said Judge's parents were not there and wouldn't be. Then he said, "We've called Marv Kulanda," as though he knew him personally. "He's on his way."

I was okay after that. They kept me and Timmy separated, though we caught each other's eye a couple times. The two fishermen who pulled Judge out kept nodding a lot, and once they pointed at me, both of them did, then shrugged, and they finally left, to fish and talk, I guess, since they walked that way into the village of shanties. I knew the stories wouldn't be the same, but not the same in a way that didn't matter to the law.

The sheriff asked me about approximate times: how long before Timmy ran for help, how long I held Judge partially out of the water—all questions I couldn't answer, and that seemed to be all right. But before he let me go he said, "Whose idea was this?" It was the first time he spoke without detachment, accusatory now, and I did not deny that it was me, though it wasn't, my father the whole time shaking his head, shaking it back and forth, no, no, insisting that could never be.

Before the first diver was helped out of the hole, he tossed Judge's mask a few feet onto the ice, and then, behind it—crumpled into a pulpy ball—what I knew was the calendar nude. I didn't know why that frightened me so much, except that it was a detail I had consciously left out, perhaps to protect Timmy's secret need to destroy the crime of her nakedness, one of the reasons we stayed there and smoked cigarettes and talked big in front of her, already outlining the plans of our story. When the sheriff unwadded the nude she fell apart, and he just shook the wet pieces from his hands. In his investigation for details, she meant nothing—a piece of newspaper, a bag, anything that might have floated by.

We left and my father said, "It's over," and I knew he'd protect me from whatever came next. Behind us I could hear them nailing my father's shanty closed, and I could see, angling beyond us from the shore, a single man, half stepping and half sliding across the ice. I knew that it was Kulanda, who should have locked his hut, who was wishing at that very moment that we had broken in. And beyond him, running between the avenues of shanties, a single dog, tall and thin and red like an Irish setter. But maybe not. Maybe he was something else, barking like that, wanting only to be heard.

JOHN EDGAR WIDEMAN

Concert

DEATH DRAPES THE STAGE LIKE ALL THOSE THINGS YOU KNOW YOU MUST do when the performance is over.

Buck called.

Your mother, man. It's your mother . . .

Shit, Buck. Don't say it. Buck your magic twanger.

Everybody in the auditorium on their feet now. Putting their hands together. You'll catch the first fast train out of here. The piano man and bass player wink, nod and mouth words at each other like lovers across a crowded room. You hear again the groan of him slicing the bow across the fat belly of the bass. Screeching halt. A trolley stop when the treacly ballad threatened to la-di-da forever and with one throaty gasp, one pen stroke the bassist ended it. One man, one vote. Everybody out. You consider the formality of their dress. Tux. Black tie. How the starched white shirtfronts sever their dark heads. Cannonballs dropped in the snow. You commiserate. Monkey suits. Monkeyshines. How many one-night stands in front of all these strangers. Who listen. Who applaud. What. Inside the elevator of their music. Going up. Down. The brothers too smooth to move. Wearing refrigerators. Laid out ice elegant on cooling boards. Got a letter this morning, how do you reckon it read? How do you reckon it read? That letter. This morning.

Can you hear me? Lots of static on the line. I can barely . . .

Why are they costumed as pallbearers? Why the morticians' manners? Have they been pulling legs so long they don't have one left to stand on? You think of Africans down on their knees scrabbling for grains of wheat dribbling from gunnysacks slabbed on a U.N. relief truck. You imagine those skeletons inside these formal suits. The high-butt shuffle of the xylophone man tells you which corner and which year and which city he hails from. Surely as the zebra's wobbly gait in his zoo pen recalls haul-assing across a Serengeti plain. The thinnest note's too heavy for those African ghosts to bear. They shiver in the shivering heat and expire. You are left alone shimmering till he bops the metal plate again. Bell ringer. Stinger. Big Bopper. Word Dropper. Quells the vibrations with his padded mallet.

One last tune. From our latest album. Available now at your record store. That was, by the way, a commercial, ha, ha. A composition we've entitled . . .

Buck, Buck.

It's ten here. Two hours difference.

If I hurry home, it won't have happened yet.

Do you remember driving into the City? From Philly over the bridges into Jersey. Flat out up the pike then the tunnel. Didn't it seem everybody going our way, headed for the same place? All those cars and trucks and buses, man. Planes in the air. Trains. Close to Newark you could even see ocean liners. Every damn form of transportation known to man, man. And every kind of high. All making it to the City. Unanimous. The people's choice. And you were there in that number. Doing it, boy. Shoom. Kicking the Jersey turnpike. Pedal to the metal. Radio already there and sending back waves. Chasing. Chased. Won't it be something when all these folks pour down through the tunnel and we're each and all of us packed into the same tight squeeze of our destination. The Five Spot. Lintons. The Village Gate. Miracle of planes trains buses cars ships arriving and checking in and checking out the scene. I can't wait. Nobody can. Ghosts boogie through the marshes. A nasty KKK greeting scrawled in four-foot-tall letters on an overpass. We see city lights braced for us. A line of hostiles on the horizon deciding whether they'll let us pass or swoop down and burn the wagons.

How long ago was that, Buck? I haven't forgotten any of it. Not that long ago, really. I was in college, first in my family, first splib this and that, the early sixties first time I checked these guys out. Now the bass player's head is bowed, his eyes closed. Is he remembering my dream? Piano man, bottom lip belled, sputters like a trumpet as he gazes down at the intricate journeying of his long fingers. I notice the bass man's hair is thinning, even worse than mine, over the crown of his skull. Brown skin dropped over his eyes blinds him. Two sightless bubbles transfix the audience. When he can't sleep he counts the fences his four fingers have jumped over, his dangling thumb along for the ride. Oh, it's a long way from May to December. So willow. Willow weep for me. I think *Ashanti* describes the bass man because the word sounds spare, sparse, taut. Quiver attached to the fiddle holds an arrow he will shoot into someone's heart. Wheels turning behind his blind eyes choose the victim. *Ashanti* because he's a warrior. Hard. Pitiless. His eyes rolled back into his skull. Madness. Ecstasy. The blank mask surveys us. Choosing a target. Nothing reveals what the hidden eyes think of us yet we know our measure is being taken, know that part of us begs to be seen by someone else in order to be real. We're in mortal danger if no mirror remembers us, reminds us what to do next.

Buck. Buck.

Listen, man. I've got something important to tell you. Your mother, man.

Wait. Let me tell you this dream I've been scoping lately. See, you call me on the phone. I'm sitting in a theater. Not a movie theater. A theater theater. Phone rings. I'm aware as I start to answer it that I'm listening to music. Jazz. Chamber ensemble jazz. Like a string quartet. You dig. Like maybe the M.J.Q. Phone rings but I don't want to miss the music. I hesitate. Or maybe I already have the phone at my ear. I'm unhappy because I'm about to miss the concert, but, you know, once I answered or decided to answer I wasn't hearing the music anyway, so shit. I say hello. Hello who is it? Kind of in a hurry. Annoyed you know because I've been interrupted. Then you come on.

Buck. Buck, is that you?

She's gone, man.

Buck your magic twanger.

Then I look at the stage. The musicians are in tuxedos. You know. Like penguins. And the darkness is not behind them. Darkness is this crisp sharp hard kind of foreground and the stage is behind it. I think maybe a steel curtain is pulled in front of the four players, four of them, a quartet. I think that's what's strange, different about the way the four of them look. They are marooned far away behind this darkness. The black curtain has been scissored precisely to surround each silhouette, then seamlessly each player's been sewn into the fabric. But a curtain wouldn't hang that way. A curtain has drapes and folds, people need room to move and breathe so what I saw was crazy. Something inside of me says no. I can't be seeing what I'm seeing, what I think I see. My eyes readjust. Do a double take, you know. Figure-ground reversal. Fish become birds, or birds fish. Except once you make up your mind which it is, ain't no going back. You say, Show me something else, this doesn't make sense. Then you're stuck with what you got. The paper-thin men and thin paper cut-out black screen come together in another way so I can deal with what was up there on the stage.

It happened much quicker than I can tell it. I never heard words, myself talking to myself. Just that blink. That click. Before I can say, Hey, wait a minute. This ain't right. Click. It's back to normal. I'm holding the phone. It's you. The players are three-dimensional again. Onstage. Not projected on a screen. Not millions of white specks and black specks floating, dancing. Their suits are not the curtain. Faces not holes punched in the snow. The stage is not wearing them anymore. I'm getting all that mess resolved in my mind. La-di-da. But it's costing me. I can't go back. Dizzy almost. My heart's thumping. I worry about everybody in the family's high blood pressure. And there's still you on the phone.

Buck. Are you there? Zat you?

I'm scared to pick up the receiver. I've already been through the conversation and I don't want to hear bad news again. The phone rings and rings but I don't hear a thing. I can't hang up. Because I haven't picked up yet. The piece playing I know the title of because the xylophone man just said it. Or part of the title. Europe's in it. Milan. Streets of Milano. Or Milano Afternoon. I heard it announced. Before. When I was paying attention. Before you rang. Before I started getting sick inside my self and looking for an exit.

Did you ever think of titles as premonitions? Threats. Destiny. Most come after I've written or told a story many times but occasionally the first words name everything else that follows. And stop me when I've said enough. A threat. A destination. I might as well say it all. A title can be like death. Like dying and being born at the same time.

The audience begins to file out. Some people stand at their seats clapping but when it becomes clear the musicians aren't going to play anymore no matter how long or loud we applaud, the trick of slapping one hand against the other, like hundreds of trained seals, starts to feel—first to one, then another and finally to the entire group—like a silly way to behave. One hand continues clapping in the void but all the rest split, leaving me stuck with the phone in mine, unplayed and exhausted passages of concert in my brain, a fear, a withering godawful fright that something terrible has happened or was going to happen.

Ping. Ping. The Chinese water torture drop of the phone no one is left to answer but me in the bright hall.

On the other hand some tunes need no introduction.

LIZA WIELAND

The Columbus School for Girls

"IT'S THE OLDEST STORY IN AMERICA," MR. JERMAN SAYS, "ONLY NO one seems to know it. When Christopher Columbus went to ask Queen Isabella to bankroll his voyage to the east, she just laughed at him, and she told him it was about as likely he could make that trip as it was that he could make an egg stand on its end. But that Columbus, he said, okay Isabella, watch closely. And he took out an egg—the one he always carried for state occasions just like this—and tapped it ever so gently on one end, not enough to shatter it, but enough to flatten that end just slightly, and there the egg stood, and Isabella gave Columbus the dough, and the rest is history."

We love this story, and we love the teacher who tells it to us and girls like us, year after year at The Columbus School for Girls. We love the way he stands over the lectern at Chapel, right in front of the red-and-white banner that says *Explore thyself!* below the headmaster's favorite words of wisdom, copied from money, IN GOD WE TRUST. We like to sit left of center and close one eye. Half-blind we see Mr. Jerman's face like a hieroglyph in the midst of wisdom, a blessed interruption, and the words say IN GOD WE RUST.

We don't care much for the other teachers, the ones who tell us to spit out our chewing gum, pull up our knee socks, and button our blouses all the way up, the ones who warn us we'll never amount to anything. We know how they fear us—we're walking danger to them, the way we whoop in the halls, the way we dance in slow circles to no music—but still they dream of having us for their daughters, of taking us home and seeing what, given the proper tools and rules, we might become. We smoke cigarettes in the bathroom. We've been known to carry gin in vanilla bottles and have a swig or two after lunch.

Mr. Jerman, though—we would be his daughters in a heartbeat. We would change our names, we would all become Jermans. We would let his wife, Emily Jerman, be the mother of us all. We see her rarely, at wind-ensemble concerts, at dances, and at field-hockey games, standing on the sidelines behind the opposing team. Tiny thin Emily Jerman, always so cold that we'd like to build a fire right at her feet. Emily Jerman, always wearing one of her husband's sweaters, smiling at us, leaning her thin bones against her husband's arm and talking into his ear in a voice we've never heard but guess must sound like baby birds. We want to be like her, so we steal our fathers' sweaters, our brothers' sweaters, our boyfriends'. We let ourselves grow thin. Emily Jerman and Bryan Jerman—we say their names over and over at night into the darkness of the Upper Five Dormitory where the air is already hazy with girls' breath. We pass his name between the beds—*have you had Bryan Jerman yet?*—like he's something you could catch.

In the morning when we wake up, their names are still hanging over us, and it's still November, always November. November is by far the cruelest month at The Columbus School for Girls. By then nothing is new anymore, not the teachers, not the books, not the rules and the bravest ways to break them. November is Indian summer, and then it's rain. November, Mr. Jerman says, is longing, and we agree. We long for Thanksgiving, but we don't know why, because it will only lead to real winter, killer winter when nothing moves. All month, we long to go back to the days when our school uniforms were new and tight across our hips, when our notebooks were empty, when no one had discovered us yet.

"Girls," Mr. Jerman says in the middle of this cruel November, "I have been thinking about you."

We could say the same thing, especially since he has been reading us Emily Dickinson these past weeks. We have come to think of Emily Dickinson as Emily Jerman and vice versa. We whisper about Emily Jerman's closet full of white dresses and her strange ideas about certain birds and flowers and angleworms. We think this must be what Emily Jerman does all day in the bungalow behind Lower Four Dormitory: she writes hundreds of poems on the backs of school memoranda that Mr. Jerman has folded and torn in quarters, just the right size for one of her poems about yellow daisies beheaded by winter, that white assassin.

"I have been thinking," Mr. Jerman says again, "that we need to do a little more exploring. We have been sitting like bumps on logs reading these poems when we could do so much more."

We look at him, making our smiles bright and trusting the way we think he must like them, letting him lead us on.

"I could take you to Emily Dickinson's house," Mr. Jerman says, and we lean forward over our desks. It feels like he's invited us into his own home. "If you're interested, I can call up there this afternoon. We can take one of the school vans. I'm sure my wife would love to come along too. She's always wanted to go there."

We can imagine. We can imagine Emily Jerman going to the home of her namesake, her other, her true self. We can imagine our own selves being the Jermans' daughters for a whole weekend, far away from The Columbus School for Girls, deep in what we think must be the savage jungle of western Massachusetts.

Mr. Jerman has a hard time convincing the headmaster to let us go. We listen to them discuss it late the next afternoon while we're waiting for tardy slips.

"Bryan," the headmaster is saying, "think about it. All of *them*. And just you and Emily. What if something happens? What if one of them goes berserk? Or gets arrested? Or smuggles along contraband?"

"Leo," Mr. Jerman says, "nonsense. The girls will be perfect ladies. It will be good for them to get out, see some more of the world. And Emily will be along to take care of any, you know, girl problems."

"I just don't think so," the headmaster says. "I'm not sure these are girls you can trust."

"Rust," we say.

"Of course I can trust them," Mr. Jerman says. "That gin at lunchtime business is all a made-up story. They're chafing at the bit a little, that's all. This trip will be just the thing. I've told their parents to call you about it."

"Oh God, Bryan," the headmaster says.

"Oh God," we say.

"Girls," the headmaster's secretary says, "you know there's none of that on school grounds."

The telephone on the secretary's desk rings in a stifled *brrrr*. We're sure it's our parents—all of them making one huge impossible conference call to tell the headmaster to keep us at this school forever, until we grow old and die. We can't stand it anymore. We forge the signatures on our tardy slips and beat it to smoke cigarettes behind Lower Four. From there we can see the Jermans' bungalow, and we keep smoking until Mr. Jerman comes home. We think his shoulders look awfully slumped, and we notice, too, the way the fiery late-afternoon light seems to have taken all the color out of his face. The front door opens, and Emily Jerman is standing there, a yellow halo surrounding her whole tiny body from head to toe. When she reaches up to touch Mr. Jerman's face, we try to look away but we can't. Our eyes have become hard cold points of darkness fixed on them, on their tenderness, and learning it. Emily and Bryan Jerman go inside their bungalow and the door closes. We watch them move from room to room past the windows until it's so dark we have to feel our way back to Upper Five, crawling on our hands and knees, lighting matches to see what little of the way we know.

At night we dream Emily Jerman has come to stand at our bedside. She is putting small pieces of paper under our pillow—Columbus School for Girls memoranda, torn in quarters. *Lie still*, she commands. *If you move, they will explode.*

The next day is Saturday, when we always have detention, and then Sunday, when we have chapel. The opening hymn is "A Mighty Fortress Is Our God." Mr. Jerman has told us you can sing most of Emily Dickinson's poems to the tune of "A Mighty Fortress Is Our God," so we try it. The headmaster glares at us, but we stare at the word RUST beside his head, rising like the balloon of talk in a comic strip. We sing to him, enunciating like there's no tomorrow, and he watches our mouths move, trying to discover our blasphemies, the mystery of us. Was there ever one of us he understood, he must be asking himself; was there ever one of us who did not have a black heart and carry a knife in her teeth?

"Girls," Mr. Jerman says on Monday morning, "grab your coats and hats, pack your bags. It's all set. We leave Friday afternoon. Friday night in Pennsylvania. Saturday at the Emily Dickinson Homestead."

We're stunned, and then we cheer until Mr. Jerman's eyes move from our faces and out to the middle distance. We turn in our desks to see Emily Jerman standing at the window. She waves to us and moves off across the garden.

"She wanted to get a look at you," Mr. Jerman says, his voice strangling in his throat.

We watch her as she gathers wood for kindling: birch, alder, even green pine. Her arms are full of wood and purple thistles, her red hair falling forward to cover her face and throat.

Oh Emily Jerman! Her name rises, almost to our lips. We burn for her, all day long, wherever she goes—our long hair fallen like hers, in flames.

By the time we're ready to leave Friday afternoon, it's getting dark. The Jermans are going to drive three hours apiece to get us as far as Harrisburg, Pennsylvania, where we've got rooms in a motel. We look out the windows and watch the back of Emily Jerman's head. She has said hello to us, but nothing after that. She rides up in front next to her husband, and sometimes their arms touch, his right and her left across the space between the seats. We stare at them when this happens, our eyes glittering and hungry, and we play charades. By the time we get an hour out of town, all we can see is night rising on the soft shoulders of the road and our own faces reflected in the windows. The highway is our own hair streaming behind us, and the moon is our eye. For miles and miles, there haven't been any lights. We're all there is in this world, just us and the Jermans.

In Zanesville, we stop for supper. Mr. Jerman drives off the highway and through a web of back streets to a Chinese restaurant—the "Imperious Wok," he calls it, glancing over at his wife, who turns to him and smiles. When we get to the parking lot, the marquee says "The Imperial Wok," and we laugh, even though we don't get the joke and we don't like them having secrets between themselves, a whole history we can never know. Inside, Mr. Jerman explains the menu and shows us how to use chopsticks. He is amazed that we've never had Chinese food before. He toasts us with his tiny bowl of tea.

When the waiter comes, Emily Jerman orders a cocktail. Mr. Jerman looks at her and raises his blond eyebrows, but doesn't say anything. We realize this is the first whole sentence we have ever heard Emily Jerman say: *I would like a double vodka on the rocks.* Her voice is surprisingly low and sweet. We have always thought she should have a high voice to go with her tiny frail body, but instead it's a voice like being wrapped in a smoky blanket. We hope she'll keep on talking. Right now we want to be Emily Jerman's daughters more than anything else in the world.

The waiter brings our food, announcing each dish quietly, with a question, like he's trying to remind himself what it is. After each name, Mr.

Jerman says "ah" and his wife laughs, a low, thrilling laugh, and we know we're going to have to spend all night in our motel room trying to imitate it exactly. She orders another double vodka.

"Dear," Mr. Jerman says, "who's going to help me drive for the next four hours?"

"We will," we say, reaching into our coat pockets for our driver's licenses. We hand them over to Emily Jerman, who looks at the pictures and then up at us, squinting her eyes to get the true likeness.

"Seventeen," she says. "Damn. I remember that." Then she laughs her low laugh—like a car's engine, we think, finely tuned.

Mr. Jerman hands around the dishes of steaming food. We still don't know what any of it is, but the strange new smells are making us not care. We feel a little drunk now, chasing gobbets of meat and snaking onion around on our plates with these wooden knitting needles. A triangle of something bright red flies from someone's plate and lands in Mr. Jerman's tea bowl, and grains of rice ring our placemats where we've let them fall. We lean our heads back and drip noodles into our mouths, noodles that taste like peanut butter. We lick the plum sauce spoon. We take tiny little sips of tea. We watch Emily Jerman get looped.

"Seventeen. Oh God, do I remember seventeen. It was before you," she says to her husband, leaning against him in that way that makes us stare at them with hard bright eyes. "I was at The Columbus School for Girls, can you imagine? Things were by the book then, no drinking gin at lunch, no blouses open down to here, no overnight trips. The goddamn earth was flat then. That's why it's called The Columbus School for Girls, to show how far you could go in the wrong direction."

"Emily," Mr. Jerman says, exactly the way he says the name in class, like he's a little afraid of it.

"Oh don't Emily me, sweetheart," she says thrillingly, her low laugh like a runaway vehicle. "I'm just giving your girls some true history, that's all."

"What was it like?" we ask.

"The same, really. We read Emily Dickinson, too. Or some of us did. 'A narrow fellow in the grass,'" she says, to prove it.

"What house did you live in?" we want to know.

"Cobalt," she says, naming a dormitory we've never heard of. "But the boiler exploded and it burnt to the ground ten years ago. Nobody likes to talk about it."

We glance over at Mr. Jerman, who seems lost to us, shaking his head.

"A girl nearly died," Emily Jerman says, looking us straight in the eye. "And the gardener did die. They were, you know, in her room. It was a big scandal. Hoo boy."

"Emily," Mr. Jerman says in a way that lets us know everything his wife is saying is true.

"He loved Emily Dickinson," Emily Jerman tells us.

"Who did?" her husband says. But we already know who she means.

"The gardener. He'd been to see her house. He had postcards. He gave me one."

"You never told me that." Bryan Jerman stares at his wife. Already we're miles ahead of him, and we can see it all: the girl who is Emily Jerman grown young, and the gardener there beside us, then the two bodies tangled together, singed, blackened by smoke.

"Fortune cookies!" Emily Jerman cries, clapping her hands. "We'll play fortune-cookie charades. It's just like regular charades, only when you get to the part about movie, book, or play, you do this."

She brings the palms of her hands together, pulls them in close to her chest, and bows from the waist. Mr. Jerman is smiling again, looking at his wife like he can't believe how clever she is. The fire, the girl, and the gardener drift from the table, guests taking their leave.

"A bit of mysterious East for you," the waiter says. "Many happy fortunes."

Look below the surface, truth lies within. Unusual experience will enrich your life. Positive attitude will bring desired result. Time is in your favor, be patient. The rare privilege of being pampered will delight you. The fun is just beginning, take it as it comes. Beware of those who stir the waters to suggest they are deep.

Our charades make Emily Jerman laugh until tears come to her eyes and run down her cheeks into her mouth. We watch her taste them and she watches us back, holding our eyes just as long as we hold hers. Then Mr. Jerman tells us it's time to get *on the road again*, singing it like Willie Nelson. Out in the parking lot, he takes his wife's hand and presses it to his heart. Light from the Imperial Wok falls on their coats, turning black to tender purple.

"See?" he says, and together they look east to where the lights of Zanes-ville die away and there are only stars and West Virginia and Pennsylvania and finally the great darkness of western Massachusetts. We stare at them, our eyes going clean through their bodies. Then we look east too, but we can't for the life of us tell what they're seeing.

Hours later, we wake to hear Emily Jerman singing along with the radio. "And when the birds fly south for a while," she sings, "oh I wish that I could go. Someone there might warm this cold heart, oh someone there might know." Her voice breaks on the last line, and we close our eyes again.

At the Holiday Inn in Harrisburg, the Jermans unload us one by one, right into our rooms, right into bed. We stay awake as long as we can listening to Emily and Bryan Jerman in the next room, imagining we can hear the words and other sounds that pass between them when they're all alone.

In the morning, it's Scranton, New York City, Hartford, and on into Amherst. Emily Jerman looks terrible, her hair hanging loose, her skin the color of old snow, but she drives first and Mr. Jerman takes over after lunch. Then she stares out the window. We think something has happened to her during the night. At first we believe it has to do with love, but soon we see how wrong we are, how lost, and for a split second we wish we'd never left The Columbus School for Girls. We've been moving east with Emily Jerman, weightless, like swimmers, but now she's holding on to our uniform skirts, and she's dragging us under. When we get to the Dickinson Homestead in the middle of the afternoon, the air is so wet with snow that we're having to breathe water, like the nearly drowned.

Emily Jerman hasn't said a word all day, but when we're all out of the van, she tells us she's going to stay put. She's been moving too fast, she says, and now she needs to sit for a while. Mr. Jerman hands her the keys, squeezes her knee, and leads us inside the house. We try to catch a glimpse of her out the window as we're standing beside Emily Dickinson's piano, listening to Mr. Jerman make introductions.

The tour guide tells us she is the wife of an English professor who studies Emily Dickinson, and for a whole year when they were first married, he would talk about her in his sleep. That, she explains, is how she learned most of what she knows about the poet, by listening in on her husband's dreams. She looks straight at Mr. Jerman.

"It's how most husbands and wives come to know anything at all," she says.

He stares back at her out of his great blue unblinking eyes, and for the first time ever, we think he looks bullish and stupid. It unhinges us, and we have to sit down on Emily Dickinson's chintz sofa.

The professor's wife keeps talking. She tells us what belongs to Emily Dickinson and what doesn't. She lets us touch a teacup and hold a pair of wine glasses the color of fresh blood. We feel as though they want to leap out of our hands and smash on the floor. We almost want to throw them down to get it over with—the same way we think about standing up in Chapel and shouting out something terrible. Then we wonder if we haven't already done it. At that moment, the back door opens and Emily Jerman walks into the hall. The professor's wife drops the guest book and its spine breaks. Pages and pages of visitors wash over the floor.

"See, Bryan," Emily Jerman says to her husband, "I told you I shouldn't have come." As we pick up the pages of the guest book, she walks over to the piano. She stays there with her back to us for a long time, and we can tell that she is crying. We want Mr. Jerman to do something, but he stays with us, listening to the tour guide wander through all her dreamed facts, and we hate him for that.

Upstairs we see the dress and the bed, the writing table, the window that looks out over Main Street, the basket used to lower gingerbread down to children in the garden. We stick our noses inside like dogs and sniff to see if the smell of gingerbread is still there, and we tell each other that it is. When the guide's back is turned, we touch everything: the bed, the shawl, the hatbox, the dress, even the glass over the poet's soft silhouette.

We watch Emily Jerman move down the hall and into this room like she's walking in a trance. We see her eyes are red and her face is swollen. The professor's wife is talking about incontinence, and then about the Civil War, but we don't know how she got there. We watch Emily Jerman, more whisper than woman's body, a sensation in this house, a hot spirit distant from her husband and from us. We stare at the two of them, and all at once we know we will never remember anything Mr. Jerman has taught us, except this: that the world is a blind knot of electric and unspeakable desires, burning itself to nothing.

As we're leaving, the professor's wife makes us promise not to miss the graveyard, and we assure her that we won't. We tell her that we have already dreamed of it, just like her husband, and she tells us to button up our blouses. It's cold out, she says.

"We'll save that for tomorrow," Mr. Jerman says. "It's too dark now."

"Oh no," Emily Jerman tells him, the light beginning to come back into her voice, "it's perfect now, perfect for a graveyard."

She takes the keys out of her coat pocket, unlocks the van for the rest of us, and gets in behind the wheel.

"I know the way," she says. "I already looked on the map."

Emily Jerman makes three left turns and we're in West Cemetery, where it's pitch dark. Mr. Jerman asks if she knows where the grave is and she nods, but then she drives us once around all the graves anyway. When we come back to the entrance road, she pulls a hard left and drives up on the grass. There in front of the van's lights are three headstones behind a black wrought-iron fence.

Emily Jerman climbs down quickly and opens the van doors from the outside. We're surprised at how strong she is, how determined she is for us to be here. She leads us to the graves, pushing us a little from behind, pointing to the marker in the middle. "Called Back," it says. She shows us all the offerings there—dried flowers, coins, somebody's ballpoint pen with its red barrel looking like a swipe of blood.

"'Just lost when I was found,'" Emily Jerman says behind us, "'just felt the world go by, just girt me for the onset with eternity when breath blew black and on the other side I heard recede the disappointed tide.'"

"Saved," Mr. Jerman says. "It's *saved*."

"Just lost when I was fucking *saved* then," his wife calls back. "'Therefore as one returned I feel odd secrets of the line to tell. Some sailor skirting foreign shores.'"

We've turned around to look for her, for Emily Jerman, but she's standing in between the van's headlights, leaning back and against the grille, so we can't see her, only the smoky mist her breath makes in the cold as she speaks.

"Do another one," we say, but she won't.

"That's my favorite," she says. "It's the only one." She tells us to leave something at the grave. She says it doesn't matter what.

There's nothing in our coat pockets but spare change, wrappers from starlight mints, and our driver's licenses. We don't know what to do. We can feel panic beginning to take fire under our ribs, and we look up first at the evening sky, clear and blue-black, then across the street to the 7-Eleven, where the smell of chili dogs is billowing out the doors. We lean over and take hold of the hems of our Columbus School for Girls skirts. We find the seam and pull sharply upward, and then down, tearing a rough triangle out of the bottom of the cloth. Cold air rushes in at our thighs and between our legs.

"Girls!" Mr. Jerman says, but his voice gets lost in the sound of his wife's laughter.

"What a waste," he says, but we tell him it isn't. At school, sewing is compulsory, and we know that with an extra tuck and the letting out of one pleat at the other seam, our skirts will look exactly the same again.

At dinner, Mr. Jerman hardly says a word while his wife orders double vodkas and tells us more about her days at The Columbus School for Girls.

"Those graduation dresses you have now," she says, "they were my idea."

We look at Mr. Jerman, who nods his head.

"I just couldn't stand the thought of black robes, and so I drew up a pattern and took it into the headmaster—who's dead now, by the way, and what a blessing *that* is."

"What did he say?" we ask.

"He said absolutely no, he wasn't going to have a bunch of girls traipsing around in their nighties. He wanted us fully covered. But I went ahead and made one dress and wore it every day. Every day for all of March and most of April. I got detention every day, too, and served them all, and finally he gave in."

We wonder why Emily Jerman would now be passing the rest of her life at a place that had treated her so badly. We think she must love Bryan Jerman beyond reason. We can't imagine that she wants to go back tomorrow, not any more than we do.

"It was a beautiful place then," she says. "The gardens were kept up. Outside was like Eden. The gardener could do anything, bring anything back to life. He was a genius."

"Emily," Mr. Jerman says, "I believe you had a crush on that gardener."

"Darling," she says, "we thought you'd never guess—didn't we, girls?"

His laugh dies to a choking sound as his wife stares at him, breathing hard and smiling like she's just won a race. The silence is terrible, beating between them, but we won't break it. We want to watch and see how it will break itself.

"To the new girls," Emily Jerman says finally, toasting us with her third vodka. We can see how, inside the glass, our own faces look back at us for a split second before they shatter into light and fire and gluey vodka running into Emily Jerman's mouth.

We don't know how long we've been asleep when Mr. Jerman comes in to wake us up. It's still dark outside. We have been dreaming but we couldn't say about what. Mr. Jerman stands beside our beds and reaches out to turn on the lamp. When he can't find the switch, he takes a book of matches from his pocket, lights one, and holds it over our heads. We think maybe we have been dreaming about that, a tongue of flame hissing above us, or about everything that is going to happen now.

Mr. Jerman tells us to put on our shoes and socks, our coats over our nightgowns, and then he leads us outside, down to the parking lot where the motel's airport van is waiting. The heat inside is on high, so we can barely hear what passes between Mr. Jerman and the driver, except when he says he couldn't very well leave young girls alone in a motel, now could he?

We know they're taking us back to Amherst, and when we pull into West Cemetery, we know why. There, exactly where Emily Jerman had parked it in the early evening, is our school van, the lights on, shining on the wrought-iron fence and the three headstones behind it. Emily Jerman is standing behind the fence, her right hand curled around one of the thin black posts rising up to shoulder height.

Two West Cemetery guards stand off to her left, motionless, watching, their bodies balanced slightly ahead of their feet and their heads hung down as if they had been running and then had to stop suddenly to keep from going over the edge of the world.

"Girls," Emily Jerman says when she sees us standing with her husband. "Look at you, traipsing around in your nighties. How far do you think you're going to get in this world dressed like that? You have to learn how to keep warm. When I was your age, I learned how. When I was your age, I was on fire. On *fire*, do you understand?"

We do. We see the two bodies pressed close, Emily Jerman and the gardener who could bring almost anything back to life. We hear his whispering and smell her hair in flames.

Mist rises in front of the van's headlights. The cemetery ground between us and Mr. Jerman looks like it's burning, but this does not surprise us. It only makes us curious, like the night birds that rise now from the leaves to ask *whose fire? whose fire?* and then drop back to sleep.

We know what will happen next. Mr. Jerman will walk through this fire and it won't consume him. He will move past us toward his wife, and we'll feel his breath as he passes, sweet and dangerously cold. This time, we'll look away when they touch. We won't have to see how they do it, or hear what words they use. We know what we need to know. This is the new world.

Light Opera

IN 1952, THE YEAR MY MOTHER FEARED SHE MIGHT LOSE ME, SHE became the time and temperature voice on the telephone. The phone company selected her, after a nationwide search, because she had a bright voice with no discernible accent, and that meant her recorded messages could be distributed throughout the country. For a while, this gave her a certain status in our town; then, the novelty wore off, and she was again Lois Sievers, the undertaker's wife, who gave piano lessons to any pupils whose parents didn't mind marching them up the funeral chapel's steps.

She used her pretty voice to put her students at ease. "This is middle C," she told them at their first lessons. "We always begin with middle C."

When she spoke to my father, which she did less frequently in those days, she used a more severe tone—muted—as if over their years together he had dulled her, as if he were a student who had sounded more flat notes than she could ever forgive.

On occasion, I dialed the time and temperature number just to hear her, and when I did, I thought she sounded like a woman I would one day enjoy meeting. What I'm saying is, you could do worse than to have that voice waiting for you at the other end of a call.

On Saturday afternoons, she listened to the Metropolitan Opera broadcasts with her friends, Mr. and Mrs. Pettyjohn, who preferred light opera to *opera seria*. The former, they said, offered them beauty and passion without any of the bother of life's gruesome tragedies.

Mr. Pettyjohn was a retired Army officer who served our town as night watchman; Mrs. Pettyjohn taught Latin at the high school. Once when I complained in her class about learning verb conjugations—bones of a dead language, I called them—she said to me, "Nothing of beauty ever dies. Once you know it, you know it. You carry it here inside you. *Aere perennius*. Translation, Mr. Sievers?"

I tried to stammer a reply, but she stopped me with a hand slapped down on her desk. "More lasting than bronze."

"Nothing lasts forever," I said. "People die."

"As long as one person knows *amo* . . . Mr. Sievers?"

"I love."

"*Amas*?"

"You love."

"*Amāmus*?"

"We love."

"Exactly, Mr. Sievers. Correct."

On those Saturday afternoons, in our living room above the chapel, my mother made tea and served it in the china cups her grandmother had brought with her from Russia.

"Perry, you should read Turgenev," Mrs. Pettyjohn said to me once.

"Chekhov," said Mr. Pettyjohn.

They sat together on my mother's loveseat, Mr. Pettyjohn with his teacup and saucer balanced on his knee, Mrs. Pettyjohn holding hers at her chin. Dostoevski was too dreary, they both agreed.

"Don't waste your time on a gloomy Gus like him," said Mrs. Pettyjohn.

Said Mr. Pettyjohn: "As for Tolstoy, remember this, Perry. Never trust a man who doesn't worship his wife."

My mother, despite my father's objections, insisted on my presence those Saturdays. I sat across from the Pettyjohns on a ladder-back chair, ready to fiddle with the tuning knob on the Philco console whenever the broadcast began to fade. Over the airwaves, I listened to that afternoon's opera-goers taking their seats, to their murmured conversations punctuated by the sounds of the orchestra members tuning their instruments. When the master of ceremonies, Milton Cross, began to announce the prologue—"When the gold curtain rises, we'll see the wood nymphs frolicking in the forest"—Mr. and Mrs. Pettyjohn would set their tea aside and clasp hands.

"You can learn something from them," my mother had told me. "All these years and they still adore each other. A man shouldn't be afraid to wear his heart on his sleeve."

Sometimes during the opera, Mr. Pettyjohn would weep. He would lay back his head, and his face would be shiny with tears.

"Good gravy!" my father said when I divulged this bit of information. "A constable of this city. A municipal official. A man responsible for our well-being."

On occasion, Mr. Pettyjohn would be so taken with the music that his angina would seize him, and he would have to slip a nitroglycerin pill beneath his tongue.

Opera, my father said, was all wailing and caterwauling and far-flung drama. "A display," he said. "A spectacle. And on top of that, it's in some pig-Latin gibberish no one can understand."

"The language of love," my mother said. "The words don't matter, only what you feel when you hear them."

One Saturday, at the end of *Die Fledermaus*, Mrs. Pettyjohn said, "We should call your husband now."

"Roy?" my mother said.

"Yes. We need to call Roy."

One glance at Mr. Pettyjohn, and I recognized the dry, fixed stare of the dead. He seemed to be looking straight at me as if any minute he would tell me to switch off the Philco, but already I could see the muscles had stiffened in his jaws and a blue tinge had spread through his lips.

I stood up, fastening the button of my sports coat. "Don't worry, Mrs. Pettyjohn," I said, in the comforting voice I had learned from my father. "We'll take care of you."

That winter, my father had offered to make me his helper—to teach me what his father had taught him.

"There are things boys shouldn't be a part of," my mother had said. "Delicate boys."

I was sixteen then, and the last thing I wanted to be known as was a "delicate boy." So when my father started assigning me duties—doorman, parking attendant, floral arranger, pallbearer—I looked upon them as responsibilities that would distinguish me. He bought me a navy blue suit, black wingtips with rubber soles, a charcoal-gray topcoat, and black gloves with a fedora to match.

"Listen to me, Perry," my mother said the first time she saw me in my new suit. "You should be careful. Believe me. I know. I want you to have friends. I want you to have a normal, happy life."

I learned my father's tools: scalpel, auger, trocar. Though he never allowed me in the embalming room, at times he would pass along some bit of information: how to fill the sunken areas on the backs of hands with injections of massage cream; how to shut a mouth by running a needle from the inside of the lower lip, in through a nostril, and back; how to lay cotton pledgets on the eyeballs before closing the lids.

My one distinction as a young man was the fact that my father was a mortician, and though I am ashamed to admit it now, I often betrayed his confidence and used those details to impress the boys I hoped would become my friends. For a time, I answered our phone with what I thought were jazzy greetings: "Sievers Funeral Home. You stab 'em, we'll slab 'em; you plug 'em, we'll plant 'em; you bag 'em, we'll tag 'em."

Then my father found out and demanded I stop: "Someday, when you take my place, everyone will know you. Rich and poor, handsome and plain. They'll come to you with their trouble and ask you to respect it. You'll have to make room in yourself for all the sorrow they'll bring you. You'll have to be an upright man, Perry. You'll have to be the kind of man people can trust."

The Saturday Mr. Pettyjohn died, I was trying to be that sort of man, noble and kind, so when my father asked me to fetch Sammy the Egg, I slipped on my overcoat and galoshes and went out into the cold night.

Sammy was the baldheaded barber who came, whenever my father called, to cut the corpse's hair. It was nearly eleven o'clock when we left his shop and made our way down Main Street to the funeral home, and Sammy kept singing "The Tennessee Waltz," a tune my mother played from time to time on the piano. He had a rich baritone voice, and despite the lateness of the hour, he allowed himself full throat.

The streetlights spread a faint bloom over the sidewalk, and Sammy and I passed through it, our galoshes squeaking on the snow. He had turned up the collar of his overcoat, so I couldn't see his face, only the smooth crown of his head. His tools—scissors, combs, clippers—rattled about in the black leather satchel he carried. For years, in his barber chair, I had felt his strong hands tipping my head forward so he could shave the wispy hairs from my neck, twisting me this way and that so he could clip and shear. "Where does the crow light?" he used to say to me when I was younger. "There," he would say, and slap his hand down on my leg with a force that would leave the red print of his fingers on my skin.

"That is a dandy song, isn't it, Perry?" His breath hung in the air, and

I could taste the sharp metal of the cold. "That's a song about a poor sap who loses his girl to an old friend. A beautiful song. That's the kind of song a man should sing to a good woman."

Over the years, he had made something of a name for himself singing at weddings in small towns across the county. It wasn't uncommon to see young brides-to-be entering his shop to engage his service. His talent, and its appreciation, had given him a confidence I envied and feared.

"Do you sing, Perry?" He stopped beneath a street light and turned to me. He smelled of talcum powder and hair oil.

"No, sir. My mother said I didn't inherit her talent."

"I suppose that would be right." Sammy narrowed his eyes and studied me. "I don't see any fire in you. You seem sort of lukewarm. No, I don't imagine you'd be the kind to carry much of a voice."

At the chapel, my father put his hand on Sammy's back, between his shoulder blades, and escorted him into the embalming room. My father's hands were pallid, the grayish white of surgical gloves. They were small and unimpressive. Still, he was always using them to touch people: a slight pressure on a wrist, in the small of the back, nudging them in the direction he wanted them to go.

Twice a month, he and Sammy the Egg played war games in our basement. On a six-by-nine-foot board they reenacted Civil War battles, maneuvering miniature soldiers across valleys and rivers and bluffs. My father spent hour after hour painting each soldier, each musket and cannon, each stone wall. I liked to watch him tracing the fine hairs of his brush along cheekbones and jaw lines. That night, when he had left Sammy to his work, we sat together in the quiet of the basement, just outside the embalming room, and I admired the patience and the steady nerve it took for him to paint each figure.

He had taught me details he had acquired over years of study, and while Sammy cut Mr. Pettyjohn's hair, my father ambushed me with a quiz.

"What was the basic infantry weapon, Colonel?"

"The single-shot Springfield."

"Range?"

"Kill a man at half a mile."

"Outstanding. And the land mines, Colonel. What were they called in those days?"

"Booby traps."

"No. Concentrate. That was later. Then they called them 'infernal machines.'"

He told me how the Union divided the Confederacy by controlling the Mississippi, how they blockaded the coast, how Sherman broke the South on his march to the sea. "Anything he could use, he took. Everything else, he burned. The man was ruthless, a devil. 'War is hell,' he said. Your great-grandfather was along on that campaign. Imagine, Colonel. Your own flesh and blood!"

When my father spoke to me of flanks and defense lines, artillery and ironclads, his voice exploded into a deep-chested song, a Gatling gun of joy. McClellan's goof at Sharpsburg, he said, was he didn't attack quickly enough. "He knew the Confederate army was divided, Colonel. He knew part of it had gone with Jackson to capture Harpers Ferry. Lee was vulnerable—only 50,000 men. McClellan had 87,000, but he waited."

"No fighting instinct," I said. "A popcorn fart in a mouse's ass."

"That's right. And what about Burnside? What was his mistake in the drive toward Richmond in '62?"

"He crossed the Rappahannock at Fredericksburg."

"Go on."

"It was the strongest point in the Confederate line. Lee massacred him."

"Bingo. Remember, Colonel. Always hit a man at his weakest spot."

That winter, my father's zest for these maneuvers had snared me. I had fallen in love with the strategy of war, with the use of cunning and pluck. Nights, while pupils played "Heart and Soul" on my mother's piano, my father and I bowed our heads over topographical maps. Together we aligned our regiments, and together we planned our attacks.

And that particular night I could hear Sammy the Egg at work in the embalming room: the snip-snip-snip of his scissors, his baritone voice. "Yes, sir," he said. "Indeed, sir." As if Mr. Pettyjohn had just offered an opinion on politics or the weather. "That's right, sir. Oh, yes, sir. You are one hundred percent hunky-dory correct about that."

The nights of wakes, Sammy would linger by the casket, eavesdropping on the mourners as they commented on the deceased's appearance. From time to time, someone would mistake him for one of the survivors. "No, sir," he would say whenever they would shake his hand and offer their condolences. "I'm not family. I just do the hair."

My father had long despised Sammy's lack of respect for the rites of death and had been casting about for another barber, one who would better revere the solemn rituals my father himself had come to admire. He had settled on Loyal Hall, a Presbyterian from Bridgeport who wore bow ties and swept his floor after every haircut.

"Loyal Hall keeps a clean shop," my father said as he listened to Sammy chattering away in the embalming room. "And he doesn't fill your ear with jibber-jabber. The next time I need someone, he's the man."

Sammy started whistling "Pop Goes the Weasel," and when I heard him, I laughed.

My father laid down his paint brush. "Perry, mourners expect a professional, considerate demeanor." He drew back his shoulders. "Never smile. Even if you mean it as a kindness, it will always come out wrong. Keep yourself under control, and never—do you understand?—never let it show that you feel someone's pain."

Sammy came from the embalming room, fastening the gold clasp on his leather satchel. "Well, that's done," he said. "Another satisfied customer. That's what I like about this job. No complaints. Hey, Roy? It's like they say about you undertakers. You're lucky. You can bury your mistakes."

My father stood and shook Sammy's hand. "Thank you for coming," he said. "Particularly at this late hour."

"Is it late?" Sammy looked at his wristwatch. "So it is. I was hoping to have a word with your missus."

"Lois?" My father said her name with a dead tongue as if he hadn't said it in a long time.

"That's right," said Sammy. "I'll only be a minute. Don't worry, Roy. I won't steal her."

We watched Sammy climb the stairs, and only when I heard him on the next flight that led to our living quarters, did I say to my father, "Why didn't you tell him about Loyal Hall?"

"Patience, Colonel," my father said. "Surrender is always a delicate matter. If it's to be accepted, it requires the proper time and atmosphere. Now, about tomorrow's battle."

We were discussing our strategy for Gettysburg when we heard my mother's shrill cry, as if in panic or alarm, and we raced up the stairs, my father leading the way.

My mother and Sammy the Egg were sitting at the kitchen table, having a glass of beer. They were laughing, and when my mother threw up her hands and tossed back her head, I thought of the girls at school—pretty and capable of spooking timid boys like me with their looks. It fascinated me to see the girl my mother had once been—in her eyes, in the blush coloring her cheeks, in the way she bit her lip when she noticed my father and me standing in the archway, watching her.

"Holy cow," she said. "Where's the fire?"

My father was panting for breath. He bent over, his hands on his knees. "I heard you scream," he said.

"That's a hoot." My mother tapped Sammy on the arm. "Isn't that a riot?"

"I just told her a joke," Sammy said. "Pull back the troops, Roy. We were just having a chuckle."

My father straightened. He ran his hand over his head, mussing his hair. I thought how silly we looked, the two of us, and I tried to justify our charge up the stairs. "I heard it, too," I said. "I thought something was wrong."

"We were just shooting the breeze," my mother said. "Sammy was telling me about his nephew."

"My sister's kid," said Sammy. "Joey Scarbo. He's coming to live with me. Be here tomorrow. His old man died in Korea, and now the kid needs a little direction. You know how it is with kids. Wild hairs."

My mother shrieked again. She slapped her hand against Sammy's shoulder. "Wild hairs," she said. "That's a scream. Uncle Sammy—*Il Barbiere di Siviglia*—he's going to take care of those wild hairs." She took a long drink of her beer. "Wild hairs," she said again. "Get it, Roy?"

"I got it," said my father.

"Lois is going to give the kid piano lessons." Sammy smiled. "We'll see if he's got any of my musical talent."

"At ease, boys." My mother raised her hand to her forehead and snapped off a salute. "Go back to whatever it was you were doing. We're shipshape here. Eh, Sammy? Believe me, Roy. Everything is A-OK."

Late that night I woke, shivering and cold. My mother had come into my room and opened my window, and the icy air was sweeping across my bed.

"Perry, come here." She was standing by the window, and the curtains were lifting and falling around her. "I want to tell you something."

Her voice was pleasant and inviting, and I couldn't help but go to it.

She pointed out the window to the sky where stars were bright above the rooftops and the trees. "A long time ago, Perry, people believed that each of the planets made a distinct musical note while it was spinning. The music of the spheres, they called it, even though no one had ever heard it. It was too majestic, they swore, ever to be heard by human ears." I could smell the warm flannel of her nightgown and a scent of roses her bath salts had left on her skin. "Do you think it's the same with our spirits, Perry? Do you think when we die, our souls spin off into space, and for eternity they make a grand music no one on earth can hear—a music so rare and dear it's not to be had for love?"

My mother, in those days, could frighten me with her passion for mysteries I felt certain would be forever closed to my ordinary imagination. "Mr. Pettyjohn's gone, Perry." She put her arms around me and pulled me close to her. "And here we are. And what can we hear?"

"Your heart."

"Good. That's music. Percussion."

"No," I told her. "It's complete systoles and diastoles. It's the heart's chambers emptying and then filling with blood. That's what stopped when Mr. Pettyjohn died."

"I know where you learned *that*." She let me go and slammed the window shut. "It chills me, Perry—honestly, it does—to see what your father's done to you."

The next morning at breakfast, my father said, "I've got a joke."

My mother looked at him as if he were someone she had never seen. She looked at him as if he were someone interesting, someone she would like to get to know.

"A joke, Roy?" she said.

"That's right. Something amusing I heard last month at that funeral directors' conference. Just let me think a minute." He cocked his head to the side and put his finger to his lips. "OK," he said. "I've got it. Listen to this: What did the corpse say to the mortician?"

I saw my mother's spine stiffen; her shoulders went back, and her chin lifted. For a long time, no one said anything. Then, finally, I couldn't take it anymore, and I said, "What? What did the corpse say to the mortician?"

My father started to giggle. "'Make it high octane. Lately, I've been running a little sluggish.'"

My mother pushed her chair back from the table.

"No, wait," my father said. "That's not right. What did Henry Ford say to the mortician? Get it? Henry Ford? High octane?"

"I think that's in bad taste," my mother said. "I don't think that's funny at all."

That afternoon, Sammy the Egg came to re-create Gettysburg. His nephew Joey was with him. He was a tall boy with wavy hair cut in a ducktail, and he was wearing motorcycle boots, a pair of Levi's slung low on his slim hips, and a red satin jacket whose back was emblazoned with fire-breathing dragons coiled around a map of Korea.

"Who's this?" My father was wearing his Union Cavalry Commander hat, the front of the blue felt laced with crossed sabers, and he brought the brim down closer to his eyes as if Joey were a Confederate spy threatening to ferret out some piece of strategy. "Reinforcements, Sammy?"

"My nephew." Sammy put a hand on Joey's back and shoved him forward until he and my father were nearly nose to nose. "Look at that hair. You'd think he was one of those doo-wop boys. Someday I'll get him in the chair. A nice crew cut, I figure. Maybe a burr."

When Joey moved, his satin jacket rustled and hissed. "Joseph Scarbo," he said, offering his hand to my father. "What were you in, Mr. Sievers? World War II, I figure. What was it? North Africa? Normandy? The Philippines?"

"Asthma," said Sammy. "A medical deferment. Right, Roy?"

My father nodded, and it was clear to me, in a way it had never been, that Sammy the Egg knew too much. "You cut enough hair," he had told me once, "you hear enough stories. You get a knack for seeing people for what they are. Secrets? Forget it. A snip here, a snip there, and I get down to the scalp. I can tell you, friend, things about yourself you forgot you even knew."

Sammy, as always, played the Confederacy. My father, from the beginning, had insisted on playing the Union, and Sammy had accepted his own role as Johnny Reb, bowing to his host with southern grace and charm.

Nothing rattled Sammy. His thick legs kept him anchored, and his bald head and grin reminded me of one of those roly-poly dolls, those inflatable clowns that always came back to you, no matter how hard you punched them. On this day, he positioned his brigades on the perimeter of Cemetery Hill, from Devil's Den to Seminary Ridge, and along my father's right flank at Culp's Hill. It was the strategy Lee had employed in 1863, and it surprised my father since Sammy rarely followed the course history had set. "It didn't work then," he always said. "Why the hell would it work now?"

His moves were often haphazard and stunning, glorious and devil-may-care, and over the winter he had captured me with the charm of his backasswards bravado. Still, the allegiance I felt myself give to him disturbed me because I could see, beneath his good-natured bluster, that he was a cruel man who enjoyed destroying my father's austere and arrogant confidence in history.

Sammy unbuttoned his cuffs and rolled his sleeves back over his arms. "Kid," he said to Joey, "I'm going to show these bluecoats a thing or two. Why don't you go upstairs and introduce yourself to Lois. You'll know her when you see her. She's the only one in this joint who's got any life."

"You're the general," said Joey. "I'm just along for the ride."

For once, my father and I had decided to depart from the facts of the battle. Instead of positioning our main line along the left wing, as General Meade had done, we had shifted our power to the right, anticipating Sammy's probable attack at Culp's Hill. "Pickett charged the left flank at Seminary Ridge," my father had said the night before, when we had finalized our strategy. "Straight into Meade's force. They could have turned the right flank at Culp's Hill, but they didn't. Why not, Colonel?"

"No cavalry reconnaissance. They never knew how much they had weakened that part of the Union line."

"Good report, Colonel. You know Samuel will try to pull his usual stunt. This time, we'll be ready."

But we weren't. There he was, the bulk of his troops entrenched along Seminary Ridge, waiting for the proper roll of the dice to permit his charge across the Great Wheat Field Farm—in a position, as Pickett had never been, to capture Cemetery Hill.

"That's a travesty," my father said.

"That's war," said Sammy the Egg. He rubbed his hands together. "Strike up the drums. Sound the charge. Let's shoot dice."

It didn't take long for Cemetery Hill to fall to Sammy's troops. "Look at that," he said when it was over. "I'll be damned, Roy. We just rewrote history."

My father grabbed onto the edge of the game board and bowed his head. Sammy took a set of car keys from his pocket and handed them to me. "Be a sport, and take these to Joey," he said. "Tell him I'm going to walk home. Tell him he can try out the Oldsmobile. Go along with him, Perry. Show him the sights. Would that be all right, Roy? Part of the terms of surrender?"

My father raised his head. "Fine," he said. "All spoils to the victor. Whatever you say."

Upstairs, my mother was sitting beside Joey on the piano bench. Her fingers were long and slender, and they trembled as she held them arched above the keys. I could see in the flared wings of her shoulder blades and the delicate sweep of her back, the lovely girl she had been when she had first met my father.

"This is a C-major scale," she said to Joey. "Now watch me." Each note sounded pure and clear in the still room, and I stood, half-hidden in the doorway, listening to my mother. "C, D, E—thumb under—F, G, A, B, C. And then back. See? Easy as pie."

If I closed my eyes, I could conjure up the sound of her singing at funerals, her soprano rising sweet and pure from the rear of the chapel. I could see her as a young bride, alone in her bedroom: laying out my father's suit, brushing lint from his jacket, choosing his necktie, buffing his shoes. But it all embarrassed me, this intimate glimpse into the life they had once had, a life that had ended when my mother had grown weary of the somber climate which had become the due course of their days together.

"My husband Roy made a rhyme once to match up with the notes," she told Joey. She played the scale again. "Pretty is as pretty does, my lovely Lois always was." She laughed, and then quickly covered her mouth with her hand. "Goodness, I haven't thought of that in years."

"That's funny," Joey said. "An undertaker who writes rhymes."

"You wouldn't think it to know him now," my mother said. "But he used to have pizazz. Do you know what his favorite radio program was? 'The Fleischmann Hour' with Rudy Vallee. Bob Hope was on that show, and his catchphrase was 'Who's Yehoodi?' I don't remember what he meant by it, but Roy loved it. He used to sneak up behind me, put his hands over my eyes, and say it. 'Who's Yehoodi?' he used to say, and I'd let my head fall back against his chest, and I'd whisper, 'Heigh-ho, everybody'—that's what Rudy Vallee always said, you see—'You are,' I'd say. 'You, Roy. You're my hoodi.'"

My mother wound the metronome on the piano and set it to ticking. "Well, that's a silly story," she said. "That's all that is. Just forget it. Sometimes my mouth just runs and runs, and I can't shut up." She grabbed the metronome's pendulum, and the room went still. "I don't have many friends. I lost one of them yesterday. It's not that people don't like me; they just don't think about getting to know an undertaker's wife."

"It's sort of creepy," Joey said. "This whole place. Stiffs all around. But it's sort of cool, too. I bet you've got stories."

My mother grabbed Joey by the arm and pulled him up from the piano bench. "I want you to hear something," she said. Before she could lead him out into the hallway, I retreated a few steps down the stairs, afraid that they would see me. But they didn't. I heard my mother pick up the telephone and dial a number. "Listen," she said.

I counted to ten, trying to decide whether I should come out of hiding. Then I heard Joey say, "It's 2:25, thirty-two degrees."

"That's me," my mother told him.

"You?"

I imagined my father downstairs in the chapel, leaning over Mr. Pettyjohn's casket. He might be using a cotton swab and some rouge to liven up Mr. Pettyjohn's cheeks, last-minute details now that he had the body in the chapel's light. I couldn't shake from my head the sight of him prancing to my mother, surprising her with his call—"Who's Yehoodi?"—and I began to grieve for such joy they had lost. What's more, I began to fear the life I would one day inherit.

I heard Joey lay the telephone receiver back in its cradle, and I came up the stairs.

"Perry," my mother said. "You little mouse. You crept right up on us."

"Sammy sent me up here to give these to Joey." I held up the car keys. "He said we should go for a ride so I can show him the sights."

"Yes," my mother said. "You two should scoot. Joey's spent long enough listening to this crazy old dame. Go on. The both of you. Get some fresh air. Enjoy what's left of the day."

Downstairs, in the foyer, Joey jerked his thumb toward the chapel doors. "Is that where you have the funerals?"

"That's right," I said. "We have a visitation this evening. Mr. Pettyjohn." I could hear my father moving about in the basement, and my mother upstairs turning on the radio. "I'll give you a look," I said. "Come on."

My father had dressed Mr. Pettyjohn in the gray suit Mrs. Pettyjohn had brought for him. I could see that much when Joey and I stepped into the chapel, that and Mr. Pettyjohn's eyeglasses and the tip of his nose just visible over the edge of the mahogany casket.

Joey's boots clomped over the polished floor. We stood at Mr. Pettyjohn's casket as if we were any two mourners, paying our respects.

"Just like the frogs in biology class," Joey said. "Pickled in formaldehyde."

"Actually it's a mixture," I said, in a voice I hoped would impress Joey with my knowledge. "Formaldehyde, glycerin, borax, phenol, alcohol, and water. That's what does the trick. Most people don't know that."

Joey lifted an eyebrow. "OK, smart guy, you know what the twilight zone is?"

It would be a few years before the Rod Serling television show of that name, and I said, no, I didn't.

"It's the lowest level of the ocean light can still reach. One more inch and you're in darkness forever. How about that? You probably thought I was a dummy, but I'm not."

I lifted Mr. Pettyjohn's hand. "Touch it," I said. "Here." I stroked my finger over the tendons that led down from the knuckles to the wrist. "You can feel where we injected cream to fill in the sunken spots."

"I don't want to touch it," Joey said. "I want that ring." He pointed to Mr. Pettyjohn's wedding band. "You're the expert here. Go on, Dr. Death. Take it off."

At that instant, a brief and dazzling moment that seized me, I fell in love with Joey—with the danger of him. I twisted the wedding band free.

"This is because we can," Joey said. "This is risk, pure and simple. That's how you know your ticker's still kicking. Meanness and ruin. That's what trips my trigger. Shout hallelujah, Perry. Jesus yes. Shits-ka-tits. Amen."

I laid Mr. Pettyjohn's left hand back over his right, taking care to leave them in that pose my father called the "at ease" posture. I could imagine him working over a corpse, forcing a limb seized with rigor mortis into a position that satisfied him, and it seemed to me a lonely and sorrowful thing to spend your life doing.

I'll say it again: I loved Joey Scarbo, loved him because he made me feel criminal, made me drunk with the joy of unbridled risk.

"Ring-a-ding-ding," he said. "Let's scram."

We escaped the still of the chapel, suffocating with its overwhelming scent of gladiolus and snapdragons and mums, and rode in Sammy's Olds 88 out the blacktop, deep into the country.

Joey steered with one finger laid across the lower rim of the wheel, as if he needed no more than that to feel the grade and roll of the road unwinding beneath us. He bumped the 88 through its gears, punched the accelerator, shoved at the limits of caution and good sense until the countryside was flashing by, and I could feel in my stomach the dip of each hill, the lean of every curve. I was no longer Perry Sievers, the undertaker's son, straight-faced and sober in his Robert Hall suit; I had spun loose from myself, lost all center and gravity, and for that terrible and frightening freedom I gave thanks.

"This is for Pettyjohn," Joey said. "This is for all the dead everywhere."

He slipped the ring over his thumb and held his hand, fingers splayed, up for my approval. "We'll keep it until this guy's wife has sunk to her lowest point—twilight-zone time—then we'll put it in an envelope and leave it in her mailbox. A gift from the dead. Special delivery. Won't she be surprised?"

I remembered the afternoons the Pettyjohns had come to our home to listen to the opera. They had been my mother's friends when too many others in our town had avoided her. Mrs. Pettyjohn, despite her stern manner in the classroom, was a good-hearted woman who believed in love, and I didn't want her to have the shock of opening Joey's envelope and seeing Mr. Pettyjohn's wedding band.

I said, "It's lousy what we've done. Give me the ring."

Joey pulled the 88 off the blacktop and sat there while it idled, tapping the ring against the steering wheel. Gusts of wind swept in from the north and rocked us. I watched the low clouds banking in the west, the sky the color of lead, and I knew we would have snow by nightfall.

"It hurts me that you should say that," Joey said. "I thought we were going to be friends."

His voice—low and sharp, a suture needle piercing skin—razored me. In any war game, my father had told me, there were a limited number of moves, and each one eliminated another. "If you get in a tight spot," he had explained, "all you can hope for is some piece of business so bold, so unexpected, you turn your fortune around."

I had fallen in with Joey and had become a thief. At that moment, I could feel my life surrounding me, my opportunities for escape dwindling. The way I figured it, I could continue to close rank with Joey and keep mum about Mr. Pettyjohn's wedding band, or I could come clean, and surrender myself to my father.

I reached over and snatched the ring from Joey's thumb. "No," I said. "We can't be friends."

I didn't know what sort of life I wanted, but I knew I didn't want Joey's life, a lowdown life full of mean-spirited intentions and underhanded tactics. I was scared because I didn't know what was going to happen next, but all he did was tell me the story of the day he found out his father was dead.

What troubled him most was the fact that he couldn't cry. "Zippo," he said. "Not a tear. I thought I was a heartless bastard. Then a few days after the funeral, a package came. You know, one of those boxes wrapped in brown paper and tied with string. It was this jacket the old man had sent me from Korea. I kept seeing him on leave, picking it out for me, folding it just so, and putting it in that box. I kept seeing him tying that string—one of the last things he would ever do—tying it tight so that package would make it across the ocean to me, and I broke down. Don't laugh. You see, I wasn't a heartless bastard after all. I'm not ashamed to tell you about it. Me, Joseph Scarbo. Swear to God. I bawled like a baby. For a minute, my old man was alive again. Let me tell you, I thank St. Christopher and the Blessed Virgin Mary that box came."

I kept staring at the cloud banks rolling in from the west. Already, sleet was spraying the windshield with its fine shot. I remembered what my father had taught me about never showing I felt someone else's pain. I closed my hand around Mr. Pettyjohn's wedding band.

"You don't get it, do you?" Joey said. "Don't you see I'm the good guy here?" He raced the 88's motor, cranked the wheel, and spilled us out onto the blacktop, tires screaming, singeing the air with the smell of hot rubber. "If you ask me, you're the lousy son of a bitch. I want to bring back the dead. All you want to do is bury them."

The 88 dipped into an S-curve, and I closed my eyes. I braced myself for the lean and twist, waited for the violent shift I trusted to sling us free.

That night, our telephone rang. My mother was playing "Mona Lisa" on the piano, and she held a chord and then let it go. "It's bad news," she said. "I know it."

My father came upstairs, rolling down his shirt-sleeves.

"This one will be felt," he said. "My, yes. Most unfortunate. A young boy."

"A boy?" My mother closed the keyboard cover.

"Joey Scarbo. Sammy's nephew. Such a shame. Snap to, Colonel."

I was sitting on the piano bench next to my mother, and I recalled the moment I had seen her sitting there beside Joey, playing scales, her trembling fingers reaching for the next note, each building on the last. It hit me, then, that she must have loved Joey for his timely entrance into her life, as if he had been sent to her to replace the friend she had lost when Mr. Pettyjohn had died.

"It's a horrible thing," she said to me. "A horrible, horrible thing." She closed her hand around my arm. "You know that, don't you, Perry? What a tragedy this is?"

The clock on the piano chimed eleven. My father tightened the knot in his necktie.

"Colonel?"

"Yes, sir."

"It's time we got started."

Although it sounds terrible to say it now, the truth is I felt a tremendous freedom, knowing Joey was dead. I felt as if someone had given my life back to me, and I wanted to tell my mother not to worry. I was going to be all right. But then she stood up from the piano bench, and she clutched her robe closed at her throat. "Go on," she said to me, and her voice was ugly and raw. "Go," she said again. "Go be his little Nazi."

I drove the hearse with care. The streets were slick with snow, and the tire chains rattled and clanked.

"Imagine, Perry," my father said. "Joey. A boy your age."

Joey had smashed Sammy's 88 on the S-curve, had clipped a bridge abutment. I imagined the 88 hurled into space, spinning an uncommon trajectory, something wild which held no claim to earth.

"Keep both hands on the wheel," my father told me. "Up high where everyone can see them. If they can see your hands, they'll know you're a square Joe. They'll know you've got everything under control."

At the Texaco, the 88 hung from the wrecker's winch. Boys with their jacket collars turned up, their shoulders hunched against the wind, circled the car. They tapped a wheel with their boots, they squatted on their haunches to see how the fenders had peeled back, how the motor had shoved itself through the fire wall.

Farther away, at a safe distance, girls wrapped their arms around their chests and stamped their feet in the snow.

When the hearse's headlights swept over them, the girls stopped shuffling their feet, the boys straightened and lifted their faces. They stared at us—the girls with their bobby sox drooping from their calves, the boys with their hands shoved into their jacket pockets, everyone's face red from the cold.

"Don't look at them, Colonel," my father said. "Come to attention."

"Sir?"

"Eyes straight ahead. Don't embarrass them. Don't let them know how precious they are in their grief."

It was after midnight when we eased the gurney, clacking along its rollers, out the back of the hearse. Joey's weight came to us, shifting and settling in the body bag. I could feel it in my arms, and suddenly the loose rattle of muscles and organs and bones undid me, and I said to my father, "I stole Mr. Pettyjohn's wedding band. I've got it here in my suit jacket. I know it was a wicked thing to do."

My father lifted his face to the second-story window where my mother's piano lamp cast a faint and distant glow. "Better classify that information, Colonel," he said to me. "Wouldn't want it to fall into enemy hands." He put a finger to his lips. "Top secret. Better keep it on the QT."

The next morning Sammy the Egg came to make Joey's funeral arrangements.

"Shouldn't we wait for your sister?" my father said.

Sammy thumped his fist against his chest. "I'm the one responsible here."

I had stayed home from school for Mr. Pettyjohn's funeral later that morning, and I was standing with Sammy and my father in the foyer, just outside the chapel. Sammy was clutching his black leather satchel. It was a frigid day, and he had brought in the smell of the cold and the damp. It was a gamey, rotten smell, and when I looked at him—the way he stood with his head bowed, the shiny egg of his skull raw and gleaming in the light—I could see how close he was to coming apart.

"And another thing." He gave the satchel a shake, and I heard the combs and clippers and scissors clank together. "I want to cut the hair."

My father shook his head. "That wouldn't be decent. You being family. No, I couldn't let you do that."

"I've got a right to do this," Sammy said. "Listen, Roy. No one else should cut that boy's hair."

"No," my father said. "That's one thing I absolutely won't allow. I'll get Loyal Hall. He'll do a good job."

Sammy's shoulders dropped; his chest fell. "Loyal Hall," he said. "Jesus Christ." He let loose a great sigh as if all the air were leaving him. He rocked back on his heels, and I had to catch him to keep him from falling. As he leaned into me, I staggered with his weight.

"Steady," my father said, coming to my rescue. "Easy now. It's all right, Perry. I've got him." The two of us ushered Sammy into the grief counseling room. We slipped off his coat and eased him into a chair.

"I promised my sister I'd look out for that kid," he said. "Make him toe the line, put him into shape."

"Tell your mother we'd like some coffee," my father said to me. "How do you like your coffee, Sammy? Black? Make it black, Perry."

"Black it is," I said.

Upstairs, my mother was having her own coffee at the kitchen table. She was still in her bathrobe, and her hair was in curlers for Mr. Pettyjohn's funeral. She was stirring sugar into her coffee, her hand making lazy circles, the spoon clicking against the cup. We hadn't spoken since the night before when she had called me my father's little Nazi, and for a moment I hesitated, afraid to approach her.

I watched her idly stirring her coffee. I knew she had tried her best to sweeten her days there above the chapel. She had listened to opera with the Pettyjohns on Saturday afternoons, she had given piano lessons, and once Sammy the Egg had told her a joke—a corny joke: "What's black and white and red all over?"—and she had been so lonely she had howled, nearly screamed with thanksgiving.

And I loved her for her loneliness, but I couldn't tell her that, because I was sixteen and I didn't know how to tell my mother I felt sorry for her. So I tapped my knuckles against the archway, and she lifted her head.

"Perry." It startled me to hear her say my name. "Did I hear someone come in downstairs? Was it Mrs. Pettyjohn?"

"No, it was Sammy. Dad sent me up to get him some coffee."

"For Sammy?" She patted the curlers in her hair. "Poor Sammy. I'll get dressed. Tell your father I'll bring that coffee down in just a jiff."

From the top of the stairs, I could see below me the toes of the over-shoes—women's overshoes—barely visible, as if their owner had tried to hide herself and hadn't done an adequate job. They were Mrs. Pettyjohn's overshoes; I could see that as I came farther down the stairs. She was standing with her head bowed, her pocketbook hanging from her arm, an embroidered handkerchief twisted in her hand. She was wearing a cloth coat and a black hat with a net veil over her eyes.

"I didn't want to disturb anyone." Snow was melting from her boots, pooling up on the carpet. She tapped her heels together. "Oh, my. Look what a mess I'm making. It is a mess, isn't it, Perry? And I didn't want to be any bother."

"A little snow," I said, trying to keep my voice airy, but not exaggerated. "Let's get those overshoes off so you'll be more comfortable."

I took her elbow and helped her to a settee against the wall.

"I know it's early," she said. "But I thought if I came, I could have some time with him. You know what I'm saying, Perry. Some more time. Before the funeral."

She lifted each foot so I could unzip her overshoes and tug them free. One of her slippers came off, and she crossed her legs and pointed her toes so I could ease it back on.

All the while, I kept thinking how commanding she was in the class-room, her pointer whacking against the chalkboard as she marched us through our drills.

"Is it all right I came?" she asked me.

I held her hand and lifted her to her feet. "Let me help you with your coat," I said, "and then you can go on in."

In the grief counseling room, Sammy the Egg was telling a story about my father.

"This was when we were kids, Perry. About the age you are now. I bet you don't even remember it, Roy. Me? I've kicked it over and over. I can't even look at you now without calling it to mind."

My father sat on the edge of the sofa, his knees together, his hands folded in his lap. "I don't know what you're talking about," he said. "Honestly, I don't have a clue."

"It was when my old man died. You were a pallbearer."

"Yes, I remember there weren't enough. I remember my father and I filled in. It was my first time."

"My old man was a drunk, Perry. That's the truth of it. I can't deny it. He was a drunk, and he didn't have enough friends to carry him to the grave. I was ashamed—I don't mind saying it. All I wanted was to get beyond that day, to get out of that graveyard and go on with my life, but then you did what you did, Roy. And now you don't even remember it, do you?"

My father shook his head. "That's ancient history."

"Not to me. I remember like it was yesterday. You took my hand. Not the way a man would—to shake it—but the way a girl would—to hold it. A sappy move like that, something you must have seen in the movies, and all I could do was stand there and let you do it."

I could hear, in his voice, the disgust Sammy had preserved and carried with him since that moment in the cemetery. I wanted to tell him I felt sorry for him, now that death had left him out in the open again, but then my mother opened the door and stepped into the room.

"Roy," she said, and my father looked up at her.

"Yes." His voice was faint, reaching out to her from the small space Sammy had backed him into with his story. "I'm here."

They spoke in muted tones, their words half-whispered, a code only people who have loved each other a long time can use.

My mother pointed to the foyer. "Please."

"A problem?"

"Mrs. Pettyjohn."

"Yes?"

"A wedding band."

Mr. Pettyjohn's ring was still in the breast pocket of my suit jacket. I had confessed my crime to my father. He had told me to keep it secret, and I had obeyed him.

"Do you know what it was like when your old man did that?" Sammy said to me after my mother and father had left the grief counseling room. "When he took my hand? That knucklehead. He was this kid with asthma, this kid no one gave a rat's ass for, and there he was holding my hand like he was Florence-fucking-Nightingale. Do you know what that was like?"

I suspected I did, but I wouldn't tell Sammy that. I wouldn't tell him because I didn't want him to know how my mother made me feel—"delicate," as if I would never survive anything ugly or brutal in the world.

"It was like nothing I can tell you. It was like he could have done anything he wanted to me, and I would have let him. He blindsided me, and somehow I knew—even a dope like me—I knew how alone I was. So alone a boy like Roy Sievers could feel sorry for me, and I could let him."

I imagined my father, at my age, holding another boy's hand, and it gave me an odd and sickly feeling to know that I would have done the same thing. We were that much alike. I thought of how he used his hands to take people by the elbows—the slightest touch—to usher them into a car, to the guest register, to the gravesite. I thought of how I felt whenever I held the door open for mourners, when I carried flowers into the chapel, when I drove a car in a funeral procession, when I helped lower a casket into a grave. The only word I could think of to describe it was "love." As corny as it sounded, that's what it was, a deep and abiding love for all those left sweet and wanting: the women who clutched my hand as I helped them into their cars; the men who let me hold their coats for them and button them as if they were children; Sammy the Egg, who a few minutes before had crumpled against me. How easy it was to love them all, everyone who came to me mourning. That was my father's secret, the one he carried with him each time he presided over a death.

Outside in the foyer, Mrs. Pettyjohn's voice rose the way it did in class whenever someone mangled a verb conjugation. "For God's sake, Roy Sievers. Robbing the dead. You. A man we should all be able to trust."

The door to the grief counseling room flew open, and my father marched in.

"Get up," he said to Sammy, and Sammy, without a word, got to his feet.

My father's voice was low, the voice he used when he spoke to mourners, but now there was an edge to it, the sharpness he used when he barked out advances during war games. "I've had my eye on you," he said. He smoothed the lapels of Sammy's blazer with his small fingers. He buttoned the blazer and gave it a tug, stretching it tight across Sammy's shoulders. "You owe Mrs. Pettyjohn an apology, soldier."

My mother and Mrs. Pettyjohn had followed my father into the room. Mrs. Pettyjohn had balled her handkerchief up into her fist; my mother was holding her by the elbow, one arm across her shoulders.

"What is this?" Sammy said to my father. "What kind of crazy stunt are you trying to pull?"

"Tell him, Colonel," my father said, and I snapped to.

"Sir?"

"Tell him what we know."

I knew what my father wanted me to say, but Sammy was glaring at me. One look at his face and I could see that we were marching into dangerous territory. A few steps more and it would be too late. I knew I could save us—there was still that chance. All I had to do was tell the truth, confess that Joey and I had stolen the wedding band, take it from my pocket. But something held me back. I wanted to think that it was courage, that I was reckless and bold, but I knew it was only because I was a coward, afraid to betray my father.

Sammy was still staring at me, and I imagined something of what Joey must have felt—the horror—that moment in the S-curve when he must have known the 88 would never hold.

"He's been stealing from the corpses," I said. "Rings and stuff. That's what he's been doing."

Sammy's satchel was on the floor by his feet. "Maybe I should check your bag," my father said. "See what you've got in here."

He leaned over to open the satchel, and Sammy jerked up his knee, catching my father in the face.

It was a quick and vicious blow, one that caught us by surprise, and I heard my mother say, "Roy." That was all. That one word—like a breath—and then my father was on his knees, holding his face in his hands, and Sammy was picking up the leather satchel and storming out the door, his shoulder knocking against me as he left.

Still holding onto Mrs. Pettyjohn, my mother again said, "Roy"—louder this time, as if she wanted him to know she was still there. Then she looked at me, and I had never seen such a helpless look on her face. I took Mrs. Pettyjohn and ushered her out into the foyer.

"It was his wedding band," Mrs. Pettyjohn said. "I didn't want to cause trouble, but I wanted him to have his wedding band. Now look what's happened."

Behind us, in the grief counseling room, my father was still on his knees. His shoulders were heaving, and my mother was kneeling beside him. She was trying to press him to her, as if he were someone lost and sweet, dear to her now in a way he had never been. Quietly, so as not to disturb them, I closed the door.

"Poor Perry," Mrs. Pettyjohn said. "The world must seem like a miserable place to you now. But don't worry. You're young. You'll survive all this. Remember, as long as one person knows *amo*, . . ."

"Yes, ma'am," I said, even though I was rotten with guilt. Inside me, where my father had told me I would have to hollow out a space for other people's misfortune, my heart was ragged and worm-eaten.

Then I heard my parents' sobs, and they were like nothing I had ever heard. I stood in the foyer, their wails rising around me—my mother's, my father's—and I surrendered. I took it in, let it fill me up: their chorus of regret and desire, their grand artillery of grief.

MARJORIE SANDOR

Portrait of My Mother, Who Posed Nude in Wartime

MY FATHER WAS THE PHOTOGRAPHER IN OUR FAMILY, THE ONE WITH A sense of occasion, and he bore this burden alone, as my mother refused to distinguish between famous moments and the rest of life. He made gallant jokes about this, calling himself "the accursed husband"; she was the only wife in their circle who didn't keep a family album, simply threw snapshots and mementos into an old shoebox where they went yellow and curled up. This is how we lost the winter and early spring of 1945, when he was stationed in California, and she was pregnant with me. *Indiana, 1945* is our family's gap, our sole unrecorded moment. He mentioned this to her once, but she was unrepentant. "Oops," she said. "'Oops' isn't sorry," my father replied, but she said no more, only gave him a look of such mild surprise that he knew she'd never admit anything. Maybe he had his own secrets, because he dropped the subject fast. After he died, she would tell me this story, but for years, all I knew was that my mother, who had never before seemed mysterious to me, could seal a piece of time like a letter and send it away.

There is, in fact, a picture from that winter—if you count the one Father asked Grandmother Eva to take on the December day he got his orders. Late afternoon, I'm guessing, and almost too dark, but he'd have seen the light fading as they ate their dinner and risen swiftly from the table. "When else, when else?" he'd cry in his exulting, worried way, his hands trembling a little as they did on even the smallest occasion, as if he still hadn't gotten over his own miraculous change of fortune. That was what he called it, so that as children we had a confused image of him as a boy in rags at a carnival booth, winning his college scholarship and our classy mother all in one night.

In the photograph he stands with his foot on the running board of a big dark car, reaching for my mother's shoulder, coaxing her into the frame. My brother Gabe, who would have been three by then, isn't in the picture—probably running wildly around Grandmother Eva's snowy yard, already impossible to catch. So it's just the two of them: my slender, nervous father in his new uniform, all dark with gleaming buttons, and my mother in something dark, too, with a white collar and cuffs, to make you think of pilgrims and convent girls. Somber, stoic, just right for the year of moving back in with her mother. Was he hoping for a romantic wartime portrait? No luck: he was still in the act of pulling her in when Grandmother Eva clicked the shutter, so that both of them appear a little tipped, off-balance. My mother's dress is all wrong, too. It blends into the twilight, leaving her face and the white collar and cuffs pale and detached, floating off from my father, the car, everything.

To move back into your widowed mother's house after four years of married life would be like being dragged into a different kind of dark: closet-dark, suffocating. Stepping back over that threshold, how do you hold on to your new self? You're not a daughter anymore but a woman who'd gotten sweaty in sex and later pushed a big baby into this world, making any ugly face you pleased. None of this would seem legitimate, even possible, in Grandmother Eva's house—my mother would have been instantly, purely, *daughter* again. It didn't matter that every week there was a postcard on the hall table, always absurdly bright, each with a beautiful blond cradling oranges or an Indian maiden strolling the courtyard of a crumbling church. The messages themselves were terse, amazed telegrams from an impossible place. *Hard to believe it's winter and we're in a war, it's so beautiful out here. Don't let Gabe grow too fast! Maybe you have some news for me? Your devoted swain, Abe.*

Your devoted swain. On the fifth or sixth postcard my mother must have frowned—if only he wouldn't try so hard. I picture her on that winter afternoon, leaning down to hand the bright card to my brother, Eva right there watching her. It happened suddenly, boredom slipping over her like a harness, her arms and legs gone heavy, grotesquely shackled by fatigue.

Eva shrugged. "There are plenty worse," she said, a remark simply meant to remind my mother that she was lucky, given the crazy world and her own impulsive nature, to have made even this mediocre marriage. But my mother instinctively pictured herself tottering on the rim of a seething pit, barely held back from falling into unimaginable disaster.

Eva took Gabe firmly by the wrist and motioned my mother up the staircase. "Go on up to your room, take a nap," she said. "I'll call you in an hour."

Sent to her room! It was as if nothing had changed—no husband, no child, no little rented cottage of her own. In Eva's house, history was a door shut tight before my mother was born—her parents' early lives long since put away in that dark bristling silence called Europe. *Enough ugliness*, Eva always said. *Why would we burden a child?* Upstairs, her girlhood bed had been carefully arranged ahead of time, a comfortable American bed with the sheets turned down and a long-sleeved nightgown laid smoothly out. It never failed in this house: down she went and slept straight through to dark. Waking up, she couldn't get her bearings, confused briefly by the ghostly shape of her bridal bedroom. My God, which way am I facing—where is the wall, where the window? I imagine it as she once told me to, like an impossible homesickness, one that reaches back and back into all the known rooms of your life, until you give up and put out your hands into a swimming darkness like the one where we begin, where there is no memory yet of any place.

Where I must have been beginning. Every afternoon, in the blue winter light, my mother was tugged into foggy sleep. "Maybe I'm under a spell," she said to Eva.

"That's what your husband would call it," Eva said grimly. "How far along do you think you are?"

"God, Mother, I'm not," she said, though in fact her period was late—but it was always late, or early. She was sick to death of counting.

"Never mind," said Eva. "You just need to get out more."

Eva had an errand in mind, something to shake my mother out of her daze: "a mission of mercy" she called it. She herself was coming down with a cold, and my mother could just bestir herself to do one small favor. There was a new refugee couple in town, and the ladies of the Temple Sisterhood had been bringing them food and nice things. The wife was apparently quite ill—a female disease, that was the Sisterhood rumor—terrible, said Eva, but at least it was nothing contagious.

"Too bad," my mother blurted out, laughing crazily.

Eva's face blanched; she grasped my mother's arm. "Bite your tongue," she whispered. "You think God can't hear in America?"

The synagogue charity league in wartime: in the corners of the sanctuary lobby were heaped bags of shrunken winter oranges; rations of coffee and sugar; potatoes, tins of stewed prunes, badly knitted mittens and baby bootees; faded, battered toys. The ladies of the Sisterhood had been assigned to the handful of refugee families in town, and on a given Saturday they could be seen marching down the sidewalk—usually in pairs for moral support, since sometimes a refugee took the charitable gesture the wrong way and threw the ladies out "unceremoniously." But then there were other times, times discussed at great length in the ladies' households afterwards, elaborated on and built up and redecorated until they were dazzling emblems of American goodness suitable for children: how such-and-such a family allowed the Sisterhood ladies to enter the apartment, sat them down at a little deal table, and wept with gratitude. Some were wary: you had to hold out friendship like birdseed on your palm, and if you were lucky, one allowed you to teach a few useful phrases of English, and oh, so heartbreaking, offered in return a few words of her home tongue—provided it wasn't German. German nobody would talk. *I'll spit first*, said the refugees. This detail the ladies did not carry home to their children.

"The husband is an artist—but don't go getting ideas," Eva said to my mother. She frowned just the way she did when my mother was a teenager, to make sure my mother got the idea of duty—even fear—mixed in with the apparent romance of the errand. Then Eva went on building her careful picture. This artist, a Russian who'd been living in France, seemed almost too lucky. Such privilege isn't right, is it, when ordinary people are suffering so? A big museum in New York City had paid for his passage and taken care of everything: money for food and clothing, even paints and canvas, very hoity-toity. Nobody in the Sisterhood had heard of him, but she was willing to reserve judgment. The museum people wanted him to live in the city, of course, and he'd tried it for a year, but he'd grown tired of the noisy streets, the trash cans always banging. This, too, was where his wife's health had begun to decline. *He chose our town.* Eva's voice was hushed now. She was proud, almost maternal about the artist's decision to leave the city.

She lowered her voice even more: Mr. and Mrs. Artist haven't chosen a temple yet, she said, and at this precise juncture, she thrust a quart jar of chicken broth into my mother's hands.

"Oh no," murmured my mother.

"Chicken soup they'll understand, artist or no artist," said Eva. She wasn't finished yet, either. Into a mesh bag she dropped oranges and two lopsided knitted caps, one slightly smaller for the invalid wife. "Childless," she said. "Maybe given the circumstances, this is for the best. I'll watch Gabe for you—go now." Eva gave her a light shove. "Hurry," she said. "Hurry back before it's dark."

Of course everything Eva said had the wrong effect: the more she shaped the story, the wilder the possibilities grew in my mother, her dreams floating up like dust gone gold in the light. She took alleys and side streets to get there. Hedges gleamed at her in the dusk; the back walls of familiar houses turned faintly pink. Sycamore, Linden, Birch—any of these might be the one that led to the house of the exiled artist and his wife, that new country where she had not yet been discovered. If only she could get rid of the chicken broth, still warm as she stepped forward, holding it up and out on the palm like a false beacon, a golden joke lifted up to the night. But Eva had trained her well: she was too superstitious to drop it.

Still, for the next ten minutes she was free of the papered walls and damask curtains of Eva's house, of the loud squat mantel clock and velvet sofa, of the spotless front parlor forbidden to children. It was a big enough gift to look aimlessly up at the stars, at the black sky, fathomless and terrible and comforting all at once, to let the mind rove. To imagine the artist and his wife making their fabled escape from France, from Paris, though she had nothing to go on. It would have to come from movies: rainy streets at night, heavy fur coats, hat brims pulled low. Then a fabulous ocean liner, its ship's horn trumpeting out the great announcement barely heard by the people on shore. But the truth was she didn't even know his name, let alone his work. Why was it that her mother had told her nothing? Not his name, not where he was from, not the sort of pictures he was famous for?

And she, herself—wasn't she equally to blame for failing to ask? And so, walking, she bowed her head, doomed to look the fool, an overgrown Girl Scout in front of these brilliant, sophisticated people—and briefly, just for a flicker of a moment, she suspected this was what her mother intended. Was it some kind of test to see if she could stand the shock of the inevitable contrast, the sudden framing of her own life? *A little disappointment never hurts*, she could hear her mother saying afterwards. *In the long run, it will make you stronger.* Even in the chill air, she felt the damp heat of future humiliation settling under her arms, in the creases of her palms.

But beneath it, already, her dreaminess was rising back up. She admitted this much to me: that while my father was away that winter she had to forcibly remind herself that she was a married woman, because she still felt like the young girl she'd been ten years before, long before she met him. Going down the sidewalk that day under the guise of a missionary Girl Scout, she was in fact a fantastic spy, a secret invader, a thief coming to snatch a rare jewel from a black velvet case, and she would have gladly made a perfect idiot of herself if only she could have walked away afterwards saying, *Now I know something I didn't know before.* What if it was all right to not love anyone in particular, she thought—to be a flying angel, observing everything with a single enchanted eye, no need to light any one place or know any given name; to be, for a minute, as close to the burning stars as you were to the cooling earth?

When the painter opened his front door, he was not wearing the paint-splattered smock and beret my mother had naively anticipated, but an old gray sweater that hung loose over his wrists. He took off his glasses, held out his hand. "I'm Lev. And you?" She felt strangely at ease, and amazed by herself, so grown-up, the hands not shaking at all. It was his face that made this possible: delicate, feline, the light-green eyes narrow and uptilted like her own. It was the curly brown hair falling around the face like a woman's, not like any man's she knew—not like my father's, in other words: my father with his dark, carefully combed hair and his nervous urgency in all things, even in sex. *The first time is no picnic*, was all she would tell me for years. Now I know how it went for her, with the roar of the great Niagara Falls beyond the wedding-night window, how he tried to be gentle, but in his rush, clumsily pinned her hair under his hand.

"Sorry!" he whispered. She knew she should laugh, but his face above hers was a mask, tense and furtive with need, and a sudden loneliness swept over her. She was surprised by the strength of her disappointment; it seemed to fling itself up and bang around the room like a crazy bird. "It's nothing, sweetheart," she said, still lying beneath him, her eyes filling up. *This is absurd*, she told herself, averting her face. *He must never know.*

At the front door, the artist was reaching out to take the chicken broth, the mesh bag with the two hats. "Angels so rarely bring chicken soup these days," he said mournfully, and my mother's face burned. Why, if he was mocking her, did he look at her so intently, as if enchanted by something that nobody else had divined? Holding the jar in the crook of his arm, he gestured her in. "A glass of tea, a cup of wine?" he said, laughing.

"I promised my mother I'd get right back—dark, I have a child—"

"No—not a child!" he murmured, vaudeville and somber all at once, his gaze so direct that she instinctively held her coat tightly to her chest. She was a little afraid—not of him, exactly, but of the long stretch of the hallway behind him that seemed to pull her in with its dank smell, foreign and vaguely familiar all at once.

On his free hand, midway up the thumb, she saw a streak of incandescent blue. "That's a beautiful color," she said shakily.

"You're interested?" he said. "Listen, come back again soon. No soup necessary for admission. My wife will want to meet you. You have something of her family's look. Russian?"

"On my mother's side."

"It would make her very happy," he said. "Please."

It took her awhile to get back there again. She had to play it slow and smart with Eva. Emphasize the *Landsmann* angle, the sick wife who wanted to meet her. "Oh, and Mother, you're right, it's not contagious," she said firmly, in the new tone she'd been trying out on Gabe. And then, as if God really were listening, she got Eva's cold on the very day she planned to go back—and so did Gabe. "It's not that bad," she cried, but Eva insisted she stay in bed lest she endanger the baby.

"Yes, Mother," she said, though this still didn't feel like pregnancy to her, here under her mother's roof. Surely by then I had begun to stir, to press and move against her, making her imagine me as a small nervous invader, a little like my father. She might have looked down and put her hand over me, but I kept kicking lightly, I refused to be still. Never mind—she didn't have to think about me yet. That night, was it a fever? A dream all dark red translucence and black, her mother's front parlor transformed by lurid red-shaded lamps, bordello fringe. Women passed through a beaded doorway, monumental women draped in veils and bearing dishes of ice and oil. *Lie down, dearie,* they said. "But it's my mother's best room! She'll have a fit—" she insisted as she lay down. They ran ice down her small childlike breasts, across her knobby hipbones—how on earth had she become a child again? They smoothed her down with oil, then ice again, preparing her for some ritual . . . then, in her sleep, a warmth, a bloom of light below that flooded belly and thighs, toes and fingertips. She awoke damp and aching, needing to urinate. Eva stood over her, a cool dry palm on her forehead. She closed her eyes, pretending to be very, very ill.

"Thank God the fever broke," said Eva, looking at her warily. "Don't move a muscle, I'll get you a drink of water."

For days after, her skin was slippery; she couldn't get clean enough. She felt Eva watching her at breakfast, at dinner, at darkfall, giving her the worried look she'd give a cloudy pane of glass. "Do you want to tell me something?" Eva said, and my mother glanced up, giving her the first of those utterly mild, baffled looks that would later be her mystery. "Me?" she said, laughing. "God knows there's nothing to tell. Gabe's the one who still has things to say. Ask him—he's fresh!"

"Don't push me," said Eva. "I'm in no mood." But my mother simply turned and smiled at Gabe—her excuse, her salvation. That day and days after, she escaped the house with him, took him out for walks in the town park, sat on a bench while he hid among the great trees he called the magic grove. His bright hair flickered at intervals, a sudden flame between the limbs, the first faint greening of the trees. "Find me, Momma," he cried. "Come in here." One day, when she ducked under the boughs, she was surprised at how private this place was, how unsuspected. Passersby couldn't see her at all. For the first time in her life, she thought, *maybe a secret isn't such a crime.*

That same day, on their way home, they came upon a tree whose long, fine red needles swooped low to the ground like the long hair of a woman bending at the waist. From this tree came a rustling, then a low, urgent cry. *I've gone crazy*, she thought, and in answer there was an endless scurrying. A pair of gloved hands parted the veil of needles and out came a soldier and a girl, gone down the sidewalk in an instant. The tree was no less miraculous: Gabe reached out to touch it.

"Feel it, Momma," he said.

The needles were impossibly soft, like human hair. She thought instantly of Eva, how even this thought would appall her, would seem a mutinous act.

"Let's make this tree our secret," she said, with much more passion than she had intended. "Not even Grandma can know."

"Our secret," Gabe repeated solemnly.

She took his hand. *If nothing else*, she thought, *I have given a child this.*

At his front door Lev took both her hands in his, warmly, warmly, then released them and opened his arms wide. Her heart beat lightly in her ears—in mine!—and she nearly closed her eyes. Open them fast, Mother—he only meant to help you off with your coat.

"Manya," he shouted. "Come downstairs, there's somebody to meet you." My mother's face was hot again, and she glanced away, down the street, and nearly prayed. She was somebody's wife, somebody's mother; he was obviously in love with his wife, and she, possibly, a dying woman. She knew this should be enough, but it wasn't, it wasn't.

A beautiful dying woman: when she came down the stairs, who could believe she was really ill? Maybe it was a story they'd put out to keep people from bothering them. Her hair floated dark around her pale, fine-featured face; everything about her was exact, concise, intentional, except her eyes—smoky black and deeply shadowed beneath. My mother was surprised: Manya had nothing whatever in common with her own family's tepid Northern coloring. Why had Lev said that? He was the one. It was Lev who had her family's looks. This joke felt suddenly sweet, purely intimate, with no ragged edge of irony to cut her.

"Are you an artist, too?" she asked his wife boldly, and they both laughed. "Not far off at all," they said. "Come, have some tea. Tell us about yourself."

She fell easily into the role of their child that afternoon—a comfortable place, from which she could look out from her idiot desire undetected, her blood singing beneath her skin even as she clasped her hands neatly in her lap. They asked her to stay for dinner, and she telephoned Eva breathlessly. *I guess it's all right,* Eva said, sighing in that way that meant my mother would pay for this later. Back in their kitchen, she wanted to say crazy things to the artist and his wife: Lev and Manya, can I stay till midnight? How long? How long can you keep me? Everything dazzled her, made her ache with envy: the rough wooden kitchen table, the heavy green plates and black teacups, a paring knife and three mushrooms in pale winter sunlight. She was almost dizzy, as if falling off the careful story her mother had built, and into a wish so fierce it might blind her.

Did they sense this? Her greed, her willingness for whatever might happen next? Because she realized that they'd both gone quiet, as if they were watching the moment slowly, luxuriantly expanding into some new shape. The three of them waited in the quiet afternoon, watching a fly buzz and land on the brightened table, buzz and depart. It was Manya who broke the silence, turning to Lev. "You remember the one you wanted to try last fall?" She turned to my mother. "He wanted me to pose for an odalisque—what an idea! I'm worn out, and why pretend, my body is not nice anymore, not nice." She leaned forward. "Though I have a feeling about you. As if you could"—she broke off with a laugh—"but no. You are very nervous, a cautious girl. I can see exactly how you were raised. It's not your fault."

My mother sat still in that fine drift of light, her hand resting on her belly under the table. She had never been less nervous in her life—what did Manya mean? She hated that, being summed up with such confidence by a stranger! But a dreamer's stunned calm was still on her, a pure amazement at being in this kitchen, in this light; nothing could break its beauty, nothing. Lev, too, seemed caught by it. He was watching Manya carefully, as if by moving too soon, he might shatter the moment.

"I'm all right," my mother said. "I've never posed, I mean. But if you . . ." She felt absurdly slow, as if trying to form correct phrases in a foreign tongue. An odalisque! She'd seen these in art books: a nude lightly veiled or not at all, reclining on her dark couch, a gold necklace at the throat, a flower in the hair, nothing else. She looked at Lev. "Will Manya stay in the room? Because if my mother ever—"

At this, Lev broke into laughter and reached out for Manya's hand. "You're right—a maiden to the bitter end," he said. He sat up straight, rubbing his eyes and looking at both of them admiringly, as if he'd come out of some long magic slumber. "Don't worry. She'll stay. And you can be sure no one will ever recognize you."

It was Manya who took charge, who guided my mother into their front room where the light would last longest, and pointed out the painted Japanese screen behind which she might disrobe—that is, if she still felt comfortable with the idea. "Of course," said my mother lightly, looking demurely down.

That day the winter dusk did not pull her down into sleep—not right away. She had time to notice the bright canvases stacked against the walls, the books in precarious piles on either side of a long blue velvet couch, the jars of brushes and vivid smears of paint, the acrid smell of solvent; to notice, before she slipped behind the Japanese screen, what was painted there: the ocean, a tree yearning its way, three women with parasols gazing back at her—surely it meant something, but she would never know what. It was strangely comforting, a mystery poised and coolly watching her till the end of time. At her feet lay a box heaped with velvet ribbons, jewels, bunches of silk violets. "Anything you see here that you like," Manya said. My mother's flesh went suddenly cool, as if she'd stepped behind a doctor's screen, but Manya handed her a bright silk kimono. "Take your time. Lie down on this couch and call us when you're ready."

She chose bravely: a tiny golden fan, a bunch of violets—nothing that would clothe or hide her.

When they came back and saw her lying down in the kimono with the violets and the fan, they stood perfectly still a moment, then burst into applause, a light, comical applause that made her feel safe and powerful, as if she were far away from them on a high stage. But in Lev, did she permit herself to see something more, a nod, a collusive smile as if to say, *you are beautiful, just right* without in the least being disloyal to his wife? They were all three like tightrope walkers, she thought, playing even the smallest moment for its grace and danger. "I feel like I'm in the circus," she said, and Lev looked at her blankly, nearly frowned, by which she knew she'd surprised him, gone a little further than expected. "You'll like this, then," he said softly. "All our props are stolen. Manya here has committed the sin of raiding your own beloved Majestic. We won't tell if you don't tell."

Manya laughed bitterly. "Here's how I'll go down in history: 'His wife, at the end revealed to be a chronic kleptomaniac, nearly shattered his career by stealing from small town theaters—'"

"Manya, slow down," said Lev. "You'll scare our novice."

He knelt down then, and arranged my mother. She felt her own stillness like a triumph, this new talent, the way this man couldn't see or hear or know the light double pulse beating in her veins, the twinning of my life and her excitement, a dark, sweet invasion. She refused to tremble for him, even when he leaned closer and put the bunch of violets into her other hand and with intolerable tenderness draped her elbow against her hip so the flowers fell lightly against the dark triangle of her pubic hair. The fan she was to hold over her head, he said, looking right at her. *Think of a Spanish dancer with her castanets.* "I am," she imagined herself saying, straight out of the fantastic silence of her skin, her secret in the world.

"Very chaste," he said. "Manya?"

Manya came forward and pushed the kimono lightly, roughly, back off my mother's shoulders.

Manya. Now my mother trembled, because Manya was looking straight into her, and her dark eyes knew. Did Lev? She couldn't tell; he only frowned, a workmanlike impatience sheathing his face.

"Let's get started," he said. "A fast sketch is all I need, and we'll send you home to your mama." And with a sharp look to her, he stood up and kissed Manya, light and slow on the mouth.

My mother did not faint. She was light and heat, a pure current of fury and desire. She held herself perfectly still.

"Magnificent," he said. "Manya, you've got an eye."

When in that hour did she begin to falter, her fingers gone numb on the little gold fan, sleep coming for her as it had to? And what, in an artist's front room, with its lush disorder of jumbled books and phonograph and bright paintings stacked against the walls, what in all this could have reminded her of her mother's squat mantel clock ticking in the front parlor's dark clean silence, the forbidden velvet sofa she once lay on as a child when her parents were out; where now she pictured my bright-haired brother lying on his belly, angrily kicking his legs? *Where's Momma? I won't go to bed, I won't, till she comes. You can't make me.* Even my father appeared to her as she lay in her pose. She pictured him in a train compartment, alone and in civilian clothes, his head nodding forward as he fell asleep, too, his slender hands for once not shaking, though tightly gripping the armrests as the train hurtled toward home, vulnerable. She was startled by a sudden sweet dinging, a light endless chiming of a clock she couldn't see. On and on it went, she could swear, nine times—or more than that! She glanced up in a panic, and strangely, her gaze fell not on Lev working at his easel, but on Manya beside him, reading in a chair. How long does it take to see the simple, terrible thing? Because gradually she noticed that the collar of Manya's blouse was damp, that Manya's fingers, under lamplight, shone on the pages of the book.

"Please, no—you're crying," my mother said. "I'll leave."

"My fault completely," said Manya, standing up. "You've been a good girl. But I, for one, am off to bed. And don't anybody try to tuck me in."

Manya stood up and walked past Lev without looking at him, but just in front of my mother she'd slowed down, stopped utterly. She leaned over my mother. "How did I miss it before?" she said quietly. And she reached out to touch my mother's abdomen with her cool wet fingers. My mother flinched, her breath knocked suddenly away. "Lev," said Manya. "Lev, you won't believe. Stop a minute." But Lev, purely vanished behind his easel, did not stop. My mother heard the scratch of his pencil, his quiet steady breathing, the true terrible distance between them. She went cold all over, but forced herself to look again at Manya's pale, haggard face, her reddened eyelids. For her my mother took a deep breath, very deliberately so Manya would hear, and submitted, while Manya's cold fingertips traveled slowly across her pale swollen belly.

"Isn't it funny," Manya said. "The very place that's killing me." She turned back to Lev. "Make it stark white," she said hoarsely. "So it hurts the eye to look there. God, I wish there were a color in the world like that." Then she stood up and walked out of the room.

"Wait," cried my mother, but Manya was gone, and still Lev worked. In the awkward quiet she saw her own smooth flesh white and exposed and avid—there was too much of it, a whole country of it swamping the room, alive and crude and insulting. She scrambled up to her feet, pulling the kimono up with her, wrapping herself in it tightly.

"Pardon, but what did you do with my clothes?" she said haughtily.

Lev sighed and put down his pencil. "Don't worry," he said calmly, as if he'd known from the beginning how it would go. "We never steal clothes. You can change behind the screen and let yourself out when you want. But you should see the sketch before you go. You might be sorry later—"

"No thank you, I don't need to see it," she said stonily. She gathered up her clothes from behind the screen—even this felt like an important refusal—and rushed out of the room. But where to go? The rest of their house had long since gone dark. She had no idea where to go. She fumbled through a short hallway, her hands blind on the walls, until she found a door and waved her hands high in the air for a light-chain. There—it was their bathroom, the linoleum a ghastly mustard yellow, the bar of soap streaked with dirt and paint—she got herself dressed, the desolate little bulb above her head illuminating every mole and crease of her belly and thighs, the darkened aureoles of her breasts.

When she came out, she saw that she was near their kitchen, and that Manya sat at the table again, her shoulders curving forward, her head down. The rest of their house was a maze to my mother now; she felt she had no choice but to go to Manya and ask the way out. But when she got there, Lev sat across from her on the other side of the table, both his hands stretched across to hold Manya's. She needn't have worried; as she came forward, neither of them looked up. The green plates and black cups were still on the table, the mushrooms on the breadboard, flat gray and stale under the harsh, ordinary kitchen light. A still life, she thought, only nobody would want to paint it.

"Goodbye," she said, and without waiting to see if they'd looked up, she opened their back door and stumbled out onto a porch. Once down, she moved her hands along what felt in the dark like a rough wild mass of hedge, until she came at last to cold metal, a garden gate she hadn't known was there. She lifted the latch and let herself out onto the sidewalk, her own town, a strangely warm and noisy night. Noisy—why? It was May, early May—there was no holiday then that she knew of. But car horns were honking, and firecrackers sputtered from the direction of downtown. *Who do they think they are?* she thought wildly. *Idiots — it's not any holiday.*

Eva was waiting for her at the front door, of course, her arms folded across her chest in her habitual posture of forbearance, but strangely, there was no recrimination in her eyes, only a deep weariness that haunted my mother as she walked past her, going in.

"Gabe?" asked my mother.

"Awake," said Eva. "I wash my hands. And by the way, your beloved husband's home, upstairs and waiting. He wanted to surprise you."

My mother said nothing, but went slowly toward the stairs. It was all as she'd known it would be: she looked into the parlor and saw Gabe exactly where she'd imagined him, on the forbidden sofa, crying and kicking his legs, refusing to look her in the eye. And the radio was on, as it never was late at night in Eva's house — a jumble of band music and excited voices, static, then a woman sobbing as she tried to speak through the jubilation.

"Mother, tell me what's happened," she cried. "Has something changed?"

"Only the whole world," said Eva, sighing. "What could it possibly matter to you?"

In all the years of our childhood, my mother made sure my brothers and I were never late for a big occasion. If we had somewhere to go — a wedding, a funeral, a formal gathering of any kind — she stood in our bedroom doorways and tapped her foot, or pleaded from the foot of the stairs, "Can't we be on time? Just this once?" Not even my father, who wanted so badly for the world to see his family whole and right, could match this panic of hers. She was never comfortable at big parties and celebrations — *ordeals*, she called them — but when the time came, she hurried us into the car so fast our hearts pounded wildly. "It matters to me," was all she'd say.

It took years, and my father's death, for her panic to fade, for her to begin to tell me things. But she would never tell me Lev's real name, or if the painting was somewhere I could find it. "I wish I knew," she told me once, in her exasperatingly mild, indifferent tone. "I don't know if he even finished it. If he did, he took it away with him when his wife died." She looked at me with pure astonishment, as if she were still a naive young woman, and all of this had just happened. "What matters is that Manya was dying," she said to me. She closed her eyes and took a deep breath. "I'm sorry. Say anything you want, but no piece of art can make up for that, ever."

Not his last name, not the name of the painting, but the rest of the story—this she would tell, blandly, dully, as if she were pulling heavy curtains across a theater stage. "It was over, everything at once," she said. A month after the armistice and a week after his wife's death, Lev sent a thank-you note to the temple: they'd taken care of Manya's cremation for him, no charge, and they would be so honored if he'd let them keep the urn with her ashes there, in their own Jewish cemetery. They would even donate a handsome engraved plaque for the memorial wall. He must have slipped the note under the door in the night—nobody saw him deliver it. "No thank you," he wrote. "You've been too generous already. She's coming with me." And then one day, without warning, he was gone—with Manya's urn, his suitcases, the big canvases, boxes, and jars. Nobody knew where he'd gone, though briefly there was speculation: back to New York, or maybe all the way to Paris. Wasn't that where all the big-shot artistic types went when they were finished using up America's little towns?

But this little bitterness didn't last long. Amidst the crazy jubilation of boys coming home and the plain fact of a husband's bereavement, who could sustain hard feelings? Never mind—let history move forward again, carrying my mother along with it. History in the shape of my father, tanned and triumphant, and not empty-handed either—he'd come back with a bundle of brightly colored real estate brochures and a quiet new confidence. Even that first night she saw it. He didn't ask her where she'd been but simply held her in a tender, certain embrace in her girlhood bed, holding before her the brochures with their scenes of California's spectacular coastline, its abundant valleys—spreading them before her as if she were his child, and this, a bedtime story. She leaned back into him; it was easy, comforting. "The fruited plains," he said. "For once they're not lying. What do you say—westward ho?"

He laid his hand on her belly then and leaned down, smiling. "Let's get you out of this trap," he whispered, and wildly she thought, *My God, which one of us does he mean?* She smiled for him, granting him his witty moment, but he took this to mean she was willing to make love and moved his hand smoothly, smoothly, down toward her sex. She flinched. "Oh, sweetie," she said, working a little shakiness into her voice. "Can you wait, can you give me a night to get used to—"

"It's the baby, isn't it?" he said tenderly, innocently, and she bowed her head in gratitude.

"Tomorrow night," she said. "I promise."

Surely she knew Lev's real name, his whole name; surely she knew enough about the painting to recognize it later. What if it is in one of her old art history books, on my own bookshelf now, in plain view and utterly hidden?

"Forget the painting, remember Manya," she said to me. I was grown by then, and she was very ill. Her eyes, as she finished the story, were as dark and deeply shadowed as Manya's must have been.

"Forget the painting," she said to me. If I can't, it's because of that moment just before she fled, the moment Lev finally put down his pencil and asked her if she wanted—no, *needed*—to see the sketch before she left. "No," she cried.

No? From everything she told me, I don't believe her. I know Lev to have been quick in all things, a little wild—maybe not unlike her. Maybe he knew something about the dark undiscovered spring at the heart of her, knew that later she would wish, just as fervently, that she had said yes. What else could he offer her, how else to say it? He turned the easel around.

Here you aren't, he must have said tenderly, in a voice with no mockery at all, a voice that would give her a gift even as it pretended to deny her. So that she saw, before she ran away, her own hand languidly covering her sex with a bunch of flowers, and her own pale torso transformed. It was true, Mother, you were no longer yourself, but an angel floating in a depth of blue, your eyes pure and austere with years of watching, your amazing body skimming the air.

Later that night you would lie with my father, his hands and yours pressed together over the place where I fed and grew, where other cells, inevitably, would one day feed and divide. You closed your eyes so he wouldn't see you crying, wouldn't see your guilt and confusion, your panic as you tried to picture the future, and couldn't—that way was dark too. It's late, Mother, but listen anyway, while I tell my children that somewhere in the world there is a painting of you and me, and in that painting your womb is not stark white and humanly cursed, but a whole dazzling universe, the burning blue-white of bones and stars.

WILLIAM GAY

I Hate to See That
Evening Sun Go Down

WHEN THE TAXICAB LET OLD MAN MEECHAM OUT IN THE DUSTY ROAD
by his mailbox, the first thing he noticed was that someone was living
in his house. A woman was hanging out wash on a clothesline, a young
girl was sunning herself in a rickety lawn chair, and an old dust-colored
Plymouth with a flat tire was parked right in Meecham's driveway. All
this so disoriented the old man that he almost forgot about paying the
cab driver. He thought for a dizzy moment that he had directed the
driver to the wrong place, but there was the fading clapboard house and
the warm umber roof of the barn, bisected by the slope of ridge, and
his name on the mailbox—ABNER MEECHAM—painted in his own
halting brushstrokes.

"Looks like you got company," the cab driver said.

Beyond the white corner of the house the woman stood holding a
bedsheet up to the line, studying him, transfixed with a clothespin in her
mouth.

"How much was it I owed you?" Meecham asked, finally remembering
the driver. He fumbled out a wallet chained to his belt, then turned slightly
to the side to study its contents.

"Well. Twenty dollars. That seems like a lot, but it's a right smart way
from Linden, and I hardly ever make out-of-town runs."

"And worth ever nickel of it," the old man said, selecting a bill and
proffering it through the window. "Twenty dollars' distance from Linden
is fine with me. If I was a wealthy man I'd have bought more of it."

"Glad to of brought you," the driver said. "You be careful in all this heat."

Meecham just nodded, picking up his suitcase and preparing to
investigate these folks making free with his property.

As he passed the lawn chair the girl casually tucked a pale breast into
her halter top and said, "Hidy. Do I know you?"

"You will here in a minute." He was a fierce-looking old man, slightly stooped, wearing dungarees and a blue chambray work shirt. The shirt was faded to a pale blue from repeated laundering, the top button fastened against his Adam's apple. His canvas porkpie hat, cocked over one bristling eyebrow, and his washed-out blue eyes were almost the exact hue of his shirt. "Who are you people, and what are you doin here?"

"I'm Pamela Choat and I'm gettin me a tan," the girl said, misunderstanding or pretending to. "Mama's hangin out clothes, and Daddy's around here somewhere."

"I mean, what are you doing *here*?"

The girl put her sunglasses back on and turned her oiled face to the weight of the sun. "We live here," she said.

"That can't be. I live here. This is *my* place."

"You better talk to Mama," the girl said. Behind the opaque lenses, perhaps her eyes were closed.

Meecham turned. The woman was crossing the yard toward him. He noticed with a proprietary air that the grass needed cutting.

"Ain't you Mr. Meecham?"

"I certainly am." He leaned on his carved walking stick. A lifelike wooden snake coiled around the staff up to the asp's head forming the curve he clasped. "I don't believe I've made your acquaintance."

"I'm Mrs. Choat. Ludie Choat—Lonzo's wife. You remember Lonzo Choat."

"Lord God," the old man said.

"We rented this place from your boy."

"The hell you say."

"Oh yes. We got a paper and everthing. We thought you was in the old folks' home in Perry County."

"I was. I ain't no more. I need to use my telephone."

"We ain't got no telephone."

"Of course there's a telephone. We always had a telephone."

The woman regarded him with a bland bovine patience, as if she were explaining something to a backward child. "There's one but it don't work. It ain't hooked up or somethin. You need to talk to Lonzo. He'll be up here directly."

"I'm an old man," Meecham said. "I may die here directly. Where is he? I'll go to him."

He found Choat in the hall of the barn, locked in mortal combat with a flat tire. Stripped to the waist, he was wringing wet with sweat, his belly looped slackly over the waistband of his trousers. He had a crowbar jammed between the tire and the rim, trying to pry them apart. Meecham noticed with satisfaction that the tire showed no sign of giving.

When the old man's shadow fell across the chaff and dried manure of the hall, some dark emotion—dislike or hostility or simply annoyance—flickered across Choat's face like summer lightning. He laid the crowbar aside and squatted on the earth. He wiped sweat out of his eyes, leaving a streak of greasy dirt in the wake of his hand. Meecham suddenly saw how like a hog Choat looked—red jowls and close-set little eyes—as if maybe fate had a sense of humor after all.

"You not got a spare?"

"This is the spare. I think I know you. You're lawyer Meecham's daddy. We heard you was in a nursin home. What you doin here?"

"I didn't take to nursin," Meecham said. "Is it true Paul rented you folks this place?"

"He damn sure did. Ninety-day lease with a option to buy."

The old man felt dizzy, almost apoplectic with rage. The idea of Choat eating at his table and sleeping in his bed was bad enough. The thought that he might eventually own the place was not to be borne.

"Buy? You wasn't ever nothin but a loafer. You never owned so much as a pair of pliers. That's my wreckin bar right there. If you think you can buy a farm of this size with food stamps, you're badly mistaken."

Choat just shook his head and grinned. A drop of sweat formed on his nose, trembled, and fell. "You still as contrary as you was the time I tried to rent that tenant shack off of you. You wouldn't rent it to me, and now I'm livin in the big house. Ain't life funny?"

"I never rented that shack to nobody. That buildin ain't but seventy or eighty feet from the main house, and I never wanted strangers livin so close. Anyway, all that must have been twenty-five years ago."

"Ever how long it was, I needed it and I didn't get it. And life *is* funny. I got a boy in Memphis, he's a plumbin contractor, does these big commercial jobs. He makes plenty of money. And you can forget about the food stamps. He buys and sells lawyers like they was K-Mart specials, and he aims to buy this place. We're goin to tend it."

"Well, I ain't seen none of this famous money. And the fact of the matter is, this place ain't Paul's to sell. It's my place and will be till I die. It may be Paul's then, but after this, I doubt it. In fact I'm pretty sure Paul's shot at this place just went up in smoke."

"They fixed it up legal."

"If I was you I'd be packin my stuff. Where's that paper?"

Choat got up. "It's up to the house."

"Then let's be for goin up to the house," the old man said.

Meecham sat on the doorstep of the tenant house in the shade and pondered his options. It was almost twelve miles back to Ackerman's Field, the nearest town and the one in which Paul did his lawyering. The old man had no telephone and no car; in actuality he owned a two-year-old Oldsmobile and a four-wheel-drive Toyota pickup, but when Meecham's driving had grown erratic, Paul had taken them into town for storage, and the old man figured by now they were somewhere in Mexico with the serial numbers eradicated. If Meecham had not shown foresight, he would have been broke as well as stranded, but at the first mention of nursing homes, he had withdrawn a thousand dollars of his savings and deposited it in a Linden bank. Folded, it made a thick and reassuring bulge now in his left front pocket.

So he had money but nowhere to spend it. He had a neighbor across the ridge, but he was too weary to walk there. Choat's car had a flat tire, but that hadn't even been factored into the equation. Folks in hell would be eating Eskimo Pies before he let Lonzo Choat haul him anywhere. He opened the suitcase. One change of clothing. A razor and a bar of soap. A toothbrush and a miniature tube of toothpaste. A tin of Vienna sausages and a package of crackers he'd bought in case he got hungry on the cab ride.

Meecham glanced toward the house. The woman was standing in the doorway watching him as if she'd learn his intentions. He looked away and heard the screen door fall to. The day was waning. Beyond the farmhouse, light was fleeing westward and bullbats winged slant-wise through the trees as if they'd harry the dusk. When a whippoorwill called, an emotion somewhere between exaltation and pain rose in him, then twisted sharp as a knife. It was as if all his days had honed down to this lone whippoorwill calling to him out of the twilight.

He sat for a time just taking all this in. Whippoorwills had been in short supply in the nursing home, and it was a blessing not to smell Lysol. Here he could smell the trees still holding the day's heat and the evocative scent of honeysuckle and the cool citrusy odor of pine needles. "Well, I've lived in tenant houses before," he told himself, and he rose and went in.

At least the lights worked. He guessed that Paul was still paying the electric bill, figured that the first one to come due in Choat's name would be the last. The old man had used this place for junk, and Choat seemed to have toted everything he didn't want down from the main house. Boxes of pictures Lucinda had saved were spilled about at random, and Meecham was touched with anger: his very past had been kicked through and discarded.

He set about arranging some kind of quarters. He placed Paul's old cot by the window for what breeze there was, then sat for a time studying snapshots—dead husks of events that were as strange to him as if they'd happened in someone else's life. An envelope of photographs of dead folks. One of Lucinda's father lying in his casket—his shock of black hair, great blade of a nose. Another of Lucinda standing by the old man's grave. Meecham studied her face carefully—it looked ravaged with grief—before he put the photos away.

He fared better in an old brass-bound trunk. Choat had missed a bet here. Meecham found Paul's old handgun, a long-barreled .22 target pistol on a .45 frame. He couldn't find any shells.

Meecham shuffled through a stack of 78 rpm records, reading the labels. Old Bluebird records by the Carter Family. Victor records by Jimmie Rodgers, the Singing Brakeman: "Evening Sun Yodel," "T for Texas." He could remember these songs from his youth, could remember singing them himself. Jimmie Rodgers, dead of TB and still a young man after all these years, and even turning a dollar off the disease that was to kill him: *That graveyard sure is a lonesome place . . . they lay you on your back and throw dirt in your face.*

He moved stacks of folded quilts from the Victrola and raised the lid. The machinery creaked when he cranked it, and he doubted it would work, but the needle hissed on the record and out came Rodgers' distinctive guitar lick. Then a voice out of a dead time but still holding the same smoky sardonic lilt: *She's long, she's tall, she's six feet from the ground. . . .*

The old man didn't hear the girl until she was in the room, a plate in one hand and a glass of iced tea in the other. Jimmie Rodgers was singing, *I hate to see that evenin sun go down . . . cause it makes me think I'm on my last go-around.* He rose and lifted the tone arm off the record.

"Mama sent this. She said she bet you was hungry, and that hot as it was, you needed somethin cold to drink."

Having anticipated nothing like this from a Choat, he took the plate awkwardly and cleared a spot for it on the coffee table. She set the tea beside it. "Well. You tell her I'm much obliged. What's Lonzo have to say about it?"

"He was down at the barn. What's that you're listenin to?"

"That's Jimmie Rodgers, the Singin Brakeman."

"What is that, hillbilly? Sure is some weird-soundin shit. Where's he out of, Nashville?"

"Out of hell, if he's out of anywhere. He's been dead and gone from here for fifty years."

"Oh. Well, how do you know he's in hell?"

"He's in the ground with the dirt throwed in his face. That sounds a right smart like hell to me."

"Lord, but you'd cheer a body up. You always in this good a mood?"

"Just when I get rooted away from the trough." He was studying the plate. He mistrusted Ludie Choat's cooking and figured her none too clean in her personal habits, but then you didn't know what was in Vienna sausage either. Here was okra that had been rolled in meal and fried. The plate also held garden tomatoes peeled and sliced, and he figured if everything else proved inedible he could at least eat the tomatoes.

"What are you doin, movin in here?"

"Yes I am. I'll have it right homey before I'm through. Curtains on the windows. I may even get me a dog."

"Daddy won't allow a dog on the place—can't stand to hear them bark."

"Hmmm," the old man mused. "Say he can't?"

"I got to get back to the house. Set the dishes on the porch in the mornin, all right?"

"All right," he said irritably, peering closely at the plate. "But I believe I recognize this as mine anyway."

At first light he was up, as was his custom, and in the dewy coolness he went up the slope behind the tenant house. At its summit he rested, leaning on his stick and peering back the way he'd come. The slope tended away in a stony tapestry, the valley lay in haze, and mist rose out of the distant hollows, blue as smoke. On this July morning each sound seemed clear and equidistant: cowbells on the other side of the woods, a truck laboring up a hill on some road invisible to him.

Meecham had moved from Alabama to Tennessee when he was a young man, had farmed for others before finally managing to buy a farm of his own. He had lived most of his life here in Ackerman's Field—fifty years and better of it—but more and more these sights and sounds reminded him of his childhood in Alabama.

Meecham entered the cool, dappled green of the woods, going downhill now, and when shade changed to light, he was in Thurl Chessor's pasture, approaching the barn and house. He went on past deceased tractors and mowers and old mule-drawn planters like museum artifacts.

Chessor was walking back toward the house with a feed bucket in his hand. Meecham had known Thurl for forty years as a farmer with no head for business, no eye for the small detail. He was apt to leave a tractor out in the weather, the intake filling with rainwater and pine needles, then curse the folks in Detroit or wherever when it wouldn't start. On the other hand, Meecham thought ruefully, Thurl was not living in a tenant shack with Lonzo Choat reared back like the lord of the manor.

Chessor put the bucket on a slab shelf and turned and studied Meecham with no surprise. "Well, I see you're back. Run off, did you?"

"Yeah."

"Are they after you?"

"After me? Hellfire, it was an old folks' home, not a chain gang. Why would they be after me?"

"I don't know. I don't know anything about it. Where'd you sleep last night? Did Lonzo let you crawl in with him and Ludie?"

"Never mind where I slept. I need to use your phone. I need to call Paul and get this mess straightened out. I've got to get Choat out of there."

"You'll play hell doin it. Or doin it quick anyway. You get him evicted legal, the law gives him thirty days. He's got a foot in the door now."

Thurl followed him into the front room where the phone was. Meecham dialed and spoke with a young woman who would make no commitment about Paul's whereabouts. The old man was put on hold for some time

SELECTED FICTION FROM THE GEORGIA REVIEW

before she came back on the line: "Mr. Meecham is engaged right at the moment."

"Then unengage him. I aim to clear this mess up and no mistake about it."

"I'm sorry, sir, Mr. Meecham is tied up. His time is very valuable."

"If I hadn't sold calves and pigs to send him through law school it wouldn't be worth fifteen cents. You get him on this phone."

There was a dawning of knowledge in the woman's voice. "Are you Mr. Meecham's father, by any chance?"

"Yes, I am."

"Well, I'm sorry, sir, I didn't understand. He's on his way to court, but I'll have him paged. He has a beeper. Give me your number, and I'll have him return your call in a moment."

Meecham read her the number and cradled the phone. Paul's got a beeper, he thought to himself. He was unsure what a beeper was but nonetheless vaguely impressed. He tried to call Paul's face to mind, but it was the child Paul had been that came swimming up from memory. Meecham sat staring at the phone and wondering where that child had gone.

He picked up on the first ring.

"Dad?"

"So you got you a beeper," the old man said.

"Dad, what is this about?"

"I want them folks out of the house, and I want them out now."

"Where are you calling from?"

"Thurl Chessor's place. They've broke my phone or somethin. Are you goin to get them out today or not?"

There was a pause. "What are you doing there? You're supposed to be in the nursing home at Linden."

"Supposed to be? I'm supposed to be where I damn well please. What is this mess you've got cooked up?"

There was another pause, longer, and this time Paul's face did come to Meecham's mind: thin but fleshed out with rich food and prosperity, tanned from the golf course, his pudgy fingers massaging his temples as if the old man was giving him a headache.

"This is too complicated for the telephone," Paul finally said. "Call a cab, and go back to the nursing home. I'll come down there"—a pause again, and the old man knew Paul was looking at the date on his wrist-watch—"day after tomorrow at the latest and explain everything about the sale."

"Sale my ass. You can't sell what ain't yourn."

"Well, obviously we need to discuss it, but as regards what I can or can't do, I'm your legal guardian and the trustee of your estate. When you started acting erratic after Mama died, I got worried about you. I figured you were a danger to yourself, and the court—"

"I'll be a danger to a whole hell of a lot more than myself unless you get this paperwork unscrambled. Hellfire, I'll do it myself. I'm not penniless. Do you think you're the only lawyer who ever hit a golf ball?"

"Tomorrow or next day, all right?"

The old man slammed the phone so hard Chessor glanced to see if it was broken. Meecham was lightheaded with rage. Black dots swam before his eyes like a swarm of gnats, and he felt dizzy and strange, as if his soul was packing up to flee his body. It seemed to him that he had scraped and cut corners just to send Paul to learn a trade that was now doing Meecham out of what had taken a lifetime to accumulate.

When he'd calmed himself, he sat on the porch with Chessor, drinking coffee and trying to formulate a plan.

"Well?" Chessor asked.

The old man sipped his coffee and sat staring across Chessor's yard toward the pear tree. The yard was a motley of broken and discarded plunder, and dogs of indeterminate breed lay about it like fey decorations some white-trash landscapist had positioned with a critical eye.

"He give me the runaround."

"Ain't that the way of the world," Chessor said.

"I got to have a way of goin. You still got that old Falcon?"

"Yeah. It runs, but I had to quit drivin it. They took my license when I kept runnin into folks. I can't see like I used to."

"What'll you take for it?"

"I don't know. Two hundred dollars? Would you give that?"

"Let's look at it."

He checked the oil and brake fluid. He checked the coolant level and listened to the engine idle. Thurl was apt to run an automobile without oil and use water for brake fluid and trust the radiator to replenish itself.

"What was that place like?"

"It was all right."

"All right? That's why you're livin in a tenant house, I reckon."

"No, it was all right. They fed you pretty good, nobody mistreated you. It was just . . . it was just a job to them, I guess. You had the feelin if you died in your sleep they'd just move you out and a live one in, and go about their business."

"You want the car?"

"I guess. Throw in that spotted dog with one ear up and the other one down, and I'll give you ten extra bucks."

"That dog ain't worth ten dollars. I'd just about knock ten off the car to get rid of him. That thing sets in barkin long about dark and don't let up till daylight."

"He may be a fifteen-dollar dog," Meecham said.

After the old man drove to town and laid in supplies—bread and milk, gallon of orange juice, soup and other tinned goods, and a hot plate to warm the soup—he was feeling fairly complacent. He had also bought a box of shells for the pistol. Sitting on the porch after supper, watching the day wane with the rusty green Falcon in his driveway and his dog dozing at his feet, Meecham felt quite the country squire. Only the thought of Paul caused him a certain disquiet, like waiting for the other shoe to drop. His son had probably figured that he'd gone back to the nursing home—but he wouldn't think that forever. Eventually he'd turn up with a sheaf of the legal papers he was so fond of.

The old man named his new companion Nipper—after the dog on the label of Jimmie Rodgers' records. It was in his mind to train the animal, but he immediately discovered that it needed very little encouragement. If he allowed it to lie on the foot of his cot, it remained quiet. If he set it outside, it began to bark. Meecham rewarded its efforts with bits of tinned mackerel, and noted with delight that when he teased the dog with a section of fish it would erupt into a fierce barking, its little black eyes bulging, ugly as something left on a beach by the tide.

Of course Choat noticed the dog right away, but he ignored it until nightfall, then came in his shambling graceless walk down the slope from the main house. "Where'd you get that thing?"

The old man was sitting on the stoop, cradling the dog as you might a child. Nipper watched Choat warily, with eyes shiny as bits of black glass. "It followed me home," Meecham said. "I guess you could say I found it."

"You better lose it then. I ain't havin no dog on this place."

"It's my place and my dog, and I guess you'll like it or lump it. He don't bark much."

"Yeah. I heard him not barkin much most of the goddamned day. It'll come up with its neck wrung, and you may not fare much better."

"He's a good boy—don't bother nobody. You hush now, Nipper."

The dog began to bark ferociously at Choat, straining against the fragile shelter of the old man's arms.

"You *learnt* that little son of a bitch to do that," Choat said. "I don't know how you found out a barkin dog drives me up the wall, but by God you did, and it's goin to cost you."

The old man felt a grin trying to break out on his face, but he abruptly swallowed hard and fought it down, for Choat had raised a fist and looked about to attack man or dog or both, his flat porcine face flushed with anger.

"You touch me and I'll have you in jail for assault before good dark," the old man said.

Choat lowered his fist and turned toward the main house. "You need put in the crazy house—and that's where you'll be fore this is over."

"You hush there, Nipper," Meecham told the dog.

The old man was abed early but awoke at eleven o'clock, as he had planned to do, and went with the dog onto the porch. Filigrees of moonlight fell through the leaves, and the main house was dark, locked in sleep. He sat on the stoop and packed the bowl of his pipe with Prince Albert. When he had the pipe going and the fragrant blue smoke rolling, he opened a tin of mackerel.

"Hush, Nipper."

The dog began to bark.

He forked out a mackerel and fed it to the dog. It stopped barking and ate the fish greedily and looked about for more. "I've done fed you," the old man said. "You behave yourself, now."

The dog began a fair frenzy of barking. After a while the porchlight came on at the farmhouse, the door opened, and Choat came onto the porch, wearing only a pair of boxer shorts. "How about shuttin up some of that goddamned racket?" he called.

"I can't get him to hush," the old man yelled. "I don't believe he's used to the place yet."

"He's about as used to it as he's goin to get. You bring him up here and I believe I might be able to quieten him down some."

"He'll be all right. I expect he'll hush by daylight."

"You contrary old bastard! I'm just goin to let you be and outlive you. You'll be in the ground before the snow flies, and I'll still be here layin up in your bed."

Choat went back in and pulled the door closed and cut off the light. When the old man went inside with Nipper, he got out the pistol and loaded it. He found a can of machine oil and oiled the action, and when he spun the cylinder it whirled, clicking with a smooth, lethal dexterity.

Sometime past midnight, the old man awoke to such bedlam that for a moment he thought he must have dozed off in a crazy house somewhere. Looking out the window did little to refute this view. Choat was beating someone with a length of garden hose. Ludie was trying to wrest away the hose, but he turned and flung her backward. All of them were screaming at the top of their lungs, the hose making an explosive whopping sound each time it struck. "You little slut," Choat was yelling. Then Meecham realized it was Choat's half-naked daughter being beaten.

There was a car parked at the edge of the yard with the driver's door open, and all of a sudden someone streaked full tilt toward it—a young man pulling up his pants and trying to evade the hose, which was now slashing at him. The boy had one hand behind him, trying to grasp the flailing hose, the other hauling at his breeches, and he was screaming every time the hose struck. He leapt into the car, slammed the door, and frantically cranked the engine. The hose was bonging impotently on the roof as the car went spinning sideways in the gravel. Glass shattered when the car glanced off the catalpa tree in the corner of the yard. It righted itself, the headlights came on, and it shot off down the road.

Choat turned his attention back to the girl. She was on her knees with her arms locked about her face and head, and by the moonlight the old man could see her naked back laced with thick red welts.

"*Hold it*," Meecham yelled. He had the window raised and the pistol barrel resting on the sill. He lifted the enormous pistol and sighted at Choat's midsection.

Choat whirled. He looked confused for a moment, as if he couldn't fathom where he was or why someone was pointing a two-foot pistol at him. "You long-nosed old bastard. I might've knowed you'd put into this."

"I'm tired of watchin you beat folks," Meecham said. "You raise that hose one more time, and if what passes for a brain in you is big enough to hit, then I aim to lay a slug in it."

"You ain't got the balls," Choat said.

Meecham lowered the pistol and fired. When the bullet thocked into the ground, a little divot jumped up and showered Choat's bare feet with dirt. Choat dropped the hose and stepped abruptly back.

"I aim to law you too, first thing in the mornin. If they don't have a law about beatin young girls with hose pipes, I aim to see one gets passed."

Choat opened his mouth to speak. Then he closed it. At length he said, "You'll regret this, Meecham. You'll be sorry ever day of your life you shot towards me."

Meecham waved the pistol barrel. "Get this circus out of my yard so's a man can get some sleep."

In the morning the old man and Nipper drove the Falcon into town. At the courthouse he told the story of the daughter and the garden hose to a deputy, and he would not leave until he had assurance that papers would be served. He was back home before noon, seated on a Coke crate in the shade of the catalpa to see what would happen.

Shortly after that a white telephone service truck parked in the yard, and a man with a toolbox got out and went into the house. Meecham was pleased at this, for once he was back in his own house he might have use for a telephone. Then, in midafternoon, a dusty Ford with a police escutcheon on the door pulled up, and a deputy got out with a folded paper in his hand. He went up the steps to where Choat had come onto the porch in his undershirt. The deputy unfolded the warrant and read it to Choat, who then took it and read it for himself, shaking his head. He began protesting that this was all just some misunderstanding. Finally he gave up and went down the steps to the cop car. When he got in, the deputy slammed the door shut and they drove away.

Ludie and the girl followed in the Choat car. The rest of the day it was quiet until just before dark, when the Choat family returned. Choat himself was driving. He got out with a six-pack under his arm, unlocked the trunk, and took out a red five-gallon can with the word KEROSENE stenciled on the side in yellow letters. When he set it on the porch, he turned and gave Meecham a look so malevolent the old man expected the grass around him to burst into flame. Choat went into the house.

That night Meecham had difficulty falling asleep. An old man's sleep was chancy at best, but that night he had begun thinking about Lucinda. He remembered when they were young, when they couldn't keep their hands off each other and the nights were veined with heat. The way he wore Aqua Velva shaving lotion to this day because she had liked the smell of it when they were going together. Then the swift squandering of days and the last time he had seen her alive.

It was on a Saturday, and he was in a hurry to get to a cattle show but she kept dragging around, trying to decide between this dress, that dress.

"Well, you best be for wearing one of them," Meecham had said. "I'm goin out to the truck, and if you're not there in five minutes, I'm gone." He had laid his pocket watch in the seat beside him, and when five minutes were gone he cranked the truck. He saw her hand pull aside the kitchen curtain, her face lean palely to the glass. Then he drove away.

Now, when finally he slept, he dreamed strange, tortured fever dreams a madman might have. He was in the undertaker's office and they were discussing arrangements: backhoe fees, the price of caskets. They were sitting on opposite sides of a limed oak desk, and the undertaker was backlit so starkly his vulpine face was in shadow. The light gleamed off his brilliantined hair. Curving bull's horns grew out of his skull, and his yellow eyes seemed to be watching Meecham out of thick summer bracken.

"Of course, there's an option we haven't considered," the undertaker said. "We could animate her."

"Animate her?"

"Of course. It's a fairly expensive process, but it's done frequently. The motor functions would be somewhat impaired and the speech a little slurred, but it's immeasurably preferable to the grave. As I said, it's done frequently, mostly for decorative purposes."

Meecham was hit by a wave of exalted joy so strong it made him dizzy. "Animate her!" he cried.

"Then it's settled," the hollow voice said out of the bracken.

Meecham dreamed he turned over, his arm falling across the animated Lucinda. Then he woke up.

"Animate her," he was saying aloud. He was crying, tears hot and salty in his throat.

The dog was lying on the edge of the old man's pillow. Its fierce little teeth were bared, its eyes bulbous, its tongue swollen and distended. There was a piece of plow line knotted about its neck, and the covers were tucked neatly under its chin.

"Jesus Christ," Meecham said. He jerked backwards reflexively, forgetting the cot was scooted against the wall, and slammed the back of his head against the window frame. He sat rubbing his head for a moment, then crawled over the foot of the bed and fumbled the pocketknife out of his pants.

He cut the plow line and massaged the dog's chest. The body was still warm, but it quickly became obvious the dog was not going to take another breath. Meecham was seized with enormous sorrow. He had killed the dog as surely as if he had knotted the line himself. If he had left the dog alone it would still be fighting over scraps in Thurl Chessor's front yard.

He laid the dog on the floor. Carrying the pistol he went through the house making sure Choat was not hidden there, while hoping all the time that he was. The house was empty.

By the time he had made his morning coffee, he had come to see things in a different light. He realized that Nipper was more than a dog. He was a pawn sacrificed in a game Meecham and Choat had invented, and Choat had simply upped the ante.

There was no taxidermist in Ackerman's Field, but Meecham heard of one in Waynesboro and drove there. The process was more involved than he had known, and he had to stay overnight in a motel. The bill for preparing and mounting the dog was one hundred and seventy-five dollars, but the old man counted it out with a willing hand. He figured that every nickel he spent would be a nickel that Paul would not get his pale, manicured hands on. In fact, the old man wished that Paul could have been with him. He would love to tell Paul that he had paid a hundred and seventy-five dollars to stuff a ten-dollar dog for no other reason than to aggravate Lonzo Choat.

The taxidermist was gifted in his art, and this new and improved Nipper was transcendent: the man had given Nipper a dignity he had not possessed in life. His mouth was closed, his little glass eyes thoughtful and intelligent. The expression on his face suggested he was thinking over some offered philosophical remark and was preparing a rebuttal.

Meecham drove back to Ackerman's Field with Nipper in the passenger seat, positioned so that the little agate eyes faced the window. "Wish I could of got some kind of barker put in you," he said. "Maybe I'll get you a beeper."

Nipper sat motionless, watching the scenery slide by: ripe summer fields already fading slowly into autumn.

When Choat glanced up from the circular he had taken from the mailbox and saw the old man and the dog on the porch, his left foot seemed to forget that it was in the process of taking a step. He stumbled and did a double take, but then his face took on a look of studied disinterest and he went back to reading the circular.

When he glanced up again, Meecham was tossing sticks into the yard and saying "Fetch, boy."

"I wouldn't hold my breath till he brought that stick back," Choat said.

"He's a slow study," the old man agreed. "His papers showed some Choat in his family tree."

"You smart-mouthed old bastard. If I could buy you for what you're worth and sell you for what you think you're worth, I'd retire. I'd never hit another lick at nothin."

"You ain't hit that first lick yet," Meecham pointed out.

Choat was looking closely at the dog. "I bet that little son of a bitch is a light eater," he said.

"He don't eat much and he's a hell of a watchdog," Meecham said. "Lays right across my feet and never shuts his eyes all night. One of these nights the fellow that tied that plow line will come easin through the door, and I'll set him up with the undertaker."

The black Lexus gleaming on the packed earth before the tenant house looked as if there had been some curious breakdown in the proper placement of things. Then the door opened and Paul got out, smoothing down the blond wing of his hair. He took off his sunglasses, folded the earpieces down, and tucked them into the pocket of his sport shirt.

"Hey, Dad."

"I figured you'd be out here the minute you learnt I wasn't in that place. What's been the holdup?"

"I just found out today. Alonzo Choat called me. He tells me you're cutting a pretty wide swath around here."

"Well. I was never one to just let things slide."

"No. You were never that."

"Did you come out here to straighten this mess out?"

"In a way. I came out here to pick you up and drive you back to the nursing home."

"Then you've wasted gas and a good bit of your valuable time drivin out here. It'll be a cold day in hell when you guile me into that place again. I get mad ever time I think about it."

"Dad, it's just till we get this straightened out. The lease has to run its course. When it expires, I'll get out of the sale and you can move back in. If we need a practical nurse to look after you, I'll hire one."

The old man marveled at how different they were, how wide and varied the gulfs between them. It saddened him that he no longer had the energy or inclination to try and discuss them. But it amused him that Paul hadn't improved much in his ability to lie. Being unable to lie convincingly to a jury must be a severe handicap in the lawyer trade.

"I don't need a nurse," he finally said.

"Perhaps not. You need something, though. Shooting a pistol at a man. Having him arrested. Setting dead dogs around the porch like flowerpots. For God's sake, Dad."

"Well, I can't say I didn't do it. But you've got the wrong slant on it. I'm not goin to argue with you, you'd just lie out of it. Don't you think I know you? Do you think I can't see through your skin to every lie you ever told?"

"I'm not leaving here without you. You're a danger to yourself, and you're a danger to other people. Goddamn it! Why do you have to do everything the hard way? You know that if you don't go voluntarily, I'll have to get papers and send people after you. Is that what you want?"

The old man was suddenly seized with weariness, a weight of despair bearing down so that it took an enormous effort to reply, just to breathe. He sat packing the bowl of his pipe and staring at the red kerosene can on Choat's porch.

"Goodbye, Paul," he said at last. "Take care of yourself."

"I'll tell you what he did do one time," Thurl Chessor said. "He was in Long's grocer store, and when they wasn't nobody watchin him, he poked a mouse down into a Cocola bottle and let on he drunk off of it. Oh, he cut a shine. Spittin and gaggin. He throwed such a fit with Long, the bottlin company give him a world of cold drinks just to shut him up—cases and cases. They drunk on them all summer, like to foundered theirselves on Cocolas."

"But do you reckon he'd burn a man out?"

"I wouldn't think so. I never heard tell of him doin anybody any real harm. He'll steal anything ain't tied down or on fire, but he's too lazy to put out much effort."

"Well. He said he was goin to. He said that tenant house would go up like a stack of kindlin and me with it. I may have leaned a little hard on him, shootin at him and all. I believe he'll try it. He strangled that dog."

"You ought to get the law then. Tell the high sheriff."

"Choat would just deny it. He's tryin to make Paul think I'm crazy. All I want you to do is just speak out if anything does happen. Will you do that?"

"Yeah. I'll do that much."

"I wouldn't want him to get clean away with it."

"No. You can have another one of them dogs if you want it."

"No, I believe I'll pass," the old man said. "I'm a little hard on dogs. Besides, I've still got the other one."

"Maybe," Chessor said. "Maybe it would be the best thing all around if you just went back. You said it wasn't so bad."

"I lied," Meecham grinned. "It's a factory where they make dead folks, and I ain't workin there no more."

Chessor was silent a time, as if considering his own bleak future as well as Meecham's. "We all got to work somewhere," he said at last.

Meecham drove back home and sat on the porch, smoking his pipe and waiting for full dark so that he could steal the kerosene can. At last the day began to fail, dark rising out of the earth like vapors. Against the sky the main house looked black and depthless as a stage prop. Beyond the Rorschach trees, the heavens were burnished with metallic rose as if all the light was pooling and draining off the rim of the world like quicksilver.

The old man worked very fast. He figured if he faltered he'd quit, give it up, let Paul be a daddy to him. He upended a box of photographs and threw on old newspapers and lit it all with a kitchen match, and when the photographs began to burn with thin blue flames, he picked up the can to splash kerosene around the room—except when he poured some, the fire leapt toward him like something he'd summoned by dark invocation. Even as he hurled the can away, it exploded. Only someone like Choat, he thought, would store high octane gasoline in a can clearly labeled *kerosene*. He could feel his hair burning, as the room filled up with liquid fire. Vinelike flames were climbing the walls, and from the foot of the burning bed Nipper watched him calmly out of the smoke, his expressionless glass eyes orange with refracted fire.

Meecham covered his face with his hands and fell to the floor. Far off he could hear someone screaming, "Help me, help me." Then he realized it was himself.

He was lying on his back staring upward into the stars. His body seemed to be absorbing the heat from the wheeling constellations as he rocked on a sea of molten lava. He could hear a voice and an ambulance siren, and after a time he recognized the voice as Lonzo Choat's.

"The old man always grumbled about how close these houses are, but if they wasn't, I never would have heard him takin on. Beats the hell out of me what he thought he was doin. He's been actin funny. I believe his mainspring may have busted. I reckon he thought it was winter, and he was just buildin a fire."

"That's a hell of a brave thing you did, Choat," another voice said. "Let's roll with him, Ray."

Then the stars were shuttled from sight, and he was sliding down the sleek wall of the night. He could feel the ambulance beneath him taking stockgaps and curves, then there was a sharp pain in his wrist, and a voice was saying, "Lay back, old-timer, this'll cool you off."

He was in a cold glacial world of wind-formed ice, ice the exact blue of frozen Aqua Velva, a world so arctic and alien that life was not even rumored. He struggled up to see.

"Help me hold him, Ray, he's trying to get up."

"Why I believe we've crossed over into Alabama," Meecham told himself in wonder, and in truth the ice-locked world was evolving into a landscape sculpted by memory. The ambulance swayed on past curving lazy creeks he had fished and waded as a boy, winding roads dusted white as mica in the moonlight.

He pressed his face to the glass as a child might and watched the irrevocable slide of scenery—tree and field and sleeping farmhouse. He studied each object as it hove into view and went slipstreaming off the dark glass to see if it might have something to tell him, some intimation of his destination.

FOR CORMAC MCCARTHY

KEVIN BROCKMEIER

These Hands

THE PROTAGONIST OF THIS STORY IS NAMED LEWIS WINTERS. HE IS ALSO its narrator, and he is also me. Lewis is thirty-four years old. His house is small and tidy and sparsely furnished, and the mirrors there return the image of a man inside of whom he is nowhere visible, a face within which he doesn't seem to belong: there is the turn of his lip, the knit of his brow, and his own familiar gaze; there is the promise of him, but where is he? Lewis longs for something not ugly, false, or confused. He chases the yellow-green bulbs of fireflies and cups them between his palms. He watches copter-seeds whirl from the limbs of great trees. He believes in the bare possibility of grace, in kindness and the memory of kindness, and in the fierce and sudden beauty of color. He sometimes believes that this is enough. On quiet evenings, Lewis drives past houses and tall buildings into the flat yellow grasslands that embrace the city. The black road tapers to a point, and the fields sway in the wind, and the sight of the sun dropping red past the hood of his car fills him with sadness and wonder. Lewis lives alone. He sleeps poorly. He writes fairy tales. This is not one of them.

The lover of the protagonist of this story, now absent, is named Caroline Mitchell. In the picture framed on his desk, she stands gazing into the arms of a small tree, a mittened hand at her eyes, lit by the afternoon sun as if through a screen of water. She looks puzzled and eager, as if the wind had rustled her name through the branches; in a moment, a leaf will tumble onto her forehead. Caroline is watchful and sincere, shy yet earnest. She seldom speaks, and when she does her lips scarcely part, so that sometimes Lewis must listen closely to distinguish her voice from the cycling of her breath. Her eyes are a miracle—a startled blue with frail green spokes bound by a ring of black—and he is certain that if he could draw his reflection from them, he would discover there a face neither foreign nor lost. Caroline sleeps face down, her knees curled to her chest: she sleeps often and with no sheets or blankets. Her hair is brown, her skin pale. Her smile is vibrant but brief, like a bubble that lasts only as long as the air is still. She is eighteen months old.

A few questions deserve answer, perhaps, before I continue. So then: The walls behind which I'm writing are the walls of my home—the only thing padded is the furniture, the only thing barred the wallpaper. Caroline is both alive and (I imagine—I haven't seen her now in many days) well. And I haven't read Nabokov—not ever, not once.

All this said, it's time we met, my love and I.

It was a hopeful day of early summer, and a slight, fresh breeze tangled through the air. The morning sun shone from telephone wires and the windshields of resting cars, and high clouds unfolded like the tails of galloping horses. Lewis stood before a handsome dark-brick house, flattening his shirt into his pants. The house seemed to conceal its true dimensions behind the planes and angles of its front wall. An apron of hedges stretched beneath its broad lower windows, and a flagstone walk, edged with black soil, elbowed from the driveway to the entrance. He stepped to the front porch and pressed the doorbell.

"Just a minute," called a faint voice.

Lewis turned to look along the street, resting his hand against a wooden pillar. A chain of lawns glittered with dew beneath the blue sky—those nearby green and bristling, those in the distance merely panes of white light. A blackbird lighted on the stiff red flag of a mailbox. From inside the house came the sound of a door wheeling on faulty hinges, a series of quick muffled footsteps, and then an abrupt reedy squeak. *Hello*, thought Lewis: *Hello, I spoke to you on the telephone.* The front door drew inward, stopped short on its chain, and shut. He heard the low mutter of a voice, like residual water draining through a straw. Then the door opened to reveal a woman in a billowy cotton bathrobe, the corner of its hem dark with water. A lock of black hair swept across her cheek from under the dome of a towel. In her hand she carried a yellow toy duck. "Yes?" she said.

"Hello," said Lewis. "I spoke to you on the telephone." The woman gave him a quizzical stare. "The nanny position? You asked me to stop by this morning for an interview." When she cocked an eyebrow, he withdrew a step, motioning toward his car. "If I'm early, I can—"

"Oh!" realized the woman. "Oh, yes." She smiled, tucking a few damp hairs behind the rim of her ear. "The interview. I'm sorry. Come in." Lewis followed her past a small brown table and a rising chain of wooden banisters into the living room. A rainbow of fat plastic rings littered the silver-gray carpet, and a grandfather clock ticked against the far wall. She sank onto the sofa, crossing her legs. "Now," she said, beckoning him to sit beside her. "I'm Lisa. Lisa Mitchell. And you are . . . ?"

"Lewis Winters." He took a seat. "We spoke earlier."

"Lewis . . . ?" Lisa Mitchell gazed into the whir of the ceiling fan, then gave a swift decisive nod. "Aaah!" she lilted, a smile softening her face. "You'll have to excuse me. It's been a hectic morning. When we talked on the phone, I assumed you were a woman. Lois, I thought you said. *Lois* Winters. We haven't had too many male applicants." Her hand fluttered about dismissively as she spoke, and the orange bill of the rubber duck bobbed past her cheek. "This *would* seem to explain the deep voice, though, wouldn't it?" She smoothed the sash of her bathrobe down her thigh. "So, tell me about your last job. What did you do?"

"I'm a storyteller," said Lewis.

"Pardon?"

"I wrote—write—fairy tales."

"Oh!" said Lisa. "That's good. Thomas—that's my husband, Thomas—" She patted a yawn from her lips. "Excuse me. Thomas will like that. And have you looked after children before?"

"No," Lewis answered. "No, not professionally. But I've worked with *groups* of children. I've read stories in nursery schools and libraries." His hands, which had been clasped, drew apart. "I'm comfortable with children, and I think I understand them."

"When would you be free to start?" asked Lisa.

"Tomorrow," said Lewis. "Today."

"Do you live nearby?"

"Not far. Fifteen minutes."

"Would evenings be a problem?"

"Not at all."

"Do you have a list of references?" At this Lisa closed her grip on the yellow duck, and it emitted a querulous little peep. She gave a start, then laughed, touching her free hand to her chest. She held the duck to her face as it bloomed with air. "Have I had him all this time?" she asked, thumbing its bill.

Somewhere in the heart of the house, a child began to wail. The air seemed to grow thick with discomfort as they listened. "*Someone's cranky*," said Lisa. She handed Lewis the duck as she stood. "Excuse me," she said. She hurried past a floor lamp and the broad green face of a television, then slipped away around the corner.

The grandfather clock chimed the hour as Lewis waited, its brass tail pendulating behind a tall glass door. He scratched a ring of grit from the dimple of the sofa cushion. He inspected the toy duck—its popeyes and the upsweep of its tail, the pock in the center of its flat yellow belly—then waddled it along the seam of a throw pillow. *Quack*, he thought. *Quack quack*. Lewis pressed its navel to the back of his hand, squeezing, and it constricted with a squeak; when he released it, it puckered and gripped him. He heard Lisa's voice in an adjacent room, all but indistinct above a siren roll of weeping. "Now, now," she was saying. "Now, now." Lewis removed the duck.

When Lisa returned, a small child was gathered to her shoulder. She was wrapped in fluffy red pajamas with vinyl pads at the feet, and her slender neck rose from the wreath of a wilted collar. "Shhh," Lisa whispered, gently patting her daughter's back. "Shhh."

Lisa's hair fell unbound past her forehead, its long wet strands twisted like roads on a map. Her daughter clutched the damp towel in her hands, nuzzling it as if it were a comfort blanket. "Little Miss Grump," chirped Lisa, standing at the sofa. "Aren't you, sweetie?" Caroline fidgeted and whimpered, then began to wail again.

Lisa frowned, joggling her in the crook of her arm.

"Well," she said, "let's see how the two of you get along. Caroline—" With a thrust and a sigh, she presented her daughter, straightening her arms as if engaged in a push-up. "This is Lewis. Lewis . . ." And she was thrashing in my hands, muscling away from me, the weight of her like something lost and suddenly remembered: a comfort and a promise, a slack sail bellying with wind.

Her voice split the air as she twitched from side to side. Padding rustled at her waist.

"Oh, dear," said Lisa. "Maybe we'd better . . ."

But Lewis wasn't listening; instead, he drew a long heavy breath. If he could pretend himself into tears, he thought, perhaps he could calm her. For a moment as sharp as a little notched hook, he held her gaze. Then, shuddering, he burst into tears. His eyes sealed fast and his lips flared wide. With a sound like the snap and rush of a struck match, his ears opened and filled with air. Barbs of flickering blue light hovered behind his eyes. He could hear the world outside growing silent and still as he wept.

When he looked out at her, Caroline was no longer crying. She blinked out at him from wide bewildered eyes, her bottom lip folding in hesitation. Then she handed him the damp towel.

It was a gesture of sympathy—meant, Lewis knew, to reassure him—and as he draped the towel over his shoulder, a broad grin creased his face.

Lisa shook her head, laughing. "Look," she said, "Thomas and I have plans for this evening, and we still haven't found a baby sitter. So if you could come by around six—?"

Caroline heard the sound of laughter and immediately brightened, smiling and tucking her chin to her chest. Lewis brushed a finger across her cheek. "Of course," he said.

"Good." Lisa lifted her daughter from his arms. "We'll see how you do, and if all goes well . . ."

All did. When Lisa and Thomas Mitchell returned late that night—his keys and loose change jingling in his pocket, her perfume winging past him as she walked into the living room—Caroline was asleep in his lap. A pacifier dangled from her mouth. The television mumbled in the corner. Lewis started work the next morning.

As a matter of simple aesthetics, the ideal human form is that of the small child. We lose all sense of grace as we mature—all sense of balance and all sense of restraint. Tufts of wiry hair sprout like moss in our hollows; our cheekbones edge to an angle and our noses stiffen with cartilage; we buckle and curve, widen and purse, like a vinyl record left too long in the sun. The journey into our fewscore years is a journey beyond that which saw us complete. Many is the time I have wished that Caroline and I might have made this journey together. If I could, I would work my way backward, paring away the years. I would reel my life around the wheel of this longing like so much loose wire. I would heave myself past adolescence and boyhood, past infancy and birth—into the first thin parcel of my flesh and the frail white trellis of my bones. I would be a massing of tissue, a clutch of cells, and I'd meet with her on the other side. If I could, I would begin again—but nothing I've found will allow it. We survive into another and more awkward age than our own.

Caroline was sitting in a saddle-chair, its blue plastic tray freckled with oatmeal. She lifted a bright wedge of peach to her lips, and its syrup wept in loose strings from her fist to her bib. Lewis held the back of a polished silver spoon before her like a mirror. "Who's that?" he said. "Who's inside that spoon? Who's that in there?" Caroline gazed into its dome as she chewed her peach. "Cah-line," she said.

Lewis reversed the spoon, and her reflection toppled over into its bowl. "Oh my goodness!" he said. His voice went weak with astonishment. "Caroline is standing on her head!" Caroline prodded the spoon, then taking it by the handle, her hand on his, steered it into her mouth. When she released it, Lewis peered inside. "Hey!" he said. His face grew stern. "Where did you put Caroline?"

She patted her stomach, smiling, and Lewis gasped. "You *ate* Caroline!"

Caroline nodded. Her eyes, as she laughed, were as sharp and rich as light edging under a door.

The upstairs shower disengaged with a discrete shudder, and Lewis heard water suddenly gurgling through the throat of the kitchen sink. Mr. Mitchell dashed into the kitchen swinging a brown leather briefcase. He straightened his hat and drank a glass of orange juice. He skinned an apple with a paring knife. Its cortex spiraled cleanly away from the flesh and, when he left for work, it remained on the counter like a little green basket. "Six o'clock," said Mrs. Mitchell, plucking an umbrella from around a doorknob. "Seven at the outside. Think you can make it till then?" She kissed her daughter on the cheek, then waggled her earlobe with a fingertip. "Now you be a good girl, okay?" she said. She tucked a sheaf of papers into her purse and nodded goodbye, extending her umbrella as she stepped into the morning.

That day, as a gentle rain dotted the windows, Lewis swept the kitchen and vacuumed the carpets. He dusted the roofs of dormant appliances—the oven and the toaster, the pale, serene computer. He polished the bathroom faucets to a cool silver. When Caroline knocked a pair of ladybug magnets from the refrigerator, he showed her how to nudge them across a table-top, one with the force of the other, by pressing them pole to common pole. "You see," he said, "there's something there. It looks like nothing, but you can feel it." In the living room, they watched a sequence of animated cartoons—nimble, symphonic, awash with color. Caroline sat at the base of the television, smoothing fields of static from its screen with her palm. They read a flap-book with an inset bunny. They assembled puzzles onto sheets of corkboard. They constructed a fortress with the cushions of the sofa; when bombed with an unabridged dictionary, it collapsed like the huskwood of an old fire.

That afternoon, the sky cleared to a proud, empty blue, and Lewis walked with Caroline to the park. The children there were pitching stones into a seething brown creek, fat with new rain, and the birds that wheeled above them looked like tiny parabolic *M*'s and *W*'s. The wind smelled of pine and wet asphalt.

Lewis strapped Caroline into the bucket of a high swing. He discovered a derelict kickball between two rocking horses and, standing before her, tossed it into the tip of her swing, striking her knee, her toe, her shin. "Do it 'gain," she said as the force of her momentum shot the ball past his shoulder, or sent it soaring like a loose balloon into the sky. It disappeared, finally, into a nest of brambles. Pushing Caroline from behind, Lewis watched her arc away from him and back, pausing before her return like a roller toy he'd once concocted from a coffee can and a rubber band. She weighed so little, and he knew that—if he chose—he could propel her around the axle of the swingset, that with a single robust shove she would spin like a second hand from twelve to twelve to twelve. Instead, he let her swing to a stop, her arms falling limp from the chains as she slowed. A foam sandal dangled uncertainly from her big toe. Her head lolled onto her chest. She was, suddenly, asleep. As Lewis lifted her from the harness, she relaxed into a broad yawn, the tip of her tongue settling gently between her teeth. He carried her home.

After he had put her to bed, Lewis drew the curtains against the afternoon sun and pulled a small yellow table to her side. He sat watching her for a moment. Her breath sighed over her pillowcase, the turn of fabric nearest her lips flitting slightly with each exhalation. She reached for a stuffed bear, cradling it to her heart, and her eyes began to jog behind their lids. Gingerly, Lewis pressed a finger to one of them—he could feel it twitching at his touch like a chick rolling over in its egg. What could she be dreaming, he wondered, and would she remember when she woke? How could something so close be so hidden? And how was it that in the light of such a question we could each of us hold out hope—search eyes as dark as winter for the flicker of intimacy, dream of seizing one another in a fit of recognition? As he walked silently from her bedroom, Lewis lifted from the toy shelf a red plastic See 'n Say, its face wreathed with calling animals. In the hallway, he trained its index on the picture of a lion, depressing the lever cocked at its frame. *This*, said the machine, *is a robin*, and it whittered a little aria. When he turned the dial to a picture of a lamb on a tussock of grass, it said the same thing. Dog and pony, monkey and elephant: *robin—twit twit whistle*. Lewis set the toy against a wall, listening to the cough of a receding car. He passed through the dining room and climbed the back stairway, wandered the deep and inviolate landscape of the house—solemn with the thought of faulty lessons, and of how often we are shaped in this way.

An old story tells of a man who grew so fond of the sky—of the clouds like hills and the shadows of hills, of the birds like notes of music and the stars like distant blessings—that he made of his heart a kite and sailed it into the firmament. There he felt the high mechanical tug of the air. The sunlight rushed through him, and the sharp blue wind, and the world seemed a far and a learnable thing. His gaze (the story continues) he tethered like a long string to his heart—and never looking down, lest he pull himself to earth, he wandered the world ever after in search of his feet.

Talking about love, I suspect, is much like this story. What is it, then, that insists that we make the attempt? The hope of some new vision? The drive for words and order? We've been handed a map whose roads lead to a place we understand: *Now*, says a voice, *disentangle them*. And though we fear that we will lose our way, still, there is this wish to try. Perhaps, though, if we allow our perceptions of love to brighten and fade as they will, allow it even if they glow no longer than a spark launched from a fire, perhaps we will not pull our heart from its course: surely this is possible.

My love for Caroline, then, is what slows me into sleep at night. It is a system of faith inhabiting some part of me that's deeper than I've traveled. The thought of her fills me with comfort and balance, like heat spilling from the floor register of an old building. Her existence at this moment, alongside me in time—unhesitating and sure—all of this, the *now* of her, is what stirs through me when I fail. My love for Caroline is the lens through which I see the world, and the world through that lens is a place whose existence addresses the fact of my own.

Caroline chews crayons—red like a firetruck, green like a river, silver like the light from passing airplanes—and there's something in my love for her that speaks this same urge: I want to receive the world inside me. My love for Caroline is the wish that we might spend our lives together: marry in a hail of rice, watch the childhood of our children disappear, and think to ourselves someday: when this person is gone, no one in all the world will remember the things I remember.

Salient point is an early and sadly obsolete term for the heart as it first appears in the embryo; I fell upon it in a book of classical obstetrics with a sense of celebration. The heart, I believe, is that point where we merge with the universe. It is salient as a jet of water is salient—leaping continually upward—and salient as an angle is salient—its vertex projecting into this world, its limbs fanning out behind the frame of another. What I love of Caroline is that space of her at rest behind the heart—true and immanent, hidden and vast, the arc that this angle subtends.

I would like to cobble such few sentences into a tower, placing them in the world, so that I might absorb what I can of these things in a glance. But when we say *I love you*, we say it not to shape the world. We say it because there's a wind singing through us that knows it to be true—and because even when we speak them without shrewdness or understanding, it is good, we know, to say these things.

The dishwasher thrummed in the kitchen, and the thermostat ticked in the hallway, and the dryer called from the basement like a tittuping horse. Caroline lay on the silver-gray carpet, winking each eye in turn as she scrutinized her thumb. Her hair was drawn through the teeth of a barrette, and the chest of her shirt was pulled taut beneath one arm. Lewis could see her heartbeat welling through the gate of her ribs. It called up in him the memory of a time when, as a schoolboy, his teacher had allowed him to hold the battery lamp during a power failure. He had lain on the floor, balancing the lamp atop his chest, and everywhere in the slate-black schoolroom the light had pulsed with his heart. Like a shaken belief or a damaged affection, the life within such a moment could seem all but irreclaimable.

The seconds swayed past in the bob-weight of the grandfather clock.

"Come here," said Lewis, beckoning to Caroline, and when she'd settled into his lap, he told her this story: In a town between a forest and the sea there lived a clever and gracious little girl. She liked to play with spoons and old buttons, to swat lump-bugs and jump over things, and her name was Caroline.

("I don' like *spoons*," said Caroline. *Spoons?* said Lewis. *Did I say spoons? I meant goons.* Caroline giggled and shook her head. "No-*o*." *Prunes?* "Nuh-uh." *Baboons?* Caroline paused to consider this, her finger paddling lazily against her shirt collar. "Okay.")

So then: Caroline, who played with buttons and baboons, had all the hours from sun to moon to wander the city as she wished, scratching burrs from her socks or thumping dandelion heads. The grownups offered her but one caution: if ever the sky should threaten rain, the clouds begin to grumble, or the wind blow suddenly colder, she must hurry indoors. The grownups had good reason to extend such a warning, for the town in which they lived was made entirely of soap. It had been whittled and sliced from the Great Soap Mountains. There were soaphouses and soap-scrapers, chains of soap lampposts above wide soap roadways, and in the town center, on a pedestal of marbled soap, a rendering of a soapminer, his long proud shovel at his side. Sometimes, when the dark sky ruptured and the rains came daggering across the land, those of the town who had not taken shelter—the tired and the lost, the poky and the dreamy—would vanish, never to return. "Washed clean away," old-timers would declare, nodding sagely.

One day, Caroline was gathering soapberries from a glade at the lip of the forest. Great somber clouds, their bellies black with rain, had been weltering in from the ocean for hours, but she paid them no mind: she had raced the rain before, and she could do it again. When a cloud discharged a hollow growl, she thought it was her stomach, hungry for soapber-ries—and so ate a few. When the wind began to swell and chill, she simply zippered her jacket. She bent to place a berry in her small blue hat and felt her skin pimpling at the nape of the neck, and when she stood again, the rain was upon her.

Caroline fled from the forest. She arrowed past haystacks and canting trees, past empty pavilions and blinking red stoplights. A porchgate wheeled on its hinges and slammed against a ventilation tank. A lamplight burst in a spray of orange sparks. *Almost*, thought Caroline, as her house, then her door, then the glowspeck of her doorbell came into view. And at just that moment, as she blasted past the bakery to her own front walk, a tremendous drift of soapsuds took hold of her from behind, whipping her up and toward the ocean.

When Caroline awoke, the sunlight was lamping over her weary body. Her skin was sticky with old soap. Thin whorls of air iridesced all around her. She shook her head, unfolded in a yawn, and watched a bluebird flap through a small round cloud beneath her left elbow. That was when she realized: she was bobbing through the sky inside a bubble! She tried to climb the inside membrane of the vessel, but it rolled her onto her nose. She prodded its septum with her finger and it stretched and recoiled, releasing a few airy driblets of soap that popped when she blew on them. *Bubble, indeed*, she thought—indignant, arms akimbo. Caroline (though a clever and a gracious little girl) could not think of a single solution to her dilemma—for if her craft were to erupt she would surely fall to earth, and if she fell to earth she would shatter like a snowball—so she settled into the bay of her bubble, watching the sky and munching the soapberries from her small blue hat.

There is little to see from so high in the air: clouds and stars and errant birds; the fields and the hills, the rivers and highways, as small and distinct as the creases in your palm. There is a time as the morning brightens when the lakes and rivers, catching the first light, will go silvering through the quiet black land. And in the evening, when the sun drops, a flawless horizon will prism its last flare into a haze of seven colors. Once, Caroline watched a man's heart sail by like a kite, once a golden satellite swerving past the moon. Preoccupied birds sometimes flew straight toward her—their wings stiff and open, their beaks like drawn swords—yawing away before they struck her bubble. On a chilly afternoon, an airplane passed so close that she counted nineteen passengers gaping at her through its windows, their colorless faces like a series of stills on a filmstrip. And on a delicate, breezy morning, as she stared through a veining of clouds at the land, Caroline noticed that the twists of color had faded from the walls of her bubble. Then, abruptly, it burst.

Caroline found herself plummeting like a buzz bomb from the sky, the squares of far houses growing larger and larger. Her hair strained upward against the fall, tugging at her scalp. Her cheeks beat like pennants in the wind. She shut her eyes. As for what became of her, no one is certain—or rather there are many tales, and many tellers, each as certain as the last. Some say she spun into the arms of a startled baboon, who raised her in the forest on coconuts and turnip roots. Some say she dropped onto the Caroline Islands, striking the beach in a spasm of sand, and so impressed the islanders with the enthusiasm of her arrival that with a mighty shout they proclaimed her Minister of Commerce. And some say she landed in this very house—on this very couch, in this very room—where I told her this story and put her to bed.

The human voice is an extraordinary thing: an alliance of will and breath that, without even the fastening of hands, can forge for us a home in other people. Air is sent trembling through the frame of the mouth, and we find ourselves admitted to some far, unlikely country: this must, I think, be regarded as nothing short of wondrous. The first voice I remember hearing belonged, perhaps, to a stranger or a lost relation, for I cannot place it within my family: it sounded like a wooden spool rolling on a wooden floor. My father had a voice like cement revolving in a drum, my mother like the whirring of many small wings. My own, I've been told, resembles the rustling of snow against a windowpane. What must the mother's voice—beneath the whisper of her lungs, beneath the little detonations of her heartbeat—sound like to the child in the womb? A noise without design or implication—as heedless as growth, as mechanical as thunder? Or the echo of some nascent word come quaking through the body? Is it the first intimation of another life cradling our own, a sign that suggests that this place is a someone? Or do children—arriving from some other, more insistent landscape—need such testimony? If the human voice itself does not evince a living soul, then that voice raised in song surely must.

Things go right, things go wrong / hearts may break but not for long / you will grow up proud and strong / sleepy little baby.

Of all the forms of voice and communion, a song is perhaps the least mediated by the intellect. It ropes its way through the tangle of our cautions, joining singer to listener like a vine between two trees. I once knew a man whose heart percussed in step with the music that he heard; he would not listen to drums played in hurried or irregular cadence; he left concerts and dances and parties, winced at passing cars, and telephoned his neighbors when they played their stereos too loudly—in the fear that with each unsteady beat he might malfunction. Song is an exchange exactly that immediate and physiological. It attests to the life of the singer through our skin and through our muscles, through the wind in our lungs and the fact of our own beating heart. The evidence of other spirits becomes that of our own body. Speech is sound shaped into meaning through words, inflection, and modulation. Music is sound shaped into meaning through melody, rhythm, and pitch. A song arises at the point where these two forces collide. But such an encounter can occur in more than one place. Where, then, is song most actual and rich—in the singer or in the audience?

Dream pretty dreams / touch beautiful things / let all the skies surround you / swim with the swans / and believe that upon / some glorious dawn love will find you.

A successful song comes to sing itself inside the listener. It is cellular and seismic, a wave coalescing in the mind and in the flesh. There is a message outside, and a message inside, and those messages are the same, like the pat and thud of two heartbeats, one within you, one surrounding. The message of the lullaby is that it's okay to dim the eyes for a time, to lose sight of yourself as you sleep and as you grow: if you drift—it says—you'll drift ashore: if you fall, you will fall into place.

And if you see some old fool / who looks like a friend / tell him good night old man / my friend.

Lewis stood with a washcloth before Caroline's highchair, its tray white with milk from a capsized tumbler. A streetlamp switched on outside the kitchen window, and as he turned to look, another did the same. The sun had left channels of pink and violet across the sky in which a few wavering stars were emerging. He could hear the rush of commuter traffic behind the dry autumn clicking of leaves—motor horns calling forlornly, a siren howling in the distance. The highchair stood like a harvest crab on its thin silver stilts. Lewis sopped the milk up from its tray and brushed the crumbs from its seat, rinsing his washcloth at the gurgling sink. All around the city—he thought, staring into the twilight—streetlamps were brightening one by one, generating warm electric purrs and rings of white light. From far above, as they blinked slowly on and off, they would look like rainwater striking the lid of a puddle.

In the living room, Caroline sat at the foot of the television, several inches from the screen, watching a small cartoon Martian chuckle perniciously as he fashioned an enormous ray gun. Lewis knelt beside her and, just for a moment, saw the black egg of the Martian's face shift beneath his gleaming helmet—but then his eyes began to tingle, and his perception flattened, and it was only a red-green-blueness of phosphorescent specks and the blade of his own nose. He flurried his hand through Caroline's hair, then pinched a dot of cookie from her cheek. "Sweetie," he said to her, standing. When his knees cracked, she started.

A set of cardboard blocks—red and blue and thick as bread loaves—were clustered before a reclining chair. They looked like something utterly defeated, a grove of pollard trees or the frame of a collapsed temple. Earlier in the day, Lewis had played a game with Caroline in which he stacked them two on two to the ceiling and she charged them, arms swinging, until they toppled to the carpet. Each time she rushed them, she would rumble like a speeding truck. Each time they fell she would laugh with excitement, bobbing up and down in a stiff little dance. She rarely tired of this game. As often as not, actually, she descended upon the structure in a sort of ambush before it was complete: Lewis would stoop to collect another block, hear the drum of running feet, and down they would go. Now, as she peered at the television, he stacked the blocks into two narrow columns, each its own color, and bridged them carefully at the peak; satisfied, he lapsed onto the sofa.

Propping his glasses against his forehead, he yawned and pressed his palms to his eyes. Grains of light sailed through the darkness, like snow surprised by a headlamp, and when he looked out at the world again, Caroline had made her way to his side. She flickered her hands and burbled a few quick syllables, her arms swaying above her like the runners of a sea plant:

in her language of blurt and gesture, this meant *carry me*, or *hold me*, or *pick me up*—and swinging into her, Lewis did just that. She stood in his lap, balancing with one smooth-socked foot on either thigh, and reached for his forehead. "'Lasses," she said. Lewis removed his glasses, handing them to her, and answered, "That's right." An ice-white bloom of television flashed from each lens as Caroline turned them around in her palms. When she pressed them to her face, the stems floated inches from her ears; then they slipped past her nose and hitched around her shoulders, hanging there like a necklace or a bow tie. Lewis felt himself smiling as he retrieved them. He polished them on the tail of his shirt and returned them to their rightful perch.

He looked up to find Caroline losing her balance, foundering toward him. Her foot slid off his leg onto the sofa and her arms lurched up from her side. "Whoa," he said, catching her. "You okay?" She tottered back onto his lap, her head pressing against his cheek. He could feel the dry warmth of her skin, the arching of her eyebrows, the whiffet of her breath across his face. Then, straightening, she kissed him. The flat of her tongue passed up his chin and over his lips, and, stopping at the ledge of his nose, inverted and traveled back down. Lewis could feel it tensed against him like a spring, and when it swept across the crest of his lips, he lightly kissed its tip. Caroline closed her mouth with a tiny pecking sound. She sniffled, brushed her nose, and settled into him. "'Lasses," she said, and her warm brown hair fell against his collarbone. Lewis blinked and touched a finger to his dampened chin. His ears were tingling as if from a breeze. His head was humming like a long flat roadway.

From the front porch came the rattle of house keys. As the bolt-lock retracted with a ready chink, Caroline dropped to his lap. She turned to watch the television and pillowed her head on his stomach.

"Home!" called Mr. Mitchell, and the door clapped shut behind him.

My brother is three years my senior. When I was first learning to speak, he was the only person to whom my tongue taps and labial stops seemed a language. I would dispense a little train of stochastic syllables—*pa ba mi da*, for instance—and he would translate, for the benefit of my parents: *he wants some more applesauce*. My brother understood me, chiefly, from basic sympathy and the will to understand: the world, I am certain, responds to such forces. It was in this fashion that I knew what Caroline told me—though when she said it she was mumbling up from sleep, and though it sounded to the ear as much like *igloo* or *allegory*—when with a quiet and perfect affection she said, "I love you."

With fingers spidery weak from the cold, Lewis worked the tag of Caroline's zipper into its slide, fastening her jacket with a tidy *zzzt*. He tightened her laces, straightened her mittens, and wiped her nose with a tissue. He adjusted her socks and trousers, and the buttonless blue puff of her hood. "All right," he said, patting her back. "Off you go." Caroline scampered for the sandbox, her hood flipping from her head to bob along behind her. When she crossed its ledge, she stood for a moment in silence. Then she growled like a bear and gave an angry stamp, felling a hillock of abandoned sand. Lewis watched her from a concrete bench. She found a small pink shovel and arranged a mound of sand into four piles, one at each rail, as if ladling out soup at a dinner table. She buried her left foot and kicked a flurry of grit onto the grass.

Brown leaves shot with threads of red and yellow skittered across the park. They swept past merry-go-rounds and picnic tables, past heavy gray stones and rotunda bars. A man and his daughter tottered on a seesaw, a knot of sunlight shuttling along the rod between them like a bubble in a tube of water. Two boys were bouncing tennis balls in the parking lot—hurling them against the asphalt and watching them leap into the sky—and another was descending a decrepit wire fence, its mesh of tendons loose and wobbling. Caroline sat on her knees in the sandbox, burrowing: she unearthed leaves and acorns and pebbles, a shiny screwtop bottlecap and her small pink shovel. A boy with freckles and cowboy boots joined her with a grimace, a ring of white diaper peering from above his pants. His mother handed him a plastic bucket, tousling his plume of tall red hair. "Now you play nice," she told him, and sat next to Lewis on the bench. She withdrew a soda can from her purse, popping its tab and sipping round the edge of its lid. Caroline placed her bottlecap in her shovel, then scolded it—*no, no, no*—and tipped it to the side. The woman on the bench turned to Lewis—gesturing cheerily, nonchalantly. "Your daughter is a*dor*able," she said.

For a moment Lewis didn't know how to respond. He felt a strange coldness shivering up from inside him: it was as if his body were a window, suddenly unlatched, and beyond it was the hard aspen wind of December. Then the sensation dwindled, and his voice took hold of him. "Thanks," he said. "She's not mine, but thank you."

The woman crossed her legs, tapping her soda can with a lacquered red fingernail. "So," she asked, "you're an uncle, then?"

"Sitter."

From the back of her throat came a high little interrogatory *mm*. In the sandbox, her son slid his plastic bucket over his head. *Echo*, he hollered, his face concealed in its trough: *echo, echo, echo*. He was the sort of boy one might expect to find marching loudly into weddings and libraries, chanting the theme songs from television comedies and striking a metal pan with a wooden spoon. "I'm Brooke," said the woman, bending to set her soda can at her feet. "And you are . . . ?"

"Lewis."

She nodded then rummaged in her purse, a sack of brown woven straw as large as a bed pillow. "Would you like some gum, Lewis? I know it's in here somewhere." Her son lumbered over to Caroline and clapped his bucket over her head. It hit with a loud thumping sound. Lewis, watching, stepped to her side and removed it, then hoisted her to his shoulder as she began to cry.

The woman on the bench glanced up from her purse. "Alex*ander*," she exclaimed. She stomped to the sandbox in counterfeit anger. "*What* did you do?" The boy glowered, his mouth pinching shut like the spiracle of a balloon. He threw the small pink shovel at a litter bin and began punching his left arm. "*That* settles it," said his mother, pointing. "No more fits today from *you*, Mister. To the car."

"Your bucket," said Lewis—it was dangling from his right hand, fingers splayed against Caroline's back.

"Thanks," said the woman, hooking it into her purse. She waved as she left with her son.

Caroline was nuzzling against his neck, her arm folded onto her stomach. Her chest rose and fell against his own, and Lewis relaxed his breathing until they were moving in concert. He walked to a wooden picnic table and sat on its roof, brushing a few pine needles to the ground. The wind sighed through the trees, and the creek rippled past beneath a ridge of grass. Silver minnows paused and darted through its shallows, kinks of sunlight agitating atop the water like a sort of camouflage for their movements. Lewis tossed a pine cone into the current and watched it sail—scales flared and glistening—through a tiny cataract. An older couple, arms intertwined, passed by with their adolescent daughter. "I'm not sure I even be*lieve* in peace of mind," the girl was saying, her hands fluttering at her face as if to fend off a fly. He could hear Caroline slurping on her thumb. "You awake?" he asked, and she mumbled in affirmation. "Do you want to go home or do you want to stay here and play for a while?"

"Play," said Caroline.

Lewis planted her on her feet and, taking her by the hand, walked with her to the playground. A framework of chutes and tiered platforms sat in a bed of sand and gravel, and they climbed a net of ropes into its gallery. A steering wheel was bolted to a crossbeam at the forward deck, and when Caroline spun it, they beeped like horns and *whoa*ed from side to side. They snapped clots of sand from a handrail. They ran across a step-bridge swaying on its chains. A broad gleaming slide descended from a wooden shelf, its ramp speckled with dents and abrasions, and ascending a ladder to its peak, they swooped to the earth. They jumped from a bench onto an old brown stump and climbed a hill of painted rubber tires. They wheeled in slow circles on a merry-go-round, watched the world drift away and return—slide tree parking lot, slide tree parking lot—until their heads felt dizzy and buoyant, like the hollow metal globes that quiver atop radio antennas. Beside a bike rack and a fire hydrant, they discovered the calm blue mirror of a puddle; when Lewis breached it with a stone, they watched themselves pulse across the surface, wavering into pure geometry. A spray of white clouds hovered against the sky, and an airplane drifted through them with a respiratory hush. "Look," said Lewis, and Caroline followed the line of his finger. Behind the airplane were two sharp white condensation trails, cloven with blue sky, that flared and dwindled like the afterlight of a sparkler. Watching, Lewis was seized with a sudden and inexplicable sense of presence, as if weeks and miles of surrounding time and space had contracted around this place, this moment. "My God," he said, and filled his lungs with the rusty autumn air. "Look what we can do."

A man with a stout black camera was taking pictures of the playground equipment. He drew carefully toward the slide and the seesaw, the monkey bars and tire-swings, altering his focus and releasing the shutter. Each print emerged from a vent at the base of the camera, humming into sight on a square of white paper. Lewis approached the man and, nodding to Caroline, asked if he might borrow the device for a moment. "Just one picture?" he asked, his head cocked eagerly. "Well," said the man—and he shrugged, giving a little flutter with his index finger. "Okay. One." Caroline had wandered in pursuit of a whirling leaf to the foot of a small green cypress tree. Its bough was pierced with the afternoon sunlight, and she gazed into the crook of its lowest branches. A flickertail squirrel lay there batting a cone. She raised a mittened hand to her eyes, squinting, and when Lewis snapped her picture, a leaf tumbled onto her forehead.

"Your daughter," said the man, collecting his camera, "is very pretty."

Lewis stared into the empty white photograph. "Thank you," he said. He blew across its face until the dim gray ghost of a tree appeared. "She is."

Though it often arises in my memories and dreams, I have not returned to the playground in many days. It is certain to have changed, however minutely, and this is what keeps me away. Were I to visit, I might find the rocking horse rusted on its heavy iron spring, the sidewalk marked with the black prints of leaves, the swings wrapped higher around their crossbars—and though they seem such small things, I'd rather not see them. The sand may have spilled past the lip of the sandbox, and the creek may have eaten away at its banks. The cypress tree might have been taken by a saw or risen a few inches closer to the sun. Perhaps a pair of lovers have carved their signet into its bark—a heart and a cross, or a square of initials. My fear, though, is that the park has simply paled with all its contents into an embryonic white—that, flattening like a photograph too long exposed, it has curled at its edges and blown away. In my thoughts, though, it grows brighter each day, fresher and finer and more distinct, away from my remembering eyes.

Caroline was nestled in bubbles. Sissing white hills of them gathered and rose, rolling from the faucet to each bank of the tub. They streamed like clouds across the water, rarefying as they accumulated—as those bubbles in the center, collapsing, coalesced into other, slightly larger bubbles, which themselves collapsed into still larger bubbles, and those into still larger (as if a cluster of grapes were to become, suddenly, one large grape), which, bursting, opened tiny chutes and flumes to the exterior—and there sat Caroline, hidden in the thick of them, the tips of her hair afloat on the surface. When she scissored her feet, the great mass of the bubbles swayed atop the water. When she twitched her arm, a little boat of froth released itself from the drift, sailing through the air into a box of tissues. She looked as if she had been planted to her shoulders in snow.

Lewis shut the water off, and the foam that had been rippling away from the head of the tub spread flat, like folds of loose skin drawing suddenly taut. The silence of the faucet left the bathroom loud with hums and whispers—intimate noises were made vibrant and bold: effervescing bubbles, gentle whiffs of breath, metal pipes ticking in the walls. Caroline leaned forward and blew a cove the size of her thumb into a mound of bubbles. The bathwater, swaying with her motion, rocked the mound back upon her, and when she blinked up from inside it, her face was wreathed in white. Lewis pinched the soap from her eyelashes. He cleaned her with a hand towel—brushed the swell of her cheeks and the bead of her nose—and dropped her rubber duck into the bubbles. It struck the water with a *ploop*, then emerged from the glittering suds. "Wack, wack," said Caroline, as it floated into her collarbone. She pulled it to the floor of the tub and watched it hop to the surface.

Lewis squirted a dollop of pink shampoo into his palm and worked it through the flurry of her hair. Its chestnut brown, darkened with water, hung in easy curves along her neck and her cheek and in the dip of skin behind each ear. His fingers, lacing through it, looked as white as slants of moonlight. He flared and collapsed them, rubbing the shampoo into a rich lather, and touched the odd runnel of soap from her forehead. One day, as he was bathing her, a bleb of shampoo had streamed into her eye, and she had kept a hand pressed to it for the rest of the day, quailing away from him whenever he walked past. Ever since then, he had been careful to roll the soap back from her face as it thickened, snapping it into the tub. When it came time to rinse, Caroline tilted her head back and shut her eyes so tightly that they shivered. Lewis braced her in the water, his palm against the smooth of her back.

With a green cotton washcloth and a bar of flecked soap, he washed her chin and her jaw, her round dimpled elbows, the small of her back and the spine of her foot. His sleeves were drawn to his upper arms, his fingertips slowly crimping. His hands passed from station to station with careful diligent presses and strokes. Caroline paddled her duck through the water, then squeezed it and watched the air bubble from under its belly. He washed her arms and her legs and the soft small bowl of her stomach. He washed the hollows of her knees, soaped her neck and soaped her chest, and felt her heart, the size of a robin's egg, pounding beneath him. Her heart, he thought, was driving her blood, and her blood was sustaining her cells, and her cells were investing her body with time. He washed her shoulder blades and the walls of her torso and imagined them expanding as she grew: her muscles would band and bundle, her bones flare open like the frame of an umbrella. He washed the shallow white shoulders that would take on curve and breadth, the waist that would taper, the hips that would round. The vents and breaches, valleys and slopes, that would become as rare and significant to some new husband as they now were to him. The face that, through the measure of its creases, would someday reveal by accident what it now revealed by intent: the feelings that were traveling through her life. He washed her fragile, dissilient, pink-fingered hands. The hands that would unfold and color with age. The hands that would learn how to catch a ball and knot a shoelace, how to hold a pencil and unlock a door—how to drive a car, how to wave farewell, how to shake hello. The hands that would learn how to touch another person, how to carry a child, and on some far day how to die.

The water was lapping against the wall of the tub. Lewis found himself gazing into the twitch of his reflection: his lips and eyes were tense with thought beside a reef of dissipating bubbles. Caroline watched for a moment, then splashed him with a palm of cupped water. When Lewis looked at her through the tiny wet globes that dotted his glasses, she laughed, and he felt some weary thing inside of him ascend and disperse, like fog lifting from a bay. He polished his glasses and his mouth curled into a smile.

When he pulled the bath plug, Caroline started—surprised, as she often was, by the sudden deep gurgle and surge. He welcomed her into the wings of a towel as the water serpent-whirled into the drain.

Number of days we spent together: 144. Number of days we spent apart (supposing that Archbishop James Usher of Meath, who calculated the date of the Creation at 23 October 4004 BC, was correct): 2,195,195. Number of days since I last saw her: 43. Number of days since I began writing this story: 3. Number of days in her life thus far: 613. Number of days in mine thus far: 12,418; projected: 12,419. Number of times we walked to the park: 102. Number of swings on the swingset there: 3; strap swings: 2; bucket swings: 1. Number of times she rode the bucket swing: 77; the strap swing: 1. Number of times she rode the strap swing and fell: 1. Number of times I pushed her on the bucket swing, average per session: 22; total: 1,694. Number of puzzles we constructed: 194. Number of towers we assembled from large cardboard blocks: 112; demolished: 111. Number of stories I told: 58. Number of diapers I changed: 517. Number of lullabies I sang: 64. Number of days I watched, while Caroline napped, Caroline: 74; the television: 23; the sky: 7. Number of times, since we met, that I've laundered my clothing: 93; that I've finished a book: 19; that I've heard songs on the radio with her name in them: 17 (*good times never felt so good*: 9; *where did your long hair go?*: 2; a song I don't know whose chorus chants *Caroline Caroline Caroline* in a voice like the clittering of dice in a cup: 6). Number of footlong sandwiches I've eaten since we met: 12. Number of Lewises it would take to equal in height the number of footlong sandwiches I've eaten since we met: 2.1; number of Carolines: 4.9. Number of times I've thought today about the color of my walls: 2; about the shape of my chin: 1; about airplanes: 4; about mirrors: 3; about the inset mirror in one of Caroline's flap-books: 1; about Caroline and the turn of her lips: 6; about Caroline and macaroni and cheese: 1; about how difficult it can be to separate one thought from another: 1; about Caroline and moths and childhood fears: 4; about my childhood fear of being drawn through the grate of an escalator: 1; about my childhood fear of being slurped down the drain of a bathtub: 2; about eyes: 9; about hands: 6; about hands, mine: 3. Number of lies I've told you: 2. Number of lies I've told you about my behavior toward Caroline: 0; about fairy tales: 0; about Nabokov: 1. Number of times I've dreamt about her: 14; pleasant: 12. Number of times I've dreamt about her mother: 3; nightmares: 3. Number of nightmares I recall having had in my life: 17. Number of hours I've spent this month: 163; in vain: 163.

Lewis tidied the house while Caroline napped, gathering her toys from the kitchen and the bathroom, the stairway and the den. He collected them in the fold of his arms and quietly assembled them on her toyshelves. Warm air breathed from the ceiling vents and sunlight ribboned in through the living-room windows, striking in its path a thousand little whirling constellations of dust. Lewis pulled a xylophone trolley from under the couch. He stacked rainbow quoits onto a white peg. He carried a pinwheel and a rag doll from the hallway and slipped a set of multiform plastic blocks into the multiform sockets of a block-box. He walked from the oven to the coatrack, from the coatrack to the grandfather clock, fossicking about for the last of a set of three tennis balls, and, finding it behind the laundry hamper, he pressed it into its canister. Then he held the canister to his face, breathing in its flat clean scent before he shelved it in the closet of the master bedroom. Lewis often felt, upon entering this room, as if he had discovered a place that was not an aspect of the house that he knew—someplace dark and still and barren: a cavern or a sepulcher, a tremendous empty seashell. The venetian blinds were always sealed, the curtains drawn shut around them, and both were overshadowed by a fat gray oak tree. The ceiling lamp cast a dim orange light, nebular and sparse, over the bed and the dressers and the carpet. Lewis fell back on the bedspread. The cable of an electric blanket bore into his shoulder, and his head lay in a shallow channel in the center of the mattress—formed, he presumed, by the weight of a sleeping body. He yawned, drumming his hand on his chest, and listened to the sigh of a passing car. He gazed into the tiny red eye of a smoke alarm.

When he left to look in on Caroline, he found her sleeping contentedly, her thumb in her mouth. A stuffed piglet curled from beneath her, its pink snout and the tabs of its ears brushing past her stomach. Her back rose and fell like a parachute tent. He softly shut her door. Returning to the living room, he bent to place a stray red checker in his shirt pocket, then straightened and gave a start: her mother was there, sitting on the sofa and blinking into space. Lisa Mitchell rarely arrived home before the moon was as sharp as a blade in the night sky, never once before evening. Now she sat clutching a small leather purse in her lap, and a stream of sunlight delineated each thread of her hair. It was midafternoon.

"Early day?" asked Lewis. He removed a jack-in-the-box from the arm of a chair, sealing the lid on its unsprung clown. Lisa Mitchell neither moved nor spoke; she simply held her purse and stared. "Hello . . . ?" he tested. She sat motionless, queerly mute, like a table lamp or a podium. Then her shoulders gave a single tight spasm, as if an insect had buzzed onto the nape of her neck, and her eyes glassed with tears. Lewis felt, suddenly, understanding and small and human. "Do you need anything?" he asked. "Some water?" Lisa drew a quick high breath and nodded.

Lewis rinsed a glass in the kitchen sink, then filled it from a bay on the door of the refrigerator, watching the crushed ice and a finger of water issue from a narrow spout. When he handed it to Lisa, she sipped until her mouth pooled full, swallowed, and placed it on a side table. Her fingertips left transparent annulets across the moist bank of the glass, her lips a wine-red crescent at its rim. Lewis sat next to her on the sofa. "Do you want to talk about it?" he asked. His voice had become as gentle as the aspiration of the ceiling vents.

"I . . . ," said Lisa, and the corner of her mouth twitched. "He said I . . ." Her throat gave out a little clicking noise. She trifled with the apron of her purse—snapping it open and shut, open and shut. "I lost my job," she said. And at this she sagged in on herself, shaking, and began to weep. Her head swayed, and her back lurched, and she pressed her hands to her eyes. When Lewis touched a finger to her arm, she fell against him, quaking.

"It's okay," he said. "It will all be okay." Resting against his shoulder, Lisa cried and shivered and slowly grew still. Her purse dropped to the floor as she relaxed into a sequence of calm, heavy breaths. Then, abruptly, she was crying once again. She wavered in this way—between moments of peace and trepidation—for what seemed an hour, as the white midday light slowly windowed across the carpet. After she had fallen quiet, Lewis held her and listened to her breathing. (She sighed placidly, flurrying puffs of air through her nose; she freed a little string of hiccups that seemed both deeply organic and strangely mechanical.) The sleeve of his shirt, steeped with her tears, was clinging to his upper arm, and his hand was pinpricking awake on her back. He could feel the warm pressure of her head against his collarbone. When she shifted on the cushions, he swallowed, listening to the drumbeat of his heart. He slid his fingers over the rungs of her spine, smoothing the ripples from her blouse, and she seemed to subside into the bedding of the sofa. It was as if she were suddenly just a weight within her clothing, suspended by a hanger from his shoulder, and he thought for a moment that she had fallen asleep—but, when she blinked, he felt the soft flicker of her eyelashes against his neck. Her stockings, sleek and coffee brown, were beginning to ladder at the knee, and Lewis reached to touch a ravel of loose nylon. He found himself instead curling a hand through her hair.

Lisa lifted her head, looking him in the eye, as his fingers swept across a rise in her scalp. He felt her breath mingling with his own. Her eyes, drawing near, were azure blue, and walled in black, and staring into his own. They seemed to hover before him like splashes of reflected light, and Lewis wondered what they saw. The tip of her nose met with his, and when she licked her lips, he felt her tongue glance across his chin. His lips were dry and tingling, his stomach as tight as a seedpod. When his hand gave a reflexive flutter on her back, Lisa stiffened.

She tilted away from him, blinking, the stones of her teeth pressing into her lip. The grandfather clock voiced three vibrant chimes, and she stood and planed her blouse into the waist of her skirt.

When she looked down upon him, her eyes were like jigsawed glass. "I think you'd better go now," she said.

Certain places are penetrated with elements of the human spirit. They act as concrete demonstrations of our hungers and capacities. A sudden field in the thick of a forest is a place like reverence, a stand of corn a place like knowledge, a clock tower a place like fury. I have witnessed this and know it to be true. Caroline's house was a place like memory—a place, in fact, like my memory of her: charged with hope and loss and fascination. As I stepped each morning through her front door, I saw the wall peg hung with a weathered felt hat, the ceiling dotted with stucco, the staircase folding from floor to floor, and it was as if these things were quickened with both her presence and her ultimate departure. The stationary bicycle with its whirring front fan wheel and the dining room table with its white lace spread, the desk cup bristling with pencils and pens and the books shelved neatly between ornamental bookends: these were the hills and trees and markers of a landscape that harbored and kept her. The windows were the windows whose panes she would print with her fingers. The doorstop was the doorstop whose spring she would flitter by its crown. The lamps were the lamps in whose light she would study for school. The sofa was the sofa in whose lap she would grow toward adulthood. The mirrors: the mirrors there were backed in silver and framed us in the thick of her house. Yet when we viewed the world inside of them, we did not think *here is this place made silver*, but simply *here is this place*: what does this suggest, we wondered, about the nature of material existence? When I was a small boy, I feared my attic. A ladder depended from a hatch in the hallway, and when my father scaled it into the darkness, I believed, despite the firm white evidence of the ceiling, that he was entering a chamber without a floor. A narrow wooden platform extended into open space, and beneath it lay the deep hidden well of my house: I could see this when I closed my eyes. Though Caroline's house suggested no such fear, it was informed by a similar logic of space: the floors and partitions, the shadows and doorways, were each of them rich with latent dimensions.

It is exactly this sense of latitude and secret depth that my own house is missing. The objects here are only what they are, with nothing to mediate the fact of their existence with the fact of their existence in my life. The walls may be the same hollow blue as a glacier, the carpet as dark as the gravid black sea, and I may be as slight as a boat that skirts the pass—but the walls are only walls, the carpet only carpet, and I am only and ever myself. In the evening, as the sun dwindles to a final red wire at the horizon, I switch on every light and lamp but still my house mushrooms with shadow. I walk from room to room, and everything that belongs to me drifts by like a mist—the wooden shelves banded with book spines, the shoes aligned in the closet, the rounded gray stone that I've carried for years . . . they are my life's little accidents, a sediment trickled through from my past: they are nothing to do with me. I look, for instance, at the photograph framed on my desk: it sports a slender green tree, and a piercing blue sky, and a light that is striking the face that I love—and how, I wonder, did I acquire such a thing? It is a gesture of hope simply to open the curtains each morning.

In truth, I don't know why it ended as it did. When Lewis arrives the next morning, the sun has not yet risen. The sidewalks are starred with mica, and the lawns are sheeted with frost, and the streetlamps glow with a clean white light. He steps to the front porch and presses the doorbell. When the door swings open, it is with such sudden violence that he briefly imagines it has been swallowed, pulled down the gullet of the wide front hall. Thomas Mitchell stands before him wearing striped red night clothes, his jaw rough with stubble. He has jostled the coatrack on his way to the door, and behind him it sways into the wall, then shudders upright on its wooden paws. He places his hand on the lock plate, thick blue veins roping down his forearm.

"We won't be requiring your services any longer," he says, and his eyebrows shelve together toward his nose, as in a child's drawing of an angry man.

"Pardon?" asks Lewis.

"We don't need you here anymore." He announces each syllable of each word, dispassionate and meticulous, as if reciting an oath before a silent courtroom. His body has not moved, only his mouth and eyes.

Lewis would like to ask why, but Thomas Mitchell, taut with bridled anger, stands before him like a dam—exactly that solemn, exactly that impassable—and he decides against it. (*You know why*, the man would say: Lewis can see the words pooled in writing across his features. And yet, though Lewis is coming to understand certain things—that his time here ran to a halt the day before, that his actions then were a form of betrayal—he does not, in fact, know anything.) Instead he asks, "Can I tell her goodbye?" and feels in his stomach a flutter of nervous grief.

"She's not here," says Thomas.

Lisa Mitchell's voice comes questioning from the depths of the house: "What's keeping you?"

Thomas clears his throat. He raises his hand from the lock plate, and his breath comes huffing through his nostrils like a plug of steam. "You can go now," he says, tightening his lips. "I don't expect to see you here again." Then, sliding back into the house, he shuts the door. The bolt lock engages with a heavy thunk.

Lewis does not know where to go or what to do. He feels like a man who, dashing into the post office to mail a letter, discovers his face on a wanted flyer. He stands staring at the doorbell—its orange glow like an ember in a settling fire—until he realizes that he is probably being watched. Glancing at the peephole, he feels the keen electric charge of a hidden gaze. Then he walks across the frost-silvered lawn to his car, his staggered footprints a dark rift in the grass. Lewis drives to the end of the block and parks. He looks into the crux of his steering wheel, his hands tented over his temples, and wonders whether Caroline has been told that he won't be returning.

On the sidewalk, he passes a paperboy who is tossing his folded white missiles from a bicycle; they sail in neat arcs through the air, striking porches and driveways with a leathery slap. Lewis walks around the house to the window of Caroline's bedroom, his heart librating in his chest like a seesaw. The sun will soon rise from behind the curved belly of the fields. The frost will dissipate in the slow heat of morning, and his footprints will dwindle into the green of the lawn.

Caroline is awake in her bed, a sharp light streaming across her face from the open bedroom door. Her pacifier falls from her mouth as she yawns. She wiggles in a pair of fuzzy blue pajamas. Lewis presses himself to the brick of the house and watches her for a few moments. Her body casts a wide shadow over her rumpled yellow bedspread, and it looks as if there is an additional head—his—on the pillow next to hers. He touches his fingers to the window. When he curves and sways them, they look like the spindled legs of an insect. He wants to rap against the glass, to pry it from its frame, to reach across Caroline's blankets and pull her into his arms, but he doesn't.

Instead, he lowers his hand to his side, where it hangs like a plummet on a string, and as a hazy form moves into the glare of the doorway, he turns and retreats to his car. Driving away, he spots a filament of dawn sunlight in the basin of the side-view mirror. He will realize as he slows into his driveway that he has just performed one of the most truly contemptible acts of his life. If he were a good man, he would have found a way, no matter the resistance, to tell her goodbye; to hand her like an offering some statement of his love; to leave her with at least this much. He could certainly have tried.

He did not, though. He simply left.

Memories and dreams are the two most potent methods by which the mind investigates itself. Both of them are held by what is not now happening in the world, both of them alert to their own internal motion. I have begun to imagine that they are the same transaction tilted along two separate paths—one into prior possibility, the other into projected. In one of my earliest memories, I am walking through a wooded park with a teacher and my classmates. I carry in my hands a swollen rubber balloon, cherry red and inflated with helium. I don't know where it was purchased, whether it was mine or how long I'd held it, but it was almost as large as the trunk of my body—I remember that. Something jostles me, or my arm grows tired, and I lose my grip. I do not think to reach for the balloon until it has risen into the trees. It floats through a network of leaf-green branches and shrinks in the light of the midday sun. Soon it is only a grain of distant red, and then it vanishes altogether, leaving the blue sky blue and undisturbed.

Remembering this moment, I often dream of Caroline. I dream her resting in my lap and dream her swaying on the swingset. I dream that she is beside me, or I dream that she is approaching. One day, perhaps, we will flee together in my car. We will pass from this town into the rest of our lives, driving through the focus of the narrow black road. On birdloud summer mornings, as a warm breeze rolls through our windows, we'll watch yellow-green grasshoppers pinging along the verge of the highway. In autumn, the leaves will fall red from the trees as our windshield blades fan away pepperings of rain. The heat will billow from our dashboard vents in winter, and the houses will chimney into the low gray sky. And on the easy, tonic nights of spring, we'll pull to the side of a quiet street and spread ourselves across our ticking hood: we'll watch the far white stars and the soaring red airplanes, ask *Which is the more beautiful, which the more true?*—and in finding our answers, we will find what we believe in.

PHYLLIS MOORE

Rembrandt's Bones

I AM SITTING HERE AT STUCKEY'S IN THE LITTLE NORTH FLORIDA TOWN where I grew up, still trying to figure out what to do with a dead girl's midterm. Yesterday, I was in my Chicago apartment trying to figure out the same thing when Mother called to tell me about Opal. I drove straight through.

"Coffee?" the waitress asks, handing me an orange menu.

"A Coke, please."

"All's we have is RC."

"RC's good."

They call it Catholic Coke here, though I am careful not to call it that myself. There are few sights uglier than that of a person who, having been raised in the South, returns after a twenty-year absence in New York, Chicago, or Los Angeles, and tries to fit back in. It's like watching a gorilla try to play a CD on a record player. There is a double remove—not only have you lost the grace of knowing how to use the current equipment, you have devolved into an entirely other, if related, species.

I take a look out the window. Matchstick pines line both sides of the highway. Outfitted in kudzu, they form two quiet columns of sleepy marching bears, a poor man's parade. This is the old Florida, the real Florida. Women carry pocketbooks, men eat hamburger meat. People here do not take aspirin, they take a tablet.

I gave the midterm on Wednesday. Last night, one of my students committed suicide. "Right after *Cheers*," one of the campus cops was quoted as saying.

What do you do with a dead girl's midterm?

Opal would know.

Opal Whiteside was a woman of reason, something absent in the tender history of my own monkey family. She wore pink slacks and Arpège. Instead of cookbooks, she kept an entire set of the *Encyclopaedia Britannica* propped on the kitchen counter, ready for action. A cloud of hair spray and intelligence followed her wherever she went, as I did through all my wide girlhood, traipsing behind like a dog without a clue. Opal Whiteside was a beautiful woman who had all the answers, and I was a plain girl with a lot of questions.

"Where do you go when you die?" I asked her once.

"You go straight to Miami Beach, order out Chinese, and wait for all eternity."

"Is it good?"

"Terribly good. In Miami, there is no need for MSG."

"Then what?"

"Then you make love with the delivery boy."

"Is it good?"

"Terribly good. In Miami, boys talk in bed."

"What do they say?"

"They say moo goo gai pan."

Sundays after church, whenever she could wrench me out of Mother's beautiful sugar-free arms, Opal would drive me out here, to Stuckey's, to drink Cokes, try on lipsticks, and talk about death and sex. Over the years I have come to think of these episodes as our Red-Vinyl-Booth Sessions—like Elvis' Sun sessions, or the Owen Bradley sessions of Patsy Cline. Opal and I were just trying to work things out.

"According to Camus, there is but one truly serious philosophical problem, and that is?" Opal's bible was *The Myth of Sisyphus*.

I remember the lipsticks, spread out on the table before me. Candy Cane Pink. Cherry Sunset. Ruby Romance. It was that time in life when any choice you made was the perfect choice.

"Suicide," I said, smiling, my eyes on the Cherry Sunset.

Besides Camus, what Opal talked a lot about was bad sex. I didn't know Camus from Camay. I was eight years old at the time and yet to become accustomed to bad sex, so I would just look at her and smile, thrilling to the red rings around my Coke straw.

"Have you decided yet?" The waitress stands poised, hunched over her order pad like a mother eagle.

"Can I ask? Do you have the salmon croquettes today?"

"I'll check with the cook."

Here is another thing I know but pretend not to. One of the local delights the menu boasts of is the salmon croquettes. They are offered with the parenthetical proviso: WHEN IN SEASON. Now, I know they make their salmon croquettes with canned salmon, as do I, as do the insane. Not even Martha Stewart is nutty enough to make salmon croquettes with fresh salmon. They're not like crab cakes, where the fresher the crab the better. The whole point of salmon croquettes is what you put on them. Look up "croquette" in the dictionary and you'll see: "A desire for tartar sauce."

The waitress returns to tell me. I am in luck. The croquettes are fresh today.

I flatten out the girl's midterm to the right of my knife and fork, iron it out with the palm of my hand, thinking, We've had a long ride, it may be hungry. The whole trip down it sat in the seat beside me, quiet like a passenger.

I was sitting at my kitchen table yesterday morning when Mother called. I pushed down the toast.

She said it was pineapple night when it happened, and they were on the pinochle cake. At least that's what I thought she said. Opal Whiteside was my girlhood hero. If Proust is correct, if objects do indeed have a life all their own, I understand the sudden lean my kitchen took to the left.

It was her heart, Mother said. Dropped dead at the card table in front of God and everybody, seventy-six years of age, never once touched her cake. "Shame," added Mother philosophically. Death, the Lutheran consequence of never having gotten into the habit—well, honey, had she?—of cleaning her plate. Feeling the need to compete with Opal's news, Mother checked off her own list of maladies, one by one, like potential party guests. Seems a certain Dr. Themo, the latest in a long line of witch doctors Mother had subsidized over the course of the years, cured her glaucoma.

"And I can see pretty well," she said.

"What do you mean pretty well," I said.

"It's a little funny in the one eye."

She applied for a library card for the visually impaired; Mother is not one to mope. Books on tape, that sort of thing. *The Clan of the Cave Bear* was checked out so she got *Les Misérables*. Indications were she was driving all over town.

"I only go places I know where I'm going, honey. Please don't use the *f* word."

"It's against the law, Mother. Blind people driving is against the law."

"I am not blind, Deborah Louise, I told you. I am impaired."

Mother was knee-deep in seaweed and psychics long before they were popular. "Science is not as smart as it thinks it is!" she likes to say. But she comes by her herbalness genuinely enough. Hospital doctors are why six of her children died in infancy—two sets of twins and two regular babies. They lie in a pretty cemetery in Tampa out by a big lake, buried in little glass cylinders like the pneumatic tubes at a drive-up bank, six silver circles in the ground. As it turned out, she wound up with just the two of us. My sister, the Homecoming Queen, and me, the heartless academic.

"You sure, honey, you want to drive down?"

"Yes, Mother. You know Chicago at this time of year. One of my students committed—"

"You don't have to tell *me* about the weather in Chicago, Miss Priss. I was *there*. I nearly froze my patootie off, and it was July! Don't tell *me*. Anyplace it gets dark in the squat middle of the day—you *are* taking those sunshine tablets?"

"Yes, Mother."

"Don't con me, kiddo. I spent good money—"

"Mother. Sweetheart. I am."

But she was off. Seasonal affective disorder, the movie. Her voice caught, sputtered, choked even from time to time, but in the end it always kicked in. It was a good engine. Dr. Themo this, Dr. Themo that. Dr. Themo and his Egyptian water therapy. Dr. Themo and the foxglove, the shark cartilage, the cauliflower tea. Dr. Themo revolutionized the medical world's thinking on the pancreas . . . no, the pituitary . . . no—

"The gizmo that regulates, you know, honey, the thingamajig."

"Kidney?"

"That's it."

Elvis would still be alive had he taken Dr. Themo's advice. Eat nothing yellow. Drink nothing brown. Take a walk on the sunny side of the street.

"Is it money?"

"No, Mother, it isn't money."

"Is it a man? Because if it's a man—"

"No, Mother, it isn't a man."

"Only one reason I can think of a grown woman'll confine herself to the inside of an automobile car and drive willingly in it for close to one thousand miles of gray Yankee highway, and that is a man reason."

"Mother, please."

"My ears are wide open. Talk."

I didn't feel much like talking about my student, acquainted as I already was with Mother's views on suicide. *Suicide, honey, it's a matter of glands.* This, the glandular argument, was Mother's standard response not only to suicide but to any ugly subject she did not wish to address: my father, my choice of attire, the 1968 Democratic Convention. *Your potassium falls off, way off, and before you can say snap crackle pop, you think there is no God.* Mother is a forward-looking person who believes in taking an active approach to life. *A glass of iron tonic and one of my broccoli burgers, and I'll show you the meaning of life!*

Mother's second argument was of a more spiritual nature. Life, for Mother, is a dinner invitation from the Host of Hosts—who for Mother is a tall, good-looking white man approximately her age with impeccable table manners and a Buick. *You wouldn't turn down an invitation from the best-looking man in the universe, now would you?*

So, instead of talking about my student, I gave Mother the news about my grant. The funding had finally come through.

"Isn't that something, sweetheart, I am so proud of you. You know your sister got her interview. She's going on *Wheel of Fortune!*"

My sister had already done *The Joker's Wild* a few years back. In pregame practice she won eighteen grand and a trip for two to Puerto Vallarta, but on the real thing she guessed Bette Davis when they asked who *Mommie Dearest* was about. Every Christmas the video was brought out and we would sit and watch my sister lose over and over again, Mother's applesauce cake fresh out of the oven and warm on our laps. You couldn't play that tape too many times for Mother. It was a great victory to have a daughter on TV.

"You pack those sunshine tablets, Missy. Put them in your pocketbook so's you have them *with*. Those are not for cure, please remember. Those are for maintenance!"

We did not go to doctors, growing up. We went to the backs of people's houses. I knew how to spell *poultice* before I knew what a polka dot was. We'd pull up into somebody's carport where babyfood jars, spewing starter shoots of herbal everything, were arranged into meaningful mandalas under pointy Spanish bayonets, the tips of which were festively ornamented with pink cups cut out from Styrofoam egg cartons. A devil boy around eight or nine would be there throwing a basketball against the carport wall, over and over again, to the sound of his own nether heart. The sound, an incantation of tin. Often, there would be a monkey.

Once there was a monkey and a rabbit, a little spider monkey that wore a diaper. The monkey and the rabbit lived together in a big cage just to the right of the carport, in a side yard littered with eyes-of-God made from cheap colored yarn. I stepped out of the car and our eyes locked, mine and the monkey's. The monkey jumped down on top of the rabbit, grabbed its ears for reins, and rode his reluctant pony all around the cage, then again faster. He threw back his tiny head, shot me a look, and laughed like Satan. The monkey's name was Mims.

"There was no monkey."

Every time I mention the monkey to Mother, she tells me I have a vivid imagination. Yesterday was no exception.

"Deborah Louise, you have a vivid imagination."

"It belonged to Myrtelene," I told her. "Myrtelene and her little son Bumpy."

"Myrtelene didn't have any son."

"Nephew, then."

"Nephew neither."

"He was in the carport. He was bouncing a basketball off the carport wall. He was like a gnome."

"Myrtelene didn't have any carport."

Unlike me, Mother does not find the past interesting because, in my version of it, she always comes out looking a little kooky—hence my nickname for her, Major Kookybird. She thinks I am criticizing, and who can blame her? What mother in these days of mother-blame wouldn't?

"There was no monkey."

"You're right, Mama Bear." I told her this because I love my mother with all my heart and all my soul. I repeated after her, "There was no monkey." But there was.

And inside the house was the lady.

The lady had me put on a slip approximately ten years too big for me. It went all the way to the floor, trailed behind like a poor girl's wedding dress. The lady told me the lord was my shepherd, I shall not want. Jalousie windows rattled in their slats. She placed something heavy and warm on my chest.

"Put your head inside and breathe deep. We're going to get that Devil out of you."

It was a pillowcase filled with boiled onions.

Myrtelene, Imogenia, Randy-Ann—each had her own idea about health and nutrition, and no matter how kooky, they all stayed well within the good boundaries of homeopathic panaceas—beet juice and the Bible, iron tonic and the colonic. The thing is, though, that what you want when you are sick and you are a little kid is what everybody else has got, a real doctor like you see on TV. You want Dr. Kildare in a bleached-white labcoat, a silver stethoscope with a Windex shine gleaming from his beautiful scrubbed neck. You want medicine—liquid, nasty, and red. You want wooden tongue depressors thrown away after each use, white surgical gloves thrown away after each use, paper hospital gowns, paper shoes, disinfected everything. You dream of being given a shot.

Not broccoli and Ben-Gay. Not Mentholatum Deep-Heat Rub smeared on a sanitary napkin and tied around your neck when you have a sore throat.

Opal put a stop to that one. She even got me to a real doctor once with Mother's reluctant okay. Yet had things been any other way I never would have met my monkey. One thing I know: I owe everything to the monkey.

The day I met him galloping around his cage on the back of that bunny, I acquired a layer of consciousness I do not believe I could have reached any other way. Look at me, the monkey seemed to say. Look at what I am doing, riding this bunny. Do you think this is a good thing or a bad thing?

I had to think.

Surely the bunny could not be having much fun. So, bad thing. The monkey was clearly having more fun than he should be having. The monkey, in fact, looked as though he would've known what to do with a whip. Really bad thing.

On the other hand, I know bunnies. Bunnies are strong. Bunnies bite.

The body weight on the bunny was twice that of the little spider monkey. That bunny could have kicked cowboy-monkey ass if need be. So. Maybe the bunny was having fun too. Bunnies get bored. Maybe the bunny even felt a certain amount of gratitude toward the monkey for coming up with the idea in the first place—for if one thing was clear, the whole thing was the monkey's idea.

I took that monkey home with me that day, in my mind that is, and he is with me still. He accompanies me to record stores—Hoagy Carmichael for me, Ween for the monkey—and to the movies—romantic comedies are about all I can take these days, give me Meg Ryan anything, but it's Tarantino and Tarantino knockoffs for the monkey. Grocery shopping—chicken again or Chilean sea bass? Raisin or sesame? Whole or skim? Even at the voting booth—Nixon? Bad thing. Carter, Clinton? Good thing, good thing. When I read in the paper about kids who kill their parents or people who blow up other people, I think, There goes somebody who never had a monkey. Or maybe had a purely bad monkey. I lucked out. Because, although he nags me from time to time since it does take me forever and a day to make the smallest of decisions, I love my monkey.

But there is another side to him.

I am not dying of leukemia nor do I have a child who is dying of leukemia. Money is not exactly no object but neither is it a big issue. I love my job. And although my boyfriend could be a bit more attentive, he is neither under federal indictment nor attempting to make a living by playing a musical instrument. Life is interesting. Friends are kind and then thoughtless and then kind again, and they make good company. Love is disappointing and then it isn't. Nothing happens and then something does. It's a pretty three-o'clock life. But sometimes, deep at night, my monkey will wake me up, wild-eyed, his spider-hair arms around my neck, and I feel a strangling. On these occasions it is not the monkey but I who ask, Is this a good thing or a bad thing? To which there is never any reply. And then I wake up.

I realize that I am sitting in the very booth Opal and I used to sit in during our red-vinyl-booth sessions. The plastic's peeling off the same place it was peeling off twenty years ago. Where the father's head goes. It's the VO5, still a seller. The funeral is tomorrow. I fudged a bit to Mother about my estimated time of arrival so as to have a chance to perform the necessary sea change. Opal's funeral coincided with spring break at my college, where Mondays, Wednesdays, and Fridays I teach art history to the completely disinterested, dispensing Rembrandt and the Renaissance part-time (code word for free). I am giddy, having driven straight through from Chicago on twenty-one hours of, as Mother said, gray Yankee highway. I had decided to drive down rather than fly; I knew I could use all the nothingness those twenty-one hours of highway hypnosis were happy to provide.

I dig in my purse for Mother's sunshine tablets, take two, and look out the window. This is a squat, shoestring Florida town. The air is bruised and full of contradiction. There is grace and rot and night-blooming jasmine—a trace of the ancient dame and her soldier son. It is the kind of place where before the day closes, you are likely to hear the word *poppycock*.

This is a word town.

It was Opal's love of words that first gave me the idea of being a teacher. Our famous sessions were all about vocabulary. In this very booth, in this very Stuckey's, every single Sunday, Opal would ask me the same question: "What is the most beautiful word in the English language?" And every week, in order to demonstrate my devotion, I tried out every single word an eight-year-old girl living a trailer-park life could brag of: *sentience, ambidextrous, ennui*. Somehow they were never enough. But there was one time, I remember, I was sure I had her.

"*Celerity,*" I said, holding my breath. It was the only word in *Pride and Prejudice* I had had to look up.

"*Celerity,*" said Opal. "Rapidity of motion or action. From the French *celer*, meaning swift. Celerity is nice, but I was thinking of something else, something simple. I was thinking *next.*"

I gave her the most intelligent *huh?* I could muster. I was incredulous—the quality or state of disbelief, from the French *credu*, meaning crudball, meaning numbskull, meaning me.

"Think about it," Opal said.

You can bet I thought about it. I loved this big, beautiful, brainy woman with all my heart, as only a plain eight-year-old girl can. While other kids were in the yard loud with kickball, I spent entire evenings in the kitchen reading the dictionary, reading everything, believing then as I believe today that the exact right word can change the world. I searched day and night for that word, the word that would make this woman sit up and take notice, the one word this woman did not know.

"Why do people answer the doorbell?" she asked me.

"To see who it is."

"Beyond the mere Pavlovian response to, as you say, Deborah Louise, see who it is, there is something else. There is a certain expectation—"

"It might be Ed McMahon. It might be a million bucks."

"It needn't take that form."

"What do you mean, form?"

"I mean it needn't take the pecuniary form you have just so adroitly pointed out, Deborah Louise."

I knew pecuniary. I knew adroit. What I didn't know was what this woman was talking about.

"Why don't we just kill ourselves, Deborah Louise? This instant?"

"I don't know," I said, ready to. To add insult to injury, Opal had informed me that the hero of *Pride and Prejudice* was not Lydia but Elizabeth.

"Think."

I was thinking. Nothing.

"What did you learn at the end of *Pride and Prejudice*?"

"Darcy wasn't all that stuck up."

"You read to the end of the whole book just for that?"

I did not tell her I read to the end of the whole book just to find one word she did not know—that recently witnessed exercise in pointlessness.

Opal tried on her patient voice. "What was your favorite part of the whole book?" she asked me.

"Lydia when she gets Wickham."

"So once she gets Wickham, once Lydia comes home married, why keep reading?"

Opal clearly had landed on Mars and had forgotten to call home so I had to celebrate the obvious for her. "To see what happens!"

"To see what happens—"

I said it. "Next."

"Same with life. People stick around, they answer the door, they answer the phone, they go to Las Vegas, they get up in the morning. They want to see what might happen."

"But your Cousin Alma—"

"One does eventually grow weary waiting for the glorious to arrive, Deborah Louise. Please pass the sugar."

Opal's Cousin Alma was married to my second cousin Buck, and when Buck died, Alma showed up at the funeral with a lady-pink pistol and shot him five times in his open coffin before they could get the gun away from her. They couldn't figure out what to charge her with.

I passed Opal the sugar.

Opal was a woman who believed in the power of sugar. She put sugar in her Coke. She liked to sprinkle it on top and watch it fizz down into the brown until it disappeared. She told me that when she died I should just fill her coffin with sugar, as she was uncertain of its availability in the next world. "A world without sugar, babydoll," she told me, "is no world whatsoever."

While Mother raisined our oatmeal with niacin tablets and wheatgermed our milk, Opal baked us sugar cakes and sugar cookies, deep-fried us sugar doughnuts. Her iced tea was famous because she didn't brew it, she distilled it. She let it sit out on her back porch in a big tin pitcher all afternoon long, three cups of sugar strong. Hummingbirds came. She called it her Florida champagne and served it in pretty colored tin glasses, and when you drank it your head swam off. Once, when she heard Mother had served us carrot cake for dessert, the first carrot cake in the state of Florida Mother would have you know, Opal church-keyed open a brand-new can of Hershey's chocolate syrup and stuck in a straw. She handed it to me and let me go, saying, "Carrots is not dessert."

It was Opal who saved my life the night of the Snowflake Princess Dance.

There I sat, furious and forlorn on my little pink bed in my little pink bedroom, up to my princess neck in cotton-candy chiffon. Mother had not gone soft on her no makeup commandment. No lipstick, no nothing. Not even for a Snowflake Princess. I sat on my bed waiting for my date, a good-looking blond boy with no personality, and riffling through *Seventeen* magazine advice—"Mayonnaise! The Poor Woman's Moisturizer!"—when all of a sudden there was something behind me. I looked up and there stood Opal.

She said, "Close your eyes and stick out your tongue. This worked for Cleopatra and it'll work for you." She dabbed something like salt on my tongue, and in seconds my cheeks and lips were rose red and stayed that way the whole princess night.

"Arsenic," she told me. "Just don't overdo it."

Then she stood back and drank a Coke. Opal happened to be one of those women who knew how to look when she drank a Coke straight out of the bottle. She was as tall as a man. She had on her famous Loretta Young skirt, navy blue with white polka dots. Womanly, but full of girl. She threw back her head—you could smell the Gulf of Mexico suddenly in the room—and took a long, slow drink, the bottle trumpeting skyward. The whole room leaned. She looked like Louis Armstrong summoning home the chariots. She looked like Dom Pérignon when he discovered champagne. When he said, "Oh my God, I'm drinking the stars."

"The salmon croquettes," says the waitress, arriving with my plate. "Will there be anything else?"

"May I have another RC, please?"

"Most certainly may."

Where the restaurant part ends, the gift shop begins. And straight ahead, at the end of my line of sight, I see—over past the saltwater taffy, the JFK key chains, all manner of highway toys—a satisfied-looking bird with a pointed beak, dipping its head down into a plastic martini glass in perpetuity, up down, up down.

I open the girl's midterm and begin to read.

It is a D-minus, which I can hardly send to the grieving parents with a note about what a great et cetera she was. She wasn't.

I could change the D to a B the way it was done in high school, but even the D-minus was a gift. She didn't identify any of the fifty slides, and she only responded to one of the four essay questions. That one response was mildly interesting, but it was shot through with inaccuracies: 1649 is just not in the sixteenth century; I wish it was.

If I could lay my hands on the same green Pilot pen I used to grade the thing with, maybe I could change the minus to a plus. But a D-plus. Wouldn't that be like pinning a sequin on a rat's ass? Bette Davis's famous line from some old movie about what it would be like to compliment Joan Crawford.

I read somewhere about a suicide's mother who pushed past police to her dead son's bathroom just to get the hair out of his hairbrush. Wouldn't this girl's mother, likewise, want every last thing? Even a D-minus midterm? At least it had her handwriting. Mightn't the handwriting have the effect on the mother of an old love letter, one you keep and read over and over again, not for the words but for the pleasure of the sight of it, the look of it, the arc and fall of the *this* and the *that*?

Or would the effect be the opposite? Might there be something in the girl's scribble that would act as an accusation? The very recognition of the hand, the way the girl made her capital *A*, might well produce a stab instead of a solace, wounding the mother every time she came across it either purposefully or by chance in a scrapbook, a file cabinet, a loose kitchen drawer.

I can't just throw it away, pretend it doesn't exist, thereby solving *my* dilemma.

The waitress returns with my RC. To my horror, she sets it down carelessly on my student's midterm.

"Sorry," she says, seeing my undisguised distress.

"Oh. It's no problem," I say.

But I am not quick enough, and because of the moisture from the bottom of the glass, the writing begins to bleed.

"I'll get more napkins."

"That's okay," I tell the waitress. "I've got it."

She looks at me, then turns and goes back to her station.

The moment is oddly emotional. I have spoken too sharply, feeling an insane desire to keep the girl's handwriting safe. Safe from what? The waitress? A napkin? It makes no sense. All I know is I want the waitress to stay away. I do not want her to see. I do not want her to ask me what it is I'm reading there. I do not want to have to say, "Oh, nothing." I wouldn't be able to say, "Oh, nothing."

The course was a survey in art history. The Venus of Willendorf through Karen Finley in a sixteen-week spin. The history of art on a yellow 78.

The class was riding high. I'd marched them up the Carolingian, down the Merovingian, and into the animal style. Gals fell silent before the cloisonné, the panther clasp, a world before buttons. Guys paid mute respect to the seriously enameled handles of war. When I put up a slide from *The Book of Kells* the whole room took a deep breath, even Randall Huddleston III. Inlaid gold? Think of it, the look on his face said, I mean in today's market. A newfound respect for art and artists alike suddenly took hold of him. You could see *The Book of Kells*, the *Hypnerotomachia Poliphili*, the duc de Berry's *Très Riches Heures*, the whole world's store of priceless incunabula all melting down into a pool of gold, and Randy with his mother's good cake pan collecting the hot liquid, cooling it into heavy gold rounds, suitcasing it off to Switzerland where it would sit in a fabulous honeymoon suite and wait pretty as a wedding cake for him and his new bride, Michelle Pfeiffer.

The girl sat in the back of the room. She never said a word, never raised a hand, never took the first note.

She was the only thing alive in that classroom.

She never even bought the text. The only book she ever brought to class was a beat-up copy of *The Idiot*. She sat there silently every Monday, Wednesday, and Friday from 10:00 to 10:50 AM reading her Dostoevski, giving him all the attention of a lover. She ignored us as hard as she could. She ignored me, she ignored Albrecht Dürer, she ignored Randall Huddleston III. She sat, in fact, as far from Randall Huddleston III as it was possible to sit. She was saving herself for Prince Myshkin.

I didn't even know what a cutter was. When my own personal brand of self-flagellation surfaces, when my Lutheran shows, I deny myself the Moët and make do with Korbel. When I want to flirt with death I say no for a month to Princess Borghese and go down the moisturizer ladder to Clinique.

This girl cut herself.

The one and only time I can remember that she ever even looked up, we were on Rembrandt. "Part of the success of Rembrandt's luminous brown," I was saying, "is due to his use of pulverized human bone." I could tell the idea struck her. Bone going to powder.

She looked up at me. And I think she wanted to know if that was a good thing or a bad thing—using human bones. I had never really thought about it. I heard myself talking, I listened to myself speak, but there had been nothing about that.

What I said was, "Next slide please." *Carceri d'Invenzione*. A series of fantastic, imaginary prisons by Giovanni Battista Piranesi. Though never constructed, these are the finest examples of his architectural renderings. Begun in 1745. Reworked in 1781.

"Lady?"

There is a boy standing at my table. He is wearing a suit. Somehow the suit is ten years too old for him. It takes me a minute. Me. I'm the lady.

"You want your game? Ours don't have all the things in it."

He is pointing to the little wood triangle, one of those highway toys Stuckey's offers for the stimulation of the long-distance traveler. There are short orange pegs sticking up out of it.

"Eddie. Over here. This minute."

And the little guy is gone. Reseated with his mother, he bows his head, seemingly benumbed by years and years of never getting anything his way. The boy and his mother are dressed in black, poor people's black, on their way to a funeral. Even the mother's barrettes are black, have been placed square and equidistant from the part, seem to know how to behave at a restaurant, at a funeral, at this and all of life's other slender occasions.

"Hand me my pocketbook." The mother is up. "And Eddie. I said don't put sugar on your french fries." The mother breezes by me to pay her bill, leaving the smell of poverty and brilliantine in her wake. I feel the little guy looking at me, looking at me hard, so I glance up.

He is holding the silver-topped sugar canister high above a mountain of french fries, and he is looking at me. I think he wants to know. If this would be a good thing or a bad thing.

And at this moment my monkey comes to me, saying that to send the D-minus to the dead girl's mother would be a bad thing. But wait. What if I were to take what the girl wrote and type it up in the form of an essay? She didn't write much, but what she did say—basically questioning Rembrandt's use of human bones, even to make what is arguably great art—would make a perfectly respectable essay, something Camus himself might enjoy. I could type it up on my computer in MLA style—her name, my name, course title, date, one-inch margins, and a nice letter-gothic face. (And may I say what a lovely century it is, since this particular solution in any other century would be out of the question.) I'll fix all the little things. I'll put 1649 back into the seventeenth century, I'll put the *d* back into "Rembrant," and voila! Then, instead of the easy, tenured-professor adjectives—*interesting, insightful*, and the ever popular *yes*—I'll make real comments in the margins and a detailed end comment about her powers of concentration. And it will be the truth, the part about the originality of her thought. I'll title it "Rembrandt's Bones" and I'll give it a B-plus. Okay, what the fucking fuck, I'll give it an A.

And this will be a small thing, a very small thing, but a good thing.

The midterm itself? It *is* a document. I can't just throw it away. And then I realize—and please remember it is me this time and not my monkey who gets this idea—that Opal will need something to read in the afterlife. I figure she'll have an open casket. Opal knew that even dead she'd be the best-looking woman there.

I look up. The boy lingers, waiting, sugar canister held high, and it seems to me at this moment that the whole wide world is on its way to a funeral. I look past the little guy to the Rebel flags and GooGoo Clusters, the alligator ashtrays and the JFK penny banks, the wooden back scratchers with faces of jokey men on the backside, the IF YOUR HEART'S NOT IN DIXIE GET YOUR ASS OUT license plates, the rows of ceramic cows and kittens—to this whole pecan divinity. I look at the boy and raise my Coke high, toast his sugar experiment.

He looks at me once, twice, then goes ahead. I watch the little guy pour.

"Is it good?" I ask, and he nods, looking at me, ridiculous with my Coke sky high. I must look like the top half of the Statue of Liberty, only a little loaded. And so we sit, this little guy and I, our hearts beating wildly. We sit and wait to see. See how much trouble we are in for, because this time we know we are both of us really going to get it. We wait to see what the waitress will say, or the manager of this crazy ceramic dream. See what a woman with barrettes like that might do. What in the world might happen next.

BARRY LOPEZ

The Mappist

WHEN I WAS AN UNDERGRADUATE AT BROWN I CAME ACROSS A BOOK
called *The City of Ascensions*, about Bogotá. I knew nothing of Bogotá,
but I felt the author had captured its essence. My view was that Onesimo
Peña had not written a travel book but a work about the soul of Bogotá.
Even if I were to read it later in life, I thought, I would not be able to get
all Peña meant in a single reading. I looked him up at the library, but he
had apparently written no other books, at least not any in English.

In my senior year I discovered a somewhat better known book, *The City
of Trembling Leaves* by Walter Van Tilburg Clark, about Reno, Nevada. I
liked it, but it did not have the superior depth, the integration of Peña's
work. Peña, you had the feeling, could walk you through the warrens of
Bogotá without a map and put your hands directly on the vitality of any
modern century—the baptismal registries of a particular cathedral, a
cornerstone that had been taken from one building to be used in another,
a London plane tree planted by Bolívar. He had such a command of the
idiom of this city, and the book itself demonstrated such complex linkages,
it was easy to believe Peña had no other subject, that he could have written
nothing else. I believed this was so until I read *The City of Floating Sand* a
year later, a book about Cape Town, and then a book about Djakarta called
The City of Frangipani. Though the former was by one Frans Haartman
and the latter by a Jemboa Tran, each had the distinctive organic layering
of the Peña book, and I felt certain they'd been written by the same man.

A national library search through the University of Michigan, where I
had gone to work on a master's degree in geography, produced hundreds
of books with titles similar to these. I had to know whether Peña had
written any others and so read or skimmed perhaps thirty of those I got
through interlibrary loan. Some, though wretched, were strange enough
to be engaging; others were brilliant but not in the way of Peña. I ended
up ordering copies of five I believed Peña had written, books about Perth,
Lagos, Tokyo, Venice, and Boston, the last a volume by William Smith
Everett called *The City of Cod*.

Who Peña actually was I could not then determine. Letters to publishers eventually led me to a literary agency in New York where I was told that the author did not wish to be known. I pressed for information about what else he might have written, inquired whether he was still alive (the book about Venice had been published more than fifty years before), but got nowhere.

As a doctoral student at Duke I made the seven Peña books the basis of a dissertation. I wanted to show in a series of city maps, based on all the detail in Peña's descriptions, what a brilliant exegesis of the social dynamics of these cities he had achieved. My maps showed, for example, how water moved through Djakarta, not just municipal water but also trucked water and, street by street, the flow of rain water. And how road building in Cape Town reflected the policy of apartheid.

I received quite a few compliments on the work, but I knew the maps did not make apparent the hard, translucent jewel of integration that was each Peña book. I had only created some illustrations, however well done. But had I known whether he was alive or where he lived, I would still have sent him a copy out of a sense of collegiality and respect.

After I finished the dissertation I moved my wife and three young children to Brookline, a suburb of Boston, and set up a practice as a restoration geographer. Fifteen years later I embarked on my fourth or fifth trip to Tokyo as a consultant to a planning firm there, and one evening I took a train out to Chiyoda-ku to visit bookstores in an area called Jimbocho. Just down the street from a bridge over the Kanda River is the Sanseido Bookstore, a regular haunt by then for me. Up on the fifth floor I bought two translations of books by Japanese writers on the Asian architectural response to topography in mountain cities. I was exiting the store on the ground floor, a level given over entirely to maps, closing my coat against the spring night, when I happened to spot the kanji for "Tokyo" on a tier of drawers. I opened one of them to browse. Toward the bottom of a second drawer I came upon a set of maps that seemed vaguely familiar, though the entries were all in kanji. After a few minutes of leafing through, it dawned on me that they bore a resemblance to the maps I had done as a student at Duke. I was considering buying one of them as a memento when I caught a name in English in the corner—Corlis Benefideo. It appeared there on every map.

I stared at that name a long while, and I began to consider what you also may be thinking. I bought all thirteen maps. Even without language to identify information in the keys, even without titles, I could decipher what the mapmaker was up to. One designated areas prone to flooding as water from the Sumida River backed up through the city's storm drains. Another showed the location of all shops dealing in Edo Period manuscripts and artwork. Another, using small pink arrows, showed the point of view of each of Hiroshige's famous One Hundred Views. Yet another showed, in six time-sequenced panels, the rise and decline of horse barns in the city.

My office in Boston was fourteen hours behind me, so I had to leave a message for my assistant, asking him to look up Corlis Benefideo's name. I gave him some contacts at map libraries I used regularly, and asked him to call me back as soon as he had anything, no matter the hour. He called at three AM to say that Corlis Benefideo had worked as a mapmaker for the U.S. Coast and Geodetic Survey in Washington from 1932 until 1958, and that he was going to fax me some more information.

I dressed and went down to the hotel lobby to wait for the faxes and read them while I stood there. Benefideo was born in Fargo, North Dakota, in 1912. He went to work for the federal government straight out of Grinnell College during the Depression and by 1940 was traveling to various places—Venice, Bogotá, Lagos—in an exchange program. In 1958 he went into private practice as a cartographer in Chicago. His main source of income at that time appeared to be from the production of individualized site maps for large estate homes being built along the North Shore of Lake Michigan. The maps were bound in oversize books, twenty by thirty inches, and showed the vegetation, geology, hydrology, biology, and even archaeology of each site. They were subcontracted for under several architects.

Benefideo's Chicago practice closed in 1975. The fax said nothing more was known of his work history, and that he was not listed in any Chicago area phone books nor with any professional organizations. I faxed back to the office, asking them to check phone books in Fargo, in Washington, DC, and around Grinnell, Iowa—Des Moines and those towns. And asking them to try to find someone at what was now the National Geodetic Survey who might have known Benefideo or who could provide some detail.

When I came back to the hotel the following afternoon there was another fax. No luck with the phone books, I read, but I could call a Maxwell

Abert at the National Survey who'd worked with Benefideo. I waited the necessary few hours for the time change and called.

Abert said he had overlapped with Benefideo for one year, 1958, and though Benefideo had left voluntarily, it wasn't his idea.

"What you had to understand about Corlis," he said, "was that he was a patriot. Now, that word today, I don't know, means maybe nothing, but Corlis felt this very strong commitment to his country, and to a certain kind of mapmaking, and he and the Survey just ended up on a collision course. The way Corlis worked, you see, the way he approached things, slowed down the production of maps. That wasn't any good from a bureaucratic point of view. He couldn't give up being comprehensive, you understand, and they just didn't know what to do with him."

"What happened to him?"

"Well, the man spoke five or six languages, and he had both the drafting ability and the conceptual skill of a first-rate cartographer, so the government should have done something to keep the guy—but they didn't. Oh, his last year they created a project for him, but it was temporary. He saw they didn't want him. He moved to Chicago—but you said you knew that."

"Mmm. Do you know where he went after Chicago?"

"I do. He went to Fargo. And that's the last I know. I wrote him there until about 1985—he'd have been in his seventies—and then the last letter came back 'no forwarding address.' So that's the last I heard. I believe he must have died. He'd be, what, eighty-eight now."

"What was the special project?"

"Well Corlis, you know, he was like something out of a WPA project, like Dorothea Lange, Walker Evans, and James Agee and them, people that had this sense of America as a country under siege, undergoing a trial during the Depression, a society that needed its dignity back. Corlis believed that in order to effect any political or social change, you had to know exactly what you were talking about. You had to know what the country itself—the ground, the real thing, not some political abstraction—was all about. So he proposed this series of forty-eight sets of maps—this was just before Alaska and Hawaii came in—a series for each state that would show the geology and hydrology, where the water was, you know, and the botany and biology, and the history of the place from Native American times.

"Well, a hundred people working hundred-hour weeks for a decade might get it all down, you know—it was monumental, what he was proposing. But to keep him around, to have him in the office, the Survey created this pilot project so he could come up with an approach that might get it done in a reasonable amount of time—why, I don't know, the government works on most things forever—but that's what he did. I never saw the results, but if you ever wanted to see disillusionment in a man you should have seen Corlis in those last months. He tried Congressmen, he tried Senators, he tried other people in Commerce, he tried everybody. But I think they all had the same sense of him, that he was an obstructionist. They'd eat a guy like that alive on the Hill today, the same way. He just wasn't very practical. But he was a good man."

I got the address in Fargo and thanked Mr. Abert. It turned out to be where Benefideo's parents had lived until they died. The house was sold in 1985. And that was that.

When I returned to Boston I reread *The City of Ascensions*. It's a beautiful book, so tender toward the city, and proceeding on the assumption that Bogotá was the living idea of its inhabitants. I thought Benefideo's books would make an exceptional subject for a senior project in history or geography, and wanted to suggest it to my older daughter Stephanie. How, I might ask her, do we cultivate people like Corlis Benefideo? Do they all finally return to the rural districts from which they come, unable or unwilling to fully adapt to the goals, the tone, of a progressive society? Was Corlis familiar with the work of Lewis Mumford? Would you call him a populist?

Stephanie, about to finish her junior year at Bryn Mawr, had an interest in cities and geography, but it was there in spite of my promotions. I didn't know how to follow up on this with her.

One morning, several months after I got back from Tokyo, I walked into the office and saw a note in the center of my desk, a few words from my diligent assistant. It was Benefideo's address—Box 117, Garrison, North Dakota 58540. I got out the office atlas. Garrison is halfway between Minot and Bismarck, just north of Lake Sakakawea. No phone.

I wrote him a brief letter, saying I'd recently bought a set of his maps in Tokyo, asking if he was indeed the author of the books, and telling him how much I admired them and that I had based my PhD dissertation on them. I praised the integrity of the work he had done, and said I was

BARRY LOPEZ

331

intrigued by his last Survey project, and would also like to see one of the Chicago publications sometime.

A week later I got a note. "Dear Mr. Trevino," it read, "I appreciate your kind words about my work. I am still at it. Come for a visit if you wish. I will be back from a trip in late September, so the first week of October would be fine. Sincerely, Corlis Benefideo."

I located a motel in Garrison, got plane tickets to Bismarck, arranged a rental car, and then wrote Mr. Benefideo and told him I was coming, and that if he would send me his street address I would be at his door at nine AM on October second. The address he sent, 15088 State Highway 37, was a few miles east of Garrison. A hand-rendered map in colored pencil which made tears well up in my eyes showed how to get to the house, which lay a ways off the road in a grove of ash trees he had sketched.

The days of waiting made me anxious and aware of my vulnerability. I asked both my daughters and my son if they wanted to go. No, school was starting, they wanted to be with their friends. My wife debated, then said no. She thought this was something that would go best if I went alone.

Corlis was straddling the sill of his door as I drove into his yard. He wore a pair of khaki trousers, a khaki shirt, and a khaki ball cap. He was about five-foot-six and lean. Though spry, he showed evidence of arthritis and the other infirmities of age in his walk and handshake.

During breakfast I noticed a set of *The City of* books on his shelves. There were eight, which meant I'd missed one. After breakfast he asked if I'd brought any binoculars, and whether I'd be interested in visiting a wildlife refuge a few miles away off the Bismarck highway, to watch ducks and geese coming in from Canada. He made a picnic lunch and we drove over and had a fine time. I had no binoculars with me, and little interest in the birds to start with, but with his guidance and animation I came to appreciate the place. We saw more than a million birds that day, he said.

When we got back to the house I asked if I could scan his bookshelves while he fixed dinner. He had thousands of books, a significant number of them in Spanish and French and some in Japanese. (The eighth book was called *The City of Geraniums*, about Lima.) On the walls of a large room that incorporated the kitchen and dining area was perhaps the most astonishing collection of hand-drawn maps I had ever seen outside a library.

Among them were two of McKenzie's map sketches from his exploration of northern Canada, four of Fitzroy's coastal elevations from Chile (made during the voyage with Darwin), one of Humboldt's maps of the Orinoco, and a half-dozen sketches of the Thames docks by Samuel Pepys.

Mr. Benefideo made us a dinner of canned soup, canned meat, and canned vegetables. For dessert he served fresh fruit, some store-bought cookies, and instant coffee. I studied him at the table. His forehead was high, and a prominent jaw and large nose further elongated his face. His eyes were pale blue, his skin burnished and dark, like a Palermo fisherman's. His ears flared slightly. His hair, still black on top, was close cropped. There was little in the face but alertness of the eyes to give you a sense of the importance of his work.

After dinner our conversation took a more satisfying turn. He had discouraged conversation while we were watching the birds, and he had seemed disinclined to talk while he was riding in the car. Our exchanges around dinner—which was quick—were broken up by its preparation and by clearing the table. A little to my surprise he offered me Mexican tequila after the meal. I declined, noticing the bottle had no label, but sat with him on the porch while he drank.

Yes, he said, he'd used the pen names to keep the government from finding out what else he'd been up to in those cities. And yes, the experience with the Survey had made him a little bitter, but it had also opened the way to other things. His work in Chicago had satisfied him—the map sets for the estate architects and their wealthy clients, he made clear, were a minor thing; his real business in those years was in other countries, where hand-drawn and hand-colored maps still were welcome and enthused over. The estate map books, however, had allowed him to keep his hand in on the kind of work he wanted to pursue more fully one day.

In 1975 he came back to Fargo to take care of his parents. When they died he sold the house and moved to Garrison. He had a government pension—when he said this he flicked his eyebrows, as though in the end he had gotten the best of the government. He had a small income from his books, he told me, mostly the foreign editions. And he had put some money away, so he'd been able to buy this place.

"What are you doing now?"

"The North Dakota series, the work I proposed in Washington in '57."

"The hydrological maps, the biological maps?"

"Yes. I subdivided the state into different sections, the actual number depending on whatever scale I needed for that subject. I've been doing them for fifteen years now, a thousand six-hundred and fifty-one maps. I want to finish them, you know, so that if anyone ever wants to duplicate the work, they'll have a good idea of how to go about it."

He gazed at me in a slightly disturbing, almost accusatory way.

"Are you going to donate the maps, then, to a place where they can be studied?"

"North Dakota Museum of Art, in Grand Forks."

"Did you never marry, never have children?"

"I'm not sure, you know. No, I never married—I asked a few times, but was turned down. I didn't have the features, I think, and, early on, no money. Afterward, I developed a way of life that was really too much my own, on a day-to-day basis. But, you know, I've been the beneficiary of great kindness in my life, and some of it has come from women who were, or are, very dear to me. Do you know what I mean?"

"Yes, I do."

"As for children, I think maybe there are one or two. In Bogotá. Venice. Does it shock you?"

"People are not shocked by things like this anymore, Mr. Benefideo."

"That's too bad. I am. I have made my peace with it, though. Would you like to see the maps?"

"The Dakota series?"

Mr. Benefideo took me to a second large room with more stunning maps on the walls, six or eight tiers of large map drawers, and a worktable the perimeter of which was stained with hundreds of shades of watercolors surrounding a gleaming white area about three feet square. He turned on some track lighting which made the room very bright and pointed me to a swivel stool in front of an empty table, a smooth, broad surface of some waxed and dark wood.

From an adjacent drawer he pulled out a set of large maps which he laid in front of me.

"As you go through, swing them to the side there. I'll restack them."

The first map was of ephemeral streams in the northeast quadrant of the state.

"These streams," he pointed out, "run only during wet periods, some but once in twenty years. Some don't have any names."

The information was strikingly presented and beautifully drawn. The instruction you needed to get oriented—where the Red River was, where the county lines were—was just enough, so it barely impinged on the actual subject matter of the map. The balance was perfect.

The next map showed fence lines, along the Missouri River in a central part of the state.

"These are done at twenty-year intervals, going back to 1840. Fences are like roads: they proliferate, they're never completely removed."

The following map was a geological one, a rendering of the bedrock of McIntosh County. As I took in the shape and colors, the subdivided shades of purple and green and blue, Mr. Benefideo slid a large hand-colored transparency across the sheet, a soil map of the same area. You could imagine looking down through a variety of soil types to the bedrock below.

"Or," he said, and then slid an opaque map with the same information across in front of me, the yellows and browns of a dozen silts, clays, and sands.

The next sheet was of eighteenth- and nineteenth-century foot trails in the western half of the state.

"But how did you compile this information?"

"Inspection and interviews. Close personal observation and talking with long-term residents. It's a hard thing, really, to erase a trail. A lot of information can be recovered if you stay at it."

When he placed the next map in front of me, the summer distribution of Swainson's hawks, and then slid in next to it a map showing the overlapping summer distribution of its main prey species, the Richardson ground squirrel, the precision and revelation were too much for me.

I turned to face him. "I've never seen anything that even approaches this, this . . . " My gesture across the surface of the table included everything. "It's not just the information, or the execution—I mean, the technique is flawless, the watercoloring, your choice of scale—but, it's like the books, there's so much more."

"That's the idea, don't you think, Mr. Trevino?"

"Of course, but nobody has the time for this kind of fieldwork anymore."

"That's unfortunate, because this information is what we need, you know. This shows history, and how people fit the places they occupy. It's about what gets erased and what comes to replace it. These maps reveal the foundations beneath the ephemera."

"What about us, though?" I blurted, resisting his pronouncement. "In the books, in *City in Aspic* in particular, there is such a palpable love of human life in the cities, and here—"

"I do not have to live up to the history of Venice, Mr. Trevino," he interrupted, "but I am obliged to shoulder the history of my own country. I could show you here the whole coming and going of the Mandan nation, wiped out in 1837 by a smallpox epidemic. I could show you how the arrival of German and Scandinavian farmers changed the composition of the topsoil, and the places where Charles Bodmer painted, and the evolution of red-light districts in Fargo—all that with pleasure. I've nothing against human passion, human longing. What I oppose is blind devotion to progress, and the venality of material wealth. If we're going to trade the priceless for the common, I want to know exactly what the terms are."

I had no response. His position was as difficult to assail as it would be to promote.

"You mean," I finally ventured, "that someone else will have to do the maps that show the spread of the Wal-Mart empire in North Dakota."

"I won't be doing those."

His tone was assertive but not testy. He wasn't even seeking my agreement.

"My daughter," I said, changing the subject, "wants to be an environmental historian. She has a good head for it, and I know she's interested—she wants to discover the kind of information you need to build a stable society. I'm sure it comes partly from looking at what's already there, as you suggest, like the birds this morning, how that movement, those movements, might determine the architecture of a society. I'm wondering—could I ever send her out? Maybe to help? Would you spend a few days with her?"

"I'd be glad to speak with her," he said, after considering the question. "I'd train her, if it came to that."

"Thank you."

He began squaring the maps up to place them back in the drawer.

"You know, Mr. Trevino—Phillip if I may, and you may call me Corlis—the question is about you, really." He shut the drawer and gestured me toward the door of the room, which he closed behind us.

"You represent a questing but lost generation of people. I think you know what I mean. You made it clear this morning, talking nostalgically about my books, that you think an elegant order has disappeared, something that shows the way." We were standing at the corner of the dining table with our hands on the chair backs. "It's wonderful, of course, that you brought your daughter into our conversation tonight, and certainly we're both going to have to depend on her, on her thinking. But the real question, now, is what will *you* do? Because you can't expect her to take up something you wish for yourself, a way of seeing the world. You send her here, if it turns out to be what she wants, but don't make the mistake of thinking you, or I or anyone, knows how the world is meant to work. The world is a miracle, unfolding in the pitch dark. We're lighting candles. Those maps—they are my candles. And I can't extinguish them for anyone."

He crossed to his shelves and took down his copy of *The City of Geraniums*. He handed it to me and we went to the door.

"If you want to come back in the morning for breakfast, please do. Or, there is a café, the Dogwood, next to the motel. It's good. However you wish."

We said good night, and I moved out through pools of dark beneath the ash trees to where I'd parked the car. I set the book on the seat opposite and started the engine. The headlights swept the front of the house as I turned past it, catching the salute of his hand, and then he was gone.

I inverted the image of the map from his letter in my mind and began driving south to the highway. After a few moments I turned off the headlights and rolled down the window. I listened to the tires crushing gravel in the roadbed. The sound of it helped me hold the road, together with instinct and the memory of earlier having driven it. I felt the volume of space beneath the clear, star-ridden sky, and moved over the dark prairie like a barn-bound horse.

JOYCE CAROL OATES

Three Girls

IN STRAND USED BOOKS ON BROADWAY AND TWELFTH ONE SNOWY
March early evening in 1956 when the streetlights on Broadway glimmered
with a strange sepia glow, we were two NYU girl-poets drifting through
the warehouse of treasures as through an enchanted forest. Just past 6:00
PM. Above light-riddled Manhattan, opaque night. Snowing, and sidewalks
encrusted with ice so there were fewer customers in the Strand than usual
at this hour but *there we were.* Among other cranky brooding regulars.
In our army-surplus jackets, baggy khaki pants, and zip-up rubber boots.
In our matching wool caps (knitted by your restless fingers) pulled down
low over our pale-girl foreheads. Enchanted by books. Enchanted by the
Strand.

No bookstore of merely "new" books with elegant show window displays
drew us like the drafty Strand, bins of books untidy and thumbed through
as merchants' sidewalk bins on Fourteenth Street, NEW THIS WEEK, BEST
BARGAINS, WORLD CLASSICS, ART BOOKS 50% OFF, REVIEWERS' COPIES,
HIGHEST PRICE $ 1.98, REMAINDERS 25¢ – $ 1.00. Hardcover/paperback.
Spotless/battered. Beautiful books/cheaply printed pulp paper. And at the
rear and sides in that vast echoing space massive shelves of books books
books rising to a ceiling of hammered tin fifteen feet above! Stacked
shelves so high they required ladders to negotiate and a monkey nimble-
ness (like yours) to climb.

We were enchanted with the Strand and with each other in the Strand.
Overseen by surly young clerks who were poets like us, or playwrights/ac-
tors/artists. In an agony of unspoken young love I watched you. As always
on these romantic evenings at the Strand, prowling the aisles sneering at
those luckless books, so many of them, unworthy of your attention. Best-
sellers, how-tos, arts and crafts, too simple *histories of.* Women's romances,
sentimental love poems. Patriotic books, middlebrow books, books lacking
esoteric covers. We were girl-poets passionately enamored of T. S. Eliot
but scornful of Robert Frost whom we'd been made to memorize in high
school—slyly we communicated in code phrases from Eliot in the pres-

ence of obtuse others in our dining hall and residence. We were admiring of though confused by the poetry of Yeats, we were yet more confused by the lauded worth of Pound, enthusiastically drawn to the bold metaphors of Kafka (that cockroach!) and Dostoevski (sexy murderer Raskolnikov and the Underground Man were our rebel heroes) and Sartre ("Hell is other people"—we knew this), and had reason to believe that we were their lineage though admittedly we were American middle class, and Caucasian, and female. (Yet we were not "conventional" females. In fact, we shared male contempt for the merely "conventional" female.)

Brooding above a tumble of books that quickened the pulse, almost shyly touching Freud's *Civilization and Its Discontents*, Crane Brinton's *The Age of Reason*, Margaret Mead's *Coming of Age in Samoa*, D. H. Lawrence's *The Rainbow*, Kierkegaard's *Fear and Trembling*, Mann's *Death in Venice*—there suddenly you glided up behind me to touch my wrist (as never you'd done before, had you?) and whispered, "Come here," in a way that thrilled me for its meaning *I have something wonderful/unexpected/ startling to show you.* Like poems these discoveries in the Strand were, to us, found poems to be cherished. And eagerly I turned to follow you though disguising my eagerness, "Yes, what?" as if you'd interrupted me, for possibly we'd had a quarrel earlier that day, a flaring up of tense girl-tempers. Yes, you were childish and self-absorbed and given to sulky silences and mercurial moods in the presence of showy superficial people, and I adored and feared you knowing you'd break my heart, my heart that had never before been broken because never before so exposed.

So eagerly yet with my customary guardedness I followed you through a maze of book bins and shelves and stacks to the ceiling ANTHROPOL-OGY, ART/ANCIENT, ART/RENAISSANCE, ART/MODERN, ART/ASIAN, ART/ WESTERN, TRAVEL, PHILOSOPHY, COOKERY, POETRY/MODERN where the way was treacherously lighted only by bare sixty-watt bulbs, and where customers as cranky as we two stood in the aisles reading books, or sat hunched on footstools glancing up annoyed at our passage, and unquestioning I followed you until at POETRY/MODERN you halted, and pushed me ahead and around a corner, and I stood puzzled staring, not knowing what I was supposed to be seeing until impatiently you poked me in the ribs and pointed, and now I perceived an individual in the aisle pulling down books from shelves, peering at them, clearly absorbed by what she read, a woman nearly my height (I was tall for a girl, in 1956) in a man's navy coat to her ankles and with sleeves past her wrists, a man's beige fedora hat on her head, scrunched low as we wore our knitted caps, and most of her hair hidden by the hat except for a six-inch blond plait at the nape of her neck; and she wore black trousers tucked into what appeared to be salt-stained cowboy boots. Someone we knew? An older, good-looking student from one of our classes? *A girl-poet like ourselves?* I was about to nudge you in the ribs in bafflement when the blond woman turned, taking down another book from the shelf (e. e. cummings' *Tulips and Chimneys*—always I would remember that title!), and I saw that she was Marilyn Monroe.

Marilyn Monroe. In the Strand. Just like us. And she seemed to be alone. *Marilyn Monroe, alone!*

Wholly absorbed in browsing amid books, oblivious of her surroundings and of us. No one seemed to have recognized her (yet) except you.

Here was the surprise: this woman was/was not Marilyn Monroe. For this woman was an individual wholly absorbed in selecting, leafing through, pausing to read books. You could see that this individual was a *reader*. One of those who *reads*. With concentration, with passion. With her very soul. And it was poetry she was reading, her lips pursed, silently shaping words. Absent-mindedly she wiped her nose on the edge of her hand, so intent was she on what she was reading. For when you truly read poetry, poetry reads *you*.

Still, this woman was—Marilyn Monroe. And despite our common sense, our scorn for the silly clichés of Hollywood romance, still we halfway expected a Leading Man to join her: Clark Gable, Robert Taylor, Marlon Brando.

Halfway we expected the syrupy surge of movie music, to glide us into the scene.

But no man joined Marilyn Monroe in her disguise as one of us in the Strand. No Leading Man, no dark prince.

Like us (we began to see) this Marilyn Monroe required no man.

For what seemed like a long time but was probably no more than half an hour, Marilyn Monroe browsed in the POETRY/MODERN shelves, as from a distance of approximately ten feet two girl-poets watched covertly, clutching each other's hands. We were stunned to see that this woman looked very little like the glamorous "Marilyn Monroe." That figure was a garish blond showgirl, a Hollywood "sexpot" of no interest to intellectuals (*we* thought, we who knew nothing of the secret romance between Marilyn Monroe and Arthur Miller); this figure more resembled us (almost) than she resembled her Hollywood image. We were dying of curiosity to see whose poetry books Marilyn Monroe was examining: Elizabeth Bishop, H.D., Robert Lowell, Muriel Rukeyser, Harry Crosby, Denise Levertov. . . . Five or six of these Marilyn Monroe decided to purchase, then moved on, leather bag slung over her shoulder and fedora tilted down on her head.

We couldn't resist, we had to follow! Cautious not to whisper together like excited schoolgirls, still less to giggle wildly as we were tempted; you nudged me in the ribs to sober me, gave me a glare signaling *Don't be rude, don't ruin this for all of us.* I conceded: I was the more pushy of the two of us, a tall gawky Rima the Bird Girl with springy carroty-red hair like an exotic bird's crest, while you were petite and dark haired and attractive with long-lashed Semitic sloe eyes, you the wily gymnast and I the aggressive basketball player, you the "experimental" poet and I drawn to "forms," our contrary talents bred in our bones. Which of us would marry, have babies, disappear into "real" life, and which of us would persevere into her thirties before starting to be published and becoming, in time, a "real" poet—could anyone have predicted, this snowy March evening in 1956?

Marilyn Monroe drifted through the maze of books, and we followed in her wake as through a maze of dreams, past SPORTS, past MILITARY, past WAR, past HISTORY/ANCIENT, past the familiar figures of Strand regulars frowning into books, past surly yawning bearded clerks who took no more heed of the blond actress than they ever did of us, and so to NATURAL HISTORY where she paused, and there again for unhurried minutes (the Strand was open until 9:00 PM.) Marilyn Monroe in her mannish disguise browsed and brooded, pulling down books, seeking what? at last crouched leafing through an oversized illustrated book (curiosity overcame me! I shoved away your restraining hand; politely I eased past Marilyn Monroe murmuring "excuse me" without so much as brushing against her and without being noticed), Charles Darwin's *Origin of Species* in a deluxe edition. Darwin! *Origin of Species!* We were poet-despisers-of-science, or believed we were, or must be, to be true poets in the exalted mode of T. S. Eliot and William Butler Yeats; such a choice, for Marilyn Monroe, seemed perverse to us. But this book was one Marilyn quickly decided to purchase, hoisting it into her arms and moving on.

That rakish fedora we'd come to covet, and that single chunky blond braid. (Afterward we would wonder: Marilyn Monroe's hair in a braid? Never had we seen Marilyn Monroe with her hair braided in any movie or photo. What did this mean? Did it mean anything? *Had she quit films, and embarked on a new, anonymous life in our midst?*)

Suddenly Marilyn Monroe glanced back at us, frowning as a child might frown (had we spoken aloud? had she heard our thoughts?), and there came into her face a look of puzzlement, not alarm or annoyance but a childlike puzzlement: *Who are you? You two? Are you watching me?* Quickly we looked away. We were engaged in a whispering dispute over a book one of us had fumbled from a shelf, *A History of Botanical Gardens in England*. So we were undetected. We hoped!

But wary now, and sobered. For what if Marilyn Monroe had caught us, and knew that we knew?

She might have abandoned her books and fled the Strand. What a loss for her, and for the books! For us, too.

Oh, we worried at Marilyn Monroe's recklessness! We dreaded her being recognized by a (male) customer or (male) clerk. A girl or woman would have kept her secret (so we thought), but no man could resist staring openly at her, following her, and at last speaking to her. Of course, the blond actress in Strand Used Books wasn't herself, not at all glamorous, or "sexy," or especially blond, in her inconspicuous man's clothing and those salt-stained boots; she might have been anyone, female or male, hardly a Hollywood celebrity, a movie goddess. Yet if you stared, you'd recognize her. If you tried, with any imagination you'd see "Marilyn Monroe." It was like a child's game in which you stare at foliage, grass, clouds in the sky, and suddenly you see a face or a figure, and after that recognition you can't not see the hidden shape, it's staring you in the face. So too with Marilyn Monroe. Once we saw her, it seemed to us she must be seen—and recognized—by anyone who happened to glance at her. If any man saw! We were fearful her privacy would be destroyed. Quickly the blond actress would become surrounded, mobbed. It was risky and reckless of her to have come to Strand Used Books by herself, we thought. Sure, she could shop at Tiffany's, maybe; she could stroll through the lobby of the Plaza, or the Waldorf-Astoria; she'd be safe from fans and unwanted admirers in privileged settings on the Upper East Side, but—here? In the egalitarian Strand, on Broadway and Twelfth?

We were perplexed. Almost, I was annoyed with her. Taking such chances! But you, gripping my wrist, had another, more subtle thought.

"She thinks she's like *us*."

You meant: a human being, anonymous. Female, like us. Amid the ordinary unspectacular customers (predominantly male) of the Strand.

And that was the sadness in it, Marilyn Monroe's wish. To be *like us*. For it was impossible, of course. For anyone could have told Marilyn Monroe, even two young girl-poets, that it was too late for her in history. Already, at age thirty (we could calculate afterward that this was her age) "Marilyn Monroe" had entered history, and there was no escape from it. Her films, her photos. Her face, her figure, her name. To enter history is to be abducted spiritually, with no way back. As if lightning were to strike the building that housed the Strand, as if an actual current of electricity were to touch and transform only one individual in the great cavernous space and that lone individual, by pure chance it might seem, the caprice of fate, would be the young woman with the blond braid and the fedora slanted across her face. Why? Why her, and not another? You could argue that such a destiny is absurd, and undeserved, for one individual among many, and logically you would be correct. And yet: "Marilyn Monroe" has entered history, and you have not. She will endure, though the young woman with the blond braid will die. *And even should she wish to die, "Marilyn Monroe" cannot.*

By this time she—the young woman with the blond braid—was carrying an armload of books. We were hoping she'd almost finished and would be leaving soon, before strangers' rude eyes lighted upon her and exposed her, but no: she surprised us by heading for a section called JUDAICA. In that forbidding aisle, which we'd never before entered, there were books in numerous languages: Hebrew, Yiddish, German, Russian, French. Some of these books looked ancient! Complete sets of the Talmud. Cryptically printed tomes on the cabala. Luckily for us, the titles Marilyn Monroe pulled out were all in English: *Jews of Eastern Europe; The Chosen People: A Complete History of the Jews; Jews of the New World.* Quickly Marilyn Monroe placed her bag and books on the floor, sat on a footstool, and leafed through pages with the frowning intensity of a young girl, as if searching for something urgent, something she knew—knew!—must be there; in this uncomfortable posture she remained for at least fifteen minutes, wetting her fingers to turn pages that stuck together, pages that had not been turned, still less read, for decades. She was frowning, yet smiling too; faint vertical lines appeared between her eyebrows, in the intensity of her concentration; her eyes moved rapidly along lines of print, then returned, and moved more slowly. By this time we were close enough to observe the blond actress's feverish cheeks and slightly parted moist lips that seemed to move silently. *What is she reading in that ancient book, what can possibly mean so much to her? A secret, revealed? A secret, to save her life?*

"Hey you!" a clerk called out in a nasal, insinuating voice.

The three of us looked up, startled.

But the clerk wasn't speaking to us. Not to the blond actress frowning over *The Chosen People*, and not to us who were hovering close by. The clerk had caught someone slipping a book into an overcoat pocket, not an unusual sight at the Strand.

After this mild upset, Marilyn Monroe became uneasy. She turned to look frankly at us, and though we tried clumsily to retreat, her eyes met ours. *She knows!* But after a moment, she simply turned back to her book, stubborn and determined to finish what she was reading, while we continued to hover close by, exposed now, and blushing, yet feeling protective of her. *She has seen us, she knows. She trusts us.* We saw that Marilyn Monroe was beautiful in her anonymity as she had never seemed, to us, to be beautiful as "Marilyn Monroe." All that was makeup, fakery, cartoon sexiness subtle as a kick in the groin. All that was vulgar and infantile. But this young woman was beautiful without makeup, without even lipstick; in her mannish clothes, her hair in a stubby braid. Beautiful: her skin luminous and pale and her eyes a startling clear blue. Almost shyly she glanced back at us, to note that we were still there, and she smiled. *Yes, I see you two. Thank you for not speaking my name.*

Always you and I would remember: that smile of gratitude, and sweetness.

Always you and I would remember: that she trusted us, as perhaps we would not have trusted ourselves.

So many years later, I'm proud of us. We were so young.

Young, headstrong, arrogant, insecure though "brilliant"—or so we'd been led to believe. Not that we thought of ourselves as young: you were nineteen, I was twenty. We were mature for our ages, and we were immature. We were intellectually sophisticated, and emotionally unpredictable. We revered something we called *art*, we were disdainful of something we called *life*. We were overly conscious of ourselves. And yet: how patient, how protective, watching over Marilyn Monroe squatting on a footstool in the JUDAICA stacks as stray customers pushed past muttering "excuse me!" or not even seeming to notice her, or the two of us standing guard. And at last—a relief—Marilyn Monroe shut the unwieldy book, having decided to buy it, and rose from the footstool gathering up her many things. And—this was a temptation!—we held back, not offering to help her carry her things as we so badly wanted to, but only just following at a discreet distance as Marilyn Monroe made her way through the labyrinth of the bookstore to the front counter. (Did she glance back at us? Did she understand you and I were her protectors?) If anyone dared to approach her, we intended to intervene. We would push between Marilyn Monroe and whoever it was. Yet how strange the scene was: none of the other Strand customers, lost in books, took any special notice of her, any more than they took notice of us. Book lovers, especially used-book lovers, are not ones to stare curiously at others, but only at books. At the front of the store—it was a long hike—the cashiers would be more alert, we thought. One of them seemed to be watching Marilyn Monroe approach. Did he know? Could he guess? Was he waiting for her?

Nearing the front counter and the bright fluorescent lights overhead, Marilyn Monroe seemed for the first time to falter. She fumbled to extract out of her shoulder bag a pair of dark glasses and managed to put them on. She turned up the collar of her navy coat. She lowered her hat brim.

Still she was hesitant, and it was then that I stepped forward and said quietly, "Excuse me. Why don't I buy your books for you? That way you won't have to talk to anyone."

The blond actress stared at me through her oversized dark glasses. Her eyes were only just visible behind the lenses. A shy-girl's eyes, startled and grateful.

And so I did. With you helping me. Two girl-poets, side by side, all brisk and businesslike, making Marilyn Monroe's purchases for her: a total of sixteen books!—hardcover and paperback, relatively new books, old battered thumbed-through books—at a cost of $55.85. A staggering sum! Never in my two years of coming into the Strand had I handed over more than a few dollars to the cashier, and this time my hand might have trembled as I pushed twenty-dollar bills at him, half expecting the bristly bearded man to interrogate me: "Where'd you get so much money?" But as usual the cashier hardly gave me a second glance. And Marilyn Monroe, burdened with no books, had already slipped through the turnstile and was awaiting us at the front door.

There, when we handed over her purchases in two sturdy bags, she leaned forward. For a breathless moment we thought she might kiss our cheeks. Instead she pressed into our surprised hands a slender volume she lifted from one of the bags: *Selected Poems of Marianne Moore*. We stammered thanks, but already the blond actress had pulled the fedora down more tightly over her head and had stepped out into the lightly falling snow, headed south on Broadway. We trailed behind her, unable to resist, waiting for her to hail a taxi, but she did not. We knew we must not follow her. By this time we were giddy with the strain of the past hour, gripping each other's hands in childlike elation. So happy!

"Oh. Oh God. Marilyn Monroe. She gave us a book. Was any of it real?"

It was real: we had *Selected Poems of Marianne Moore* to prove it.

That snowy early evening in March at Strand Used Books. That magical evening of Marilyn Monroe, when I kissed you for the first time.

GEORGE SINGLETON

Which Rocks We Choose

LUCKILY FOR EVERYONE IN THE FURTHEST BRANCHES OF THE FAMILY
tree, the mule spoke English to my grandfather. Up until this seminal
point in the development of what became Carolina Rocks, a few generations of Loopers had tried to farm worthless land that sloped from the
mountainside down to all tributaries of the Saluda River. From what I
understood, my great-great-grandfather and then his son barely grew
enough corn to feed their families, much less take to market. Our land
stood so desolate back then that no Looper joined the troops in the 1860s;
no Looper even understood that the country underwent some type of a
conflict. What I'm saying is, our stretch of sterile soil kept Loopers from
needing slaves, which pretty much caused locals to label them everything
from uppity to unpatriotic, from hex ridden to slow witted. Until the mule
spoke English to my grandfather, our family crest might've portrayed a
chipped plow blade, wilted sprigs, and a man with a giant question mark
above his head.

"Don't drown the rocks," the harnessed mule said, according to legend.
The mule turned its head around to my teenaged grandfather, looked
him in the eye just like any of the famous solid-hoofed talking equines
of Hollywood. "Do not throw rocks in the river. Keep them in a pile. They
shall be bought in time by those concerned with decorative landscaping,
for walls and paths and flower beds."

That's what my grandfather came back from the field to tell everybody.
Maybe they grew enough corn for moonshine, I don't know. My own
father told me this story when I complained mightily from the age of
seven on about having to work for Carolina Rocks, whether lugging,
sorting, piling, or later using the backhoe. The mule's name wasn't
Sisyphus, I doubt, but that's what I came to call it when I thought it
necessary to explain the situation to my common-law wife, Abby. I
said, "If it weren't for Sisyphus, you and I would still be trying to find
a crop that likes plenty of rain but no real soil to take root. We'd be
experimenting every year with tobacco, rice, coffee, and cranberry farming."

Abby stared at me a good minute. She said, "What? I wasn't listening. Did you say we can't have children?"

I said, "A good mule told my grandfather to quit trying to farm and to sell off both river rocks and fieldstone. That's how come we do what we do. Or at least why my grandfather and dad did what they did." This little speech occurred on the day I turned thirty-three, the day I became the same age as Jesus, the day I finally decided to go back to college. Up until this point Abby and I had lived in the Looper family house. My dad had been dead eleven years, my mom twenty. I said, "Anyway, I think the Caterpillar down on the banks is rusted up enough now for both of us to admit we're not going to continue with the business once we sell off the remaining stock."

When I took over Carolina Rocks we had already stockpiled about two hundred tons of beautiful black one- to three-inch skippers dug out of the river. I probably scooped out another few hundred tons over the next eight years. But with land developers razing both sides of the border for gated mountain golf course communities, in need of something other than mulch, there was no way I could keep up. A ton of rocks isn't the size of half a French car. Sooner or later, too, I predicted, the geniuses at the EPA would figure out that haphazardly digging out riverbeds and shorelines wouldn't be beneficial downstream. Off in other corners of our land we had giant piles of round rocks, pebbles, chunks, flagstones, and chips used for walkways, driveways, walls, and artificial springhouses. Until my thirty-third birthday, when I would make that final decision to enroll in a low-residency master's program, I would sell off what rocks we had quarried, graded, and—according to my mood—divided into color or shape or size. I had decided on Southern Culture Studies, and the department chair of the one particular low-residency program I looked into wrote that I should mention the degree with purpose, as if capitalized, no matter what. Maybe I should've taken his advice as an omen.

Anyway, I never really felt that the Loopers' ways of going about the river rock and fieldstone business incorporated what our competitors might've known in regard to supply and demand, or using time wisely.

"Hey, Stet, can we go back to trying our chosen field?" Abby asked. She wore a pair of gray sweatpants and a MoonPie T-shirt. Both of us wore paper birthday cones on our heads. "Please say that we can send out our résumés to TV stations around the country. Hell, I'd give the news in Mississippi if it got my foot in the door."

She pronounced it "Mishishippi." She wasn't drunk. One of our professors should've taken her aside right about Journalism 101 and told her to find a new field of study or concentrate in print media. I didn't have it in me, either, to tell Abby that my grandfather's mule enunciated better than she did. When she wasn't helping out with the Carolina Rocks bookkeeping chores, she drove down to Greenville and led aerobics classes. I never saw her conducting a class in person, but I imagined her saying, "*Shtep, shtep, shtep.*"

"It's funny that you should mention Mississippi," I said. I thought of the term *segue*, from when I underwent communications studies classes as an undergraduate, usually seated right next to Abby. "I'm going to go ahead and enroll in that Southern Culture Studies program. It'll all be done by e-mail and telephone, pretty much, and then I have to go to Mississippi for ten days in the summer and winter. Then, in a couple years, maybe I can go teach college somewhere. We can sell off this land and move to an actual city. It'll be easier for you to maybe find a job that you're interested in."

I loved my wife more than I loved finding and digging up a truckload of schist. Abby got up from the table, smiled, walked into the den, and picked up a gift-wrapped box. She said, "You cannot believe how afraid I was you'd change your mind. Open it up." I kind of hoped it was a big bottle of bourbon so we could celebrate there at the kitchen table as the sun rose. I shook it. I said, "It's as heavy as a prize-winning geode," for I compared everything to rocks. When hail fell, those ice crystals hitting the ground were either pea gravel or riprap, never golf balls like the meteorologists said.

"I'm hoping this will help you in the future. In *our* future." Abby leaned over backward and put her palms on the floor like some kind of contortionist. "I don't mind teaching aerobics, but I can't do that when I'm sixty. I can still report the news when I'm sixty."

Sixschtee.

I opened the box to uncover volumes one, two, and three of *The South: What Happened, How, When, and Why.* Abby said, "I don't know what else you're going to learn in a graduate course that's not already in here, but maybe it'll give you ideas."

I might've actually felt tears well up. I opened the first chapter of the third volume to find the heading "BBQ, Ticks, Cottonmouths, and Moonshine." I said, "Man. You might be right. What's left to learn?"

I'm not sure how other low-residency programs in Southern Culture Studies work, but immediately after I sent off the online application—which only included names of references, not actual letters of recommendation—I got accepted. An hour later I paid for the first half year with a credit card. I e-mailed the "registrar" asking if I needed to send copies of my undergraduate transcripts, et cetera, and she said that they were a trusting lot at the University of Mississippi–Taylor. She wrote back that she and the professors all believed in a person's word being his bond, and so on, and that the program probably wouldn't work out for me if I was the sort who needed everything in writing.

I called the phone number at the bottom of the pseudo-letterhead but hung up when someone answered, "Taylor Grocery and Catfish." I had only wanted to say that I, too, ran my river rock and fieldstone business on promised payments, that my father and grandfather operated thusly even though the mule had warned to trust nothing on two legs. And I didn't want to admit to myself or Abby that perhaps my degree would be on par with something like that art institute that accepts boys and girls who can draw fake pirates and cartoon deer.

A day later I received my first assignment from my lead mentor, one Dr. Theron Crowther. He asked that I buy one of his books, read the chapter on "Revising History," then set about finding people who might've remembered things differently as opposed to how the media reported the incident. He said to stick to southern themes: the assassination of Dr. Martin Luther King, for example; the sit-in at Woolworth's in Greensboro; unsuccessful and fatal attempts at unionizing cotton mills; Ole Miss's upset of Alabama. I said to Abby, "I might should stick to pulling rocks out of the river and selling them to people who like to make puzzles out of their yard. I have no clue what this guy means for me to do."

Abby looked over the e-mail. I was to write a ten-page paper and send it back within two weeks. "First off, read that chapter. It should give you some clues. That's what happened to me when I wasn't sure about a paper

I once wrote on 'How to Interview the Criminally Insane' back in college. You remember that paper? You pussied out and wrote one on 'How to Interview the Deaf.'"

I'd gotten an A on that one: I merely wrote, "To interview a deaf person, find a sign language interpreter." That was it.

Abby said, "There's this scrapbooking place next door to Feline Fitness. Come on in to work with me, and I'll take you over there. Those people will have some stories to tell, I bet. Every time I go past it, these women are sitting around talking."

We sat on our front porch, overlooking the last three tons of river rock I'd scooped out, piled neatly as washer–dryer combos, if it matters. Below the rocks, the river surged onward, rising from thunderstorms up near Asheville. I said, "What are you talking?" I'd not heard of the new sport of scrapbooking.

"These people get together just like a quilting club, I guess. They go in the store and buy new scrapbooks, then sit there and shove pictures and mementos between the plastic pages. And they brag, from what I understand. The reason I know so much about it is, I got a couple women in my noon class who showed up early one day and went over to check out the scrapbook place. They came back saying there was a Junior Leaguer ex–Miss South Carolina in there with flipbooks of her child growing up, you know. She took a picture of her kid two or three times a day, so you can flip the pictures and see the girl grow up in about five minutes."

I got up, walked off the porch, crawled beneath the house a few feet, and pulled out a bottle of bourbon I kept hidden away there for times when I needed to think—which wasn't often in the river rock business. When I rejoined my wife she'd already gotten two jelly jars out of the cupboard. "There's a whole damn business in scrapbooks? Who thought that up? America," I said. "Forget the South being fucked up. America."

"You can buy cloth-covered ones and puffy-covered ones and ones with your favorite team's mascot on the cover. There are black ones for funeral pictures and white ones for weddings. There are ones that are shaped like Santa Claus, the Easter Bunny, dogs, cats, cars, and Jesus. They've even got scented scrapbooks." Abby slugged down a good shot of Jim Beam and tilted her glass my way for more. "Not that I've been in Scraphappy! very often, but they've got one that looks like skin with tattoos and everything, shaped like an hourglass, little tiny blond hairs coming off of it. It's for guys to put their bachelor party pictures inside."

I said, "I wonder if they have any bullet-riddled gray flannel scrapbooks for pictures of dead Confederate relatives." I tried to imagine other scrapbooks but couldn't think of any. "Okay. What the hell. When's your next class?"

We drove down the mountain the next morning, a Wednesday, so Abby could lead a beginner aerobics class. Wednesdays might as well be called "little Sunday" on a southern calendar, for small-town banks and businesses close at noon for employees to ready themselves for Wednesday night church services. My common-law wife took me into Scraphappy!, looked at a wall of stickers, then said, "I'll be back a little after noon, unless someone needs personal training." She didn't kiss me on the cheek. She looked over at the six women sitting in a circle, all of whom I estimated to be in their mid- to late thirties.

"Could I help you with anything?" the owner asked me. She wore a name tag that read Knox—the last name of one of the richer families in the area. In kind of a patronizing voice she said, "Did you forget to pack up your snapshots this morning?"

The other women kept turning cellophane-covered pages. One of them said out loud, "Pretty soon I'll have to get a scrapbook dedicated to every room in the house. What a complete freak-up."

I had kind of turned my head toward the stickers displayed on the wall—blue smiling babies, pink smiling babies, a slew of elephants, Raggedy Anns and Andys, mobiles, choo-choo trains, ponies, teddy bears, prom dresses, the president's face staring vacantly—but jerked my neck back around at hearing "freak-up." I thought to myself, Remember that you're here to gather revisionist history. I thought, You want to impress your professor at Ole Miss–Taylor.

But then I started daydreaming about Frances Bavier, the actress who played Aunt Bee on *The Andy Griffith Show*. I said, "Oh. Oh, I didn't come here to play scrapbook. My name's Stet Looper, and I'm enrolled in a Southern Culture Studies graduate program, and I came here to see if y'all wouldn't mind answering some questions about historical events that happened around here. Or around anywhere." I cleared my throat. The women in the circle looked at me as if I had walked in wearing a seersucker suit after Labor Day.

The Knox woman said, "Southern studies? My husband has this ne'er-do-well cousin who has a daughter going to one of those all-girls schools up north. Hollins, I believe. She's majoring in women's studies." In a lower voice she said, "She appears not to like men, if you know what I mean—she snubbed us all by not coming out this last season at the Poinsett Club. Anyway, she's studying for that degree with an emphasis in women's economics, and I told her daddy that it usually didn't take four years learning how to make a proper grocery list."

I was glad I didn't say that. I'd've been shot, I figured. The same woman who almost-cursed earlier held up a photograph to her colleagues and said, "Look at that one. He said he knew how to paint the baseboard."

I said, "Anyway, I have a deadline, and I was wondering if I could ask if y'all could tell me about an event that occurred during your lifetime, something that made you view the world differently than how you had understood it before. Kind of like the Cuban missile crisis, but more local."

One of the women said, "Hey, Knox, could you hand me one them calligraphy stick-ons says 'I Told You So'? I guess I need to find me a stamp that says 'Loser.'" To me she said, "My husband always accuses me of being a germaphobe." She held up her opened scrapbook for me to see. It looked as though she'd wiped her butt on the pages. "This is my collection of used moist towelettes. I put them in here to remember the nice restaurants we've gone to, and sometimes if the waitress gave me extras I put the new one in there, too. But even better, he and I one time went on a camping trip that I didn't want to go on, and as it ended up we got lost. Luckily for Wells, we only had to follow my trail of Wet Naps back to the parking lot. I don't mind bragging that that trip was all it took for him to buy us a vacation home down on Pawleys Island."

I wished that I'd've thought to bring a tape recorder. I said, "That's a great story," even though I didn't ever see it being a chapter in some kind of Southern Culture Studies textbook. I said, "Okay. Do any of y'all do aerobics? My wife's next door teaching aerobics, if y'all are interested. From what I understand, she's tough, but not too tough." I heard my inner voice going, Okay, none of these women is interested in aerobics classes, so shut up and get out of here before you say something more stupid and somehow get yourself in trouble.

I stood there like a fool for a few seconds. The woman who complained about her baseboard started flipping through pages, saying, "Look at them. Every one of them." Then she went on to explain to a woman who must not've been a regular, "I keep a scrapbook of every time my husband messes up. This scrapbook's the bad home repair one—he tries to fix something, then it costs us double to get a professional in to do the job. I got another book filled with bad checks that got sent back, and newspaper clippings for when he got arrested and published in the police blotter. I even got ahold of some of his mug shots."

I felt like I was standing next to a whipping post. I said, "Okay, I'm sorry to take up any of your time." The place should've been called *Strap*happy, I thought.

As I opened the door, though, I heard a different voice, a woman who'd only concentrated on her own book of humiliation up until this point. She said, "Do you mean like if you know somebody got lynched, but it all got hush-hushed even though everyone around knew the truth?"

Everyone went quiet. You could've heard an opened ink pad evaporate.

I pulled up one of those half stepladder/half stool things. I said, "Say that all again, slower."

Her name was Gayle Ann Gunter. Her daddy owned a car lot, and her grandfather owned it before him, and the great-grandfather had started the entire operation back when selling horseshoes and tack still made up half of his business. She was working on a scrapbook that involved one-by-two-inch pictures that grade schoolers hand over to one another, and she had them under headings like 'Uglier than Me,' 'Poorer than Me,' 'Dumber than Me'—as God is my witness. She said, "We're having our twentieth high school reunion in a few months, and I want to make sure I have the names right. It's important in this world to greet old acquaintances properly."

I said, "I'm no genius, but it should be 'Dumber than I.' It's a long, convoluted grammar lesson I learned back in college the first time."

The other women laughed. They said, "Ha ha ha ha ha" in unison and in a weird, seemingly practiced cadence. Knox said, "One of the things that keeps me in business is people messing up their scrapbooks and having to start over. I had one woman who misspelled her new daughter-in-law's name throughout, the first time. She got it right when her son got a divorce, though."

"This was up in Travelers Rest," Gayle Ann said. She kept her scrapbook atop her lap and spoke as if addressing the air conditioning vent. "I couldn't have been more than eight, nine years old. These two black brothers went missing, but no one made a federal case out of it, you know. This was about 1970. They hadn't integrated the schools just yet, I don't believe. I don't even know if it made the paper, and I haven't ever seen the episode on one of those shows about long-since missing people. Willie and Archie Lagroon. No one thought about it much because, first off, a lot of teenage boys ran away back then. Maybe 'cause of Vietnam, I guess. And then again, they wasn't white."

I took notes in a professional-looking memo pad. I didn't even look up, and I didn't offer another grammar lesson involving subjects and verbs. For some reason one of the women in the circle said, "My name's Shaw Haynesworth. Gayle Ann, I thought you were *born* in 1970. My name's Shaw Haynesworth, if you need to have footnotes and a bibliogeography."

I wrote that down, too. Gayle Ann Gunter didn't respond. She said, "I haven't thought about this in years. It's sad. About four years after those boys went missing, a hunter found a bunch of bones right there about twenty feet off of Old Dacusville Road. My daddy told me all about it. They found all these rib bones kind of strewn around, and more than likely it was those two boys. This was all before DNA, of course. The coroner—or someone working for the state—finally said that they were beef and pork ribs people had thrown out their car windows. They said that people went to the Dacusville Smokehouse and couldn't make it all the way back home before tearing into a rack of ribs, and that they threw them out the window, and somehow all those ribs landed in one big pile over the years." She made a motorboat noise with her mouth. "I'm no expert when it comes to probability or beyond a reasonable doubt, but looking back on it now, I smell lynching. Is that the kind of story you're looking for?"

Abby walked in sweating, hair pulled back, wearing an outfit that made her look like she just finished the Tour de France. She said, "Hey, Stet, I might be another hour. Phyllis wants me to fill in for her. Are you okay?"

The women scrapbookers looked up at my wife as if she had zoomed in from cable television. I said, "We have a winner!" for some reason.

"You can come over and sit in the lobby if you finish up early." To the women she said, "We're having a special next door if y'all want to join an aerobics class. Twenty dollars a month." I turned to see the women all look down at their scrapbooks.

Knox said, "I believe I can say for sure that we burn up enough calories running around all day for our kids. Speaking of which, I brought some doughnuts in!"

I looked at Abby. I nodded. She kind of made a what're-you-up-to? face and backed out. I said, "Okay. Yes, Gayle Ann, that's exactly the kind of story I'm looking for—about something that happened, but that people saw differently. How sure are you that those bones were the skeletal remains of the two boys?"

A woman working on a giant scrapbook of her two Pomeranians said, "They do have good barbecue at Dacusville Smokehouse. I know I've not been able to make it home without breaking into the Styrofoam boxes. Hey, do any of y'all know why it's not good to give a dog pork bones? Is that an old wives' tale, or what? I keep forgetting to ask my vet."

And then they were off talking about everything else. I felt it necessary to purchase something from Knox, so I picked out a rubber stamp that read "Unbelievable!"

I'm not ashamed to admit that, while walking between Scraphappy! and Feline Fitness, I envisioned not only a big A on my first Southern Culture Studies low-residency graduate-level class at Ole Miss–Taylor, but a consultant's fee when this rib-bone story got picked up by one of those TV programs specializing in wrongdoing mysteries, cold cases, and voices from the dead.

Since I wouldn't meet Dr. Theron Crowther until the entire graduate class got together for ten days in December, I didn't know if he was a liar or prankster. I'd dealt with both types before, of course, in the river rock business. Pranksters came back and said that my stones crumbled up during winter's first freeze, and liars sent checks for half tons, saying I used cheating scales, et cetera. After talking to the women of Scraphappy!, I sent Dr.

Crowther an e-mail detailing the revisionist history I'd gathered. He wrote back to me, "You fool! Haven't you ever encountered a little something called 'rural legend'? Let me say right now that you will not make it in the mean world of Southern Culture Studies if you fall for every made-up tale that rumbles down the trace. Now go out there and show me how regular people view things differently than how they probably really happened."

First off, I thought that I'd done that. I was never the kind of student who whined and complained when a professor didn't cotton to my way of thinking. Back when I was forced to undergo a required course called Broadcast Station Management I wrote a comparison–contrast paper about the management styles of WKRP in Cincinnati and WJM in Minneapolis. The professor said that it wasn't a good idea to write about fictitious radio- and television-based situation comedies. Personally, I figured the management philosophies must've been spectacular, seeing as both programs consistently won Nielsen battles, then went on into syndication. The professor—who ended up, from what I understand, having to resign his position after getting caught filming himself having sex with a freshman boy on the made-up set for an elective course in Local Morning Shows, using a fake potted plant and microphone as props—said I needed to forget about television programs when dealing with television programs, which made no sense to me at the time. I never understood what he meant until, after graduation, running my family's business ineffectively and on a reading jag, I sat down by the river and read *The Art of War* by Sun Tzu and *Being and Nothingness* by Sartre.

I said to Abby, "My mentor at Ole Miss–Taylor says that's a made-up story about black kids and rib bones. He says it's like that urban legend about those vacation photos down in Jamaica with the toothbrush, or the big dog that chases a ball out the window of a high-rise in New York."

Abby came out from beneath our front porch, the half bottle of bourbon in her grasp. She said, "Of course he says that. Now he's going to come down here and interview about a thousand people so he can publish the book himself. That's what those guys do, Stet. Hey, I got an idea—why don't you write about how you fell off a turnip truck. How you got some kind of medical problem that makes you wet behind the ears always."

I stared down at the river and tried to imagine how rocks still languished there below the roiling surface. "I guess I can run over to that barbecue shack and ask them what they know about it."

"I guess you can invest in carbon paper and slide rulers in case this computer technology phase proves to be a fad."

All good barbecue stands only open on the weekend, Thursday through Saturday at most. I got out a regional telephone directory, found the address, got directions from MapQuest, then drove around uselessly for a few hours, circling, until I happened to see a white plume of smoke different from most of the black ones caused by people burning tires in front of their trailers. I walked in—this time with a hand-held tape recorder I'd gotten for opening a new CD down at the bank, I guess so people can record their last words before committing suicide, something like "Two fucking percent interest?"—and dealt with all the locals turning around, staring, wondering aloud who my kin might be. I said, loudly, "Hey, how y'all doing this fine evening?" like I owned the place. Everyone turned back to their piled paper plates of minced pork and cole slaw.

At the counter a short man with pointy sideburns and a curled-up felt cowboy hat said, "We out of sweet potato casserole." A fly buzzed around his cash register.

"I'll take two," I looked up at the menu board behind him, "Hog-o-Mighty sandwiches."

"Here or to go?"

"And a sweet tea. You don't serve beer by any chance, do you?"

"No sir. Family-orientated," he said. He wore an apron that read, "Cook."

I said, "I understand. I'm Stet Looper, up from around north of here."

An eavesdropper behind me said, "I tode you."

"By north of here I mean just near the state line. I'll eat them here. Anyway, my wife introduced me to a woman who told me a wild story about two young boys being missing some thirty-odd years back, with something about a pile of bones the state investigators said came from here. Do you know this story?" I mentioned Abby because any single male strangers are, in the sloppy dialect of the locals, "quiz."

"My name's Cook," the cook said. "Raymus Cook. Y'all hear that? Fellow wants to know if I heard about them missing boys back then. Can you believe that?" To me he said, "You the second person today to ask. Some fellow from down Mississippi called earlier asking if it was some kind of made-up story."

I thought, Goddamn parasite Theron Crowther. "I'll be doggone," I said. "What'd you tell him?"

"That'll be five and a quarter, counting tax." Raymus Cook handed over two sandwiches on a paper plate and took my money. "I told him my daddy'd be the one to talk to, but Daddy's been dead eight years. I told him what I believed—that somebody paid somebody and that those boys' families will never rest in peace."

People from two tables got up from the seats, shot Raymus Cook mean looks, and left the premises. One of them said, "We been through this enough. I'mo take my bidness to Ola's now on."

Raymus Cook held his head back somewhat and called out, "This ain't the world it used to be. You just can't go decide to secede every other minute, things don't turn out like you want them." At this precise moment I knew that, later in life, I would regale friends and colleagues alike about how I "stumbled upon" something. Raymus Cook turned his head halfway to the open kitchen and said, "Ain't that right, Ms. Hattie?"

A black woman stuck her face my way and said, "Datboutright, huh-huh," just like that, fast, as if she'd waited to say her lines all night long.

"You can't cook barbecue correct without the touch of a black woman's hands," Raymus said to me in not much more than a whisper. "All these chains got white people smoking out back. Won't work, I'll be the first to admit."

I thought, Fuck, this is going to turn out to be just another one of those stories that's bloated the South for 150 years. I didn't want that to happen. I said, "I'm starting a master's degree in Southern Culture Studies, and I need to write a paper on something that happened a while back that maybe ain't right. You got any stories you could help me out with?"

I sat down at the first table and unwrapped a sandwich. I got up and poured my own tea. Raymus Cook smiled. He picked up a fly swatter and nailed his prey. "Southern culture?" He laughed. "I don't know that much about southern culture, even though I got raised right here." To a family off in the corner he yelled, "Y'all want any sweet potato casserole?" Back to me he said, "That's one big piece of flypaper hanging, southern culture. It might be best to accidentally graze a wing to it every once in a while, but mostly buzz around."

I said, of course, "Man. That's a nice analogy." I tried to think up one to match him, something about river rocks. I couldn't.

"Wait a minute," Raymus Cook said. "I might be thinking about southern literature. Like Faulkner. Is that what you're talking about?"

I thought, This guy's going to help me get through my thesis one day. I said, "Hey, can I get a large rack of ribs to go? I'll get a large rack and a small rack." I looked up at the menu board. I said, "Can I get a 'Willie' and an 'Archie'?"

I thought, Uh-oh, though it took me a minute to remember those two poor black kids' names. I thought, This isn't funny, and took off out of there as soon as Raymus Cook turned around to tell Miss Hattie what he needed. I remembered that I'd forgotten to turn on the tape recorder.

On my drive back home I wondered if there were any low-residency writing programs where I could learn how to finish a detective novel.

I told my sort-of wife the entire event and handed her half a Hog-o-Mighty sandwich. She didn't gape her mouth or shake her head. "You want to get into Southern Culture Studies, you better prepare yourself for such. There are going to be worse stories."

Wershtoreesh. I said, "I don't want to collect war stories."

"You know what I said. And I don't know why you don't ask *me*. Here's a true story about a true story gone false: This woman in my advanced cardio class—this involves spinning, Pilates, steps, and treadmill inside a sauna—once weighed 220 pounds. She's five-two. Now she weighs a hundred, maybe one-o-five at the most. She's twenty-eight years old and just started college at one of the tech schools. She wants to be a dental hygienist."

We sat on the porch, looking down at the river. Our bottle was empty. On the railing I had *The South: What Happened, How, When, and Why* opened to a chapter on a sect of people in eastern Tennessee called "Slopeheads," which might've been politically incorrect.

I said, "She should be a dietician. They got culinary courses there now.

She should become an elementary school chef, you know, to teach kids how to quit eating pizza and pimento-cheese burgers."

"Listen. Do you know what happened to her? Do you know how and why and when she lost all that weight?"

I said, of course, "She saw one of those before-and-after programs on afternoon TV. She sat there with a bowl of potato chips on her belly watching Oprah, and God spoke to her." I said, "Anorexia and bulimia, which come before and after 'arson' in some books."

"Her daddy died." Abby got up and closed my textbook for no apparent reason. "Figure it out, Stet. Her daddy died. She *said* she got so depressed that she quit eating. But in reality, she had made herself obese so he'd quit creeping into her bedroom between the ages of twelve and twenty-two. Her mother had left the household long before, and there she was. So she fattened up and slept on her stomach. When her father died she didn't tell anyone what had been going on. But when all the neighbors met after the funeral to eat, she didn't touch one dish. Not even the macaroni and cheese."

I said, "I don't want to know about these kinds of things." I got up and walked down toward the river. Abby followed behind me. I said, "Those my-daddy-loved-me stories are the ones I'm trying to stay away from. It's what people expect out of this area."

When we got to the backhoe she climbed up and reached beneath the seat. She pulled out an unopened bottle of rum I had either forgotten or didn't know about. "There were pirates. You could write about pirates and their influences on the South. How pirates stole things that weren't theirs."

I picked up a nice skipper and flung it out toward an unnatural sandbar. Then I walked into the water up to my knees, reached down, and pulled two more out. I thought, pirates, sheriffs, and local politicians. I thought, the heads of Southern Culture Studies low-residency programs. I reached in the river and pulled out rock after rock. I threw back the smaller ones, as if they needed to be released in order to grow more. I flung up perfect stones to the bank. An hour later, I had enough rocks piled up to cover two graves, but I would need a mule to dredge up enough for the appropriate roadside memorials.

Contributors

LEE K. ABBOTT (b. 1947) is the author of seven collections of short fiction, most recently *All Things, All at Once: New and Selected Stories* (2006). His work has appeared in nearly one hundred periodicals, as well as in the *Best American Short Stories, O. Henry Awards: Prize Stories, Best of the West,* and the *Pushcart Prize.* Twice a winner of NEA fellowships, Abbott is Humanities Distinguished Professor in English at Ohio State University.

T. C. BOYLE (b. 1948) is the author of twenty-two books of fiction, including *The Women* (2009), *Wild Child* (2010), and *When the Killing's Done* (2011). Since 1978 he has been a member of the English Department at the University of Southern California, where he is Distinguished Professor of English. His stories have appeared in most of the major American magazines, and he has been the recipient of a number of literary awards, including the PEN/Faulkner Prize, the PEN/Malamud Award, and France's *Prix Médicis Étranger* for best foreign novel.

KEVIN BROCKMEIER (b. 1972) has published seven books since 2002: three novels, *The Illumination* (2010), *The Brief History of the Dead* (2006), and *The Truth about Celia* (2003); two story collections, *The View from the Seventh Layer* (2008) and *Things That Fall from the Sky* (2002); and two children's novels, *Grooves: A Kind of Mystery* (2006) and *City of Names* (2002). He lives in Little Rock, Arkansas, where he was reared.

SIV CEDERING (1939–2007), an exhibiting sculptor and painter, a book illustrator, and a writer of songs and TV programs for children, was the author of eighteen books and four volumes of translations. Her honors included three Poetry Society of America awards, Pushcart prizes in both fiction and poetry, and several grants from the New York State Council on the Arts.

FRED CHAPPELL (b. 1936) has written more than two dozen books, most recently *Shadow Box: Poems* (2009). *The Fred Chappell Reader* was published in 1987 by St. Martin's Press. Among his many awards are the T. S. Eliot Prize, the Bollingen Prize for Poetry, and the *Prix du Meilleur Livres Étranger* of the *Academie Francaise*.

HARRY CREWS (b. 1935), a native of Bacon County, Georgia, is the author of nearly twenty novels, from *The Gospel Singer* (1968) to *An American Family: The Baby with the Curious Markings* (2006). Crews's published nonfiction includes the first volume of his auto-biography, *A Childhood: The Biography of a Place* (1978), and three essay collections. A substantial section of a second autobiographical manuscript, "Assault of Memory," appeared in *The Georgia Review* (Winter 2007). Crews was inducted into the Georgia Writers Hall of Fame in 2001.

JACK DRISCOLL (b. 1946) has two short-story collections, *The World of a Few Minutes Ago* (2012) and *Wanting Only to Be Heard* (1992, reis-sued 2008). Also the author of four novels and four collections of po-ems, Driscoll taught for thirty-three years at the Interlochen Center for the Arts in Michigan.

PAM DURBAN (b. 1947) is the author of *All Set About with Fever Trees and Other Stories* (1985), *The Laughing Place* (1993), and *So Far Back* (2000), winner of the Lillian Smith Book Award. She has also won the Townsend Prize for Fiction, a Whiting Writers' Award, and the Mary Roberts Rinehart Award for Fiction. Currently, Durban is the Doris Betts Distinguished Professor of Creative Writing at the University of North Carolina.

WILLIAM FAULKNER (1897–1962), winner of the Nobel Prize for Lit-erature in 1950, wrote "A Portrait of Elmer" in the mid-1930s, but it was not published until its appearance in *The Georgia Review* some forty-five years later. The story was subsequently printed in Joseph Blotner's *Uncollected Stories of William Faulkner* (1979).

ERNEST J. GAINES (b. 1933) has authored eight books of fiction and several other works, most recently *Mozart and Leadbelly: Stories and Essays* (2005). His third novel, *The Autobiography of Miss Jane Pittman* (1971), was made into a highly praised television movie in 1974. Gaines has held writing fellowships from the Guggenheim Foundation, the NEA, and the Rockefeller Foundation, and he is now Writer-in-Residence Emeritus at the University of Louisiana–Lafayette.

WILLIAM GAY (b. 1943) was a previously unpublished writer when "I Hate to See That Evening Sun Go Down" first appeared in *The Georgia Review* in 1998. The story became the title piece of his 2002 collection, and it inspired a feature film— *That Evening Sun*—written and produced in 2009 by Georgia native Scott Teems and starring Hal Holbrook. Gay is also the author of three novels.

GARY GILDNER (b. 1938) has twenty published books, among them *Blue Like the Heavens: New and Selected Poems* (1984), *Somewhere Geese Are Flying: New and Selected Stories* (2004), and *The Bunker in the Parsley Fields* (1997), which received the 1996 Iowa Poetry Prize. He has also received a National Magazine Award for Fiction (for work in *The Georgia Review*), Pushcart prizes in fiction and nonfiction, the Robert Frost Fellowship, and two National Endowment for the Arts Fellowships.

DONALD HALL (b. 1928) served as Poet Laureate of the United States in 2006 and received the National Medal of Arts in 2010. He has authored more than thirty works of poetry, fiction, nonfiction, and drama as well as eleven books for children; his many honors include two Guggenheim fellowships, the *Los Angeles Times* Book Prize for poetry, and the Ruth Lilly Poetry Prize.

JIM HEYNEN (b. 1940) is the author of several collections of short-short stories, including *The Boys' House* (2001), *The One-Room Schoolhouse* (1993), and *The Man Who Kept Cigars in His Cap* (1979); he has also published short stories, poetry, essays, and novels for both adults and young adults.

T. E. HOLT (b. 1952) holds a PhD in English from Cornell University and an MD from the University of North Carolina, where he currently practices medicine and teaches at the UNC Medical Center. His collection of short fiction, *In the Valley of the Kings*, came out in 2009, and he has also published a handbook for amateur astronomers, *The Universe Next Door* (1985).

MARY HOOD (b. 1946) is the author of two story collections—the Flannery O'Connor Award–winning *How Far She Went* (1984) and *And Venus Is Blue* (1986, reissued 2001)—and a novel, *Familiar Heat* (1995).

BARRY LOPEZ (b. 1945) has thirteen books to his credit, among them the National Book Award–winning *Arctic Dreams* (1986). He has published eight works of fiction, including *Resistance* (2004) and the novella-length fable *Crow and Weasel* (1990). Lopez's interdisciplinary writings have earned him honors and awards from the American Academy of Arts and Letters, the Academy of Television Arts and Sciences, the Guggenheim and National Science foundations, and the Association of American Geographers.

JAMES LEWIS MACLEOD (b. 1937), whose ancestry includes the first Presbyterian minister born in Georgia, was himself ordained in the Presbyterian Church in 1963. *A Season of Grace*, his book of religious meditations dedicated to his friend and mentor Flannery O'Connor, appeared in 1978; essays from a forthcoming book on O'Connor appeared in the Spring–Fall 2010 issue of *Shenandoah*.

LEE MARTIN (b. 1955) has published a story collection, *The Least You Need to Know* (1996), and four novels: *Break the Skin* (2011), *River of Heaven* (2008), Pulitzer Prize finalist *The Bright Forever* (2005), and *Quakertown* (2001). He teaches at Ohio State University.

PHYLLIS MOORE (b. 1953) is the author of the short-story collection *A Compendium of Skirts* (2002) and has been the recipient of numerous Florida and Illinois arts council grants. She received her PhD in English from the University of Illinois at Chicago and is a former cochair of the MFA in writing program at the School of the Art Institute of Chicago; she currently directs the School of Liberal Arts at the Kansas City Art Institute.

NAOMI SHIHAB NYE (b. 1952) has published six poetry collections, including National Book Award nominee *19 Varieties of Gazelle: Poems of the Middle East* (2002). In addition to winning two Jane Addams Book Awards for her books for young readers, Nye has been a Lannan Fellow, a Guggenheim Fellow, and a Witter Bynner Fellow, as well as the recipient of a Lavan Award from the Academy of American Poets and numerous other honors.

JOYCE CAROL OATES (b. 1938) has composed some one hundred books in multiple genres, including the novel *Little Bird of Heaven* (2009), the story collection *Sourland* (2009), and the memoir *A Widow's Story* (2011). The 2009 recipient of the Ivan Sandrof Award for Lifetime Achievement from the National Book Critics Circle, Oates is the Roger S. Berlind Distinguished Professor of the Humanities at Princeton University, where she has taught since 1978.

FRED PFEIL (1949–2005) was a teacher, an activist, an editor, and the author of five books of fiction and nonfiction, including the story collection *What They Tell You to Forget* (1996) and *White Guys: Studies in Postmodern Domination and Difference* (1995). He taught for many years at Trinity College in Hartford, Connecticut, where the Fred Pfeil Community Project, an alternative living experiment, has been established in his honor.

MARJORIE SANDOR (b. 1957) won a National Jewish Book Award for her second story collection, *Portrait of My Mother, Who Posed Nude in Wartime* (2003); her first book was *A Night of Music* (1989). She has also published a volume of essays, *The Night Gardener: A Search for Home* (1999), and a memoir, *The Late Interiors: A Life under Construction* (2011). She currently directs the MFA program in creative writing at Oregon State University.

GEORGE SINGLETON (b. 1958) has published *The Half-Mammals of Dixie* (2002) and three other collections of stories; two novels, including *Novel* (2005); and a book about writing titled *Pep Talks, Warnings, and Screeds* (2008). The recipient of a Guggenheim Fellowship in 2009, he lives in South Carolina.

JESSE STUART (1906–1984) wrote more than forty books: novels, short stories, poems, children's stories, and autobiographical works; his novel *Taps for Private Tussie* (1943) sold more than two million copies. Kentucky, his lifelong home, has honored him by establishing the Jesse Stuart Foundation in Ashland to promote his work and beliefs; in 2003 the foundation released *New Harvest: Forgotten Stories of Kentucky's Jesse Stuart*.

JOHN EDGAR WIDEMAN (b. 1941) has garnered many honors for his twenty-plus books, among them PEN/Faulkner Awards for *Sent for You Yesterday* (1983) and *Philadelphia Fire* (1990). His nonfiction book *Brothers and Keepers* (1984) received a National Book Critics Circle nomination; his memoir *Fatheralong* (1994) was a finalist for the National Book Award; and he has received a MacArthur grant, the Rea Award for the Short Story, and the American Book Award for Fiction. Wideman's latest book is *Briefs: Stories for the Palm of the Mind* (2010).

LIZA WIELAND (b. 1960) has three collections of stories, the latest of them *Quickening* (2011), and three novels—among them *A Watch of Nightingales* (2009), winner of the Michigan Literary Fiction Award. She has earned grants from the NEA, the Christopher Isherwood Foundation, and the North Carolina Arts Council, as well as two Pushcart prizes.